NOTHING SAVE THE BONES INSIDE HER

CLAYTON LINDEMUTH

Hardgrave Enterprises
Chesterfield, Missouri

NOTHING SAVE THE BONES INSIDE HER/Clayton Lindemuth -- 1st ed.
ISBN-13: 978-0615933702

For Georgena, the kindest, most generous, supporting, and best cooking mother a son could want.

*I took her wrist and got my hand on her neck and I couldn't
think of nothing save the bones inside her.*

—ANGUS HARDGRAVE

MAUL Prologue

Maul shouldered aside five brothers and sisters for a place at Tobacca's nipple, which he chewed like a discarded strap of leather. She nipped his nose and he sank sharp puppy teeth into her clipped ears. Maul wore a battleship gray coat, bullied his normal-sized siblings, failed to learn fear, and seemed oblivious to pain.

The alpha of their small pack, Mighty George, had died in the ring shortly after pairing with Tobacca. A gruesome forty-eight minute grinder had removed most of his face and proven his stamina, determination, and intelligence. Trusting years of warrior conditioning, with both front legs broken, he wriggled across a syrup of shit and blood to meet his opponent. Mighty George died game ten minutes later, choking for breath, his jaws clamped on his opponent's breast.

Mighty George's valiant death proved the bloodline, but set back his owner's dream. "Ticky" Bilger was a short man with a tick that pulled his right cheek toward his left eye. His voice trilled an octave higher than other men's and his belly flopped over his belt like a giant breast with an inverted nipple. Had he been born in a litter of pit bulls, his master would have used him as a bait dog. Born to the human world, he considered his flaws evidence of exceptionality and cultivated them.

A day came in Maul's life when Ticky pulled him from ferocious play and wrapped a grimy bicycle drive-chain around his neck, making several circuits, and fastened the end to the beginning with a twisted piece of coat hanger. Ticky spun Maul with a hard smack to his rump and got down on his elbows to jeer in the dog's face.

Ticky's son Pete watched with bottle cap eyes.

"These sons a bitches don't fight 'less they're good and mad," Ticky said. "You got to humiliate em from the time they can walk to the time they can't."

"Why the chain?"

"Fighting dog needs a good neck. Lookit him. He loves this shit."

Maul growled with small-toothed rage and Ticky's hand flashed from his side to Maul's head, knocked him end over end.

"You got to be careful when you discipline a dog," Ticky said. "Too much, and he'll just piss puddles."

Pete smiled.

Maul added pounds quickly and Ticky rewrapped the chain every few days to keep his airways unimpeded. He suspected Maul had a bit of Mastiff blood. To kill parasites, Ticky fed him cow or hog liver, busted a pair of eggs on top, and razzed him with a stick to hearten his appetite. If Ticky had no liver, he fed Maul extract from a brown bottle. When Maul carried his head as high as his littermates, Ticky replaced the bicycle chain with a rusty length of torus links from the garage.

Maul promised to be Ticky's contribution to blood sport, his ticket to the ranks of professional dog men, but legendary breeder Mason Smith stood in Ticky's path. The man had no sense of humor and had never forgiven Ticky for knocking up his youngest daughter; had never forgotten a midnight drive to a doctor in Philly to get the baby cut out. He had a memory like a woman and, unfortunately for Ticky, was the only local fight organizer of renown.

It would take something special to gain his approval, or some trick to avoid his attention. The answer would come. Meantime, Ticky assigned the daily chore of exercising Maul to Pete, usually in the back yard on a device that resembled a mule-driven grain mill, called a catmill. Pete would harness Maul to the beam, which jutted fifteen horizontal feet from a central, rotating post. A counterbalance of cement blocks hung on the other side. Almost within reach of Maul, a neighborhood cat dangled in leather straps, hissing and powerless to flee.

Pete's first time running the catmill, he held the screeching cat in leather gloves and strapped it in, then wrapped him in a rag. He brought out Maul and the rag was on the ground. Maul dragged him toward the tomcat and it was an act of seeming divine providence that Pete was able to secure the dog in the harness. He'd planned to remove the rag in a semi-official ceremony, stepping aside and letting Maul run. Instead he lost his balance and the dog was off.

Maul lunged. The mill jerked the cat away and Maul gnashed inches behind; the faster he ran the more fleet became his adversary. Pete cursed encouragement. The frenzied cat hissed. Maul redoubled his effort. The chains about his neck jangled. Slobber dripped from his jaws. He circled round and round, each lap slowing, but the cat remained just shy of his bite, screeching and waving tiny talons. When Maul stopped, the cat swung away; he charged and it rocked closer. Maul heaved. The cat neared. His jaws smashed shut and missed. He skidded. The cat screeched. He sprang. Another miss. Over and over until he could lunge and snap no more, and collapsed, each panting breath lifting a cloud of dust.

"Damn you!"

Pete prodded him. Nudged him. Kicked him. Donned leather gloves again and held the cat before him. The tom clawed Maul's nose and Pete tossed the cat in a cage until the next day.

Another of Pete's favorite calisthenics pitted Maul against his feline tormenter in an all-wire birdcage, suspended from a backyard tree with a rope running through the center of the cage, the excess hanging below. Maul leapt, caught the rope in his jaws and swung free of the ground until his strength waned.

The cat enticed him with breathy hisses, and Maul snarled back with maturing rage. Age ripened his wrath, until at five months his fury was so acute and his strength so developed he ratcheted up the rope by whipping his body and adjusting his jaws to lock each half-inch gain, until his paws beat the cage.

Maul's training progressed to his sixth month. Ticky ran from the house to a squabble of a fervor he'd never before heard. Wrapped in heavy chains, Maul stood over the mangled corpse of a male sibling. Ticky clubbed Maul with a baseball bat, careful not to break bones, and segregated him. Bait dogs weren't easy to come by—from this day onward he would expect Pete to keep Maul crated except while training.

A day came when, after running around the catmill for a hot hour in the sun, Maul's ambition flagged. The chains were heavy that morning and to the degree a sport dog could be attributed

a variability in mood, Maul's had darkened. The relentless training exhausted him and his natural intelligence flagged, but even
through the fog of endless toil a dim realization emerged: he
would never destroy the cat.

The tom shared this knowledge, and lulled to a sense of security, urinated onto Maul's circuitous path. Maul stopped, as if his
warrior spirit was unable to bear the humiliation. His neck bore
the weight of a fifteen-foot chain; he panted in the late-morning
heat. Pete rushed to kick him and Maul bared his fangs.

Pete crossed the yard to the shed, slipped his hands into
leather gloves. Trod across the dirt to the suspended cat and
loosed it from the harness. He tied it at the base of the birdcage
tree. The cat mewed and as Pete walked away from him and
toward Maul, hissed.

Maul, nine months old and sixty-eight sinewy pounds,
watched with rapt eyes and trembled in a pointer-like pose. Endless jumping exercises had converted his rear legs to ropes of electric muscle. His neck was meaty like a buffalo; his jaws could
crush bone. Maul strained forward so hard Pete had to knee him
in the chest to break the tension on his collar enough to unclip
him. Maul crossed the lawn in two twelve-foot bounds and be-
headed the cat in a single biting rip.

Ticky grumbled, but took heart from Pete's description of
Maul's instant and unbridled brutality. As the dog's training advanced, Ticky would need more bait animals, and he fed Maul's
siblings every day for that purpose, though he gave none liver
and eggs. Meantime he'd have to drive to Dubois and find another stray cat—or with luck, a poodle. Ticky hated poodles.

The lunge test came two months later. Two dogs, each tied short
of the other, were released from their masters' restraining arms

in a test of mettle. A young dog eager to close with a senior male could be trusted to enter the pit aggressively and avoid embarrassing his owner. Maul launched like a rocket and when the rope jerked him shy of his quarry, raged.

Maul dispatched two siblings in backyard rumbles over the next month. He flew into fury at the sight of another animal, and the untrained puppies were defenseless. Ticky stopped wasting them.

For Maul's first birthday, Ticky arranged an unsanctioned, private match with a local two-year-old, untested pit named Sonny. His breeder, Abe Conry, had given Sonny the usual training, beatings, and bait cats, but the dog had never conquered the lunge test. Sonny outweighed Maul by eight pounds, and Conry hoped a taste of Maul's blood might stir Sonny's ambition.

Rules called for a simultaneous release. After that, the referee deemed the contest over by death, cowardice, or in a rare exception, a dog's owner could forfeit the match and spare his defeated dog.

An animal demonstrated cowardice by fleeing the fight circle or, given the opportunity to attack, by turning away. Some localities permitted three turns; Ticky and Conry agreed to no limit, provided when the dogs were separated to their corners, the turning dog proved his pluck by aggressively closing with his enemy.

A cur that fled the pit earned a death sentence, delivered immediately with requisite cruelty to staunch the breeder's embarrassment. Shame among dog men lingered, for they derived great satisfaction from creating, as products of their own intelligence, sweat, and determination, a class of animals uniquely suited to destroying other animals. The dog measured the man. Both the coward and the champion reflected upon their owner.

Conry and Ticky met inside an unused barn on Conry's property. Pete and Conry's boy sat on a rail, out of the way.

The refereeing was consensual. They were, after all, gentlemen.

A pair of sixty-watt bulbs lit the small barn; dust filaments drifted through the light. Maul walked unsteadily from the pickup truck, the first time in his memory without neck chains. His head floated high and his energy swelled; he sniffed friskily and picked up the scent of another dog. Maul froze; his throat vibrated. His back hair lifted and he pulled the lead.

Ticky guided him to the far side of the enclosed room; one hand looped through the leash with the excess coiled around his arm. His other hand clasped Maul's collar.

Metal tinkled outside and a moment later, man and dog entered. Maul bristled; adrenaline shot through him. He sensed this moment consummated a year's training, strength struggles, leaping, hanging from a tire, running, weights chained to his neck, rending cats and puppies. His instincts were tuned to destruction.

He smelled the other dog's fear.

His adversary dropped his muzzle and growled. The other man slid the barn door closed while the dog slunk to and fro, his nose inches from the floor, as if the deception hid his superior size and weight.

The noise and posturing, Maul sensed, were dissembling. He understood the width of the dog's shoulders and smelled his age. Instinct calculated his opponent's height and strength, but Maul's direct cogency was limited to the other dog's fear. It was palpable.

The dogs knew each other's minds.

Maul's felt his master squatting behind him, arms interlocked around him. His collar had vanished while he'd mused about his foe. The other man squatted beside his dog, restraining him with a single arm across his chest. Both men stank an acrid odor of anticipation.

The last time, Maul had been stopped short of his adversary. But in this novel setting with an unknown rival, he sensed deliverance. This time he would not be restrained. Maul glanced back; his master's right cheek twitched. Maul strained forward.

"Git 'im!" his master's boy cried.

Maul lunged, dragging Ticky center ring.

"You dumb sumbitch!"

Maul struggled to close the four-foot gap.

Ticky shouted and released him. The other man rolled away from his dog. Maul reared on hind legs and descended upon his foe. His rival lifted his anvil head, but Maul feinted and clashed shoulders; they collapsed into a whirl of tangled legs and gnashing teeth until seconds later Maul sank his fangs into the other's throat.

The fur was dry. When the first delicate taste of blood touched Maul's tongue—teasingly faint, like a wisp of buck scent carried a thousand yards—he clamped deeper and jerked. His rival's muzzle aimed skyward. The man-child on the beam yelled "Gitim!" like when Maul killed a bait dog, and Maul squeezed his jaws tighter. Blood spurted in his mouth and he gagged, wheezed, and added pressure. His opponent quickly ceased his struggle.

The other dog's master stroked his throat, his eyes shifting from Maul to Ticky, then Maul. "Forfeit."

Ticky stepped to Maul with a pry stick. "That's it you crazy son of a bitch."

Maul sensed him from the sides of his vision. His mind was on blood and a feeling of joy that came from his master.

ONE June 1957

The Lord had answered and His words portended suffering. Emeline Margulies bent at her waist and knocked dirt and crinkled grass from her stockinged knees. She had been deep in prayer, kneeling in the field because the Lord was always closer outside, on the hill behind the house.

She held a bloodied finger before her. Bending, she studied a splotch of red on her stockings and pressed the center, where some unknown wound had occurred. She felt it now.

On the ground where her knee had pressed lay the white stone that had lacerated her. A narrow streak of blood crossed the face of the rock. She recalled a scripture from Revelation about a white rock with a name written under it—the name the Lord would give her, known to her alone.

She stared down the field. "Should I look at it now, Lord?"

She observed the clouds, one after another, then turned and beheld the row of trees beside the field. She listened to the deepest recesses of her mind. Nothing. Just moments ago the Lord had spoken with clarity she'd never before experienced, and now He was silent.

"I'll come back later."

Emeline's thoughts returned to the reason she had prayed. Angus Hardgrave had asked her to marry him. Angus Hardgrave.

She hadn't known him until recently.

Immediately before her father's death she'd decided that if she was to be alone in a fallen world at eighteen years of age, she would have to depend heavily upon the Lord. But because the Lord and she had different ways—she being rebellious—she had little hope of seeing the footsteps He prepared for her to walk in. Without the Lord's help, she wouldn't know where to put her feet. She resolved not only never to cease seeking the Lord's will, but to remain open to suggestions from places that might ordinarily cause trepidation. The Lord could communicate through any number of channels, other believers, nonbelievers, even dreams, apparitions and visions. And although the most convincing exchanges with the Almighty usually took the form of a simple, nagging voice in her mind, Emeline determined to pay attention to everything and hope the Lord would not give up on overcoming her stubbornness.

Thus, when Angus Hardgrave accosted her, she fought her natural revulsion and listened with divinely attuned ears.

As a girl she'd heard stories about the Hardgrave clan and their war with a brood of McClellans. The stories carried a note of long past lore, told when the moon was full and family and neighbors would sit on the front porch smoking pipes, sipping iced tea, and speaking in special haunted tones for the children.

In high school she'd heard a story about Angus, something to do with his wife running away—but the memory was faint and she couldn't recollect if it was him or some other poor man.

Marry Angus Hardgrave? Lord? I want to be obedient, but I don't know what you want.

So she'd walked in the fields behind the house, along the wood line, where the Lord had sometimes been willing to converse with her. She'd felt the Lord's presence so acutely that she'd dropped to her knees, closed her eyes and bowed her head. She told Him everything He already knew, and His answers came in waves of awareness, each insight building upon the previous, culminating in an understanding that existed beyond her capacity to articulate.

She understood with clarity. The Lord was specific in his command that though she loved neither, she was to marry Angus Hardgrave, not the other man she knew, lip-biter Brad Chambers.

The Lord reminded her of His trustworthiness, and told her that because she was a sinner she would doubt. However, by His grace, He would enrich her by deepening her understanding of His ways. In the end, her knowledge of good would be as deep as her experience of evil.

She knocked dirt and dried grass from her knees and turned toward her house on the bottom of the slope below. So many questions. It was her house now that her father was gone, and the Lord was telling her to marry Angus Hardgrave. She stopped.

Lord, what do I do with the house? I don't understand how this solves anything. And what about Brad Chambers? Is Angus going to take care of him?

She walked stiffly, knees unwilling to bend. She didn't need the Lord to answer.

He said she would doubt.

He said she would fear.

TWO

The walnut tree told me when Emeline Margulies turned eighteen. Law-wise in Pennsylvania, a girl burns her ships at eighteen. Her daddy was dead and she was alone, so I bound her with spells, talk of blue spruce situated off the front porch, small-mouth bass jumping bugs at the lake, and how sunshine bounces from the water to the orchard and turns pear blossoms gold. She bought every word and wiggled close. I took her wrist and got my hand on her neck and I couldn't think of nothing save the bones inside her.

I stand with her in a stone church a block from Madison. Pastor Denny thumbs to a folded page and Emeline presses a fistful of daisies to her heart. I look at the white petals and she looks at me. My eye patch still throws her. She pretends, but she sees it first and switches to my left eye. She blinks three times. Rubs her hand down her side.

Pastor Denny says, "From Ephesians we are told, '*Wives, submit to your husbands as to the Lord. For the husband is the head of the wife as Christ is the head of the church.*'" Denny faces

Emeline and says, "That means you got to do as he says. Angus—you got a ring?"

I drop my hand to my pocket. Emeline's face is pale.

Denny says, "...to be your lawful, wedded wife, until by death do you part?"

"Yes sir," I say. "'Til one of us is dead."

Denny repeats the oath to Emeline. She peers hard into my eye. Movement flickers at my extreme peripheral, but I don't turn my head.

Emeline gulps air. "I do."

I ease the band onto her finger. She lowers her arm and curls her hand. I'll see a jeweler at some point, get the ring resized.

"You can kiss her now."

I take her elbows, press my face to hers. She ain't been kissed much, I suspect. Every time I get a grip on her skinny arms my mind goes elsewhere and I see things I want to take right now. I don't close my eye, and she don't close hers, and maybe she understands and maybe she don't. I glance back and a fella I don't know leans against the wall by the entrance with his leg hiked up like James Dean. He slips out and next I look at Emeline her eyes are closed.

Pastor Denny nods; I take Emeline by the hand and face the witnesses. Her older sister Martha, in town to collect inheritance. George, summoned from the barbershop with shaving cream on his ear. The pastor's wife Nancy, dense as a sack of soggy cowshit but topheavy enough it don't matter what she says.

I step from the platform, Emeline in tow. As we pass Martha shakes her head and Nancy Denny says, "It ain't right, Emeline. Think what you're doing."

My fingers tremble and I clamp my hand to the door jamb.

"Don't worry about them." Emeline shades her eyes, faces north and south, then lingers a moment on a new 1957 red and white Fairlane gleaming at the curb. "What'd you expect from a pair of hens but a bunch of clucking?"

I spit on the church steps. "Not much."

She looks at the spit puddle, blank. Then, "How old are you, Angus?"

"Forty-six, I think." I check my pocket watch and lead her across the macadam road to the First National Bank of Walnut, Pennsylvania. We step onto the speckled stone floor. The door swings closed and I release her wrist. She trails me to the lone teller and our footsteps echo from the marble walls. I push my passbook below the brass grill.

"Move her money to my account," I say. "We're married."

"All right," says the teller.

Emeline pulls my sleeve like a small bird might, if it wanted my attention. "Angus, I don't have my pass book."

"They don't need it. You come in here just yesterday."

She leans to me. "We didn't talk about this."

"Everything?" the teller says.

"Close the account."

He notes a ledger. "I'll just need Missus Hardgrave's signature." He passes a slip through the slot and I scribble, "Emeline Hardgrave."

"But—" She clenches fists at her sides and her brow is jetted up like a mad blue jay's.

"We got to put her name on this account," I say. "Make it joint."

"I'll draw up the papers. Money's moved, account's closed. And congratulations on the wedding."

"Gimme a ten spot."

"Ten?"

I wink—looks like a regular blink, I suppose. "We got to celebrate."

Emeline watches me fold the ten. I take her hand and lead her to my truck, open the door for her. She stands outside and I walk to the other side, swing under the steering wheel. She climbs in, slams the door, plants her hands on her lap.

"I don't brook sass in public," I say.

She waits.

"I apologize," she says. "I haven't had a man in my corner since Papa... I apologize."

I start the F-100. "Not in public, not nowhere." My temple aches and I press it. She rolls down the window. Her head tilts toward her knees and her lips move. In the weeks I've known her she's prayed five hundred times and that's good. More she talks to him, less she talks to me.

The church stands a block removed from Madison, the only through-street in town. A mile in either direction, Madison becomes State Road Sixty-Four. Eight miles south sits the Hardgrave Estate. She wanted to talk poetry, so I told her about the wet warm feel of a Holstein milker's nose. I talked about the hearth. The sanctity of a woman's womb. Her pap had died a month past and the cycle that closed with him would renew with us.

We courted a week and I learned how she tended her father and scribbled poems at night before bed. She's got secrets, that one. But the walnut tree on Devil's Elbow—a spur peninsula on Lake Oniasont, right below the house—showed me an image of me telling her about the land and Emeline's eyes swelling and her lips pursing, so I talked 'til I run out of lies. Rich brown soil, hunting game, fruit trees and the smell of corn dripping with butter. I slipped my arm around her back, felt her heat, and promised ducks floating on the lake under white clouds.

She seized my hands when I said we should marry, and a light crossed behind her eyes. Marrying was the last thing she'd thought of, she said, except the lord put the idea to her first.

We pass a silent moment outside the church, sitting in my F-100. "Who's that Fairlane belong to?" I shift the truck into gear. "See it around more and more."

"I don't know."

"Forgot something." I kill the engine and cross the street to the state store, and return with two paper bags. I stow one behind the truck seat, slip a fifth of Wild Turkey from the other, and crack the seal. After a quick gurgle I rest the bottle between us. Emeline leans closer to the open window.

The F-100 chugs along. I steer with my knees, fish a tin of Copenhagen and offer her a pinch.

Emeline wrinkles her nose.

I thump the tin, look through the side view mirror. Down by the Fairlane, the fella from the church stands with his hands at his side like he's used to hefting a pipe. I pack my lip full of snuff.

"If I asked," she says, "would you give up tobacco?"

These kinds of questions don't mean shit on their own, but add twenty together, you get boxed in. Then hell breaks loose.

"Our love would suffer."

"Papa... used tobacco."

"Your Pap gave me my first chew."

"What?"

"Sure did. Never touched it 'til I sold him a mess of walnut logs. Must've been in what, forty-seven?"

"You knew Papa?"

"Just enough. Worked with him over a weekend, sawing a big old walnut tree on my land. Said he was setting up a wood shop for his golden years. He offered his tin and I took it, and ain't quit yet."

"This is my driveway coming up."

I look at her. Turn.

The gravel leads through a shaded grove of eastern hemlock that smells like black earth. Forty yards from the road, the drive-way loops to the milk house and rounds within a dozen feet of the farmhouse front porch.

We're here to fetch her honeymoon suitcase, and we'll return for the rest of her things. Two hours ago, she left this house an unwed woman; now she's owned.

"Ever since Papa died, I've remembered a single stanza. I memorized the whole poem, of course, but all I recall is four lines." Her voice goes soft. "*I shall sleep, and move with the moving ships, Change as the winds change, veer in the tide; My lips will feast on the foam of thy lips, I shall rise with thy rising, with thee subside...* While my father withered away upstairs, I hid from his moans in the living room. I wrote silly poems and compared them to Swinburne's. But now I'm so happy I don't need poems any more."

I study the house from lightning rods to stone foundation. A paper flag sticks between door and jamb.

Emeline touches my shoulder. "I'll be right along." She climbs out of the truck. "My bag isn't heavy."

Wondering about the note stuck in the door, I say, "I'll fetch it."

"I'll just be a minute."

Emeline runs up the steps. I work a stray grain of Copenhagen back to the pouch of my lip. She hides the folded paper with her body and snatches it when she opens the door.

I sit in the truck and spit at the grass. Time to see the old man's tools. At the barn I drag open the twelve-foot sliding door.

Secrets.

In 1947 when I was three years back from the war and Emeline was tall as a tomato plant, I sold a lightning blasted walnut to Old Man Margulies. The tree reached deep into Hardgrave history, but I was hard up and helped saw ten-foot logs and load them onto Margulies' truck. The crotch took a tractor, a giant tripod we made of three oak trees, and a horse to maneuver it to the truck bed. Margulies busted a leaf spring hauling it out. He paid a sawmill to cut eight, six, and four-quarter boards that he'd turn into fine furniture once he sold the Farmall dealership and retired. I'd have to stop by one day and see the shop.

Indeed.

The sun lights a broad shaft of dust at the barn entrance. I run my fingers across the tacky cast iron top of a DeWalt table saw, then scrape the metal with my fingernails. Paste wax curls under, like it was put on heavy to protect. I buff the metal with my shirttail and the iron gleams. A few feet away stands a Rockwell shaper, a drill press and an edge belt sander. Tools on the walls, and everything maintained. No corrosion. The rafters support maple and walnut—the same walnut I sold Margulies—maybe four hundred board feet.

I spot a white Farmall A, parked against the—

"Angus? Where are you?" Emeline's voice drifts into the barn.

I glance through the open door and nod. She heaves her suitcase to the truck bed and joins me.

"I've been keeping these tools for two years. The last time Papa stepped outside the house he showed me where to rub the wax. He taught me to turn on the motors and let them exercise, is what he called it."

I drop to my haunches and study the base of the table saw. "You got your gear?"

"In the truck." She stands with hands clasped. "I thought we were leaving for Pittsburgh straight off."

I lead her out and close the sliding door.

"I didn't see your bag in the truck," she says. She reaches for my arm. "We *are* going to Pittsburgh?"

"Changed my mind. You got things to do."

I open the passenger side truck door.

Emeline braces a palm on the bed. "You promised, Angus. I've never been to the city. Last night you promised." Her brow wrinkles. "What *things* have I to do?"

I cross to the driver's side. "You got to get that house ready to sell, for one."

"That house hasn't been mine but for two weeks. I'm not selling it."

I clean the chew from my mouth with a hooked index finger. She raises her hand to her breast and scratches, probly where she tucked the paper note.

We trade stares a long minute. She lifts her hand to her breast again and stops, and turns part sideways and meditates on the house. Her lips move silent again. I think of the walnut and the tools and how hot her skin was when I touched it last night, and I got to own this woman right now. I got to drag her somewhere. I can almost feel her neck in my hand.

At last she faces me. "Maybe we could picnic at the lake? You described it so beautifully."

"Let's do that."

Driving with the Wild Turkey bottle between my legs, I pull onto Road 64. To the left, a breeze roils a wheat field. Miles come and go. A forest borders the field. We approach a house set twenty feet from the road. Mrs. McClellan sits on a porch swing eyeballing me. Got so many wrinkles it'd take two square feet of face to pull her skin taut. Sheriff's car is in the drive, part on the grass. The driver door hangs open.

"What do you suppose is going on?" Emeline says.

I slow the truck, enter McClellan's driveway. My land sits adjacent and I prefer the law to stay off it.

"We might be able to help," Emeline says.

I step out of the truck and recall the past.

I came home from France in forty-five and visited a cemetery memorial the McClellans set up because their son Larry never came home. This was the first I paid respects since trying to push his guts back in his belly on the beach, and I'm still getting used to my eye patch. Mrs. McClellan sneaks to my blind side, beats my shoulders with balled up hands, saying, "You did this!"

I back away and her husband Mitch is behind her. She charges me and I'm looking at Mitch to control his woman. Larry was almost a brother, and I could just as easy been saying she got Larry killed by raising him a coward. Finally, Mitch says, 'Leave the bastard alone. He ain't worth it.'

Since then Mitch has had the general good sense to keep clear of me but I caught him a half dozen times stealing walnuts from the tree on Devil's Elbow. Years back his family disputed the property lines, and though the courthouse shows I own the cussed land and the tree sitting on it, Mitch McClellan for years went around telling folk it was his birthright. When I sawed and sold the older, bigger walnut in 1947, it was partly for spite.

I blink a stiff long blink and the memories float off through the corn field.

I'm two feet beyond the truck when I hear Emeline open her door. She's quick to my side and takes my hand.

"What you want?" Mrs. McClellan says.

"Something going on?"

"Bugger off."

"Sheriff Heilbrun here?"

"Ain't it plain?"

I look to the woods around the house. "Where's Mitch?"

"That's the question," she says, and her bottom lip quivers. "Be gone!"

I take Emeline by the elbow and she tugs away and kneels beside the old woman. "Can we help you?" Emeline says.

"See if you can help yourself." The old woman eyes me. "Be gone." McClellan sniffles, rocks back and forth on the swing. Emeline rests her hand on top of McClellan's before walking away.

I back out of McClellan's driveway.

We pass a quarter mile of cornfield. I slow. Courting Emeline I told her my house was perched on a knoll above Lake Oniasont. Apple and pear trees dot the slope on the left, and to the right, a hardwood forest spans miles, all the way to the big lines running from the Warren power plant. When storms come, six inch waves lap the pebbled beach and in summer heat you can look across the water and the whole thing is glass-flat, except an occasional small mouth bass jumping at a bug. Yellow butterflies float like bubbles of sunlight and at dusk, fireflies glitter green across the fields.

I downshift and take the driveway. Emeline catches her breath. There's corn on our right and a forest that gives way to pasture and barn on the left. We putt over ruts that jar the bone. Small in the distance, the house stands proud of the horizon, and a hodge-podge of brown Jersey and black and white Holstein cows graze by the barn. Rust-pocked hull of a pickup seems to float on weeds beside the barn, then beyond, a slope-sided chicken coop comes into view. A dozen birds strut and peck the ground.

Everything I billed, and then some.

I park and Emeline steps out. She looks across the orchard, the lake, the house. Blue spruce trees stand like sentries off each porch corner. The lowest limbs brush the ground and frost-colored needles extend to the top whorl, half again higher than the two-story house. A blue jay studies Emeline with a beady black eye and welcomes her with a jeer.

I yank her suitcase from the truck bed. She stands on the porch, looking around. The lawn grows more ragged as it reaches the lake. She turns, taking in the apple and pear trees. Her eyes follow the porch rail, the flaking paint, and the dry rot where posts meet boards. Under her feet, the grey paint is worn to the wood. She looks inside the house through a window needs washed.

"What's that from?" She nods at a chestnut smudge on the wall.

"Ike. Most useless dog ever was. Just laid there all day long."

"Where is he?"

"Put him down a few months back."

"Oh, that's terrible... I'd like a dog."

"Got my eye on one. Let's get inside."

She opens the screen door and stops. I bump into her ass and get a vision like I pissed on a hot fence—see her hands bound and eyes like headlights when you turn em off and they glow for another second or two.

Emeline eases inside and takes it in. A Philco radio stands against the outer wall, with three chairs arranged in a semicircle. Beyond the chairs, the opposite wall is a built-in bookshelf, loaded with the same books that educated the likes of Thomas Jefferson. She glances at a stone fireplace with a mantle clock and a Sharps rifle mounted above. She steps into the kitchen, where the chimney forms part of the wall.

"Snug come winter," I say. "Forgot the dishes. Let me carry this case upstairs and I'll get you stationed."

"How does one man have so many dishes?" She unfolds her hand toward plates stacked lopsided on the table; to the sink, where four cast iron pans rust half submerged. "And all of them dirty?" She views the whole grand sweep; cornbread crusts, fish bones, dried mashed potatoes, then she opens the screenless window above the sink and shoos black flies.

"Kitchen needs a woman's touch."

I head up the stairs with her suitcase.

Jacob rambles up the porch steps and enters the house as I near the top of the stairs. He's in bare feet and dirty pants that stop short of his ankles. He stands as high as Emeline's breast, and looks like an eight-year-old beat with a grow-stick. A streak of mud crosses his face like a battle scar.

"You Emeline?"

"I'm Emeline." She looks at me with a half smile, eyes bright for the unexpected... but holds her look with me long enough to say this ain't what she bargained for. I continue up the stairs as she faces Jacob. "What's your name?"

"Jacob."

"You live nearby?

He snorts. "Course. Me an' Deet."

I rest the suitcase at the top of the stairwell and step back down. "This is Jake. Deet's in the field. Come upstairs and see where you're situated."

Jacob says, "Mitch McClellan blowed his head off."

"If I had a head like his, I'd want rid of it."

Emeline glances at me, kneels, takes Jacob's hands. "How do you know?"

It's been half a year since a woman touched him. Jacob looks to me. "I seen him."

"Child," she says, and embraces him. Jacob watches me, arms limp at his side. I'm thinking I should've drained the dishwater to get rid of some of the smell. Jacob pulls his head back from her.

"What'd you see, boy?" I say.

"I was fishing. I heard the shotgun."

"Where was you fishing?"

"West a bit."

The west side of the lake curls around with a clear eyeshot of the walnut tree. "See him do it?"

Jacob nods. "He sat down to whittle. I didn't pay him no mind. He's always there—when you ain't around."

"Why ain't you ever said so?"

"This's the first he blowed his head off." Jacob pushes away from Emeline and goes to the refrigerator.

Emeline brushes back hair that's fallen to her nose. I lead her up creaky steps to a hickory hallway that ain't seen oil soap in six months, turn into the last bedroom and put her bag in the closet. "There's space in the top two dresser drawers. You'll want to change before you start supper. I'll get things red up, and tonight we'll sit at the lake with a bottle."

"Were you going to tell me you have two sons?"

"I said something about that last night."

She sits on the edge of the bed and the springs twang. "Seems like a man ought to tell a woman he's got two kids before he marries her." She flattens a fold in the quilt. "Though Jacob looks like a fine boy."

"Dumb as a frog in cold water. Got his momma's brains."

"Where is she?"

I feel the cords in my neck all stiff. I think of bones and teeth and human frailty.

"I didn't mean to snoop. I should have expected surprises. We didn't exactly take our time."

I nod. I could take her wrists and have her, but I want to let it build.

"Don't fret about the kitchen," she says. "I'll clean it. I'll just be a few minutes.

THREE

I fetch a mess of rope and a double-bladed axe from the barn. I crafted the handle a year ago—hardened hickory sapwood over fire, shaped it with a drawknife, paid special attention to the bump of shoulder below the head. I sanded until the grain was slick and rubbed it daily with linseed oil until the finish glowed, then locked the twin-bladed head with a wedge. Homemade haft stretches a foot longer than stock from the store. I stand six-four, and if the bit has a razor edge I'll sever three-inch maple in a single swing.

Crossing the house again I linger by the porch and look into the kitchen through the window Emeline left open. Jacob sits at the table chewing bread smeared with apple jam.

"How old are you, Jacob?" Emeline says.

"Eight."

"Did your Papa tell you who I am?"

"My new momma."

"Did he say anything else?"

"We need a woman for dishes and laundry. And other needs."

Emeline takes in the kitchen. I have electricity—and not many in the country do, with the Eisenhower program only ramping up. She draws water at the tap. Townsfolk 've had hot water forever, but not out here. She lifts a black telephone from its cradle, prominent beside the kitchen entry. Her home in Walnut don't have a telephone. She said her old man had one at the Farmall dealership but wanted his house quiet. After he sold the business they went without. She holds the handset to her ear and the corners of her mouth move up.

Her smile fades as she replaces the telephone, steps to the stove and wipes it. She peers at the grease smudge on her finger, the floor, the walls, hutch. She opens a pantry door and pulls a lanyard from a bulb at the rafters. I circle to the other window. All at once she's dragging a stool from below the bottom shelf, climbing it, elbows flapping, rearranging Campbell's soup and a bag of beans.

She slams a can into the shelf a half dozen times and Jacob jumps out of his skin.

"Jacob honey, I need you to get me a grocery bag or something."

"What for?"

"I said so."

"I mean, what you want to put in it?"

"Mice."

"Just give them to me." He holds cupped hands above his head.

"They're bloody, Jacob."

"Aw c'mon. Let me have em. Please?"

She lowers a fuzzy nest of leaves and string, swallows like to hold back bile, and places the nest in Jacob's hands. "Toss them in the field."

"I wanna fish with em."

"Do that, then. Jacob? Where's the broom? Mop?"

"The cellar." He runs out the door.

She touches her belly and leans against the doorjamb a long minute with her eyes clamped shut, like she's already out of breath. Got a lot of work ahead, to be short on breath now. She wipes her eyes and I puzzle until Jacob leaps the steps and takes off toward the barn.

"Hey!"

Jacob spins. I wave him closer and he holds up his prize, an adult and four hairless, blind, smashed baby mice. I tousle his hair. "Get outta here, little shithead."

Figured Sheriff Heilbrun would have been up to the house by now. He ain't come so I head down the trail to the lake. He faces the walnut on his haunches and I get a thought in the back of my mind that the walnut knows all about death, and if I ever knew as much as that walnut I'd know too damn much.

Heilbrun always looks tense on account of his narrow, high shoulders, but it could be his proximity to the walnut throwing him off. Or maybe it's the axe in my hand, and rope in the other.

The walnut tree don't look any worse for a shotgun blast but that's 'cause Mitch's head took the brunt. From forty yards the only thing looks different is a gallon jug on its side. Mitch's body's already moved. Heilbrun stands as I near. His look goes to my axe and he opens his mouth and I answer.

"Gonna gather some brush for a fire."

He nods to the ground in front of his knees where Mitch McClellan ended his life. "Ugly," he says.

There's a mess of blood and brains on the bark and the ground. To the side where Mitch pitched over the grass and leaves are almost black. Flies buzz around us, brought in by the blood.

Lot of history on the Devil's Elbow.

Heilbrun holds a Y-shaped sprig in his fingers, maybe a half-inch in diameter and eight inches long. He raises it to eye level. "Whittled this right here. There's shavings on the ground, spread out. Probly leaned on the tree, and the shavings fell to his belly. Then he slumps over, and all these chips fall to the side."

"What is it?" I listen but don't hardly hear. The dirt calls me from twenty feet away. I get a notion I'm liable to start talking and not know a damn thing I'm saying. This ground's had a lot of death on it. The tree, the graves. Other history, before my time.

He pokes the sprig toward me. "Used it to depress the trigger."

"Pretty clear suicide?"

"Where was you about four hours ago?"

"Church. Got married."

"No shit? Again?"

Married again? Again? Why, we ain't twenty feet from the last. Meanwhile I can almost feel Emeline's hot skin, and can almost taste the salt on her neck, and I got Heilbrun talking like he knows more than he knows. I want her neck in my hand and her wrist in the other. I reach to the walnut and plant my hand firm, and wait until I'm all easy-does-it, and Heilbrun smiles. I got a picture come to me from the tree but this ain't the time, sheriff eyeballing me. I can make out a photograph of myself a ways off and then I see Emeline's ass got a man's hand on it.

"Real happy for you," Heilbrun says.

I loose my hand from the tree and the vision's gone. This ain't like the others—but I never let go so fast 'cause the damn sheriff was next to me before.

"Real happy," Heilbrun says again. His look is peculiar and I suppose mine is too.

"I'll be seein' you." I leave him there.

FOUR

D evil's Elbow is a small knob formed by a hillside creek
that empties to Lake Oniasont. Name's a hundred fifty
years old and amounts to a clever way to say things at
the elbow ain't the same as elsewhere. Devil's Elbow shapes what
goes on around it. I wouldn't be surprised if the fallen angel himself coaxed the shotgun into Mitch's hands, and lullabied his ears
full of music.

I harvest firewood here every summer and now collect dried
brush from the refuse. I clean brush from branches, rest the poles
on a stump, and chop four-foot lengths. A loose pile grows to the
side and when it stands two feet I sit on a flat stump and reju-
venate on Wild Turkey.

The house's fallen to disrepair since Lucy Mae ain't been
around, but her nonstop clucking got on my nerves. Discovering
Emeline and negotiating a wedding in a single week was genius,
and I wish I could claim it, but the idea come to me sitting in
the walnut tree. Since I took to sitting in the tree things've been
looking up whichever way I look. Last week at the derrick, Merle

invited me to a dog fight. He's been cagey for years but last week came around.

"You ought to see em go. Those pits's some *game* sonsabitches; I tell you, they don't even quit when they're dead. They jaws lock."

Next fight's tomorrow after work. "Don't think I'll be interested," I said.

"I cleaned up. Bet on this red nose. Went in with five, came home with ten."

"Don't have the money to lose." Played Merle like a fiddle.

I look at the logs. A deer fly stings my neck. I swat, touch the bite with a whiskeyed fingertip. Fools like Merle make here-and-there money betting on fights. Smart man makes all-the-time money betting on the betters. By uncanny coincidence I got money the same time I got an invitation. Believe I'll investigate these fights.

Another gulp of Turkey in my belly and I fill my arms with firewood. Cross the stream on a series of flat rocks and emerge on Devil's Elbow near the walnut tree, thirty yards below the rotted stump of the senior tree I sold to Emeline's father a decade ago. I pass leaves with Mitch McClellan's blood, the bark with his brains and a chunk of skullcap with hair.

This surviving tree descended from the one I cut. A hundred years ago, some wily walnut escaped harvest by squirrel or man. The junior tree stands forty feet tall, full and round. The trunk splits into two heavy limbs. As a boy I curled in the crook and watched fish snap at bugs floating on the water. Through the years the walnut on Devil's Elbow has become a sort of oracle. Some of my best ideas, like courting Emeline, seeped into my head while I was cradled in the branches.

I stand at the lake's cobbled shore just beyond the walnut's shadow. There's sweat on my neck and my hair sticks. The tree wants me to deflower Emeline nearby. Wants me to keep a hand on the bark while I take her, or better, wants me to take her on its leaned-back limb. I know this like I know the sky is blue. My arms are full of wood and I think, I'm indebted, but I don't want to poke her where my neighbor just blew his brains out.

To the west a knoll ends with a steep bank. I follow the rocky waterline and toss my armload of scrub and return for another. Ten minutes later I drop a second armful to the pile, arrange the smallest sprigs into a teepee and fill it with tinder of dry grass and twigs. The sun stands midway between zenith and horizon. I make a final trip for my bottle of Turkey and stop at the walnut.

I can't smell anything. Copenhagen dulls the olfactory—but I figure ripe blood would cut through. I climb to my sloping perch on the horizontal branch and stretch my back against the bark. I drink, fold my arms at my belly, close my eyes.

Things are turning around, for damn sure. At forty-six I don't have a whole lot of time and can't say what I want it for. But I do have a dream, and I've struggled closer to it with each wife and year. Every time I sit in the tree I can see it clear as day.

White fence along the road, my house coated in fresh paint, maybe a foundation set in bricks instead of fieldstones. A double layer of red paint on the barn, all the missing boards filled in, a pasture spread far off to the right, replacing twenty acres of forest. And finally, by the walnut tree, a gazebo where I'll smoke a pipe and bark orders at an Irish foreman. He'll come to me with fear on his face, bowed like a page. I'll sit on a rocker, fishing pole, loyal dog at my side. Irish'll say, "Mister Hardgrave, sir, all four hundred head are fed, sir, and you'll have sixty smokin' hogs come fall." I'll wave and he'll shamble away. In a just world, I'd have been born in a city and I'd have gone to college. In this world, I didn't know what college was 'til it was too late. Before I earned the G.I. Bill I'd married an American fraulein who pooped out a son and named him Dietrich while I was off fighting the Hun.

The walnut tree groans in a breeze and I feel an image coming. It builds up a swirl of colors that don't make sense, and then resolves like a vacuum cleaner's just sucked out the fuzzy. These pictures don't last long and I've learned to pay attention. It seems like things are fulminating and somehow my role is important.

I see a photo of myself, but like I never lost my eye. I see a bloody brute of a dog wearing an eye patch. There's Deet, touching Emeline's hip like it's all he can do not to lay her on the table.

And I see a red and white Fairlane tooling on gravel.

FIVE

"Pap, Pap!" Jacob runs down the trail from the house. I roll off the limb and land in a clump. "Miss Emeline's got the Sharps!"

I rub my elbow.

"Says there's a man in the woods!"

"A man?"

"Got a bead on him right now."

I brush my legs, press a fist to my eye and gouge away the bleary.

"Pap, you got to come now!"

"Hold your cussed horses."

Jacob's already turned and running back to the house. I walk. Emeline shouts "Angus!" from inside. At the porch steps I scan the tree line beyond the barn, the rippling corn, the orchard. I step inside. Emeline's got a rifle through the window over the sink, aimed at the pasture to the left of the barn.

"You shoot a milker, I'll beat you ugly. What's going on?"

"There!" she says, "Do you see him?"

Outside there's not a damn thing. Not a damn thing. I stand back, take in the kitchen. She's begun her work, starting with the cupboards, counters, stove. Soapy dishwater fills the sink. Emeline blows hair from her eyes and swabs her brow with her sleeve.

"That Sharps is just as liable to blow up in your face as fire downrange. It don't go off the wall. Now who is it you see?"

"A man. With black hair."

"Probly the sheriff, or one of his crew." I lift the rifle from her hands, step to the living room, and replace it on the mounts above the mantle. "This fella you saw. He on the other side of the pasture?"

"By that gray stump," she says.

Back at her side, I crane forward. Blink.

"He must have slipped into the woods while you were coming. Aren't you going to run him off?"

I rough my hair.

"He could be in the barn by this time."

"Don't know what he'd want in the barn." I face her. "What color clothes he have on?"

"Blue jeans, I think. A white shirt."

"C'mon, Jake. Let's take a look."

"Aren't you going to take a rifle?" Emeline backs from the window, out of sight.

I kick driveway dust and part from Jacob at the pasture, throw my leg over the barbed wire fence, plod toward the stump. Jacob scurries on the driveway. Cattle graze a few yards off. Ahead in the woods a white-tail's ass flashes as he bounds away. My back to the house, I take a leak. Jockey my trousers, wave to Jacob.

A minute passes before I'm back at the house. Emeline's got a shooting stance, elbows on the kitchen table, legs braced wide, aiming the Sharps at the cellar door.

"A man running flat-out could cross a mile while you were out there," she says. She cranks back the hammer with her thumb.

"Woman! I know damn well I give instructions on this carbine."

"He's downstairs! I heard him!"

"Who?"

"I don't know!"

I lift the Sharps from her clutch and lean the barrel next the hutch. "Downstairs?"

She nods.

"Jake—run outside. See if the door's locked."

Jacob bolts.

"I don't care if the door's got iron bars. I heard him."

I throw open the cellar door and march into darkness, grope the wall with one hand and wave the other in front. A cobweb snares my fingers; I clasp a handrail. Each step carries me further into cold and damp. Smells like mold. The handrail ends. I reach with my foot and find cement, then face the light from the kitchen entrance and raise my arms. My fingers close on a string and I pull. A yellow bulb glows and the reluctant blackness recedes.

I turn a circle: ahead, a square door to a potato cellar; to the right, a room with darkness forbidding as a locked door; on the left, a workbench with scattered junk; behind, the chimney foundation and beyond, in shadows so deep they only resolve as I step closer, shelves. Below a blue rat poison dispenser, the corner of a suitcase bears the inked shape of a rose. Should've burned the damn thing, and the two below.

Emeline's brushed the dust with her hand, by the marks. She's seen the monogram, penned in ink many times over, as a child makes a thick letter from a thin pen: L.M.M.

I return to the kitchen. Emeline stands with a cleaver from the knife block.

Jacob stands at the kitchen entry. "It's locked."

"You was runnin' hot water," I say. "It's the pipes."

"Pipes?"

"Jacob, run along." I wave my arm. "Copper expands with hot water. Pipe squeaks against the holes in the trusses." I step to her. "Who was you expecting, Miss Emeline?"

"I didn't run water when the noise happened."

"The basement door's secure. Who'd you think you saw?"

"No one in particular."

"Secrets ain't too good, see. We got to have trust. There's no other way for a man and woman to live in the same house."

She looks to the floor.

"I'm heading back to the woods. You see him again, get his name. Hell, invite him to supper. Just don't touch my fuckin Sharps."

Passing the hutch I dislodge the carbine. Make a grab but miss and it clatters against a bucket and discharges, the angle perfect for the lowest center pane in the window. Now my fuckin ears ring. I lift the Sharps, press palm to temple. Feel the bulge of veins in my neck.

"Oh Lord Jesus. I'm sorry." Emeline rests the knife on the counter.

"Yeah. You talk to the lord."

I cross to the living room, replace the carbine on its mount.

SIX

I'm on the porch resting on an Adirondack chair. Emeline cooks as she cleans. By suppertime I smell ammonia, mashed potatoes, gravy, breaded venison and onions, and a side of boiled carrots. Plus she's mopped the floor.

The sun dips into the horizon. My older boy Deet drives the tractor into the barn bay and comes to the house. He's spent the day on the back forty, cutting first hay. His skin is sunburned and his hair hangs limp. A sheathed buck knife clings to his hip. He kicks dirt from his boots, hocks a loogey to the grass, ignores me. The porch light goes on. Emeline must have watched him approach. He goes inside.

Deet's her age, roundabout.

"Deet?" she says.

Silence. I'm looking away from the house but I can see him sure as I can see the lake. He studies her. She got a regular woman's face but her hips and rack are special. Next he sees the work she's done in the kitchen. And then he adds it up.

"How old are you?"

I want to turn and read her face, but I let things play.

"Eighteen."

"Shit. You could be my wife."

I watch through the window with the bullet hole. Deet grabs a glass from the drying rack, fills it with water, downs it without stopping. He does this every night. Too ornery to take water with him to the field.

"Would you mind cleaning your shoes and not tracking mud?"

"Sure, Ma." He refills the glass, drinks again, and lifts the lid from the cast iron skillet. Slips his deer knife from its sheath, spikes a strip of venison and eats.

"There'll be no more of that," she says. "You'll find a place at the table, like the man of the house."

Deet snorts and looks out he busted window to me. He holds his look long enough to challenge but lets it go before I rise.

Jacob arrives from the lake with a fishing pole, leans it against the house and I follow him inside.

"You want to get cleaned up for supper?" She says to Deet.

He. looks at his hands. His pants. "What's your name?"

"Emeline."

"Sure. Emeline."

I step to the stove and fork a cut of breaded venison. I sniff it, and drop it to the pan. "Miss Emeline, maybe you could have food on the plate when I come in?"

She looks out the window, lets a long breath escape. "Everyone does things differently; it takes a little time to learn new ways." She swipes my plate.

"In the future," I say.

Emeline heaps potatoes. "Gravy?"

"On the table."

"Aren't you going to wash up?"

I study my fingernails, flip my hands palms-up and spit at a blotch of pine pitch. "Deet, you get the hogs and cows fed?"

He nods.

"Jake—the chickens?"

"Yessir."

"Clean out the coop?"

Silence.

"Well?"

"Nossir."

Emeline's busy filling plates. I unbuckle my belt. "Outside."

I follow Jacob to the door, take him to the end of the porch. He braces against the wall and endures three wallops without commotion, and confirms he's the toughest little shit ever lived. We go inside and Deet's staring at the table. Or Emeline's ass. I can't tell.

Jacob smirks at Emeline, wiggles onto his chair.

"All right, dammit. Let's eat."

"Stop!" Emeline says. "Lord we thank you for your bounty and ask you to bless all who live here. We thank you for your redeeming grace and—"

"Miss Emeline. I said it's time to eat."

Deet's outside helping Jacob clean the chicken coop. Emeline's at the sink. I open the hutch door. "You move my whiskey glass? The one with the turkey?"

"In back, on the right."

My cuff catches another glass; I watch it drop to the floor and shatter then I sit at the table and pour. I glance at Emeline, then the window shot out on account of her disobedience, and the shards at my feet. "Our love affair's been hard on glass."

Emeline fetches the broom and dustpan. She sweeps and picks fragments from the gaps in the floorboards. "You get a fire ready, down at the lake?"

"All but lit."

"I'll just be a minute cleaning up. Why don't you go down and start the fire, and relax?"

"Miss Emeline, this being our first day, you ought to know I don't tolerate henpeckin', nebbin', or proddin'."

She studies my face and offers a tentative smile. "Angus, that was a suggestion."

I lift my glass, swirl the fluid. "You drink whiskey?"

"Never tried." Emeline carries glass fragments to a bin on the porch. When she returns, I have a second glass on the table, both half full. I work an ice cube tray at the refrigerator door.

Emeline runs the sink full of dishwater while I rap the metal tray on the tabletop. I drop a chunk of ice in each glass. She scrubs dishes and bumps my stomach with her elbows. I press against her bottom and rest my drink on her shoulder. Scrape my stubble on her neck. Press against her back and take her wrist in my hand like a rope might in a few minutes.

"May I have a taste of that?" she says.

I lower an arm across her front and press the inside of her thigh.

"Angus, the window." She wiggles away. "'Sides, I want to see the fire."

I put the whiskey to her lips while her hands work in suds. Tip it and she gulps too fast. She chokes and breathes hoarse. Teary, she looks to the darkness outside and says, "Let's build that fire, Angus. If you've a mind."

I've a mind.

SEVEN

Emeline yawned. The clock read four-thirty. Through the kitchen window red taillights drifted toward the road. Angus worked at an oilrig in Franklin and drove two hours to get there. He told her last night at ten. This morning he barely said a word except he'd be home by dark, or not.

She rubbed her wrists and though she stared at a rubbery fried egg, in her mind she saw darkness and felt the animal terror of being bound wrist to ankle, crushed under his weight, pinched and sobbing. She put the thought away. Following the Lord required resolve. The world was cruel but it was cruel for everyone.

Emeline pierced egg with her fork, spiked a strip of hog sidemeat that remained after Angus took his fill, and ate. Her stomach rolled and she waited. When the nausea subsided she gathered and washed dishes, then made a mug of second-strain coffee. The boys slept upstairs; outside, not even morning birds stirred. The sun wouldn't rise for another hour.

With the comforts of her Bible and coffee, she curled her legs and cold bare feet on the living room sofa. She opened the curtain behind her to a gray, moonlit lawn with mist rolling from the lake. The yellow lamplight seemed bright now, and she flipped to her bookmark at Deuteronomy 6, Moses talking to the people.

Ye shall observe to do therefore as the Lord your God hath commanded you: ye shall not turn aside to the right hand or to the left. Ye shall walk in all the ways which the Lord your God hath commanded you, that ye may live, and that it may be well with you, and that ye may prolong your days in the land which ye shall possess.

No mistaking the tone of authority. Read Deuteronomy and you know you're dealing with the LORD. Contrasted with Angus, who last night after retiring called out, "I'm gonna spit in the air!" Emeline ducked under the covers only to gag on the smell of raw sewage. That, after he'd trussed her and ridden her like an animal for a half hour by the lake.

Emeline rested her hand on her belly. She looked outside at the darkness. Angus had arrived as a specific answer to prayer, and upon further prayer, she'd accepted his proposal. In trouble, she'd turned to the Lord and He said *"trust me,"* and she had. Her struggle was continuing to trust Him, for the Lord never revealed everything at once. He confirmed little steps and her faith grew. Except marrying Angus Hardgrave felt like a big step.

The Lord had said to marry him.

Doubt was blasphemy. She bowed her head.

Lord, I trust you and will wait for your plan. I married Angus like you told me to but I don't know what angle you're taking and I might need you to give me the power to keep believing. I'm not seeing how any of this works for the good of anyone.

The wait was an opportunity to grow in faith. The Lord had said she would doubt and fear. In the gray light she felt numb. Heaven and salvation were easy, but earthly living required deeper faith.

Deet stretched. The beautiful girl from his dream became his father's new wife.

Emeline.

Below his bed, a canvas knapsack contained everything he needed to escape: a change of clothes, pliers, fishing line, hooks, and ten dollars he'd accumulated by hoarding sidewalk pennies and the dimes his father paid for working the farm. Plus a two-dollar bill he'd swiped from the old man's dresser one afternoon last doe season when he'd seen Angus teach Jacob a lesson he called Human Frailty.

Angus and Jacob were in the barn and Deet arrived as Angus said, "The hardest part of the human body is the tooth. Lookit this big old molar. Watch." Angus laid the molar on the barn floor and crushed it with a roofing hammer. "See that? There's your lesson. Yessir." The tooth had belonged to Jacob's mother, and had resided in her mouth until a few hours earlier. Deet had seen the two dollar bill on Angus's dresser and paid it no mind, but witnessing his father murder his third wife, and then teach her son the Frailty Lesson with her tooth made Deet return and swipe the money.

The canvas bag under his bed held everything he'd need to meet life on his own terms, everything except the knife that hadn't left his hip since he'd seen Angus drag a body from the barn to the lake.

Leaving would be a hell of a thing. It'd be an admission that his understanding of the world wasn't right enough to stand up for. He couldn't quite get his mind around that kind of cowardice—yet he was ready to go. Winter had descended like a cold hurricane that night. Wind drove ice pellets against the window panes. Drifts of ice nuggets locked the door. All last summer the old-timers at the barbershop had said local weather followed a thirty-year cycle, and the last bad winter was 1927. Snow drifted six feet, so cold that trees snapped in the wind. One geezer told of finding a trophy buck in the spring of '28 that he'd hunted for years, starved to death. Deet considered that hard, versus the warmth of his bed and venison in the skillet. It had always been apparent that Lucy Mae irritated the living shit out of Angus, and being around Angus all his life, Deet understood that only women need worry about him.

If he ran, he'd never survive without stealing a car and heading south. Even in all his winter clothes, maybe kifing a rifle and a box of shells, he'd freeze or get found out. As long as Angus didn't act up, Deet's departure could wait until spring.

Four months passed and the land thawed. Angus worked at the derrick most days and only returned at night. Deet remembered that December day, seeing his father with Lucy Mae's body and the subsequent Frailty Lesson, but during the day-to-day solitude of tending the farm, one thought stayed his leaving. What of the livestock?

Deet planned to take Jacob, but he couldn't bring the hogs and cattle. The thought of the livestock slowly starving as Angus drank himself unconscious left only one alternative. Before leaving, Deet would have to slaughter Pete, the old moss-horned bull; Gretel, the three-year Holstein milker; Loozyannie, a Jersey with soft eyes and a strange smile so pretty you could kiss her—in cold blood, or turn them loose to wander the land. The hogs would thrive. Angus fattened those pegged for slaughter on acorns every fall. But the cattle would graze the small pasture to dirt in a week.

As spring deepened Deet spent every day dragging a plow or harrow from a steel-wheeled tractor, his guts scrambled from bouncing, his skin burned from sun. In early spring he'd work most of the day before his thoughts turned to slaughtering the animals, but as spring wore on he had more time to reflect on the fact he was working like a sharecropper for a slave's wage, and he confronted earlier and earlier in the day his dread of killing the animals.

Two weeks ago he rose from bed and his first thought was no more, he wouldn't do it anymore. He'd packed a bag and stuffed in under the duffel. He'd plotted the sequence, the timing, the destination. Last night would have been the slaughter, and today he and Jacob would have been a hundred miles away.

But Angus went to town and came back with a wife.

Emeline woke on the sofa to the smell of cinnamon and oatmeal. Deet and Jacob clattered spoons on bowls. Her feet were cold.

Yesterday before bed Angus had harried her unpacking. While she was barely awake Angus tripped on her suitcase, cursed, and carried it to the basement. She'd spent a few moments sitting upright, wondering what day it was and why she lay in an unfamiliar bed, and then realized she was a married woman with obligations. Her first duty was to see her husband fed before he left the house. She dressed but couldn't find stockings or her suitcase. Meanwhile Angus had already risen and left the room, and the thought of earning his reproof stirred her to arrive in the kitchen barefoot to fix his breakfast.

She'd prepared a meal while he brooded over his headache, and after he left she had fallen asleep trying to read her Bible. Now that the boys had wakened her, more than anything she wanted warm feet.

"Good morning, Jacob. Good morning, Deet."

"Morning," Jacob said.

Deet chewed bread.

Emeline went to the hutch where yesterday she'd found a tall, yellow-brown beeswax candle and a box of matches. She lit the wick, descended to the basement and turned on the light at the foot of the steps. She noticed the cord that carried electricity to the light socket appeared new. Turning, she found some of the seams in the stone foundation were wet. The corners of the cement floor glistened. She looked for other light fixtures on the joists but found none; but she did spot shiny copper pipes through the trusses. A stone stair led to a slope-doored exit. She pressed against it and found it locked from outside. Leaning a moment she wondered that Angus would spend money on running water and electricity, but not paint or basic repairs. Had he come into money?

Or wanted to make the house more appealing for a town girl?

Her suitcase rested on the shelf where she'd found the others yesterday when she'd ventured downstairs looking for a broom and cleaning supplies. She dragged it to the floor and removed her stockings from an elastic compartment. The candle flickered. She tapped the pockets for other stowaway garments and returned the case to the shelf, on top of the one with L.M.M. penned on the shoulder. She brought the candle closer. The next shelf down supported another suitcase, and lower, a fourth. Dust caked each in successively deeper coats, and the one on the bottom seemed fuzzy with mold.

Emeline looked at her bare feet, now numb, on the cement floor. She placed one foot on top of the other and looked at the cobwebs between the support timbers, the shadow-filled recesses, and back to the suitcases. L.M.M. A corroded silver Christmas tree stand, an iron with a frayed cord, a stack of empty photo frames. A blue warfarin dispenser: De-Ratter—De Mouser. She remembered her mother telling her a story about a boy who'd eaten a warfarin pellet, thinking it was a candy. How a boy could mistake rat poison for candy was impossible to guess, but judging from what little boys became when they grew up, it wasn't out of the question. Either way, it killed him.

The candle cast light where she'd seen only shadows yesterday. She lifted a jar of nails from the workbench, revealing a coffee can of rusted wrenches behind it. A dirt-filled pail balanced haphazardly on a mason's trowel, half over the edge. Rust thick as paint covered everything.

She climbed the stairs.

"Jacob, I'd like for you to open the basement door outside, get some air downstairs."

"Pap says keep it closed. Don't want snakes or mice in the basement."

"Do snakes eat mice?"

"Yeah."

"Then open the door and trust the world to work the way the Lord made it."

Jacob looked at Deet.

"Stretch a few boards from the barn across the bottom of the doorway, and nothing will get in," Deet said. "Right, Ma?"

She punched his arm. His eyebrows cut low—a look that on other boys preceded pulling pigtails. She scowled. "Jacob, get the boards like Deet said. And Deet, I don't appreciate your tone."

The telephone rang. Emeline paced to the stand by the kitchen entrance and watched. It clanged again; she lifted the handset to her ear.

"Yes?"

The operator connected.

"Emeline? This is Nancy Denny. Are you all right, dear?"

"Of course. We made a fire last night."

"Don't tell me about it. I rang because a young man stopped by church this morning. A sweet, clean-cut young man. It was the strangest thing; he asked right out if I knew a place to lease."

"Uh, you don't say?"

"You'd be prudent to set aside some money for yourself. He's clean cut. He shaved."

"What's his name?"

"Bradley Chambers. He graduated from Walnut in '52, and went straight to the war. Korea. Now he works at London Cleaners."

Emeline's free hand fell to her belly. "Where does he live now?"

"He's staying at the Dubois Young Men's Christian Association—until he finds a place."

"I can't. He sounds nice, but I can't."

"I told him I'd show him your place if you didn't object."

"I object! Nancy, I haven't even got my things out."

"Who else are you going to find? Why, it's like the Lord is dropping him in your lap. Pastor Denny is driving to fetch you right now. Things are difficult, with your Papa just passed—but you're not making any sense. Run off and marry Angus Hardgrave. You're his fourth wife! You ought to be going to movies and eating hamburgers. Wasn't three years ago you were playing hula-hoop."

"It's a funny thing. Pastor's wife not understanding when a girl wants to be obedient to the Lord."

"The Lord told you to marry Angus Hardgrave?

"He did."

"Pray again. You misunderstood."

"Did you say Pastor Denny is coming here?"

"Left ten minutes ago. I thought you'd be delighted."

"Oh, Nancy; this is too soon."

"Did you know Bradley in school?"

"He was several grades ahead of me, and he was terrible."

"Well, wars change men. What harm can come from meeting him?"

Emeline pressed her abdomen. "You'd have to know Brad Chambers."

EIGHT

S mall talk failed. Pastor Denny regarded her with a quiet sideways glance as he turned onto the driveway of Emeline's house and parked behind a red and white Fairlane. Nancy stood on the porch, partially eclipsing the rigid figure of a man with black hair and a brow that looked run over by a harrow. Emeline inhaled, twisted and searched the driveway behind. She opened the car door.

Nancy flew down the steps and hugged her. She pressed her cheek to Emeline's and rubbed her back. "Are you okay, dear?"

"I'm fine."

Chambers rested his elbows on the side rail; a careful smile balanced on his lips. He looked like he had that night, black shoes, blue jeans, white shirt. She could almost smell his cologne from here, could almost feel his knees riving hers, his thudding pulse, his—

He studied her in return. His eyes bore the appreciation of a cattleman judging a blue-ribbon calf.

"Mister Chambers, we have a misunderstanding. I won't be leasing the house."

"Miss—Hardgrave, is it? All I need is a room, and Mrs. Denny was polite enough to show me that you have some rooms with no one in them."

"You've been in my house?" She stepped closer. "Nancy and I didn't communicate very well. I must have left her with the impression I'd be receptive to a boarder. I am not. Especially to a man—"

"You and me should talk inside—"

"Maybe you should—"

Nancy touched her shoulder. "It can't hurt to talk to him, Emeline."

"Oh, I'll talk to him." She climbed the steps. Chambers followed her inside and closed the door. "I saw you in the woods, yesterday," she said.

"Only 'cause I wanted you to."

Emeline peeked through a lace-curtained window. Outside, Pastor Denny sat in his car and Nancy leaned on the fender and searched for something inside her purse. Chambers crept behind Emeline. "I thought we had a nice time together."

She turned, clasped his head in both hands and pressed her jaw to his. She bit his lower lip and pulled back. That's what it was like a month ago. Pain. Fear. He grunted, hit her shoulders. Opened his mouth. She shoved him away. "It wasn't a *nice time*, Brad."

He seized her arms. "You're mine, Emeline. You said so. You don't think I can forget all that?" Blood appeared at his bottom lip.

"I said that before—"

"Before I made you mine. I'm not letting you go."

"You have to. Or you'll deal with my husband. You think you're the meanest person you ever met, but you don't know Angus Hardgrave."

Chambers released her.

She stepped backward.

"What if I bend you over right here with the preacher outside? Huh?" He dropped his hand to his belt, pressed toward her.

She swung her open hand and misjudged the distance. Her palm connected like a punch; Chambers touched his jaw and spat blood to the counter top. He advanced two steps, cocked his arm. Emeline stood beside the window, arm lifted as if to shatter glass.

"Oh, you're clever little cunt, Emeline." He pushed the curtain aside. "Clever from the get-go. Well, I'm not letting you get away."

"I'm Mrs. Angus Hardgrave. Get out of my house."

"This ain't over by a damn stretch." Chambers opened the door and slammed it behind him.

Emeline watched through the window. Chambers stalked to his car and if he said anything to Nancy, Emeline didn't see. The Fairlane's rear tires sprayed rocks as the car fishtailed down the driveway.

NINE

Dim lights make black suits and dresses look the blacker. I'm in Groesly's Funeral parlor, shuffling toward the line. Ahead is a closed casket made of red oak, a photo on its lid.

I knock a nub of dried blood from my chin. Face itches from shaving soap. It wasn't enough that Emeline drug me here; she drug me to the bathroom first and tried to shave me with a straight razor. Times, I don't know where the steel in her spine comes from. I took the blade from her and shaving out of sorts, nicked the cleft on my chin.

Voices quiet as I near and buzz when I pass. The McClellan clan spreads over Walnut and Jefferson counties and every one of them is here. They stare. I'll pay my respects to Mitch and leave—and it'll be the last I owe my youth companion, the long dead Larry McClellan. That's more than the rest of the clan wants. Our families have a history that won't die, even when we do.

The most recent flare up was in 1916. Mitch's father Jonah McClellan, a seven-foot giant, downed a shot of rye at a town pub and vowed he'd destroy the Hardgraves. By then, Jonah had created a rural pussy empire. He brought organized harlotry from the cities to the towns, and had a system of brothels with all the clout and protection of the ones he'd studied in Pittsburgh. His girls worked four towns. He sold women first, and if his patron thirsted for something to make the rest of his life more palatable, Jonah sold him a jug of home-stilled whiskey. The recipe was a secret, and involved walnuts from the tree I cut and sold to Margulies.

Jonah McClellan's big triumph in the feud came when my grandfather's black sheep daughter, my aunt Elsa Hardgrave, moved to Dubois and spread her gizzy at Jonah's bidding. Jonah disappeared shortly after word got out, and there wasn't a soul in Walnut County didn't suspect my grandpap dispatched him. Jonah's body remains undiscovered.

When I was a boy the clans speculated Larry and me being friends would end the old days. The Hardgraves were in decline anyway, me being the last. The McClellans spread like weeds. But when Larry died, no one believed I shoved his intestines back in him and cried like a woman. There's something changes when you see a man cut up and dying like that, and though part of you carries on and blubbers, the saner part gets real cold.

Ahead in the box rests the bones and flesh of a man I didn't like and never forgave. A man who raised the coward I lost my eye trying to save. *Leave the bastard alone...*

Widow McClellan sits on a wooden chair at the head of the casket. A small girl hugs her. A man, woman, and a boy wait by the box. They study the black and white photo, and the boy points at me. His mother swipes his hand and stares. His father touches the photo and turns.

I've never seen them, but the McClellan type is familiar. Their faces are narrow, more angles than curves; lips thin and brows high. They're tall, like their grandfather, and like me. Other people turn.

"Here to pay respects, like you," I say, and scratch my neck. The room is silent. Emeline squeezes my hand. She's got a lot of sand in her guts but her face telegraphs fear as more and more eyes flit from my face to the widow.

I study their looks and it dawns on me these men and women are not angry.

The widow observes her kin, follows their faces to me. Her white brows drop as she focuses, then her forehead tightens and her jaw goes slack. She wobbles to her feet and steps toward me, arm open toward me. Her face changes a thousand times until she stands two feet away, looking up. She reaches; her hand cups my jaw. She shakes her head.

"No." she says.

She drops. I clutch her shoulders and she slips to her knees.

"Hey!" someone shouts.

They think I've dropped her. I stagger with bent knees and back and leave her on the chair. Family throngs beside her.

A man jerks my shoulder. His fist connects sideways with my head. I catch myself on the casket. The photo topples into my hands. I wipe my nose and bloody the frame. It's Mitch, with twenty fewer years and a clean shave.

I recognize my face in his. Cleft chin; cleft nose.

From behind, Emeline wraps her arms around the man who struck me. I study the photo. The closest McClellans understand the truth that shook the widow to her core and yanked the floor beneath me. "Leave the *bastard* alone," Mitch said all them years ago. I look from the photo to the men and women and to the photo again.

I had a beard so long I forgot my face.

Three men hold Emeline's arms and shoulders. She struggles and as silence retakes the room they release her.

My hand shakes. I return the photo to the casket. I don't know that I'll find peace without a little whiskey and a conversation with the walnut on Devil's Elbow. Get some shit straight.

TEN

My neck is stiff as a horse's hardon and my shoulders are cinched up from a full day of hoisting pipe, throwing chain, running the cathead. I'm the motorman and work for Merle, the driller. Sunup to sundown. Twelve hours of my best labor, earning dimes on the boss man's dollars so some Oil City asshole can eat prime rib and pour brandy from cut glass.

So now I'm McClellan? Don't mean a damn thing. Hoot Hardgrave, the man that raised me, was a malingering broke back and I almost wanted to be one of the other clan anyway. Least Jonah McClellan had stones.

I lean against the rig, wipe grime from my fingers and take a pinch of Copenhagen.

Karl, the derrickman, scoots down the ladder and looses a clump of dirt that shatters on a rung and rains like brown hail. The mudman, a drifter from Alberta we call Sarge says, "Gimme a rub, eh?"

"Buy your own fuckin rub, *eh?*"

Merle approaches from the clutch. "You want to see them pits, tonight?"

I shrug. "Where?"

"Ten mile off. My brother-in-law organizes everything."

I follow Merle on Route 322 through forest and farmland and turn on 257 to Seneca. We chug ten minutes on a narrower road, then five more on pair of tire ruts cut through black mud, screwing counter-balance around the hill. The sun sets through a hemlock canopy. Land turns gray. Finally the road opens to a hollow with orange lanterns hanging from low branches. I park alongside Merle between three-foot hemlock trunks.

A score of men shoot the shit, swat deerflies, drink whiskey, smoke corncob pipes. Merle says "hello" to someone and wanders away. I scope my surroundings.

An enclosure stands at the center of the assembly with walls made of discarded oak pallets, held vertical by steel spikes driven into the ground. Two pallets pivot like doors at opposite sides; the rubber cords that secure them hang loose. The earth in the middle is bare and stinks as if blood and perpetual shade keep the dirt raw and festering.

A man in leather gloves leans against the bed of a pickup. I nod; he dips his eyes. A metal crate sits in the bed. I lean close and study the silent dog inside. It has a head like a pit viper, broad and strong, and a red nose.

"He ain't very big," I say.

"Ain't seen you around."

"Which dog's he matched with?"

"Bilrod's shepherd. You was smart, you'd put your money on Killer, here."

"What's he weigh?"

"Sixty."

"And the shepherd?"

"Look for yourself."

I read Killer's lines. His hips are narrow and his shoulders broad; his chest is muscled like a bulldog's; a scar traverses his top right shoulder to lower left. His chest trembles and his eyes look stone mad. He presses his nose against the mesh and his whine drops to a railroad rumble. My neck hair stands. His eyes sit flat in his head and he stares like he could murder me through the wire if he tried hard enough, and shit if I ever saw a dog looked so smart I almost believed him. I appreciate that same shit, Killer, yes I do.

Yes I do.

"How old's this fella?"

"Two."

"Kinda young?"

"This is his third match. You only git a third when you win your second."

Truck headlights approach single file on the trail and park between trees. Never seen so many men in the same wood. I search out the next pickup with a crate. Owner's away. Behind the wooden slats is another pit, smaller than Killer, also got a red nose. A white splotch on his chest interrupts his brindle coat. He's familiar. He lays curled in the back of the crate, unmindful of the excitement. Mid-step to the next truck, I stop and pursue a thought. Will the brindle's lack of enthusiasm predict how much fight he brings to the ring? I'll remember that splotch.

The next crate holds a grizzled German shepherd that looks about a hundred and twenty pounds with a scarred grey muzzle, ragged flaps for ears, and coal beads for eyes.

I cant my head and listen. Of the men, motors, and dogs, the dogs are the quietest, maybe like soldiers figuring the generals will immortalize their battlefront courage with rear-echelon words. I rap the cage and the shepherd snarls, but when I fail to

further aggravate him, he sniffs toward the fight circle and ignores me.

"You don't want to be doin' that," Merle says, approaching
from my blind side.

"You don't want to surprise me from that side," I say.

"These boys protect their dogs better'n their women. Time
you meet Charlie—he makes book."

"I'm watching tonight." I spit.

"Suit yourself. We start in a bit. Boys from Oil City bringing
dogs in; must have got lost. Charlie sent his kid out the main
road to fetch them."

I nod at the shepherd. "What's a fighting dog like that go
for?"

"You say fighting dog, but you're looking at a big-boned Nazi-
dog. Shepherds don't know shit about fighting. You couldn't give
me one. Now, you take a pit bull pup from a champ like Thunder,
that red nose in the GMC step side—he got a white patch—a
pup in that line will fetch seventy-five dollars."

"For a dog."

"Pit bulls ain't dogs. They know more about war in their little
toes than a platoon of jarheads like you knows in your whole
body. They're *pit* bulls—bred to hang from a bull's nose while
the butcher slits his throat and bleeds him. Takes a lot of game
for a sixty-pound dog to latch on to a fifteen-hundred pound bull
and hang by his teeth. Stones the size of cannonballs. Lookit the
jaws on them sonsabitches. They lock; takes a breaking stick to
bust them loose. And they don't feel pain."

"Still. Seventy-five dollars for a dog?"

"If he wins, you make fifty times that betting on him, then
studding him. Now, that's a champion. Charlie don't even fight
Thunder any more, just brings him out here to show him off."

"What's your cut?"

"I don't make no cut. However—Charlie is taking bids for the pick of the next litter, due shortly."

I follow Merle to his truck; Merle drops the tailgate and we sit. "Where's your dog?" I say.

"He's a face-licking puss. These fellas breed killers. Any one of them would murder my pup inside a minute."

"Don't you have a pit?"

"Yeah, but you got to train them to fight. You got to condition him."

"Wish you'd make your mind up. That shepherd's seen a round or two."

"He's never fought a pit."

"How you know?"

"He's alive."

"Bullshit."

"You watch."

A caravan of lamps approaches on the hillside, bouncing headlights into our eyes. Men grumble it's time to get started. A breeze carries diesel exhaust. I slip from the tailgate and fetch a fifth of Turkey from behind my truck seat. Merle drinks, passes the bottle back, and I gulp a long snurgle.

A boy trots in front of the arriving trucks. At the bottom he ground-guides the vehicles around stumps and logs. When the last engine stills, the Oil City boys mingle with kindred spirits from Franklin and Seneca and familiarize themselves with the animals.

Darkness folds us in a ring of black, held back by orange kerosene light. Charlie strides to the center of the pit. Men close in around the pallets and Charlie circles as he speaks.

"All right boys, we got some good matches tonight. You know it's a shame we got to come this far out, but the ladies and society folk don't understand sport."

Men carry dog crates from the backs of pickups and position them at gates on opposite sides of the ring.

Men laugh, and Charlie raises his hands. "That's alright. Smells better out here, anyway. Mickey's got a half-barrel in the blue Dodge. Afore we commence, I know some of you, and some I don't. We got to get on the same page. We're about to commit our beloved champions to battle. These dogs live for fighting, and we love em for it. Envy em, really.

"Every one of you is spoken for by a fella I know and trust, else you wouldn't be here. But since maybe a couple of you boys has never seen an honest blood spectacle, I got to make myself clear. You got a problem with blood, or glory, or two thorough-breds going shoulder to shoulder to see which is best, then just consider yourself uninvited. Go on. Get the hell outta here and keep your trap shut. I mean it. 'Cause if someday your conscience tells you to run your dick-licker, we'll have Armageddon problems, you and me.

"Now, let's get these dogs a-fighting. First up we got Killer the shepherd and Killer the pit. You boys have to think of different names, for shit's sake. Well, then again—give it ten minutes, maybe not. Shepherd's had four *unsanctioned* fights and won. He's six year old, and this is his first run in with a pit. Three to one. Mort? How many has Killer the pit won? Both? All right, get your money out."

An Oil City boy calls, "I'll put three on Killer." Men laugh. Charlie works his way around the ring and men place bets.

I nudge Merle. "You got skin in this?"

"Hell fuck course I do. Don't know why Charlie lets these other breeds in. They're all but useless."

Charlie finishes noting a name and number and climbs over a pallet. Leaning into the ring, his arm poised high, he meets the eye of one dog owner then the other. He drops his arm.

"Go!"

The gates swing open. The shepherd leaps ten feet and clashes with the pit bull. The shepherd cuts a gash on the pit's neck and meat glistens, but the pit twists aside and whirls with the blow, spins to the shepherd's hind leg and crunches his ankle. The pit pulls, jerks, gnashes.

Jaw open, the shepherd spins and loses his balance. The pit springs. Shoulders collide. The shepherd lurches. The pit clamps jaws on his throat. The shepherd rolls and kicks; the pit tightens his jaw hold with each twist. The shepherd breathes in choked gasps; he kicks; wheezes blood bubbles from his nose. He blinks.

The pit bull's owner—Mort—grins.

Merle says, "Lookit—ain't sixty seconds and he quit. I'd take a pit over a half dozen shepherds."

"You want your dog?" Mort says.

"Let them finish," the shepherd's owner says. "He ain't done. Yet."

"You ain't leaving him in my woods." Charlie says. "I can't have a bunch of dogs rotting all over the place. Dead or alive he leaves with you."

"Ah, hell." The shepherd owner waves. "Go ahead."

Mort enters the circle, kneels at the dogs. He works a pry-stick into the pit's growling mouth, and pushes against the dog's lower jaw until it releases. The pit bull stands, breathes heavy a moment and lunges. Mort restrains him with his arm.

"You got to admire that," Merle says, and I remember our orders in the infantry, to close with and destroy the enemy. I get a hot feeling in my head brought on by the smell of blood and earth, and I hear sounds and taste salt and I want to go home.

Bind Emeline by the wrists and bend her bones.

The shepherd rests on his side, lungs heaving. His neck is red and matted, but the carotid is intact. He'll live.

The pit lunges against Mort's arm and the shepherd responds to the motion. He jumps to his feet and slashes at the pit but catches Mort's arm instead.

Mort pushes the dog off and in the same motion, draws a .38 out of nowhere and fires a slug into the shepherd's head.

The men are silent, save one who grouses, "Mite tight for gunplay."

"The hell!" the shepherd owner finally says, pressing against the oak pallets. "You can't do that!"

Mort pulls his torn sleeve, exposing a bloody arm. "Get your fucking dog out the pit."

"Least you don't got to change his name," someone says.

The shepherd owner drags his Killer by the paws. Charlie enters the ring and exchanges bills with the men on his list. Voices rise in discord. I turn. The crowd quiets and Charlie's voice rings above the others.

"All right, listen here. Listen here. Don't place bets if you don't have cash in your pocket. You lose and I come for funds and you don't have them, I'll take you out in the woods and shoot you." He pats a holstered pistol on his hip. "All right? All right."

Charlie walks the fighting pit and when he arrives at where he started, calls out, "Where's Tim Fields?"

"Here!"

"You owe me twenty bucks." Charlie tracks down others as men back trucks to opposite sides of the fight circle and men help lift crates to the ground.

"Next we got two pits, so maybe this'll last more'n a minute. Todd Sager brought Rebel tonight. Rebel's had three fights, and comes from an unknown line out of Potter County. He's the brindle red-nose. It's Rebel against John Murphy's white pit. John, you name that damn dog yet?"

"I call him Skeeter."

"That's a hell of a name."

"Lookit his nuts."

Charlie laughs. "Skeeternuts, huh? He's only had one fight, but he's a big somebody, and I guess that makes his balls look small, or something. You all know Thunder, the Champion Thunder, ahem, well, Thunder is Skeeternuts' daddy. And by the way, I'm taking bids for pick of the litter due in three weeks. Top bid's forty-five. Skeeternuts here was the litter runt and he turned out big enough, except his balls. Odds two to one, favor of Skeeternuts."

Charlie huddles ringside as men approach and place bets. He writes notes, and when he meets a face he don't recognize, says, "Show me cash... All right."

I gulp Wild Turkey and elbow closer to the pit. Rebel—the one with a calm temperament—has a white splotch on his chest. Two to one, favor of the dog with tiny nuts. I shake my head.

Charlie drops his arm, "Go!"

Crate doors swing open and the dogs explode at each other. They meet face-to-face, rearing on hind legs, and scrap. Rebel nips at Skeeter's muzzle but the bigger dog pushes him back and they drop aside and clash again. After two minutes the dogs' muzzles and ears bear each other's blood. They fight on, a never-ending whirl of muscle and rending teeth.

"Skeeter's tired," I say to the stranger beside me.

"He's winded, sure."

"Same odds! Same odds!" Charlie calls.

The dogs circle one another, panting. Skeeter parries an attack and counters with a slash to Rebel's face.

"Oh, shit," Sager says. He's a squat man with a high voice. "Shit."

"Lost an eye," Merle says.

Rebel staggers, twists, and Skeeter charges his shoulder from his sighted side. Rebel squares himself and ducks; the dogs tumble, neither finds advantage.

When they stand again, their ears are mangled and their shoulders are matted. "That blood came from the shepherd," I say. "See that soppy ground?"

Skeeter jumps at Rebel's hind leg and it cracks in his jaws.

"It's about attrition," Merle says. "Other animals will slash and pretend, but pit break bones, rip arteries, bust windpipes."

Skeeter releases the leg and they continue. Now they're on their sides, gnawing each other. On their feet, still chewing. I glance at my watch, then the moon, creeping beyond the trees. Time slips and the dogs chase glory.

"Skeeter busted Rebel's leg," a man says. "See how it hangs?"

Rebel fights on three legs and doubles his fury. He pins Skeeter but before he finds the white dog's throat, Skeeter clamps his windpipe from below.

"They got jaws like a bear trap," Merle says. "Just a matter of time, now. See Rebel work his mouth? He can't breathe worth a shit."

"You don't know that!" Sager yells. "Let them go to the end."

Murphy shrugs.

Rebel thrashes and wriggles and twists. His teeth find Skeeter's neck.

"That little son of a bitch has some fight in him," I say.

Merle shakes his head. "His leg's busted. His eye's gone."

Skeeter snaps a tighter grip. Too slow, Rebel pushes away. Skeeter's teeth sink new holes in his neck, now wide and deep across his throat. Skeeter clenches and Rebel wheezes tiny blood bubbles through his nose.

Johnny Murphy says, "It's over. Rebel's done; no use letting him die."

"You want a draw, pull him off." Todd Sager squeals. "You want the win, you got to let him go."

Murphy shrugs at Charlie. "Let them finish."

Rebel struggles. With each wiggle, Skeeter's teeth clamp tighter on his throat. Solemn men watch and Rebel's harsh, gurgling gasps fill the air.

"He got some lungs," I say.

"He's fighting on gameness, now. Nothing else left."

Skeeter's iron jaws seal Rebel's windpipe. Minutes pass, marked every few seconds by Rebel's waning bursts to free himself. Finally, Rebel's entire body spasms and he is still. Skeeter holds tight; Rebel don't move.

"Son of a bitch," Sager says.

"Skeeter wins," Charlie says.

Murphy jumps in the pit with a pry stick. "Let up!"

Skeeter releases on command and Murphy studies his dog's wounds by the crate entrance.

Sager rushes into the pit and kicks Rebel's gut. Blood spits from his nose. Sager grabs Rebel's hind legs and drags him from the pit, leaving him off to the side.

"You ain't leaving him in my woods," Charlie says.

Merle and I peer close, got the best angle. Merle elbows me. "That kick—"

"I seen it."

"That kick re*sus*citated him," Merle says. "Look, he's breathing again."

Sager heaves Rebel to his truck's rear tire. "Can I get hand with this crate?"

I lift it with him. Sager huffs and jerks, his face flushed. We hoist and I push the pen across the truck bed. "Lot of fight for a little dog."

"Son of a bitch cost me thirty bucks! 'Champion bloodline,' that no-good breeding bastard said. Dog's a worthless coward."

I offer my bottle of Wild Turkey and Sager accepts.

"Well, you can't leave him here. Charlie's clear on that."

"I'll dump him side of the road."

Charlie calls names behind us. I'm silent.

"Gimme another pull on that bottle."

I give it to him. "You got other dogs?"

"I put every penny in Rebel. I ought to shoot him for the satisfaction."

"Maybe you ought to sell him."

"Couldn't get fifty cents."

I pull two quarters from my pocket and slap them in Sager's hand.

Sager don't know whether to cuss or keep quiet so I give a long look that ought to help, then carry Rebel to my truck, lay him on the passenger floor and study his wounds. Rebel growls like a cat purrs. Blood shines on his face and shoulder, but most of the color comes from the shepherd, I suspect. Rebel's injuries are limited to a busted leg bone, a tattered ear, a jellied right eye, and puncture holes about the throat. He come close to suffocating, but now breathes free. If I can keep infection out his eye and shore up his leg, he'll heal.

I gather a few short sticks from the ground and rags from behind the seat, and splint Rebel's leg. The dog growls. There's a coat I ain't wore in five years tucked under the seat: I fish it out and arrange padding under Rebel's leg. Take a pull of Copenhagen and drive home.

On the road I think about Rebel's bloodline and then my own. It occurs to me I got a better line than I thought. I don't know if Mitch McClellan was my daddy or Jonah, and I don't care—though deep inside it's got to be Jonah.

If ever there was a son of a bitch you'd want for your daddy, it's Jonah McClellan.

It's a quarter after eleven. I pull the F-100 front of the barn. Emeline sits by the window looking yellow in lamp light. She turns at my headlamps.

I slide the barn door open and back the truck part inside. After five minutes Emeline joins me. I'm hammering plywood. "I could eat the ass end out a dead groundhog. Supper ready?"

"It's a little dry..."

"Look in the truck."

She opens the door. She looks to me and back to Rebel. "What happened, you poor brute?"

"Don't get your face too close. That's a fighting dog."

"What are you doing with a fighting dog?"

I stand beside her. "He'd be dead if I wasn't doing something with him. In the house, upstairs hall closet, there's an ace bandage. I need it."

Emeline touches Rebel and his throat rumbles; his tail thumps the metal under the seat. She wipes blood from her hand on his haunch. "What's his name?"

"Rebel."

Emeline stares at the dog. I dislike the set of her jaw. And her stance.

She shakes her head. Turns back toward the house. "I'll warm your supper."

"Bring the bandage first."

In a few minutes she returns with medical supplies. "Your supper's on the table. I'll nurse the dog."

I sip whiskey and watch with satisfaction.

In a small tub she whips cayenne pepper and Plaster of Paris to a batter. She cuts an ace bandage into segments, wraps Rebel's leg in wax paper, and applies a cast. Rebel licks the un-set plaster, sputters and rubs his tongue with his paws. Emeline scratches between his ears.

"Don't love that son of a bitch too much. That's a rock there, or something. That's a cornerstone.

ELEVEN

O ver the following days Emeline fed Rebel slabs of beef fat, milk, eggs mixed with rice—anything she could find to strengthen him. His eye was a swollen, red tangle of gel. She rubbed the bony perimeter with Bag Balm and taped a patch, but Rebel scratched it off. She wrapped gauze around his head, only to find it shredded when she saw him next.

Rebel always grumbled lazily when Emeline rubbed his belly. He seemed to lack the demeanor of a fighting dog, and because Angus never took action without a purpose, the only reason she could fathom that he would bring the crippled dog home was that she'd said she wanted one. That didn't answer how Angus happened upon a mangled 'fighting dog,' but it was a small comfort.

Each day at dusk, Angus returned from work and checked the barn before he came in for supper. Wednesday night he arrived home early. On Thursday, Jacob confessed to Emeline that Angus had taken a belt to him for petting Rebel.

She closed her eyes and too easily imagined her husband suspending Jacob by his coverall straps and lacing his behind. "What did he say about loving on the dog?" Emeline said.

"Fight dogs don't get pet."

"Why'd you pet him?"

"So he'd let me see his mussed up eye."

"You'd best listen to your father when he tells you something. Animals don't change their stripes."

Saturday morning she rose with Angus and the boys at five. Conversation was spare. Angus grabbed a couple rolls and a thermos of coffee and said they'd return in a few hours.

Emeline mashed bread into a bowl of eggs and took it to Rebel, almost expecting him to be gone with the others. She climbed over the plywood wall and dropped to her knees in the hay. What a mess. She closed her eyes and touched Rebel's short hair, heard the steady thump of his tail, his deep, satisfied sigh. He ignored the food while she sat beside him.

The day after Emeline buried her father had been sunny and she had walked slowly to Prescott's Grocery store, wandering footsteps and wandering thoughts. During her father's long illness she had been responsible for taking care of him and the property, a burden made easier by his decades of wisdom. Now that he was gone she was happy for him. He was with the Lord, but she missed his good judgment. She trusted the Lord in everything, but she missed her earthly father.

A red and white Fairlane crept into the corner of her vision, driving slow next to the curb, the way boys did when they wanted to talk but were too cool to walk beside a girl. The red hood glimmered a reflection of the tree limbs above; the fat whitewalls crunched over roadside pebbles. She looked straight ahead to Prescott's Grocery.

"Get in," Brad Chambers said.

She knew Chambers. He'd goosed her in seventh grade and reached from behind and grabbed her right breast in eighth. He'd grinned like no hard feelings and she'd remembered his smile more than the violation. Right after that he left school for good, though he was far from graduating.

Inclined to ignore him until he drove away, Emeline remembered that she had decided to trust the Lord to guide her path, and that meant being open to things she wouldn't otherwise consider.

"Come on," he said. "Let me give you a lift."

She'd walked to town six times over the last three weeks, and each time, the Fairlane had been parked at London Cleaners, off to the side where the owner parked. Once as she left the grocery Chambers stood in the entry and nodded at her while adjusting himself with an air of great confidence, as if there was nothing on Earth so mundane as Emeline's opinion.

His hair was short on the sides but greased on top and teased forward up front. He looked good, driving alongside her, calling, "C'mon, Emeline; let's just talk a minute."

She turned while she walked. "Do I know you?"

"I'm Brad. Been off to the war, and then places."

"I remember you. You stole frogs from biology and hid them in the girls' restroom."

He grinned.

"You set off the fireworks in the boys' restroom. You hang around restrooms too much for me."

"Aw, that was just fun. Let me give you a ride. I'm going to the cleaners and you're going to the grocery. They're practically side by side."

The empty road stretched another half mile before town.

"War's been over four years," she said. "Where you been, all that time?"

"Places. All over." Still driving, slowly he leaned across the front seat and unlatched the door.

Her eyes measured the diameter of his arm. "Where are you staying?"

"The Y in Dubois, 'til I get a place."

"Why not with your folks?"

"I hate the bastards, that's why." He looked ahead and though he continued to match her speed, was silent.

"I didn't mean to pry. I'd like a ride, thank you."

Chambers stopped the car. Emeline climbed onto the seat and flattened her skirt.

"I won't stay in Walnut long—that's a guarantee," he said. "Just until I get my bearings."

He seemed intent on some thought that he couldn't shape into words. Emeline enjoyed the breeze. A moment after she entered the car, Brad parked in front of Prescott's Grocery. "I'd take you home, but I'd be late for work."

"I'm used to walking. Thank you for the ride."

"Just a second. I want to take you to the drive-in."

"Ask me later."

Chambers took her hand and held her stare a long time before releasing her.

Inside the grocery, Willard Prescott stood behind the counter, his brows knit. His watery eyes followed Emeline as she moved from aisle to aisle. Basket filled, she stood at the checkout.

"How's your Pappy?" Prescott said.

"He died yesterday."

Prescott shook his head. "That cancer's no good at all." His fingers tapped register keys. He opened his mouth and then closed it, then gave her the slip.

She passed him a few bills.

"You be careful with that fella from the cleaners. I saw you come from his car—you don't have anyone to keep an eye on you, so I don't mind telling you. That one ain't right."

She *had* been careful. Or thought she'd been careful.

Emeline wiped her eyes and rubbed Rebel's belly. "You mangy puppy dog." She pulled a flake of plaster from the edge of the cast. Rebel climbed to three legs and licked her face.

A breeze came from the lake. She'd spent so many hours making the house livable that she hadn't yet found a few moments' holiday at Lake Oniasont, other than her wedding night by the fire. Emeline reminded Rebel to eat his breakfast then wandered across the lawn and down the slope to the pebbled beach. Tiny waves rippled; the lake stretched three quarters of a mile in the shape of a stretched grub worm.

Hills rimmed the northern and southern shores; the land sloped steeply to the water and the slow press of time abetted the water as it ate the earth, until the grade became steep and the roots lay bare. Trees leaned and by the time they were ready to die from old age the water had gently eroded the earth from their roots and they collapsed to the water, here and there, log bridges to the depths.

The eastern and western shores were not so forbidding. Angus had said on their engagement night that his family lived beside the lake two hundred years. It probably didn't change anything if it was true that he was a McClellan, for they had been there just as long. Angus hadn't mentioned it since the funeral.

Emeline walked to the ashes where they'd celebrated beside a blazing campfire, and stood on the matted grass. The fire had burned for hours, far longer than Angus could wait.

She stood in the shade of an old walnut tree, larger than any she'd ever seen. That night it loomed above, a black mass blotting the stars. Angus spread the blanket flat at the trunk, out of the firelight, and staked his claim on Emeline where the ground smelled of blood. In receiving him, Emeline staked her claim as well. Angus was now the father of the child that grew within her. She felt a tinge of remorse for not being honest, but the Lord hadn't addressed the matter of paternity, only the larger issues of her faith in Him and her marriage to Angus. As for remorse, she'd have to wait for the Lord to tell her to feel it. Otherwise, this was His plan. Her role was to obey.

Stepping under the walnut tree's shadow was like stepping into dusk. Moss grew on the north side of the bifurcated trunk. Above the crotch, the limb on the hill-facing side extended horizontal with the ground and offered an inviting view of the lake. She pressed her fingers into the craggy bark and scrambled to the lounge-like limb.

Aboard, her legs dangling, she pressed her hand to the tree. A cloud crossed her mind. Her skin tingled as if chilled by cold raindrops and she beheld a visage of Brad Chambers: pale, suffering, bleeding at the leg. His breath came in tight gasps and his half-lidded eyes were weighted with accusation.

She released her grip on the walnut tree and the image vanished.

Suddenly aware of the creased bark stinging her skin through her thin dress, she leapt to the ground and stumbled. Ahead was a massive rotted stump surrounded by gangly birch trees vying for sunlight. Emeline brushed dirt from her shins and studied the ground, the lack of walnuts. Maybe Jacob had gathered them.

She stepped to a sunken depression of grassless dirt. Though camouflaged with scattered leaves and fallen twigs, she could not mistake the shape, the lack of grass, the muddiness. It was a grave, small, as if for a child.

Maybe Angus had buried his dog Ike here.

Emeline studied the walnut tree and felt as if the Lord was speaking to her, but garbled in her mind. A chill ran through her and maybe this was what the Lord had predicted before she married Angus, that she would be afraid and would come to know evil. Her gaze moved along the trunk, skyward into the deep green canopy; the higher she looked the darker it became. She was aware of the moistness of the earth stuck to her palms and the living musk of the ground where her knee had torn it bare. Something about the tree attracted her, as if...

She backed away. The Lord wasn't in it.

The farther she removed herself from the walnut tree, the righter she felt, and she wondered. Did the Lord send her to Angus so that she might win his soul away from whatever abstract darkness possessed it? Or Jacob's soul? Deet's?

Men of God walked with Him, and Angus plainly didn't. Maybe the Lord's purpose was as finite and graspable as that— maybe her appointment was to save Deet for the Lord.

Because whatever force was in that walnut tree, it wasn't Him.

TWELVE

"Hold her, now! Don't let her drop!" I say. Inside the barn, Rebel thumps plywood with his tail. Deet stands at the tailgate, his fingers slide along the base of the cabinet saw. It's six feet long and more than two wide with a cast iron top looks like a football field. Sturdy and precise, a gem of a table saw. I jerk the other end free of the truck and the saw drops a foot before Deet catches it.

"Aw, shit Pap!"

We shuffle across the barn floor; Deet's back bows and his eyes roll back under the strain. He drops his end of the saw. I ease the other side to the floor. Deet rubs his fingers. Rotates his shoulders. I wipe dust from the waxy iron table. "You got your breath? Thinking it ought to sit over there, a few feet off the wall."

"Looks pretty good right here."

"Let's move."

I lift the table; my arms stretch at the joints. Deet struggles.

"C'mon, damn you!"

"I'm pullin' my shoulders out." Deet can't lift the saw so he tugs and it slides an inch at a time. Again and again; finally the machine is in place. Deet slumps against the wall, unsheathes his knife, and cuts a piece of torn skin from the side of his index finger.

Over at the plywood Rebel beats hay dust into the air. I lean forward, take the brute's head in my hand and study his bad eye, then his good one. He growls; I cuff his nose.

Jacob arrives, interested in the saws but not the work of moving them. He stands beside the plywood. "Mrs. McClellan wants you to mend a cupboard."

"What?"

"She hollered when I was on my bike. Says a cupboard fell off'n the wall and busted open. Wants you to fix it."

Some kind of truce? An opportunity to question what I know? Or tell me what I don't?

I search the cross-supports above, empty save a bullet-shot rowboat. A white electric line runs from a light bulb to the breaker box on the bottom level, then to a single outlet posted on a vertical beam a few feet away. "I'm gonna have to rewire this whole place."

"We got an extension cord," Deet says.

I step into a grain storage room that I converted to a tool shed by building a table into the wall. Move greasy wrenches, screwdrivers, chisels, and rags until I find the extension; back in the bay, I stretch the cord from the outlet to the saw and drop the plug to the floor.

Before moving the table saw from Margulies' place, I removed the blade. I fetch it from the truck cab and hold it at an angle. The teeth fail to reflect light—the blade ain't been used since Margulies last sharpened it. I slip the disc onto the arbor, tighten the reverse thread nut, spin the blade. At the back of the saw, I thump the triple belts. Connect the extension cord, come around to the front and flip the black switch. The blade whines quiet above the motor's hum.

In the corner of my eye, Jake drifts toward Rebel.

"Somethin' purty 'bout the sound of a sharp blade," I say.

Deet comes to the table, tilts his ear.

"You'll know when you hear a dull one. Leastways I do."

"You gonna cut something?"

I grab a warped pine board leaning against the door, look for nails, and slide it along the table saw's fence. The blade spits sawdust to the floor. I press the kill switch and hand the board to Deet.

"Let me try." Deet stands in front of the saw, turns on the power.

"You got to adjust the fence or there'll be nothing to cut. Loosen here, and slide along the rails, like so." I shift a few feet back. Jacob climbs the beam over Rebel's pen.

"Jake—no horseplay around the tools, y'hear?"

Deet places the board on the table.

"That's right," I say, "black is 'on'. Press the board against the fence and flat to the table. Fingers clear."

Deet powers the saw and shoves the board forward. The blade twangs and the motor bogs.

"Easy, feed it slow; let the motor catch up. Don't get so damn close with your fingers."

Plywood claps against the floor and I spin to the sound. Jacob rolls on his back in the hay and Rebel scampers toward the bay door. I lurch after the dog and he skids into Deet's legs.

The blade plunks.

"Shit!" Deet hops back, squeezes his thumb at the base. Blood runs like it's poured from a cup. Rebel shoots out the door. I glance at Deet's hand, then out the bay door—Emeline crosses the lawn and Rebel's body wobbles as he runs full-tilt with a cast. He reaches her and worms on his back. Jake cowers at the back of the barn. I kill the motor and take Deet's slippery hand. Blood hides the wound. His face drains white.

"Aw, shit. Shit!"

I sponge blood with my shirttail. "Lotta fuss for a half-inch of thumb. Go inside and have Emeline slip a bandage on it. We got two, maybe three trips yet and I want to be done by noon." I turn. "Jake, fetch that dog. Then I'm gonna tan your fuckin hide."

Deet wanders down the dirt ramp. Emeline runs to Deet but watches me while she's doing it. She takes his elbow in her hand and hurries him to the house.

All that fuss. I step to the truck where a couple boxes of hand tools and the shaper still need unloaded. It's an awkward machine with a pig iron frame supporting a cast iron table, got a motor mounted off the back. I jump into the bed and lug the shaper to the tailgate, then, standing on the barn floor, bear-hug the iron base and lurch to the far wall.

Passing the table saw on my trip back to the truck I notice a mess of blood on the barn floor where Deet bled. I think on that blood, and other blood, and get a pinch in the back of my mind like it's time to be getting on with things.

Rope and wrists and such.

THIRTEEN

Emeline held Deet's hand. "Hold your thumb under the water." The basin splashed pink; his thumb ended with a flat spot at the last joint.

Deet jerked.

"Keep it under cold water." She hurried upstairs, flung open the hall closet, knocked brown bottles aside. Surely a house of country men had a bottle of Mercurochrome—there! She returned cradling gauze, bandages, and tape at her breast.

Deet's face had regained color; he leaned at the sink with his elbows resting on the basin edge, his hands joined together to staunch the flow and brace his thumb under running water. "Look how clean that blade cut. See that?"

She dabbed the wound with a towel. Deet pressed his chest to her shoulder. He shifted his weight and a moment later his good hand rested on her hip.

Emeline dabbed directly on the flat of the wound and Deet jumped. He faced away, his whole body rigid with pain.

"That's not a good idea," she said. She dabbed a folded square of gauze into Mercurochrome and taped it over the top of his thumb, then wound it in tape. "You should sit down a few minutes and collect yourself. Have a roll. Just pulled out of the oven."

She gathered a knife and butter, and turned to the slap of the closing screen door.

On the porch, Emeline looked toward the barn, then saw Deet trudging on the trail to the lake.

Pine sawdust fills the air with a clean scent. I haul an awkward armload of hand planes and lathe chisels from the truck to the workbench in the old corncrib. Come out patting dust from my shirt and feeling it stick to the sweat on my brow. Emeline stands at the table saw right on top of a half cup of Deet's blood ain't yet soaked into the floor. Her pap bought these tools when she was seven and probly built her bedroom furniture with them. The way her eyes rest on the machinery, she's thinking she swore before God to stick by my side 'til one of us is dead—that was the vow—but everything is more real now that pap's tools is in my barn. "Something eating you?"

"You didn't mention you were taking all this."

"I don't mention when I take a shit neither. You want me to leave the whole wood shop to sit and rust? These tools mean business, and woman, there's one thing you need to get planted in your head quick. Don't let yourself be a burden."

"Business? What kind of business?"

"Widow McClellan needs work done. There'll be others."

"These are my Papa's tools."

"Your pap's dead."

She recoils like she didn't know. She stares into my eye patch. "You have a good job at the well."

"A good job? Busting my back day in and out? Mind just a wandering. Drive two hours each way for the privilege? No man signs up for that less he's got nothing better. These tools mean something better."

Emeline holds her hands behind her back. She moves sideways a little, unwilling to retreat but unwilling to advance. "I didn't see it that way."

"Come here, real quick." I grab her arm. She smells of powder. "Don't! Not here! Not now."

She pushes against my chest and I lock her close with an arm behind her back and use the other to grab everything good at once. She squirms as I lean in and when she gives up resisting I push her off.

"One of these days you'll get the side of your head knocked in."

"You're my husband and I'll obey you. But I won't be had in a barn. Now we're talking about these tools. You go ahead and move them if you want, but I want the furniture Papa built. We have space in the spare rooms."

My brow twitches. I adjust my eye patch strap cutting above my left ear, and feel a pinch where it crosses my temple. "This is the first you said about furniture. Let it rest. I'm moving the shop today."

"Don't you want to know how bad Deet's hand is?"

"He nicked it."

"Took off the top of his thumb. Do you even know how to use these saws?"

I cuff her good. She rocks sideways a step; her face is red and her eyes are hot and there's something in this woman needs knocked out before it gets proud.

"Mind who you're talking to. Next time there'll be a row of knuckles with it. Talk at me like I'm some dirt farmer."

Her eyeballs glow wild and I can make my hand print in red on her cheek where the blood come to the surface. She says, "Something I want to have a conversation with you about."

"A conversation."

"Yes. Since we married you haven't once taken me to church on Sunday."

"Your math's good."

"When we were courting you said you would take me to church, regular."

"Well goddam, woman. What'd you expect?"

"Well, you've plainly given away your soul but aren't you at least concerned for your sons?"

Too many fucking words.

"Their salvation," she says. "And even your own. You've done evil in this lifetime, Angus Hardgrave; I'd have to be blind not to see and a liar not to confess it. But it isn't too late to get right with the Lord. If not for yourself, think of your sons. They don't know any better but to look up to you. What kind of role model do you make?"

I don't know what makes her bones so straight and uppity. Pride or something. But I got to admit I'm confused a moment by her tactics and I'd ruther she was crying off in the corner somewhere.

Rebel growls. He stands with his forepaws on the plywood ledge and his head angles at the barn wall. Car wheels crunch rocks outside. I move to the bay entrance.

"We're not done talking yet," Emeline says.

The driver kills the engine. It knocks. The man gets out, slams the door and crosses in front of the car toward the house. He wears a short-sleeve business shirt and a tie. He raps the front door, waits three seconds and raps again. I reach in the driver's side of the truck cab and pull a bottle of whiskey. Gurgle from the bottle and tramp down the gravel slope. Emeline trails.

"What you want?" I call.

The man starts, straightens his tie and bustles down the steps. Patches of scalp shine through his gray hair and he scoots like a dog with short legs.

"Ah, Mister Hardgrave. Fred Cayer," he says, and offers his hand. "I understand you got married."

"What do you want?"

Fred drops his hand. "I had a lovely visit with your neighbor, Missus McClellan. She insisted I stop by—said you need to come by and fix her cabinets."

"You come here for that?"

"No, Mister Hardgrave. No, Angus, I came by because you are a newly married man, again, and I know you'll be interested in buying a life insurance policy to protect your wife for that terrible, unexpected day—we all know it's coming, but we don't know when. Friend," he tucks a business card in my shirt pocket, "I have the authority, vested in me by the chairman of Eastern and Northern Life, Walter Reynolds Whittaker the Third, Juris Doctor, to insure you this very moment. You look forty, that right? Good health?" He flips a numbers book open, tabs through the pages, and gazes at the sky while he computes. "You'll be insured for five hundred dollars upon receipt of a dime—a dime! Five hundred dollars for the pretty lady if you drop dead today, this minute, guaranteed; I swear on the Bible."

"You shouldn't do that," Emeline says, behind him. "Swear on the Bible."

"Yes Ma'am." He waves his arm at Emeline. "Angus? Friend, how'll she get by without you?"

I swat a deerfly. "She'll marry someone else."

"That's not true. She'll grieve! Where'll she find the money for the funeral, the casket? And after that, food and bills? Mouths to feed." Fred pulls a deck of smokes from his shirt pocket. He lights one, and his eyebrows shoot up. "Eastern and Northern is a hundred years old—and we're a mutual company, by the way, so while your money grows in the policy, it earns dividends like a savings account at the bank."

"I don't need insurance."

"Ah! You've taken precautions. Great! Have you protected yourself in case something happens to her? Women die as much as men. Sometimes, more. Man like you—she'll be in a family way soon, if she ain't already, and childbirth has its hazards; what do you say? Just a dime a week for seven hundred fifty dollars. Guaranteed. I can take her application right now."

"Covered today?"

"Conditionally. The home office reviews the application. I'll bring the policy the next time I come by. I collect premium two weeks at once; it cuts my windshield time, see?"

I nod at the paper. "Fill it out."

"That's right. I tell my customers, 'you never know.' And this will pay no matter how she passes. God forbid, of course." Fred rests the form on the hood of his car, asks Emeline's birth date, completes the rest without another question. He checks a few blocks and marks an X at the bottom. "Sign here, Missus Hardgrave."

"Do I really need life insurance, Angus?"

"Oh—it's not for you, Sweetie," Fred says, placing his hand at his heart, cigarette smoke crawling from his mouth. "We buy life insurance for the people we love."

"What about you? How much life insurance do you have?" she asks me.

"Just sign that so Fred can be on his way with his ass intact."

"I'll need the first two-weeks' premium..."

"You'll get it when you bring the policy."

"I—well. Hm. I can do that—but only for special customers. If I'm sure you won't leave me hanging."

"Do or don't. Our business is done."

"Just sign here, Ma'am."

"Angus, I don't want to. Not yet."

I take the pen from Fred's hand and scribble on the form. "There. Get along."

"I'll drop by one evening, couple weeks out, and collect—but I'll need a whole month's premium. Now, shouldn't we talk about more coverage for you?"

"If you want to pick your face off that barn wall."

Fred grins, puzzled. I fill my lip with a wad of tobacco and Emeline follows me back to the barn. She watches the insurance man climb in his car and drive the loop toward the road.

"Look after Reb's leg," I say. "I got maybe two more loads. You see Deet before I leave, send him along."

She opens her mouth.

"We're not talking about the lord anymore."

She closes her mouth then opens it again. "There's a ladies' bicycle on the porch. Could you bring that back? I'd like to pedal to the neighbors' for a proper 'hello.'"

FOURTEEN

I check my pocket watch and look over Margulies' mostly-empty barn. This final trip will finish by mid-afternoon, and I'll worry on that white Farmall later. I sate my empty stomach with a gulp of whiskey. "Let's get the drill press."

"You want to grab this lumber today?" Deet chins toward the rafters. "If that Farmall starts, we can throw them on the trailer out back."

"If its tires wasn't flat."

We carry the drill press to the truck and place it laterally on the bed, load a home-made lathe, then a horizontal belt sander. We fill gaps with hand saws, drill bits, squares, levels, a plumb, screw drivers, a five gallon drum of shellac flakes just waiting for the alcohol to make em useful, boxes of screws and nails, files, and pipe clamps. At the front porch, I wheel Emeline's bike to the truck and hoist it on top of the other cargo.

Deet says, "Where's that whiskey?"

"Up front."

"Think I'll take a pull."

"Suit yourself."

Deet wriggles onto the tailgate and uncaps the bottle. "You know the Loomis boys make hooch? They sell it at the hook shops."

"You go to them hook shops?"

"I don't believe I'll ever pay for a woman."

"You will. One way or another."

"Almanac says this year'll be a bumper; maybe stillin's worth a try."

"Stillin'," I say. "Mitch McClellan made some of the meanest corn whiskey you ever tasted. He give me a nip before I went off to war. Take the rust off a nail. Boiler's in the woods, even yet. After the last revenuer took an axe to it, Mitch just quit. Musta had a basement full of it."

"Yeah, well, corn's shoulder-high. We got maybe two months to get it all together."

"Something to think on," I say.

"Think on? There's no way it don't make sense."

"Well, there's one way. You ain't old enough to consider the cussed government. You put the money in, make something worthwhile, and they'll come along with axes and shotguns blasting the whole works, and haul you off to jail 'til you pay a ransom. The only way to do it is if you know they won't catch you, and I haven't figured that one out yet."

"How long's it been since McClellan run his still?"

"Couple years."

"You don't think they forgot, yet?"

"Something to think on. Let's see if Emeline kept this Farmall the way she kept the table saw."

In the back corner of the barn bay, a Farmall sits on flat tires with old, parched rubber. I blow dust off the engine block, wipe a swath with my hand, revealing shiny white paint.

"'47 A model," I say. "Seven hundred dollars, brand new."

"Why's it white?"

"Who gives a shit? Look at that—Super model. Emeline's Pap used to deal them."

"Think she'll run?"

"Farmalls run. Might take a little sweet talk, but she'll run." I climb aboard. "Padding on the seat." I tap the tank and listen to the wavering echo of fuel. "Little low, and probly stale. Didn't I see a fuel pump on the side of the barn?"

"Think so. You run one of these before?" Deet says.

I press the clutch, wiggle the shifter, extend the throttle full out and then in. I press the starter. Nothing. "Get the cables out the truck."

Deet glances over his shoulder. "They won't reach. Why'd Margulies park it in the back, anyway?"

I look at the hay bales stacked across the bay. "Turn the truck around and pull in, just shy of the wall, there."

Deet goes to the truck and I push the tractor. The flat tires hold like cement; I sit on a front wheel. Deet eases the truck forward and kills the motor. He stares outside. Visible in the aperture between the truck fender and barn door, a red and white car rolls to a stop. I step to the door. A young man approaches and regards me coolly.

It's the fella from the back of the church.

"Brad Chambers." He offers his hand. "You own this place?"

"That's right."

Chambers stands two feet away, still offering his hand. I give it a quick snap.

"Well, uh, what's your name?" Chambers says.

"Hardgrave. I already got life insurance."

Chambers laughs. "I'm looking for a room. Pastor's wife said this place was empty, and I pulled in when I saw you."

"What you have in mind?"

"I can look after the place and pay twenty dollars a month."

"'D'ruther it sit empty. Normal rents is four times that."

"I can be handy."

I pull Copenhagen from my pocket. "Lend us a hand in the barn."

Chambers follows. "What's that? '47 A model. Still white?"

"Don't know the history," I say. "Wife's daddy dealt in Farmall."

"That French fella?"

"Margulies."

"That's right, and Pitlake bought him out in '49," Chambers says. "Margulies must've slipped one of the show models home."

"Why?"

"Dealers are supposed to paint them red before they sell them."

"Get back of the left wheel and give a push," I say.

Chambers takes one tire, Deet the other. I say, "Heave!"

The tractor rocks forward, but the giant rear tires have settled to the rims. We relax. The tractor rocks back.

"Another two of us could move it," Chambers says.

I reach to the engine, touch a black hose then a wire fastened to the head, as if examining the engine might conjure from the wary tractor a secret that will help me move it. "Deet, didn't you carry a block and tackle to the truck?"

"That's right."

"Get it."

"Why not just get an air compressor?" Chambers says. "What farm doesn't have a compressor?"

"Deet, scout about and see."

On the far side of the barn bay, hay bales rise in a corner pyramid. Maple and walnut boards stretch across the loft; their ends protrude over the edge. All that remains in the bay is the tractor, a twelve-foot workbench, and a broom in the back corner. Deet trots down the steps to the lower level.

"Where you work?" I say.

"London Cleaners. Running uniforms, pressing suits."

I release a slow string of tobacco spit to the barn floor.

"Might go to college somewhere, use my G.I. Bill." Chambers studies a distant spot on the wall. "Somewhere."

"Korea?"

"That's right."

"You poor bastards hit some shit."

"Some. Commander was a crazy wop named Calavano, wanted to make up for missing Hitler. First Sergeant Knudsen didn't have the rocks to put him straight. Marched a platoon like a bunch of stupid Redcoats straight into a hillside with more fucking Chinks than we had bullets."

"Can do, *sir*." I salute. "Yes sir."

"Anyway, Calavano worshipped Patton, told a story about him and MacArthur in the First World War, standing on top of a hill as artillery came in all around. He thought that was just boss. Calavano lost his marbles. Said Eisenhower had Patton killed. But after what I saw, men with their bellies hanging out, legs laying fifteen feet away, still shaking, I wouldn't put it past one man to kill another to steal what's his, you know? After what I saw."

We are quiet.

Footsteps pound the stairs. Deet appears in the doorway. "Found a compressor. I'll roll it around."

"Fairlane sounds like it has some blasting powder under the hood."

"She's a hottie."

"Let me take a peek."

I carry the Wild Turkey to the car. "Lookit that. Fairlane Crown Victoria." I sip from the bottle and pass it to Chambers.

"I guess it's after noon," he says and drinks. Chambers reaches in the driver's window and pops the release.

I feel along the bottom for the latch, lift and prop the polished hood. "I was afraid you'd have a straight six in here."

"Nah; bent eight. Two hundred seventy two cubic inch—runs like a cat on fire, and that's for damn sure."

"Start her up. Give her a goose."

Chambers slides into the seat. The engine turns and a moment later, races. I lean forward, mindful of the fan blowing my hair, and nod at the throaty rumble. Chambers joins me. "Took all my Army money to buy it."

"Sounds purty." I sit on his perfect wax job.

"What do you say to the room?"

Deet tows a black and white compressor around the barn corner. Chambers kills the motor and we mosey back to the barn.

Working together we fill the tires, replace the oil, flush the fuel filter, and fill the tank with several trips to the pump outside with a five-gallon can. Chambers pulls the battery caps and tops each hole with water from a basin on the first floor, then readies the jumper cables.

"Let's push it forward," I say.

The tractor rolls easily. Chambers connects the cables between truck and tractor. I wave him to the seat. Chambers works the clutch, shifts the throttle to the left, then the right, then back a quarter distance to the left. He exhales.

"You got her." I nod. "Give her a little choke, blip that lever for a revolution—then ease off. Just get the gas flowing."

"What do you say to that room in the house?"

Chambers waits, and when I say nothing, moves the choke and presses the starter. The motor grinds with a great rhythmic heavy whoop, and dies.

"Let her charge a few minutes," I call. "Meantime, Deet, take an extension cord and fill the tires on the trailer. Check it out good."

Chambers edges forward. "What do you say to the room, Mister Hardgrave?"

"Make it thirty a month, so I don't feel like I'm getting took."

"All I got is twenty."

I shake my head. "I'll expect you to look after the place. There's a push mower in the shed by the house, rakes and such. Twenty's it?"

"Twenty."

"This is just 'til I decide what to do with the house. Could be a few months, could be a week. I'll be taking things out, but you can move when I see the first rent."

Chambers opens his wallet and hands me a ten-dollar bill. "I'll have the rest end of the month. Two weeks."

"That'll work."

FIFTEEN Maul

A t dusk Ticky Bilger rewarded Maul with a fresh-butch-
ered cow's heart and watched the blood on his snout
glisten.

A car door slammed and Ticky crossed to the gate. His brother
Vic leaned against the fender and held a bottle.

"Hey ya old man how ya doin? I'm headed for New York and
stopped to say a big hello..."

Ticky slapped his brother on the arm and led him into the
enclosed back yard. "Doin' fine, doin' fine—How's life in the big
city?"

"Lights and ladies."

"Business?"

"Real good. Passin' through to New York."

"What line of hustle you in, these days?"

"Little this, you know. Whole lotta that." Vic drank and
passed the bottle to Ticky. "Progress with the dogs?"

"Got the meanest sumbitch in the state right here. Flat licked a dog holdin' eight pounds and a year on him." Ticky led Vic to the pens and sipped from the bottle. "In seventy seconds. This is him."

"They got poodles in Chicago'd spank this pup." Vic peered close to the pen. Maul growled.

"You let him mouth off at people?"

"I don't give a shit about people; he's a dog killer."

Maul leaped at the cage. Vic jumped, then rapped the mesh with his palm. "Dumb fuck."

"You shoulda seen him."

"I bet. Say, I ain't eat all day."

Ticky led Vic to the house. Vic paused on the porch, pressed a nostril and blew snot to the bushes.

"How'd we both have the same momma and you didn't get no bringin' up?"

"Oh, I got it; just ditched it in Chicago. If you ever left Pennsylvania, you would too. Do you lotta good."

"You didn't use to go around honkin' all the time. How you went from bookworm know-it-all to a slick-talking huckster, I don't know."

Vic opened the refrigerator and drank milk from the jar.

Ticky shook his head. "That gonna sit on whiskey?"

"Christ, I don't care." He found a block of cheese and sat at the table. "Got any bread?"

Ticky tossed a loaf to the table.

"I need your help, big brother."

"I knew it."

"I'm pert nigh stranded. Crawled up the driveway on fumes. Need you to spot me gas money to New York."

"I ain't made of money, for crissake."

"Well, maybe not, maybe so. I thought a business man like you—"

"What's in New York?"

"I'm in the delivery business."

"And can't afford gas."

"Now hold on—"

"Vic, I give you money and I never see it again. That ain't how to do a brother, but it's how you do me. You got some gall, owing me two hundred already, and coming here strutting like a cock in a hen house."

"This delivery's a special deal. Lemme show you. It's in the trunk." Vic tossed Ticky his car keys, left the bottle but took some bread and a slab of cheese, and followed Ticky outside. "Check the trunk."

Ticky opened it. "A suitcase."

"Open the suitcase."

"What's this?"

"That, big brother, is cocaine; made on the other side of the earth, come across the equator, through Mexico, ferried across the Rio Grande, up to Chicago, and I'm the last leg of the trip, like the Pony Express, almost. I got to get the goods to my people in New York, else I'm done for."

Ticky waited.

"I'll bring a thick wad of cash back through, you can bet your sweet ass."

"This why you're blowin' snot on my bushes?"

"I got a little of my own, you know. They gimme a little of my own. That's all. Christ, no; I don't use their shit."

"Let me see what you been takin' on your own."

Vic smiled tight. "You want a try, that it?"

"I want to see what you got."

Vic opened the passenger door, reached under the seat, tossed a folded envelope to Ticky. Ticky opened it, lifted the flap, smelled inside. Dabbed a wet finger. Touched his tongue.

"Get a good snort up your nose," Vic said.

"You got speed?"

"Speed? Shit, that ain't even outlawed, is it?" Vic tossed a bottle of pills.

"I'll be hangin' on to these 'til you get back—a couple of days, right?" Ticky tossed Vic a roll of bills.

SIXTEEN

Emeline punched a double batch of bread dough, spread flour on the cutting board, folded the glob on itself, and punched it again. Through the window, she watched Angus set up Papa's tools in the barn. Not another word had passed about her furniture, but the barn overflowed with tools.

Jacob scraped his chair from the table.

After a week of nonstop work, Angus's kitchen smelled like a harvest, spice and flour and sugar. His drab living room was clean enough to invite a guest over without a twinge of shame. The bedrooms were red up. The bathroom—which she'd found looking like a barn stall and smelling like a cesspool—why, she could eat a ham sandwich while looking at the base of the toilet without the slightest revulsion. Oh...Angus Hardgrave's house was *clean.*

The eve of their wedding, when Angus described the orchard, picking apples before the frost, sunrises over the lake, she saw it all as if spread out in some comfortable dream. All the warmth she remembered as a child, now hers as a wife and mother. Pumpkins and venison and snow. Fresh eggs. She punched the dough and her wrist ached.

"Why you angry?" Jacob said.

"I'm not angry. I'm making bread. Why aren't you in the barn?"

"Pap don't want me in the barn. Says I'm in the doghouse."

"I don't think he's angry anymore. Your father can be impatient, but he's not angry."

Emeline thought of the night Angus learned he was the grandson of Jonah McClellan. It hadn't seemed to register a change in him. She wondered, if she had grown up in a family that was at war with another, would finding out she was the child of the enemy mean something to her? Of course it would. All sorts of alignments would change. She would begin to question everything she thought was good about her family. Everything sacred would be suspect. She would take a fresh look at her family's opponents with a desire to find something redeeming.

But Angus didn't change at all. He never struck her as introspective and didn't communicate his thoughts, so it was impossible to guess. But there had been no outward change. No moment caught musing. No kind word toward the widow next door.

As if bidden by the Lord she wondered if that was because Angus was already as irredeemable as Jonah McClellan. Was the whole family lost?

"Can I ask you something, Jacob?"

He nodded.

"Have you ever gone to church?"

"What for?"

"To learn about God."

"There ain't no god. Just god damn. Ask Pap."

"Someday I want to take you to church. Until then, I want to start a Bible study with you and Deet every morning."

"Aw, no way."

"Yes."

"But—"

"I don't want to hear another word about it. We'll begin tomorrow morning. Make sure you tell Deet. I don't know where he is half the time. Now I want to ask you one more thing. Did you ever have a little brother or sister?"

Jacob shook his head.

"Did something happen a year or two ago and you lost a brother or sister?"

"Huh-unh."

"Did your Papa bury a dog, or an animal down by the lake?"

Jacob's jaw tightened. He bolted from the kitchen. Emeline watched the window. Jacob strode toward the field to the left of the barn.

She kneaded dough and thought about the grave under the walnut on Devil's Elbow. She thought about Angus spending so much time at the tree, and taking her there on their wedding night.

The strangeness here was different than any she'd experienced. It was like Angus, Deet, and Jacob lived in punctuated moments that never cohered into... life. She hoped so much that the Lord had come with her, with His plan. Because so far, it seemed like everything Hardgrave was just random ugliness and evil.

SEVENTEEN

I bite the corner of a four-quarter maple board and show Deet the impression.

"Well?" he says. "Soft?"

"Hard. Look. Barely dented. Good hard maple—machines damn near like metal."

"Won't it dull the blades?"

"Yeah, but you build with hard maple, you got something. You can always sharpen a blade."

We stow boards in the barn loft in the same order we found them at Margulies': the longest, widest, and heaviest on the bottom. The rough-cut maple is generally knot-free, but empty knotholes and sections of dry rot render a quarter of the walnut useless. The boards are gnarled and warped, and milling them flat and straight will take hours. But the rich color and the leather and gunpowder smell invite me to make sawdust.

One ten-inch wide crotch board caught my eye when we were loading it at Margulies and unloading it now, the last on the trailer. Margulies must have set it aside special, otherwise it would have been unloaded first, with the other heavy cuts. A black and brown knot ripples across the bottom four feet, long and skinny, so turbulent it's like to drag your eyes under and drown them. The plank is six feet tall and maybe three inches thick, and heavy as a dead man. I lean it against the wall.

"Take a look at that," I say. "That's character."

Deet sits with his legs hanging over the loft.

The board won't work for commercial furniture—people that don't know jack shit about wood insist on straight-grained lumber. But that crotch will be a jewel. The ripples and rolls, even through the sawmill finish, promise a spectacular piece.

Something in the board speaks to me. The swirls and pattern suggest something that can't be.

"You can c'mon down; that's the last," I say. I rock the planer stand across the barn floor and position it with a dozen feet clear for in-feed and output. I rotate the elevating screw and the cutter box lifts from the steel table. Slip my hand inside, press the blade, and show Deet the blood on my finger.

"Margulies kept his tools right. How about you plug me in?"

I lower the screw until the indicator points a hair over three inches, then back off an eighth turn. The crotch board rests on the in-feed. I flip the toggle and the motor whines. I summon Deet with a wave. "Support the board! Don't lift; don't pull!"

Deet assumes a limber stance facing the output slot.

The rollers jerk the board forward but the cutters are too high and it slips through with nary a shave. I spin the screw counterclockwise and feed the board again. The blades bite the walnut and spray black shavings at Deet.

Deet stands the board on end and I study a long bowl untouched in the middle. I run my fingers across the shaved edges, both directions, smooth as the bottoms of Emeline's tits. I lower the cutter a thirty-second and pass the board through again.

With each pass the bowl flattens and the grain picture resolves like I'm blowing dust from an old painting. Chocolate colored shavings pile at Deet's feet. I work faster scarcely believing what I see, and hide my eye from Deet's each time I retrieve the plank for another pass under the cutters. The fevered motor whines. Something in the board is damn hard to cut. The scent of sawdust and electric, copper and magnets fills the air.

Bone.

Finally, slack-jawed Deet holds the board as if looking at a portrait.

Encased in the wood is a spine, with a purple glow like the sheen on old roast beef.

I fish my Copenhagen.

"Looks like some animal got buried in a tree," Deet whispers. "Ain't these ribs, here, each side, one on top of the other?"

I take the board and flip it. The bones shimmer like the inside of a clamshell. I press a vertebra, each the size of a fist and hard as a rock. The length and dimension indicate a large man. I hold the board to my stomach and align the lowest vertebra with my hip. This man bests me by six inches, maybe, making him close to seven feet.

Whiskey might put things in perspective. I rest the board on the bench and Deet studies the markings. I gulp Wild Turkey, wipe my mouth with my sleeve and get walnut and bone shavings in my mouth, and the walnut leaves an aftertaste I can't clean with whiskey, and it ain't at all bad.

"You think a deer or something got petrified?" Deet says.

I drink again and swallow a little Copenhagen spit with it. Run my fingers along the bones. Do math, subtract years. I nod at the board.

"Say hello to your Grandpap, Jonah McClellan."

I tramp along the cornfield with the lake over the grassy slope to my left. Fireflies glow green where the forest abuts the field. I lengthen my stride and follow the deer path through knee-high weeds. On cue, a spooked deer flashes its white tail. I squint but fail to make out antlers from the forest. The deer crashes through a blackberry thicket.

A hundred yards shy of the road, a footpath used by generations of McClellan and Hardgrave boys cuts to the left. Larry McClellan died on Omaha Beach. The machinegun bunker that got him looked like an eye set deep below the hillside's brow. Larry was a few years my junior, but growing up in the country, a boy and his neighbors is fast friends—even if they don't know they're half brothers, and even if they belong to a rival clans. I took shrapnel in my eye carrying him to cover just so he could bleed to death in peace.

I came home and Mitch McClellan told me a joke. He called me a bastard at the cemetery and I didn't get the punch line for twelve years.

It is dusk. I turn into the forest and watch the ground for protruding roots. Fifty yards ahead, a fractured yellow window shifts with the sway of branches. In a couple minutes I tramp across the widow's porch. A dog growls inside and the dry-rotted floorboards creak. The porch light comes on; the curtain rustles; a lock slides and the door swings open.

"Only sent for you two day ago." Widow McClellan shuffles aside. "Hurry 'fore the moths get in!"

Outside of Mitch's funeral, this is the first we've been this close since she beat my chest at Larry's grave. I stand at the entrance and look into her kitchen. She limps to the table and drops to a chair. A dog stands at the living room, head low, a growl floating in her upper register. I give her a quick study; she appears the same as Rebel, a pit bull.

"Don't appreciate you sending that insurance man to my house."

"If you'd have come when I asked—"

"Jake said you busted a cabinet door."

"Don't you see it on the counter? Hinge came loose and when it hit the floor, the whole thing come apart."

I whistle. "You got your stiles free on each end, and the panel's falling apart. Looks like old glue dried out. What?" I pull the frame apart. "Mortise and tenon on a cabinet door? Take some doing, but I can fix it."

"Well, I won't pay you an arm and a leg."

I don't have a notion what the widow is up to. "We'll work something out. Two weeks, if I don't get any time weeknights."

I step to the porch. She holds the door. Damned if that isn't a red nose pit bitch, growling and eyeballing me.

EIGHTEEN

A ngus had left for his long morning drive to the oil derrick. Emeline held her fist to Deet's door. She hesitated. Had Jacob told him about the Bible study?

She rapped three times. "Time for Bible study, Deet."

Further down the hall she stood at the next door. Rapped. "Time for the Good News, Jacob."

She returned to the kitchen and emptied the coffee pot into her mug, taking what remained after Angus filled his thermos. An egg spattered in bacon grease on the stove; she slid it onto a bread crust and chewed slowly. Her stomach turned at the salty grease.

While she waited for Deet and Jacob on the sofa, Emeline found her bookmark and began reading.

She woke at dawn to a faintly lit and utterly silent house. Without checking their rooms she knew they'd snuck out. She looked upward. Her eyes filled with tears and she didn't move as they dripped from her lashes and streamed down her face. She stared at the ceiling as if the Lord was behind it, and He would soon give her an insight that would make sense of it all. This very morning she'd browsed her favorite chapter in Ephesians, which reminded her that the Lord had a plan for her life, with good works prepared like footsteps she should walk in. But the harder she sought direction, the more cagey the Lord seemed. The more tantalizingly distant and unfathomable. She couldn't doubt what He'd said—but she did doubt what she'd heard out there in the praying field. Did He really promise that He was trustworthy and following Him would bring her closer? Because this wasn't close at all.

She stared at the ceiling, thoughts cascading through her, none of them a prayer, and yet, every one of them heard. For the Lord knew everything.

Emeline looked out the window. The sunlight arrived through her tears like a scattered burst of yellow, and she smiled, and coughed phlegm. She would trust the Lord as He had commanded.

For Jacob and Deet she would pray. Maybe things would change. They were at places in their lives that weren't conducive to pondering the Almighty. She would be a model for them. She would live on God's grace and show them what a disciple looked like.

She closed her eyes and prayed.

Lord, give them time.

The ride to town was eight miles, longer than she'd ever ridden a bicycle. She walked up hills and coasted down, pedaled across flats circumfused by light green fields of wheat. Her fingers grew numb in the breeze and the rushing wind whipped tears from her eyes. An hour and a half after she started, her jacket bundled in the handlebar basket, she coasted the final stretch, slowed at the gravel driveway, and turned toward her house.

A red and white Fairlane sat by the steps.

She dropped her bicycle on the gravel and ran to the door. It was unlocked. Angus had a key, but how had Chambers gotten inside? Did she dare enter? She shoved the door open. Her heart raced. Violated again. The living room smelled foreign. The kitchen was dark; the hallway, lit. She charged up the staircase.

"Who's there?" His voice came from the bathroom. He stepped to the hallway wearing a towel around his waist, a toothbrush in his mouth.

"What?" She stepped closer. "Get out!"

"Hey, I'm supposed to be here."

She drove her palms into his chest. He braced his arm at the doorjamb. She pushed again and he swatted her forearms aside.

"What do you mean *supposed to be here?* Get out of my house!" she pushed again; as if humoring her, he retreated to the sink and lifted his arms to face level.

"Careful, Emeline Hardgrave. Go talk to your old man."

"I'm going to the sheriff."

He swiped her arm, twisted it behind her back and crushed her to his chest. "You'll go nowhere 'less I say so." His free hand clutched her rump. "But now that you're here, how 'bout you and me have some fun?"

She stamped her heel to his naked foot and missed. She spun and he released her. Emeline backed into the hallway. "I'm going to the sheriff. You touch me again you better kill me."

"I love you enough, you know... Whichever way you want things to come out."

She gaped. "You aren't right, Brad."

"No, I suppose not." He stepped closer.

Emeline backed a step. Chambers swung and his fingers grazed her arm. She fled and he raced after her; his towel flapped exposing a black mat of hair and a pug-nosed snake. Emeline missed the top stair and swung her arm shy of the rail.

She tumbled.

A blade of pain shot through her leg and blackness closed on her mind like night laying siege to a waning candle, and she lay heaped on the foot of the stairwell.

"Papa?" she cried, but he didn't answer. Emeline squinted to squeeze the agony from her mind. Realization flickered: she was alone. She felt wetness on her skin, stickiness, and smelled the richness of her blood.

Her ears rang; the tone pulsed with each heartbeat. She moved her leg and blackness swelled again.

"There you go, child, you're okay." Doctor Fleming stroked her cheek with rough, old knuckles.

She opened her eyes. Chambers stood behind Fleming, upside down in her sight. Time had passed. He was dressed. She lay crumpled on the floor at the stairwell.

"There, there, dear," Fleming tottered as he squatted beside her and she felt the urge to protest the old man doing this for her, but her voice failed. His black bag lay by her head.

"You have a compound fracture, Emeline, and you must listen. I have to take you to my office, and you will feel pain. Can you be strong?"

The white-haired doctor's sanity and gentleness struck her. Her eyes crested with tears. She inhaled. Nodded. Chambers kneeled, worked his thick arms under her back and thighs. He wore cologne. His jugular swelled as he lifted her.

Her right shinbone protruded white and bloody through her skin and her leg hung beneath, already stiff and contracting. Blackness overtook her again.

Emeline wakened in Fleming's office to unflagging, but endurable pain, with her leg immobilized below the knee in a thin cast.

"Hello, child," Doctor Fleming said.

Her first cogent thought was that she was not a child. Doctor Fleming was a quirky soul, liable to cite Gray's Anatomy or Shakespeare with equal zeal. He'd treated Papa, and though gentle, never minced his meaning.

"Am I okay?" she said.

"I'll have to see you every day until we're sure you're not getting an infection, and that will mean removing this cast and applying a new one each time."

She accepted his prescription in silence.

"I'll drive her home," Chambers said.

"Thank you," Fleming said.

Emeline shifted; her leg was like a log. "I'll ride my bike."

"Oh no, Emeline. Your leg is broken all the way through."

"Let me get you to the car," Chambers said. "Doc, can you get the door?"

Her heart hammered. Pressure swelled in her head. "Doctor, I should telephone my husband," she said. "For propriety."

"I'll telephone for you. But will he answer?"

"He'll be at the oil well, right Mrs. Hardgrave?" Chambers said. He lifted her.

"Let this young man take you," Doctor Fleming said.

"Doctor!" she said. "Crutches?'

"I don't have any to give you. We can order a set."

Moments later she sat on Chambers' front seat next to the door handle that bruised her scalp, the edge where she wrenched her shoulder, the radio knob still broken from her knee.

Chambers reached between his legs; a spring twanged and the seat rolled back, opening more legroom. Pain stabbed her shin. Did the baby in her womb share the agony?

"I mentioned your fall to Mister London and he let me off for the morning. I'll take you to the doctor's on my lunch breaks this week, and get you home after my shift."

She watched the words form in his mouth and drift out, every one of them perfectly normal, and spoken as if he and she were best friends only now venturing into romance. He spoke a phantom reality as if she might confirm it.

Emeline looped her index finger through the door release. She waited. As long as he drove toward the Hardgrave farm...

They came to wheat fields, then cornfields. She cast a hopeful eye, but Deet had no reason to be in the fields; the corn was shoulder high and until harvest, he could be anywhere, working in the barn, fishing at the lake, courting some girl in town.

"I talked to Angus about staying in the house," Chambers said. "Paid a half-month's rent. Ten dollars. I got a right to be in that house."

Emeline clamped her teeth.

"He didn't mention that to you, did he? Ole Angus? You might stop and think about what kind of man you married. I'm a lot of things, but I'm not a squatter. And falling down those steps was your own fault."

About to point out the Hardgrave driveway, Emeline refrained. Chambers drifted almost to a stop before turning.

Doctor Fleming had given her a capful of a new children's painkiller, Tylenol, and had sent her home with a bottle, but as the Fairlane bounced over the rock driveway, pain jabbed through the monotonous throbbing she had gotten used to.

Deet emerged from the barn with sawdust clinging to his pants and a red blot on his thumb bandage. He appreciated the car then stooped and met Emeline's eyes. His smile faded.

The Fairlane stopped with a gentle rocking motion and a billow of dust overtook them.

Deet stooped at Emeline's side and looked through to Chambers. "What's going on, Brad?"

"She slipped and busted her leg. Give me a hand getting her out."

"How'd it happen?"

"She stopped by the house and didn't know I'd already moved in. Guess I surprised her."

"Fell down the stairs, did she?" Deet stood upright and Chambers exited the driver's side. The open window framed Deet's torso and arms. They talked over the roof of the car.

"I'll carry her out," Brad said. "You might not be able to lift her."

Deet eased the door open, touched below her cheekbone. "Oh, Emeline. That's gonna be a shiner." He cradled her legs and lower back, and extracted her from the seat, careful not to bump her cast on the door. His touch was proper. But she detected something else, a rigidity that Deet projected in order to what? Demonstrate his strength to Chambers? Or her?

Being carried was like floating over a sea of agony, and every time her legs dipped, pain frothed higher. Deet's arms quivered as he climbed the steps. She rested her head against his shoulder. He whispered, "You really fall?"

She nodded. "I did. He was half naked and—"

"Shh."

Deet stood sideways as he worked the screen door handle. Brad trailed to the porch.

"Don't bring him inside," she whispered.

"Did he hit you?"

"No."

Deet lowered Emeline until the sofa cushions supported her. He rested his wounded thumb at the belt loop by his knife and turned to the sound of the screen door spring.

"She'll need to see Doc Fleming every day this week," Chambers said, and spoke louder for Emeline, "So I'll come get you on my lunch break. See you tomorrow, Em."

"I'm sure she appreciates that, but I'll take her in."

"Thanks, Dieter, but we got things squared away. I'll be here tomorrow at noon."

"I don't think that's very smart. You bring her here all beat up and tell me you're gonna be back tomorrow? I don't think so."

The screen door separated them.

"She slipped," Chambers said. "She'll tell you that."

"Thanks for helping out."

Emeline watched both the door and the window by the writing table. Chambers stood where she couldn't see him. After a moment, his heels struck the porch and he crossed the window, scowling.

She looked at the sawdust on Deet's clothes and in his hair. "What were you doing?"

"Pap said to build a pen for some mutts."

"A pen for Rebel? How are you doing that, when you just cut off half your thumb?"

"Trial and error. What happened?"

"I fell down the stairs. I didn't know Angus rented the house to Chambers. I saw his car and went inside. I ran from him and fell down the stairs."

"Why run?"

"I didn't expect to see him."

"You saw the car. You expected someone."

"I don't want to talk about this."

Deet ran his fingers through his hair, then stood with his hands loose at his side. "Did you go there to see him?"

"No!" She recoiled. Her leg throbbed.

"Then you need a better story to tell Pap. Why was you even in town?"

"I wanted to buy corn meal."

"Corn meal."

"Deet, I won't be questioned. Wrap some ice in a hand towel if you want to help."

"It wasn't a question, and you don't know what help you need."

"What's that mean?"

"You better think of a better story." He turned and at the door said, "You don't know what you married."

Melted ice dampened Emeline's hair and a warm, wet towel covered her eye. The whine of a saw blade carried through the screen, but she awoke to rapping on the door.

"Yoo-hoo!"

The house was dim but Emeline recognized the pastor's wife Nancy Denny by her silhouette. She carried a basket and before they exchanged words Emeline knew baked chicken was nearby.

"Where's the light switch?"

"By the door. Lower."

The lights came on and Nancy rushed to her side. "Oh you poor thing; Doctor Fleming told me everything."

"I'm fine." She'd wakened several times and rung the cowbell Deet had left on the coffee table, but the saws in the barn never stopped.

"That smells so good."

"Did you have lunch?"

She shook her head. "I shouldn't eat dinner until my husband comes home."

"You think he'd know if you just took a little bit? I'll fix you a plate and moosh around what's left so he won't know what we started with." She found the kitchen and a moment later rattled plates and silverware. Nancy returned to Emeline with a plate of paprika-red chicken, mashed potatoes and gravy, with a side of peas.

"Would you mix the peas with the potatoes?"

Nancy rolled the green orbs into the potatoes, scooped a spoonful. Emeline took it from her and ate.

Emeline searched Nancy's face. What mechanics of character made a woman good and a man bad? Or a boy mostly good while another was evil? One patient and caring, the other fascinated by tearing wings off flies, stepping on ants, raping girls? She swallowed. The potatoes were lumpy and the gravy was salty. Perfect.

"Thank you."

Nancy watched her. "You're welcome." She hesitated. "It's none of my business..."

"Maybe."

"Did you meet Mr. Chambers? On purpose?"

Emeline groaned. "I didn't know he was there."

Nancy filled the spoon with white meat and potatoes and passed it to her. "You've been funny about him—changing your mind about him renting."

"I didn't change my mind!" Her leg pain flared and heat washed across her face. She forced the mouthful down. "I didn't change my mind. Angus rented the place to him, I guess. I stormed in like a fool thinking he was squatting. He chased me and I fell down the stairs."

Nancy nodded, wiped the corner of a doe eye. "Did you have a black eye before you went there, this morning?"

"I fell down the stairs."

Nancy leaned conspiratorially close. "Only two weeks have passed. We can get you out of this."

"Out of what?"

"This mistake." She glanced about the room. Exhaled.

"This mistake was an answer to prayer, Nancy Denny, and it was done in a house of God." Emeline winced. "Would you get that bottle on the end table? Says 'Tylenol.'"

Nancy pressed her shoulder. "You don't have to be this brave."

Emeline adjusted her weight. The sofa cushions sagged and the support joist pressed her mid-back. The damp, rough upholstery irritated her arms.

"I've seen a lot of troubled girls," Nancy said, passing the Tylenol. "I recognize trouble."

Emeline drank from the bottle. "Give me more of those potatoes and gravy. Please."

Nancy obliged. "Your daddy passed away and a month later you married a man you didn't even know. A *bad* man. I tried to tell you. You could've had any of a half-dozen nice young boys in town, and you chose Angus Hardgrave. Didn't even know you were Mrs. Hardgrave Number Four. Didn't even know what happened to his eye. And you don't want to, either."

"It was from Normandy," Emeline said.

"Not Normandy. Paris. When he found out his son had a Nazi name."

"What?"

"I shouldn't say this—but I have to. You just run off on a whim. Now look at you. Beat up, broken down, and defiant as a game cock—"

"That's not—"

"But it's going to get worse and worse! Each time you get your back up, like you're doing now, he's going to knock you down! This man has history." Her voice broke. "He didn't shave for your wedding. What kind of man is that?"

"I made him shave for Mitch McClellan's funeral."

Nancy rolled her eyes. Emeline took the spoon from the plate and ate peas and potatoes.

"You're going to disappear like Lucy Mae. I can't bear the thought."

"That'll be a trick in this cast."

Nancy wiped her cheeks. Shook her head. Feigned a smile.

"Lucy Mae. What a dear. Wasn't hardly more than a child when he married her, and looked like one, not four feet tall. At the wedding she was the tiniest woman I ever saw."

Nancy studied Emeline, then sat upright and patted her arm. "I'll warm the oven so Angus has something to eat when he comes home, and maybe that'll stay his hand."

NINETEEN

I park in front of the barn. Light's on and the smell of sawdust and burnt blades comes through the open truck window. I told Deet to size boards for a kennel, though he might waste a truckload of lumber learning the tools.

Supper can wait. Fixing the widow's tenon and reassembling the rails, stiles, and panel is an easy job—but not with new tools. Might take an evening or two. I swallow Wild Turkey. Though the whiskey tastes as good as it ever has, it's like slipping a wet dowel in a square hole. The corners stay dry. Part of me ain't satisfied. I pack my lip with snuff.

Rebel's head pops over the plywood pen at the far end of the barn bay; he watches with one eye and grins. I can't help but grin back, him one eye, me one eye. So long as his nuts are whole, his value is secure.

Deet kills the table saw motor. He looks at the dark outside and all of a sudden starts toward the bay door. Dust floats in a yellow glow over a stack of boards he's sized. "That's a lot of cutting. Rips too. You size em right?"

Already at the foot of the slope by the truck, Deet says, "I wasn't thinking. We best get inside and look after Emeline. She's busted her leg."

"Busted?"

"Fell down stairs at her old place. That fella with the Fairlane brought her here. Her leg's busted good, and she's got a shiner."

"I wish I'd seen it."

"Seen your wife smacked around, that it?"

"Watch your tongue. I'd maybe put a shiner on him, is what I meant." I nudge the stack with my toe. "What about these boards?"

"She just dropped by her place on the way to the grocery."

I nod. "What about these boards?"

Deet looks toward the house. "Everything's sized like you said. You didn't write out the floorboards, but I did the math and I'm finishing them now."

"Got a good idea how to put it all together, do you?"

"It's in your drawing." He paces back inside the barn.

I lift a board, hold a square to the cut, then eye-plumb the rip. "Got the warp out. Guess you figured how to use the jointer?"

Deet nodded.

"Maybe you got a knack. Let me show you this panel door."

"Emeline's inside. Ain't been checked on for a while."

I feel my brow pinch under my eye patch. "Is she dyin' right this cussed minute?"

We move to the workbench. I arrange the pieces of the cabinet door and hold the left stile for Deet to examine. "This is a mortise. See the bottom slot? That's where the tenon goes. Just like the birds and the bees. Slip it in, like so. Good and snug. You got to cut this tenon flush, put a mortise in here, and size a floating tenon."

"Two slots, and one—"

"That's right. Drill the holes, chisel em square, and size the tenon by hand so the outsides are flush, you follow?"

"Like this?" Deet holds three machined blocks of maple, and assembles them in the manner of my proposed joint.

I take the unit from him. Break it apart. Study the craftsmanship. "When you do this?"

"Gave it some thought this morning."

"Yeah, right. Why don't you fix that door tomorrow?"

Deet looks toward the house.

"Then get the pen done."

I move over to Rebel, check his eye. "Let's see about Emeline."

A minute later I enter the house. Smell chicken. I cross the living room to Emeline, pull a blanket from her and peer at a cast on her leg.

"How you feel?"

"It hurts."

"You lived in that house all your life. How'd you slip?"

"I didn't know you'd let the house out. I ran when he came out the bathroom."

I take her chin in my hand. "Looks like a knuckle-made shiner to me."

"Well, you'll have to talk to the stairs, 'cause they're the ones that did it."

"Unh. How'd you cook supper?"

"Nancy Denny brought chicken over. It's warming in the oven." She looks away. "I need help...I haven't been upstairs all day."

"What?"

"The toilet. You got to carry me, Angus."

I look at her leg and then her face. "Didn't they give you any crutches?"

"Doctor Fleming didn't have crutches. The bone was right through the skin, meat and all. I can't breathe without it screaming pain like murder at me. Angus, you got to carry me right now!"

I shift back and forth, bend, and slip my arms beneath her. She embraces me around the neck. I lift, prop my knee on the couch. Stand.

"How long the doctor say you got to stay off it?"

"He didn't. I have to go in every day for him to clean it."

"That's a load of bullshit. How we gonna pay for that?"

"We'll use the money from my bank account. Or we'll sell a saw. Or we'll take the money Brad Chambers gave you to live in my house."

I pitch sideways and rap her foot to the banister. She buries her face in my shoulder, bites my collar. I twist and knock her foot against the wall. I feel the vibrations of her scream in my chest, and her damp sobs through the cloth.

"Mind your tongue, Miss Emeline."

In the bathroom, I hold her over the toilet while she lifts her dress and sits. Her eyes are red and tears shine her cheeks. Her piss splashes loud against the toilet bowl, and she lifts her face and her eyes draw tight on mine.

"Angus, you got to treat me better."

TWENTY

Deet pushed the barn's sliding door open. Facing the house, he bent at the waist and allowed his arms to hang. The scent of lumber mingled with crisp morning humidity. Beads of dew glittered on tufts of grass. Even the packed dirt below his feet smelled rich.

Blood rushed to his hand and his thumb throbbed. A dot of pink had already seeped through the gauze. Angus had left without helping Emeline, so Deet had carried her to the bathroom. He remembered feeling her skin under her nightgown and the satin brush of her hair against his cheek. Her sweat was perfume.

He stood. The sun had broken over the lake a few minutes before but the air remained cool. He rubbed his arms and flipped the light switch inside the barn.

Rebel stood at the corner of his plywood pen, paws over the top, tail drumming the wood. Deet crossed to him and scratched behind his ears.

"I'm building you a palace."

Rebel growled.

"Wasn't much of a fighter, huh?"

He turned to the shop. A five-inch drift of maple sawdust lay under the table saw, white like snow, and a similar pile sloped from the base of the jointer. A half-dozen other tools, as yet untouched and unknown, waited with gleaming blades. He dragged his fingers across the table saw, thumped the blade and listened to it ring. The sawdust looked good enough to have with milk and brown sugar.

He moved to the twelve-foot workbench and studied Widow McClellan's disassembled cabinet door. His test-run solution, which Angus had acknowledged, lay beside the broken tenon.

Deet puzzled over how the tenon could have broken. Falling from the cabinet would have dinged the corner. Dried glue would have made the joints loose. Seemed like the only way to break it was on purpose.

Nonetheless it provided an excuse to use the tools.

Working with quick precision, Deet removed the broken tenon, drilled holes, and chiseled a slot that was its exact inverse. He fashioned a floating tenon—a quarter inch wafer that would fill both the new mortise and the old, and rasped the edges to a hand-in-glove fit. He inspected the product, then walked outside to study his second project of the morning.

On Sunday after unloading the wood with Angus, Deet had parked Margulies trailer on the barn's north side. He now studied the flatbed. Rectangular holes sized for two-by-four inch posts lined the sides. He counted them and returned to the barn.

He climbed the ladder to the loft where they'd stowed Margulies lumber. Looking upward as he climbed, his gaze found the old boat stowed above. A bullet hole that dated to last December reminded Deet of his vow to leave Angus behind. And yet here he was, swooning over his father's wife. Destruction awaited, yet how could he leave Emeline to his mother's fate?

Or was he willing to stay because Emeline's skin smelled like paradise, and if he waited he knew he could have her?

Emeline fidgeted with a pair of pillows propped against the head-board. The clamor of saws that had penetrated the windows all morning had finally stopped a half hour ago. A wind-up clock tick-tocked on the dresser. Each percussion thumped her bladder. Hours had passed since Deet had said he'd check in.

Jacob was off Lord knew where. Playing at the walnut tree? He'd taken to disappearing for hours at a time, and gave smart-aleck answers when questioned.

Emeline squeezed. Her bladder felt like a balloon filled with a barrel of water. How would Angus respond if she diddled in bed? And how was it, again, that Doc Fleming didn't have a single crutch at his office? The clock ticked. She stared at the minute hand—and the pain in her leg pulsed with maddening inescapability. Emeline watched the door, willing it to open.

The putter of the tractor motor came from the window, and eventually reached a crescendo. Deet must have parked immediately below. The downstairs door clattered and footfalls approached on the steps. Tapping sounded.

"Help me to the bathroom!"

He lifted her and negotiated around the bedroom door. He had sawdust in his hair and smelled musky like a boy, not as acrid as Angus. He rested her on the toilet, eased her cast to the floor. Stood beside her.

"I can do the rest," she said.

He stepped to the hallway and latched the door. "Time to get you to Doctor Fleming's," he called.

"Angus said I'm not to go. I'll ask him again later."

"I don't give a rat's ass what he said. That leg gets infected, it's coming off."

She rocked side to side and hiked her gown. Searing pain flashed with each movement. Cold sweat stood on her brow and she grew faint. She sat until her legs tingled and her bladder was at peace, then pulled her panties up. Every heartbeat roused agony. A red flush swelled at her knee. Dizzy, she focused on breathing.

"Deet!"

He opened the door.

"Help...me...up."

"Shit Em, your leg's infected. See the red streak." He cradled her and stood; removed her from the small bathroom. "Easy does it; watch your toes. Have you had aspirin today?"

"I left a red and white bottle by the sofa downstairs. It's for pain." She pressed her forehead to his shoulder.

Deet carried her down the stairwell and lowered her beside the coffee table; she grabbed the Tylenol bottle and twisted the cap as he continued to the door. She drank from the bottle.

Her leg felt like she'd immersed it in fire, and she watched the cast almost touch the wall, the banister, the whole time imagining the flames that must be devouring her flesh under the plaster. The tractor engine chugged behind her. Deet swung her around to take her down the porch steps and she recognized the trailer— Papa had taken town children on haunted hayrides every year until he sold the distributorship—but what Deet had done to it made the pain disappear for a moment. She kissed his cheek.

He'd cut posts for the side slots, stretched rope between them, and lined the perimeter with hay bales. A pool of loose, golden hay filled the middle, and he'd stretched blankets on top of half. Tethered to a corner post, Rebel lay in the sun, tongue lolling.

"It's wonderful," she said.

With her balanced in his arms, Deet climbed a plank ramped from the ground to the end of the trailer, stepped over a bale, and rested Emeline on a blanket. Rebel snuggled close and licked her face.

"Think you'll be comfortable?"

"Deet, this is wonderful—but my leg's on fire. It hurts... Could you work a little more hay under my knee?"

He lifted the blankets and manipulated tufts below.

"What's wrong?" he said.

"How do we hide this from Angus? You can't go to this trouble every day."

"What's to hide? If he doesn't want his wife to be well, I suppose he can go to hell." Deet pushed hay below her leg until the cast was as high as her head. "That should help."

Rebel rested his head on the inside of her arm. She stroked his belly.

"All good?" Deet said.

She nodded.

He walked the linkage between trailer and tractor like a tightrope artist, scaled a rear tire, then climbed aboard the Farmall seat. He gave a backward nod and increased the throttle. "This thing takes off kinda sudden, but it'll run smooth after that." He put the tractor in gear and released the clutch. The trailer jumped.

Emeline closed her eyes and squeezed Rebel. He whined and she felt his grainy tongue on her cheek. Still with her eyes closed, she felt a cool breeze and had the sensation of rapid motion, but the wagon never bounced. Grass swooshed against the sides. She peeked. Deet had avoided the rutted drive by taking the edge of the field.

Emeline gulped more Tylenol, rested her head against a pillowy fold, and closed her eyes with morning sunshine on her face. *Lord, thank you for being so good to me.*

⚜

Looking over his shoulder as he neared the curb, Deet slipped the throttle lever back and chugged to a stop in front of Doctor Fleming's office. The doctor occupied half of the bottom floor of an ornate, gilded age mansion—or what passed for one in Walnut— which at one time belonged to Giuseppe Marconi, proprietor of Marconi Macaroni.

The outside was yellow brick with wood siding; the inside, dark-stained hardwood floors, knee-high hand-tooled baseboards and crown molding painted eggshell white.

Deet propped the front door open with a rounded river rock left on the porch, and carried Emeline through a moment later. The place smelled of coffee.

The door opened and Fleming waved them through the office to the visiting room.

"Here, yes, this is fine," Fleming said.

Deet placed Emeline on the leather-upholstered table. Fleming lifted her dress to her knee, and turned to Deet.

"You'll have to wait in the antechamber, son."

"Where?"

"The entrance—you'll find chairs and reading materials."

"Em?"

She nodded. Deet took a chair and studied the molding, wondered what kind of tool could make a pattern so exquisite. He picked up a copy of *Time*. "Rex Harrison in My Fair Lady," he

read. The elegant woman perched over Harrison's shoulder resembled Emeline. Deet brought the photo closer. Emeline was
better, more meat on the bone. He tossed the magazine aside and
shuffled through a stack of older copies, grabbed another at random, this one with a picture of an admiral with a statue beside
him. He flipped through the pages.

"The Big Corn Crop," he read. He'd better take a look.

Somehow, the story was about Lawrence Welk. Deet pitched
it, grabbed a newspaper from an adjacent seat and turned to the
commodities numbers. The federal support level for corn had
been cut eleven per cent in February, and the nation's corn crop
was likely to be a bumper. The Hardgrave acres would produce
top numbers. If the big growers out west had the same good for-
tune, the surplus would drive down the price per bushel.

He read the paragraphs again and the muscles in his back and
shoulders rebelled. Jarring hours on a steel-wheeled tractor, in-
nards bouncing, sun baking his skin. A whole life of it waited.
Tilling, planting, harvesting, stacking the corn poles. All betting
on the uncertain premise a market would be ready to buy whatever surfeit his ambition produced—and his father would pay him
dimes.

He'd planned on being south by now.

Maybe the woodshop would provide a way out. The shop had
every tool he could imagine. His skill would improve in time.
With luck he'd earn a few jobs. Woodworkers had to make good
money. Hardgrave land extended a full mile into the forest, with
enough maple, beech, oak, cherry, chestnut, and ash to never run
out. No seed costs, no vagaries of the growing season. He just had
to learn the craft.

Let Angus scramble his guts in the fields.

Outside, footsteps shuffled by the door. A fist rapped; the door
flew open.

"That your white Farmall out front, boy?"

Deet looked up from the newspaper. Stood. The man had him by a foot and a hundred pounds of belly.

"That ain't your tractor," the man said. "Who's your old man? That tractor ain't allowed to be white."

"Who thinks he's in charge of what color my tractor is?"

"Farmall, boy. I own the dealership. You can't have a white Farmall, and that's all there is to it. International Harvester has it in the by-laws. In the corporate constitution. The only white Farmall is on the dealership floor. End of story. Now who owns that tractor?" His head jerked around and his back stiffened. "Wait a damn minute. Just wait a damn minute." He went back outside.

Deet followed.

The man stalked to the tractor. Rebel stood at the corner, head low looking through a bare slit of eye.

"Shut up," the man said to Rebel. He waved his arm. "This is my tractor—I own the damn thing. This is the '47 A-Model been missing from the books since I bought the place."

"Lay a hand on it and I'll do something about it."

"Don't need to. I've studied that serial number on my books every month for nine years."

"Where's the number? On the tractor?"

The man sniggered. "Go to the back, at the seat support. Left side."

Deet found the small metal plate. "What's it read? You tell me."

"One eight three, eight one four."

"One eight three, eight one four. So you memorized it before coming in to find me."

"Yeah, right after I fudged nine years of ledgers back at the dealership. That's my property, son. I've been writing that number every year. You know anything about ledgers? Inventory? Ah, Shit. Who's your father? I need to know, or I'm going to find Sheriff Heilbrun."

The man grasped his arm and Deet twisted away, shoved him against the tire. Rebel strained at the edge of the hay bale beside them.

"You don't want to make that mistake again," Deet said, hand resting on the butt of his deer knife. They were still. "His name's Angus Hardgrave."

"Don't know him. Where's the farm?"

"Figure it out your damned self."

"Tell your old man I'll be along."

Emeline waited on the leather table. The pain while Fleming cut away the cast, debrided her wound with peroxide, wiped balm, bandaged and recast her leg—all without nudging the broken bones' delicate ossification—had been nearly unbearable. She watched the shiny spot on his head, the white hair. He grunted and mumbled terribly vanilla stories. The new cast, this one also very thin, was hardening.

"Why not use a splint, if it has to come off each day?"

"Two things. A splint would not immobilize your leg to the degree the cast will. Also, there would be more pressure points on your leg, and more pain. Now, blood flow is terribly important—even more so with infection. The rapid swelling, the redness, inflammation, racing heart, wooziness—these are all indications. The bone will mend, but the infection is very bad."

He removed a brown bottle and a needle from a wall cabinet, filled a syringe, held it to the light, depressed the plunger until fluid leaked from the point. "Have you learned of penicillin?"

"A Frenchman discovered it. Pasteur."

"No, a Scot—Sir Alexander Fleming. My namesake." He pressed old, flat fingers to her shoulder. "You should eat more." He leaned her toward the wall and supported her with his left arm, and pulled her dress high with his syringe hand. "You're going to feel a tickle."

Fleming pressed the needle into her rump. He chuckled. "If you can't see me for any reason, rub bread mold on the wound. The antibiotic comes from mold. I'm teasing, of course. But it is simply amazing. Amazing."

Doctor Fleming placed the syringe on a stainless tray. "Questions, Emeline?"

She shook her head.

"The pain will lessen. The redness will disappear over a couple of days, and the Tylenol I gave you will do the trick. You might have a hot toddy to help you sleep. I want you to come here tomorrow."

She nodded.

He stood, opened the door. "Deet?"

Deet arrived a moment later.

"You may carry out your step-mother."

Emeline's face had more color than when Deet had carried her in. After seeing to her comfort in the trailer, he steered toward home and watched the hills and fields roll by. The man who'd laid claim to the Farmall might be trouble—but in the worst case,

Angus had another tractor, though its steel rims made riding it a bucolic torture. In little more than a half hour, Deet steered into the field along the driveway. He parked at the farmhouse steps.

"Can you put me in a chair on the porch?" she said. "The weather is lovely."

Deet noticed the scent of evergreen. He situated her on a low Adirondack-style chair with a wide, sloped back, facing the blue spruce off the corner of the porch, and overlooking the lake. "You must feel better."

"Why?"

"You look better."

"The break was infected." She squeezed his hand. "You kept me from being a peg leg."

"That bad?"

She nodded, looked at his hand, released it.

He studied the lake. "You need anything, now?"

"Water, maybe? Sun's dried me out."

He brought a pitcher and a glass, then filled it. "I've got work in the barn. Holler if you need anything."

She pressed her lips to a thin line.

"What?"

"As if you'd hear."

"I'll check on you. Promise."

Deet carried her smile in his mind until he reached the barn. Inside, he pressed close to a knothole in the wall. She sat on the porch, her dress hitched on the chair seat, her plaster cast white against her knee. Her other leg was exposed as well—such a gentle curve. He wavered from the board; she blurred. He glanced sideways. Listened. The barn was empty. He gaped again.

What had she said, earlier, when he'd cut his hand and accidentally rested the other on her rump?

That's not a good idea, Deet.

Not a bad one, though.

He breathed deep to clear his mind.

She stared at the barn, at this very spot, as if she knew he watched her, and that action revealed her. His thoughts resolved and he could finally categorize her. She was an angel—not just a heavenly beautiful woman, as he'd believed earlier. Her strength called upon a hidden force.

He crossed to the workbench. The Widow McClellan's panel door lay in clamps. A half-dried, leathery bulb of glue pressed from the new joint. Deet removed the pipe clamps and sliced the glue with a chisel blade. He studied the door from every angle and found not a single blemish in his work. This was real, not like tilling land, planting seed, and hoping for rain. This was progress and satisfaction all at once, taking something straight from a picture in his mind to something that would have honest utility in another person's life. Corn was real but it took all summer. There was nothing creative about corn.

On the floor to the right lay the boards he'd sized and cut for the kennel, arranged for assembly. He carried a bucket with number eight wood screws to the stacked kennel parts.

Deet looked to the loft where the tip of rowboat prow hung over, then to Emeline sitting on the porch. He pictured the pain that flickered behind her eyes and imagined a separate Emeline within her—an entirely distinct girl crated inside an abominable marriage like some ogre's plaything. A girl who looked to him because she recognized her plight and that he was the only man who could save her.

How could it be right to leave her with Angus?

At the workbench, he twisted the crank on a red Millers Falls eggbeater-style drill. Meticulously oiled gears spun. The chuck whirled. He placed it on the bench and lifted instead a Black &

Decker quarter inch hand drill. Slipped in a bit and hand-tightened the chuck.

He held the drill at his hip like a holstered pistol, then whipped it level. "It's time to account for the things you done," he said, aiming at the wall.

Deet depressed the trigger and the drill screeched.

He lowered it and dragged the extension cord behind him to the boards. As he studied them his mind replayed the silliness of pointing the drill, pretending to be a man.

He cleared his throat. Pressed together his lips.

He would stay, and when the need arose, he would defend Emeline.

TWENTY ONE

The shop light is on and as I step from the truck I hear the whine of a hand drill. I circle to the basement side entrance, lean against a hog sty and gulp from the bottle of Turkey I've nursed since Franklin. Almost out. The whiskey hits my stomach like a tube of dimes and lays inert. I need a chew, or a smoke, or something to take the edge off. It ebbs and flows and now it's back. I get my mind on something thin and soft and I got to get a hold of it.

I want to feel a woman bite my chest and scream.

It's *that* I want. Wild Turkey usually does the job, but my need is more severe since I planed the board with Jonah McClellan's spine.

In the pen, a brick-red Jersey sow I never named watches me. She'll farrow in a week; of the ten or so piglets, I figure to keep five to replace the ones I smoked last fall. I'll sell the rest.

Isn't right, having to follow up on Deet. Jake, I understand. It took daily thrashings for me as a boy to learn farm rules. We do most everything by hand, and it's a labor-intensive proposition, even with the new tractor. But Deet thinks he's better than farm work, and sometimes don't give a task his full energy.

The sow grunts. I grunt back, spit fresh-cut phlegm to her side.

My boar and three sows require a trough of water and ten pound of corncob and soybean a day. Near the side entrance an iron bathtub sits below a chute that transports shucked corn from the floor above. A table beside the tub supports a device that looks like a sausage-grinder, for ripping kernels from the cob. I assigned operation of the machine to Jacob. Deet's supposed to come in after and scoop buckets of grain for the livestock each morning and night.

The tub is almost empty. The trough is low.

The sow grunts.

"That's a powerful question," I tell her.

Sometimes doing right is helping people get what they got coming.

I exit the barn. Moonlight breaks from behind a cloud and I see Margulies' flatbed trailer. I run my fingers along the bales, feel the edge of the posts, their width. I sniff them. Deet sawed the only two-inch walnut plank into posts, but only a foot high. What in hell possessed him? I tramp upslope to the second story bay and barrel in.

Deet has framed the kennels, two separate runs of six crates each. He looks up from attaching a floorboard. I stop short. "Ho there! What the hell you doing?"

Deet finishes drilling a screw. Stands chest out, brow wrinkled. Hand floats beside his knife. His grin is confused. Proud. Maybe.

"Hogs ain't fed? The cows? But you got time to cut up a high-dollar board for a fuckin hayride? Wonder why the hogs are skin and bones and the stalls are cruddy with shit."

I swing.

Blood runs from Deet's lip and he stands a foot back, but jaw jutted a little farther now.

"Check your eyes, boy! And make a move for that blade, you'll be pulling it out your heart."

"I built your kennel and fixed your cabinet door." Deet brushes past me. "Guess I'll feed your fuckin hogs."

"Where's Jake? Part of your chores is seein' him do his."

Deet disappears down the stairs.

"I won't tell you again!"

I squat beside the kennel frame. Deet's turned my pencil drawing into architecture. The doors open tailgate-high for ease loading dogs on the truck. All that remains is to install the floors, walls, roof, and put in the wire outhouse section of the floor. The dogs will venture onto the mesh to do their business and their shitpiles will fall to the ground, and Jake can use buckets to get them to the field.

Deet's stacked the remaining components close to their home on the frame. Even with his chores, he'll finish within a day or two. I rest a hand square against the closest corner of joist and leg. Switch to the opposite corner, twelve feet away. Perfect.

Deet's mechanical aptitude comes from his Kraut blood.

I turn to find Rebel regarding me from his makeshift plywood crate.

"What?"

Damn dog wags his tail. What's the point of a fighting dog that meets his master with a lolling tongue? I stand at the crate and the one-eyed bastard searches me. I punch his blind side, connect with his skull. Rebel slams to the floor and trembles.

I got an edge Wild Turkey won't touch. I can feel a bout of darkness coming in.

The finished panel door lies on the workbench, with a flat shine that suggests a half-buffed coat of paste wax. Though the mortise and tenon joint is hid, the surfaces are flush and square without any glue leakage. I press corner to corner, then shake it. The panel don't rattle or play.

With a triple-braid of bailer twine and a Phillips screwdriver in my pocket, the cabinet door tucked under my arm, I follow the edge of the field, turn the corner by the wood, and walk under the heavy shadow of overhanging limbs. Can't see for shit. Stumble and catch myself. In the woods I hold my hand afore my face; the glow of the hemlock splintered moon gives me bearing on the path I walked as a boy.

I beat the Widow McClellan's door.

"Come in before the moths do. Thought you said two week."

I rest the cabinet door on the counter. "Speed like that'll cost you."

The red dog lifts her head from the floor and growls.

"I'm an old woman. Won't cost much, or you can keep it."

I hold the fixed door to the vacant spot. "Looks better than the rest."

She sits at the table. "There's coffee still warm."

I find four screws in my pocket, twist them into the existing holes, then open and close the door with an easy motion. I eyeball the bottom alignment against the other doors. "Perfect," I say.

"A good man does good works."

I open the next cabinet door, tighten each hinge screw, and open the next.

"My, but you're thorough."

I finish the upper cabinets and start the lower level. "These musta been built fifty years ago, from the joinery."

"Woulda been in '15, after Mitch and me tied the knot. He had the kitchen remade right after the wedding, since we wasn't getting a new house. It's been his since Jonah—"

"Disappeared altogether." I close the last cabinet. "All tight. Now, job like this—six hours of shop time—that's worth six dollars."

"Six hours! Six dollars!" She grabs her breast with one hand and balls the other into a fist. "Pull the door down and keep it!" She struggles to her feet.

"I didn't do all this work not to be paid."

"I got to eat!"

"Everybody got to eat. You got anything worth six dollars?"

"It ain't what I got, it's what I'll give, and I wouldn't give more than—" she looks around.

I study the dog roused from the floor by commotion.

"That mutt," she says.

"That's how you do a Christian neighbor?" I say. "I'll take the mutt, and we'll be through."

I yank the coil of bailing twine from my trousers. The dog's growl sounds like it comes from deep in her guts. I reach for her collar and she nips my hand. I drive a fist to her skull. She drops and I loop the hemp through her collar and jerk her upright. Bony ass head.

I stop and look at the widow as she releases a long sigh. She shakes her face and hobbles to a dark pine hutch, stoops, and withdraws a gallon jug. "I guess you done me right with the door," she says. "Craftsmanship—the kind that shows a man's character—is worth more'n a flea-bit dog."

My eye follows the black splash in the jug. "Make your own stain, did you?"

"That, Angus Hardgrave, is mother's milk to a whiskey man, and you're no stranger to the spirit."

"Worship regular."

She fetches a lead crystal glass, uncaps the black whiskey. "Mitch, bless his soul, 'stilled this himself, back in the day. He loved his walnut whiskey." She pours from the jug.

"They found a bottle by him, wasn't that right?"

"An empty bottle." She hesitates as the whiskey reaches the half-way mark, then smiles and fills it close to the rim. "Course those damned revenuers axed his still." She offers the glass. "I know you'll love it as much as he did. Smell it, first."

I take the crystal from her gnarled hand and meet her eyes as I bring the rim to my lips. The smell overtakes me. Rich, like walnuts, dissolved into flammable vapors. I think of the board with Jonah's bones. Iridescent surface oils reflect my eye. I flash to the photo of Mitch that topped a red oak casket. The fluid touches my lips, pours into my mouth, numbs my tongue. The flavor overwhelms my senses, paralyzes my giddy throat.

I choke, "Walnut shine?"

She smacks her thigh. "Them walnuts come from the tree on Devil's Elbow! Have another!"

The thirst that's haunted me since I ran my fingers over the shimmering spine-board vanishes. Walnut whiskey is a square peg going in a square hole. The corners get their fill.

"Bottom's up," the widow says.

I drink in gulps, note the fire in my throat and stomach, and the heat spreading across my face. I'd take hell if it felt like this.

I gulp. The dog whines. The widow beams. I watch her. Has she forgotten that forty-seven years ago, her husband wandered across a cornfield and sired a bastard?

"Take the whole glass!" she says. "Don't have a belly for it, myself. And I won't feel right without you take the jug. You don't know how much I appreciate you."

TWENTY TWO

The widow closes the door behind me. The yellow bulb blinks off and the porch posts, the trees, the lily-pad path of stones across the lawn—vanish. I feel for the step and tramp across grass. The bitch pit bull tugs toward the forest; I got the jug of walnut whiskey in my left hand and the twine in my right. I raise my leash hand to shelter my eye, though the lowest boughs are twenty feet above. I got a newfound clarity but I suspect my judgment will suffer.

As a boy I climbed one of these ancient hemlocks. I was ten, and I'd clenched my bare ass three hours, hanging over a limb, stung raw by skeeters, waiting for Larry McClellan to cross below. I dropped pinecones as practice to get my ass situated right. Larry came along and I timed it perfect. I shat on him from thirty feet and never confessed until we rode a plywood Higgins boat to Omaha Beach. Larry said "No," and shook his head. It was a treed black bear, though he couldn't explain the corn in the shit. Machine gun bullets cut him to pieces a minute later—Larry shat on from above, one last time.

I jerk the leash, unscrew the jug, gulp, cough.

"Here's to you, Lawrence fuckin McClellan."

My voice startles an animal at the juncture of forest and field—a whitetail deer, from the flash of the tail in the moonlight. The bitch heaves and I fall forward holding the uncapped jug high in salute. The bottle splashes but remains upright. My knee hits a root; I slide forward and catch a mouthful of pine needles. Bitch tugs and wheezes against her collar until I regain my feet and yank the line and flip her.

She whines. I blink. My feet don't feel like the ones I came on. The pit bull surges and I wrench the twine. "Hiya!"

I turn the corner at the field. With grass to my right and corn on my left, the sky opens above and the moon lights my path. A few minutes later I arrive at the barn. Deet works inside and meets my eye.

"Where'd you get that one?" he says.

"The widow insisted." I land the jug on the workbench and lead the dog to Rebel's corner. "How long 'til that kennel's done?"

"Tomorrow, if I can get the chicken wire."

I take the bitch by the muzzle and squint into her eyes. "Snap at me and I bust your head."

The dog blinks. I reach under her ribs and haunches and toss her into the pen.

"She's squat enough," Deet says. "Red nose, like Rebel."

"Maybe seventy pound. Monster of a pit. Any luck, they'll get together. Fill these pens." I lean against the wall. Rub my eye.

Deet shakes his head. "What's in the bottle? You look peaked."

"Walnut shine."

"Took Emeline to see Doctor Fleming today." He pauses. "She said you told her not to go."

I hoist the jug, swallow. "Women lie."

"She'd have lost her leg without I took her in today, and I'm taking her again tomorrow." He fidgets with a claw hammer at the bench, lays it on its side, but the handle remains in his hand. "Another thing. I was in Doc Fleming's waiting room and a fellow busted in and claimed the Farmall's his—said the serial number from his head."

I laugh. "I'll kill him."

"You might get some sleep first. You look like shit. I'll need money for the coop wire."

I find my wallet and hand Deet seven singles.

I finger the jug loop and leave the barn. Pull a corduroy jacket from the truck seat, drape it over by shoulders, and head down slope. The water washes against beach stones. I remember Larry McClellan. Sorry son of a bitch. I drink. Shat on from above. Ain't we all.

A frog splashes a gurgled response. I can't make it all the way out but I believe he was saying life ain't fair.

The walnut tree on Devil's Elbow blots the sky. I veer to the trunk and throw my arm into the crotch, make a fist. I hang, head lolling, bottle stretching my thumb joint until my hand is numb and I recline. The roots prop my elbows like armchair rests. My head against the bark, I tip the jug and swallow, cap it, and stow it between my legs. The water laps. The tree groans. I belch.

I close my eyes and feel a cold, giant hand rest on my shoulder. I sleep, and see things.

Jacob watched a shadow on the ceiling. His open bedroom window faced the forest; the lake was to the left, out of sight except for a thin line of water visible beyond the trees at Devil's Elbow.

The breeze smelled of fish. The house was silent. Jacob usually waited for Angus to begin snoring before venturing out, but tonight the absence of snoring was palpable. The old man hadn't gone to bed. That meant he was outside, somewhere. Maybe in town, maybe by the lake. Maybe slipping his peeper to a hog in the barn. He could be anywhere.

Jacob's mattress springs creaked with every roll, every deep breath. He'd experimented to find a quiet exit procedure. Without massing his weight at the center and unduly stretching the springs, he rolled over the edge, caught himself on the floor with one arm and leg, and eased from the mattress. He pulled on clothes that were scattered on the floor and pressed his ear to the window screen.

A sound came from the lake—faint—a hundred yards away, carried over the dense night air. It was Angus. Jacob smiled. He popped the screen free of the bottom slot and wiggled the frame; leaning through, he lowered it to the roof and climbed out. Slid his toe along the wall, found shingles and dropped catlike to the roof of the side addition.

He jumped to the ground and circled to the lake side of the house. There he waited until Angus sawed an exhalation, then he followed a foot trail down slope through the grass.

Jacob paused. The sound came from the walnut tree. He looked back to the house, then across the foggy lake. The snores were loud, now, only a dozen yards away; he heard the imprint of his father's large nose on the snore; the individual chokes and snuffles mired in each grinding gasp.

Jacob stretched to all fours and willed his knees and elbows forward. His father slept at the walnut tree, but the shadow held no human outline. Jacob stared at the crotch where an old limb jutted out like the family black sheep, where Jacob sometimes laid and watched the lake. Where Angus left him hanging one morning three years ago, overall straps looped over a railroad spike driven into the tree, as punishment for wetting his bed.

His old man was nowhere; everywhere. The snoring distended like the black mass of limbs above. Angus choked on his noise and grunted. Jacob froze. Angus kicked like a sleeping dog, betraying his shadowy form embraced in the trunk folds. The snores resumed; Jacob crept closer.

The odors of whiskey and a pile of rotting fish guts Jacob had left nearby a few days earlier mingled in a comfortable pungency. He propped his head on his hand and remembered his mother, Lucy Mae. Her voice was like maple syrup. She ran off last winter. Angus dumped her clothes in the burn barrel the next day. Jacob pleaded to save them because she might come back.

"She won't be back," Angus said.

"It's cold—she has to!"

"She ain't coming back. Now git!"

Angus pushed him aside and went to the house for another armload. Jacob stole Lucy Mae's coat and slipped around the house. He slept with it, buried his nose in the fuzzy collar and smelled her.

Jacob opened his eyes and studied his sleeping father.

TWENTY THREE

Deet rose long before dawn, tended the animals, fixed Emeline and Jacob an oatmeal breakfast, assigned the dishes to Jacob, helped Emeline to the toilet.

"Deet—" Emeline said through the door, "did Angus come home last night?"

"Just after dark. Took the door I fixed over to McClellan's. Came back with a dog and a bottle."

"He never woke me."

"Considerate."

When she finished, he carried her downstairs and left her on the sofa with her Bible and a cup of tea. "Just holler if you need me," he said.

Deet found Jacob petting Rebel in the barn.

"You cost me grief last night—didn't shuck your corn. I'm shouldering extra with this woodshop, so today you're gonna do enough corn to fill the tub, and then you're gonna clean the hog stalls."

Jacob patted Rebel's head. "Reb's getting skinny. You been feeding him since Emmy busted her leg?"

"Ain't you?" Deet crossed to the dog's corner.

"No."

"Pap ain't. Son of a bitch. Well, go in the house and find something—and bring some water." Deet scratched his head. "Was there another dog here when you came in?"

"No."

In his mind's eye, Deet followed the bitch's probable escape route, downstairs and out the back. They never closed the barn's lower exit to the pasture. She maybe spent the night on McClellan's porch. If the widow hadn't been outside yet, the dog might still be there. But then, what sort of deal had Angus struck? Maybe Pap had *borrowed* the dog overnight. It was Angus's own fool ass that hadn't secured her.

"Get some food and water from the house."

Deet screwed floorboards to the kennel frames until ten, then checked to ensure Jacob still ground cobs into kernels in the tub. The boy looked sullenly at him.

"This right here is why you want to do good in school. You'll wind up like your Pap and me. Don't know nothing but how to grow callus." Deet grabbed an ear of corn and tore the dried husk. "How come you been having such a time with your chores? Where you been?"

"Nowhere."

"I bet you been walking two miles around the lake every day to see Tony Antonuccio. You soft on his sister, what's her name?"

"No. Her name's Regina."

"Rej-eye-na. Don't worry if you don't get her. All girls got a regina. So far as I know."

Jacob frowned.

Deet slapped his back. "Your secret's safe. Just do your chores so I don't get my ass peeled." Deet tossed the shucked cob into the bin and went outside to the Farmall.

Emeline brooded on the hayride to Doctor Fleming's. There was a grave a hundred yards from where she slept every night and three Mrs. Hardgraves' dusty suitcases in the basement.

No, four.

A baby in her belly, and a husband staying out all night long.

The tractor chugged down the road and wind tangled her hair. She watched a long stem of hay trembling in the wind. No marriage proved as sweet as the engagement. Papa had always said wanting something was better than having it. If she listed the blessings in her life, she'd run out of ink. But still—what new husband stayed out all night?

Deet parked. As he lifted her from the trailer, she said, "Would you buy me a journal at the drugstore? I've run out of space."

"A diary?"

She nodded and curled her arm around Deet's neck. She rested her temple on his shoulder. He lifted her from the blankets, held her firm to his chest and she breathed the sweetness of a young man whose body was primed for work and seemed hungry for it. Not like her husband, whose sour smell called to mind hardship, and whose scarred hands were almost preternaturally cold. She and Deet worked well together; he positioned her at the door, she twisted the knob and nudged it; he pushed through with his back. Doctor Fleming emerged into the waiting room a moment later, and waved them through to the visiting room.

Deet left her on the padded table. "I got a few errands, but I won't keep you waiting."

She smiled at Deet and the doctor turned from her to watch Deet exit. "Everywhere you go, Emeline, the boys are enamored with you. Did your daddy warn you?" Fleming furled her dress to her thigh and studied her flesh at foot and knee.

"Warn me?"

"Men. Young men. Mature men."

"I'm beyond warning now."

"That confirms my suspicion. You are entirely naïve—and because I delivered you and have watched you grow from a little pumpkin to a beautiful young woman, I will tell you what you need to hear."

"What?"

"Science has confirmed an elegant truth—and by that I mean *simple*—that men exist with only one purpose. Procreation. From the moment a boy becomes self-aware, one passion consumes him. Man's greatest achievements—architecture, art, athletics, business, war—all have been inducements for some girl to lie down with him."

"War? What?"

"When these constructive, or deconstructive achievements fail to bring a woman of free accord, that is, when a man believes himself insignificant, he turns to force."

"Doctor Fleming—"

"You—how do I say it? I am an old man. I have been joyously free of the prison of which I speak for years. I no longer desire to procreate."

She turned away, smiling.

"I am an old man, Emeline, listen to me."

"But, Doctor Fleming, what's that got to do with me?"

"You've heard of Helen of Troy—a woman so beautiful her face launched a thousand ships? You've heard of the mythological sirens, whose voices drove men insane? You are such a woman, Emeline, in a nest of men already mad to possess you. Their minds are devious little engines solely employed toward capturing you. Your husband? Four wives. Your chauffer? A breeder in his prime. Your tenant? A man returned from a horrible war, with scars. Each man wrestling his insignificance. Forgive my candor. A man lays claim with his achievements or his strength, and your suitors have little of the former."

"Why are you telling me this?"

Doctor Fleming cut away the thin cast, beginning at her foot. He was silent until he snipped the final segment, spread it like the chest cavity of a slaughtered beast. "You must exercise caution around your men, Emeline."

Yesterday the pain had been so severe she'd turned away. Today she looked. Her shin was a red and pink swirl of serrated flesh.

Fleming cleaned the wound, applied an ointment. "The infection has subsided." He covered it with gauze. "I'm going to do something new." He cleaned the inside of the cast with alcohol, slipped it around her leg, and wrapped an ace bandage around the plaster. "We'll try this for three days. You mustn't put your weight on it. Come see me if the pain approaches what you felt yesterday, or if you see red lines above your knee."

"You believe these men will hurt me?"

"Possessing you is more important than loving you. I am sorry. Biology makes us beasts until we are so old we have no use for our... biology."

"That can't be true of all men."

"All men? We're only discussing three, and for those I am certainly correct. Be careful."

Deet traced his finger over a coil of half-inch copper tubing. He'd bought a diary at the drugstore, dog feed and heavy gauge chicken wire at Agway, and a roll of tar paper at the builders. Now he visualized a still: copper from boiler to doubler; twenty feet of coil inside a cooling tank, with a shut off valve at the end. A lot of copper.

He left the hardware store rubbing his hands, thinking of cutting wood and smelling sawdust. Madison Street, Route 64, was a quarter mile of old-style storefronts, the same as any other Pennsylvania town. Its history extended well over a hundred years. A barber worked each end of town. The Walnut Macaroni plant, housed in a three-story brick building set a block back, employed more townsfolk than any other business. Adjacent stood St. Luke, the largest Catholic church in town, and opposite, the Presbyterian church where Angus married Emeline.

Doctor Fleming's office was on Madison, on the way home after the hardware. Deet stopped the tractor. Emeline waited in the visiting room. He carried her to the trailer.

"Doc give you bad news?"

"I'm fine. It's lunch time."

"Got an appetite myself."

Deet cut the steering wheel, checked traffic. Released the clutch and glanced over his shoulder at the rear tire spinning close to the trailer corner as he chugged through a semicircle turn.

"Where are we going?" Emeline called.

Deet grinned at folks on the sidewalk and stopped at the only red light in town. Ahead on the left was Pitlake's General Farm Supply Company—the Farmall dealership. He'd seen the place for years but had never been inside. The Hardgraves didn't buy new farm equipment. Their first tractor, when Deet was three, was a jalopy stripped of everything but its frame, axles, and engine. They made do. They invented.

The smell of singed beef and onions pulled Deet's eyes to Tony Ianolio's Burger Shack, ahead on the right. The traffic light became green. A hundred yards ahead, he circled through the Burger Shack lot and parked next to the road, broadside to the Farmall dealership. He killed the engine and spun on his seat.

"Ever been here?" he said.

She shook her head; her hair bounced and her lips pulled back, dimpling her cheeks. "Well, maybe once or twice."

"Neither've I. Smells good, don't it?"

Deet climbed down. "Wait here." He crossed the lot and stood at the window, looking at the menu board inside. A town kid waited on him. He decided Emeline would like a cheeseburger with fries and Coke.

"Dollar fifty."

Deet gave up the two-dollar bill he'd saved for his escape. Emeline beamed as he neared.

He climbed onto the trailer from the side and crawled close to Emeline. Reclining against a bale, he propped two paper cups in the blanket folds between them. She accepted a burger with bulging eyes and flared nostrils, unfolded the waxed paper, and bit into it.

Deet watched her. She chewed, made a sated face. Moaned. "This is so good. Aren't you going to try yours?"

"Me? No, I bought two for you."

She punched his arm. "Don't be ridiculous."

He unwrapped the other; nodded across the street. "That dealership used to be your Pappy's?"

"That's right. Um-hmm." She filled her mouth with burger.

"And you only come here once or twice?"

"Papa was frugal. That's how he stayed in business." She smiled.

"You know Pitlake—the fella that bought it? He came up yesterday while you was in the doctor's office and said he owned this tractor. Said he carried the serial number on his books since the beginning. Why would he say that?"

"I don't know him. Pitlake?"

"He said he was Pitlake. Wait a minute. That's him there, talking to the bald fella on the right side of the lot. That's him."

"Papa brought the tractor home when I was too young to notice."

"Pitlake said he's carried it on his books for years."

"He's looking this way."

"You know why your Pap parked it in the back of the barn, like he was hiding it?"

"Hiding? We didn't have guests to our barn."

"Angus is gonna have to deal with this fella, and what you remember is all he'll have to go by."

"This tractor's been ours since before Papa sold the dealership. I can write a thousand dollars in my checkbook ledger, and copy the numbers every day for a year! What do you think the bank is going to say when I go there and demand a bunch of made up money?"

"Didn't mean to get you riled."

"Well you did. I'm fed up with vultures. Soon as Papa died, they swooped in for his money because they'd rather cheat and steal than work an honest wage."

"Easy, Em." He noticed a glaze of sweat on her brow.

She pointed. "You take me over there right now!"

"I haven't had a bite of my burger."

"Finish it this second and take me over there."

Both Pitlake and the bald man watched. Pitlake turned and the other followed him inside the dealership.

"This is Angus's fight, now."

"I'm not asking if you're man enough. I'll tell him myself."

He glared, unbuttoned his top shirt button. "It ain't about being man enough. I'll go whup on him right now if I've a mind to."

Her gaze fell. "I get angry." She twisted her side to the Farmall dealership. Opened her mouth. Closed it. "Your sandwich good? You try the potatoes?"

"I guess they're pretty good."

"You haven't had one."

"No." He climbed from the trailer and mounted the tractor. Started it. Pitlake watched from the dealership door, behind a row of red tractors. Deet chugged onto the street.

Emeline sat on the porch. The familiar blue jay yammered a string of avian profanity. The turmoil with the tractor and the pain from her leg weighed on her. She had a belly full of cheeseburger and cola, and they weren't making friends.

Doctor Fleming's words troubled her.

Clouds rolled over the lazy lake; the air that followed was thick with humidity. She yawned. Deet backed the trailer to the barn entrance and unloaded rolls of tarpaper and chicken wire, then removed the slats and piled the hay bales lower on the slope. Finally he backed the trailer into the barn bay, leaving the front end visible from where she rested. Minutes passed with Deet out of view, and then a dark object crept across the trailer. It was a kennel.

"How did you lift that?" She glanced sideways for Jacob but she was alone. Deet worked inside the barn, a shape in the shadows, bucking angrily against the weight of the kennel. He emerged into sunlight and raised his arm to his brow. Emeline touched her sternum. He went back inside and she stared at the lake.

From the back of her mind a thought thrust forward and she saw the black walnut on Devil's Elbow. She closed her eyes and sunlight patterns flickered on her eyelids. The walnut called to her with an image of herself lounging in the cool shade. She smelled the lake air, the forest. An image resolved as sun amoebas floated on her closed eyelids. A shadow of the walnut tree became a cloaked man with broad shoulders and a face made of sawdust and hard angles. His eyes were dark caverns and he did nothing but stand and study her—as if he could know her mind.

If she opened her eyes she would see him.

The sticky lake breeze brought the sound of rickety springs and tires on stones. The apparition vanished. Emeline opened her eyes. On the driveway, a blue car led a plume of dust. The windshield reflection hid the inhabitant.

Deet watched at the barn door. Emeline looked back toward the car. Pitlake? She shifted her legs and pain shot from her shin to her side, as if a bolt of electricity had burned everything between. The car stopped. Deet turned back to the trailer but watched over his shoulder. A woman exited the passenger side.

"Oh, Lordy child, it's good to see you!" the woman called, still unrecognizable, leaning into the blue car's back seat.

"Thank you for coming," Emeline said. "So good to see you."

A man waved through the driver's side window and cigarette smoke rose from his hand. The woman carried a tray. Emeline had met her at church but couldn't recall her name. Before the woman's foot struck the porch Emeline said, "I'm so glad you stopped by!"

The woman carried a tray with several dishes. Her countenance was like a marble piece the sculptor had decided at the last moment to make smile, after the rest of her face was chiseled to a frown.

"Inside?"

"Kitchen's on the right."

The woman thumbed the screen open and carried the tray inside. "You want this to warm in the oven, Sweetie?"

"Thank you but just leave it on the table. Angus doesn't come home until after dark." Emeline smelled beef roast.

The woman emerged and dragged a chair next to Emeline. "So," she said.

"Thank you. I can't tell you—"

"Nonsense. Least I could do."

The woman knit her hands together. "That leg looks painful." She leaned forward. "Lord, I know what it's like to fall down the stairs."

"You what?"

The woman glanced to the blue car.

"I slipped when I saw a strange man in my house in town," Emeline said. "I didn't know Angus—my husband's not a church-goer, and you may not know him—"

"Oh, I know him."

"—had let out the house."

They were quiet. Emeline queried her eyes.

"Well, I'll be running. Charles is in the car..."

Charles...Kirk. Charles and Hannah Kirk.

"Hannah—stay a little longer, won't you?"

Hannah simpered. "Of course, dear. This is such a lovely perch. The lake, the clean smell from the trees. You never can smell enough corn field, either. That's what I always say."

"You said you know Angus?"

"Went to school with him. Used to tingle to look at him."

"Is that so?"

"All the girls did. He's different now. But it's not my place to tell you that."

"Different how?"

"He was a regular Tom Sawyer showoff before the war."

"He doesn't talk about it."

"He saw dreadful things, no doubt, but I suspect it was something else. He married right before the war, a blonde named Adolfina, of all things. He should have known."

"What? Known what?"

"Well, he calls his son Deet, doesn't he?"

"That's right."

"It isn't my place to tell you this. But I swear someone better. While he was off fighting the Hun, Adolfina gave his son a Nazi name."

"Oh."

"It wasn't a year or two after he came home with his eye missing that she ran off. Of course, rumor was she'd had a paramour, and when she disappeared, Angus didn't seem to mind."

"Where'd she go?"

"Some say she went to her brother's place in Arkansas."

"What did Angus do?"

"I don't know if he hit her. Not her. But the other two—"

"I meant what did Angus do after she left?"

Hannah raised her right hand. "Well that's exactly what I was saying. He married two more women and beat them both. The one I saw myself. On Main Street, broad daylight, and he gave it no more mind than spitting on the grass. Big old Angus, stooped over, dragging Lucy Mae by the wrist like a dog on a leash. She traipsed away to cross the road, and he tugged hard, like that, and jerked her straight. He let go and she turned again, and he lashed out. She staggered back and kept walking from him. He was cussin' mad, and looked around to see who was watching. I was alone or I'd have give him the what-for."

"I don't believe it."

"Oh, I would have. Anyway, Lucy Mae disappeared shortly after. That's why I needed to come see you myself." Hannah patted Emeline's forearm.

Emeline shook her head. She spoke slowly. "You know Hannah, I accepted my husband's proposal after consulting on bended knee with the Lord, and He's never been more clear."

The older woman snorted. "Oh, you pathetic darling!"

Emeline blinked.

"You married a man and you got to stand by your decision. But that doesn't mean you can't make a second decision after the first. Things change. We mustn't be afraid to make a new... precedent. You see how Charles waits on me like I'm a queen?"

Emeline nodded.

"Last time he struck me I waited until he passed out. I woke him up with his thirty-eight pistol in one hand in scissors in the other, and I told him if he ever hit me again I'd catch him sleeping, slice off his family jewels and nail them to his forehead. He still drinks himself stupid, but he hasn't raised a hand toward me since. Now Emeline, is Angus hitting you?"

"It was so nice of you to stop by, and thank you for the supper plates."

Hannah frowned, gulped. "You got some deciding to do. And I'm going to run along before the storm hits."

After returning Emeline to her chair on the porch, Deet had hauled the kennel frames outside and positioned them along the barn wall facing the orchard at the lower level entrance. The barn would protect the pens from harsh weather and they would be visible from the house. Deet tapped nails. The pen rooftop was narrower than the thirty-six inch tarpaper, and one sheet covered. Looking at the sky, it was a good thing. White clouds raced and in the last five minutes gusts had started blowing sawdust into his eyes.

Emeline waved from the porch and he went to her.

"Can you take me into the house?"

He cradled her. Inside, she pointed to the sofa and he draped her there. As he extracted his arms from beneath her, she kissed his cheek. "You've been so dear."

He kissed her mouth. She withdrew, pushed his arms. He slipped his left arm underneath her and stroked her neck.

"Deet, this is wrong!"

"I know." He kissed her again and she didn't respond. "Don't pretend it was just me."

"We're wrong, so many ways."

Emeline wanted this to happen. Deet felt it in her fingernails and in her mouth. Yet her plaintive look checked his desire. He pulled away. Exhaled. "I'm going to the barn."

A tear fell to her cheek and hung there, and she crossed her arm to her breast.

He squeezed his eyes closed. "Why did you come here?"

"I married your father, Deet."

He turned, marched to the kennels. Her hair smelled like fruit or honey and lingered in his mind more than her lips or the small of her back. Her scent followed, somehow, and her hair still tickled his nose.

"She won't survive without you," he said. "Jackass."

TWENTY FOUR

After a gulp of walnut whiskey I rest the uncapped gallon against the swell by the stick shift. I take a hard curve on Route 322 out of Brookville and headlights flash in the oncoming lane. I swerve and the whiskey tips. My fingers swat empty. The jug rolls into the foot well; I rattle to the curb, grab it by the neck. A half-inch of liquid swishes at the bottom. The rest drips through my rusted floorboard.

The sun is gone from the sky before I pass Hazen, but it don't matter 'cause the sky is black with storm coming on. The wayward jug leans against my hip like a faithful dog, with my steadying hand across its shoulder, pinky through the loop. Through the day, despite the worst obstacles we've faced in months—two busted bits and a headache sent from hell just to fuck with me— I've found a steady nursing of walnut whiskey buoys optimism, almost like the clarity I get when I sit in the tree and meditate on things.

And now I'm all but out.

The Ford's yellow headlamps creep along. I tip the jug high, coax the last swallow, then the last drops, and return it to my side.

I thump the steering wheel. The air is rich from spilt walnut whiskey and my mind twinkles with insights. That bitch I got from the widow will be in heat within a month or two. I'll keep the first batch of dogs—every one. I got a theory about why men bet on dogs, and I don't need a winner to make dough. Fact is, a loser's better. Victory is nothing without loss and in blood sport the loss is permanent. Men come to see the loser. The walnut showed me how to profit from it.

That shop in my barn—I don't have the time to work it, but Deet sure as hell does, and better, he has a Kraut's way with tools. The cabinet door he fixed showed craftsmanship that'll fetch a premium. I'll get the word out, drop a hint at the barber shop. Or take Emeline to church and let her cluck some business from her society friends. Get some use out of religion.

Something Deet said a week ago comes back. Excess corn isn't worth jack shit at market, but a single good run of whiskey would pay for a still with profit left over. Didn't the widow say Mitch used walnuts from my tree? Maybe to keep tongues from wagging I'll buy tubing, barrels, yeast, and sugar in Franklin and Oil City, or at stores spread out along the way.

Two hours after leaving the derrick I swerve onto my drive. Headlights catch a shadow by the barn; I push the clutch and lean to the windshield as the Ford drifts to a stop. Deet's installed kennels on either side of the barn's first floor entrance—where I'd imagined them. Motor running and headlamps on, I hop out. First pen I come to, Rebel beats the chicken wire with his tail. He stops when he sees me.

The screen door at the house flaps closed and Deet joins me.

I steady myself against the kennel. "Got the roof on 'fore the rain. This ain't a bad piece of work, entirely."

"Not a bad piece of work at all," Deet says.

I heave against the corner. The kennel don't budge. "Where's that bitch I brought last night?"

"Thought you let her go. She was gone first thing."

"Why didn't you fetch her?"

"Didn't know what kind of arrangement you made to get her."

I open Copenhagen, loose a preemptive spit, fill my lip. "I'll visit the widow after supper."

At the F-100, I reach through the window and kill the engine. The scent of spilled whiskey wafts. I swipe the empty jug and upend it; not a drop falls. I probe inside the neck with my tongue.

Deet walks away, that damn buck knife at his side.

I open the passenger door and scoop whiskey-mud from the floor, hold it to my nose and inhale. Go to the house. Deet sits on the porch and follows me inside.

"Cows and hogs fed? Chickens?"

"That's right. Jacob's doing real good."

"Not 'til I straightened his shit out." I stand in the entrance, look at Emeline stretched across the sofa, and back at Deet. I study Emeline. "You must feel better. Got down them steps aright."

"Deet carried me. He's the only way I can get anywhere. Doc didn't have any crutches."

"That so?"

Deet nods.

"You carried her?"

"She can't walk." Deet stands beside the sofa.

"Unh." My eye falls to Deet's chest, his arms, back to his eyes. "You got a new project in the shop. Set of crutches. You ain't carrying my wife nowheres." I jab Deet's shoulder. "Clear?"

"Angus!" Emeline says.

"I said clear?" I shove Deet. Emeline shrieks and folds her legs. Deet falls against her cast and she wails. Deet regains his feet and grits his teeth and faces me.

"Go ahead and bite your lip! I see you! Gonna take on the old man! This is my house. My house!"

Deet squeezes his hands into balls.

I reach to him, peer into the boy's steady eyes. I wrap my fingers around his throat and squeeze 'til his face turns red. The artery in his neck bulges. His hands hang limber at his side and Deet stares like he's daring me to do the job. I stare back daring him to fetch his knife.

"You build a fuckin crutch," I finally say, and push him away. He falls to his ass and sits.

I stand on the porch, my mind hot, then go to the truck. A minute later I cut onto Widow McClellan's drive. The dog ain't at her doorstep, and I wouldn't be surprised if the old woman denies the bitch came home. That story won't float tonight. I bang the door. It cracks open. I force my hand around the edge.

"You liking the whiskey?" McClellan says.

"Ain't bad."

"Suspect you're after the dog, then," McClellan says. She opens the door and I fall inside with it. The pit bull growls at the entrance to the dining room.

"Bitch snuck off. That how you raise a dog?"

"What'd you do? Stick her in the barn?"

"You got a piece of twine?"

"Didn't bring any tonight?" She says. "Maybe in the basement, if you fetch it. I don't use the steps no more."

"Where'll I find it?"

"You got an edge, tonight. There's a ground-level window. Bear left 'til you see what you come for."

I step past the bitch pit bull, find the light switch by the cellar door and rattle down the stairs. Gulp the dank air and search the wall. See a bench below an open window. To the left, a stack of shelves supports a row of black, dusty jugs. I count twelve, and can feel the spit run in my mouth. I glance to the stairs, then up to the kitchen. The pit bull's shadow looms on the wall.

Standing on the bench, I hook my thumb through a jug loop and hold it to the light bulb. Black as tar. Gorgeous.

And I happen to be out of walnut whiskey.

Footsteps sound on the floor above. "Take another jug of that whiskey, if you like! I got a couple to spare."

"Mighty kind." I poke the side of my fist to the screen tacked to the window frame, then push three jugs through. Nine more on the rack, and she'll be dead without ever missing them. Slowly, avoiding the careless clank of glass, I push three more through.

Fair pay for having to come back for an unmitigated cur. I cut a five-foot section of twine from the coil on the adjacent shelf and climb the stairs.

"Dark as hell down there," I say.

"I wouldn't know," she says. "Why didn't you take a jug of whiskey?"

I tie the twine to the bitch's collar. "Didn't care for the bite. I'll be off."

McClellan closes the door and leaves the porch light on, bathing the front yard in an amber glow. Six jugs of whiskey wait in darkness beside the house. I open the Ford and the smell of whiskey greets me. "Soon," I say.

The dog jumps in; I thump her ass and she scoots. On the stretch to my driveway I look over my shoulder. The light is still on.

A minute later I lock the bitch in the kennel next to Rebel. "You two get real friendly."

Jacob rocked to the right. Bed springs twanged. Something was going on outside—he could feel it. He rolled over the mattress edge and forty seconds later jumped from the add-on roof to the ground. Crouching in moonlight, he scanned the forest, the lake, the field. He breathed in short gulps. Nerves taut, he crept to the corner and peered at the barn. Pap stood in front of the new kennels. It looked like there was another dog.

Jacob crawled closer.

Angus loped the ramp to the barn entrance and gawked across the cornfield to a faint yellow glow in the woods beyond. He grumbled something the wind didn't carry.

Jacob flattened against the earth as his father entered the truck and drove without lights. The truck pulled to the side of the road before reaching the forest by the Widow McClellan's.

Jacob slipped between corn stalks and watched.

Through the window I watch the widow seek her maker's council. Hands clasped on the book on her lap, eyes closed, she moves withered lips in prayer.

Other side of the house, I tuck a gallon jug under my right elbow and carry one in each hand. At the Ford I prop two jugs against each other at the foot well and grip the third's cap. Can't wait for the taste. Cap's rusted. I unbuckle my belt, whip the leather from my pant loops, coil it around the cap. With the jug braced between my knees I twist; the leather tightens until the cap breaks loose. I wipe rust from the threads and drink.

Good like I don't deserve.

I drink again; my mind swims in the fluid. I replace the cap, leave the jug on the seat and creep along the forest wall. Approach a few steps toward the window. The seat is empty.

McClellan prays no longer.

Jacob stole across pine needles to the edge of the widow's lawn and remained in the shadows. Something shiny reflected the porch light from the far side of the lawn. It was Angus, stalking the widow in the open. Jacob's heart raced. The widow sat on the porch, her head low and her eyes lidded, and then she looked toward Angus. Jacob slipped to all fours and crawled forward. Angus walked as if he didn't see her. Jacob's voice climbed in his throat but he stifled a warning cry.

Angus stopped. He'd seen her.

My arm-hair tingles. The old bat rocks in a chair on the porch. With the light so bright beside her she can't have made my shape against the forest, but her head swivels to me and an ugly smile crosses it.

I advance a step. Dried leaves conspire against me, pin me. I consider the way I've come then look ahead along the trees. Onto the grass, to the dim edge of light. The old woman jumps.

"Who's there?"

Closer.

She stands from her rocking chair. "I got a gun inside!"

Closer.

She flings open the door, reaches across the threshold. I veer, leap around the corner. She spins with a shotgun at her hips and points at the empty lawn. I watch from around the corner, low.

"I ain't afear'd to use it!" she calls.

I grab a fist-sized rock beside my foot and chuck it to the lawn. McClellan fires. In the yellow orange flash I make the Jacob's face, over by the trees she's fired into.

The shotgun smoke tastes sharp.

I leap. She twists, eyes bulging, and I drive my fist to her face. The old woman crumples. Moans and cries and it's all the same sound. I carry her inside, up the stairs. She mumbles, coughs blood.

"Where's your room?"

She ceases coughing and regards me with flat eyes.

I push a door open. Elbow a light switch. Larry's old room, unchanged in all these years since he died in Europe. I'd forgotten his room, somehow. I carry her farther down the hall, push open the last door, drop her on the bed. I wrench the pillow from beneath her head.

"Dear God," she says.

"You're mistaken."

I press the pillow to her face. Lightning flashes and booms so loud I jump and give her another gulp of air. She wriggles. Of all the things I've killed she's most like a kitten. Minutes pass. I breathe and she don't. I've never been so aware of my surroundings as right now. An ache accumulates at the back of my mind, an unfulfilled desire. Six jugs rest on a shelf in the basement, and the thought of all that walnut whiskey so close maddens me. I withdraw the pillow, press my palm to her sternum, nuzzle two fingers under her jaw.

The widow is dead.

At the front door I reload the single-shot Remington with another sixteen-gauge shell from a box by the door, wipe the stock and nestle the barrel at the corner by the wall. In the basement, I grab the remaining jugs of whiskey. Two minutes later I'm in the truck.

The rain comes steady, not hard, but enough to get wet. Lightning flashes and I got that feeling creeping on me like it's time to find the rope and pay my old lady a visit. I feel good.

Better'n I got a right too. Yessir.

TWENTY FIVE

J acob sat with his hand wrapped around his arm, still watching McClellan's house. Raindrops clung to his thin eyebrows. A long time had passed since Angus carried away the black jugs.

His father had punched an old woman.

Jacob wiped his fingers on the wet grass. His back was soaked in cold rain, but hunched, his belly was dry. A single bb had struck his arm and the rest of the radius of lead had blasted into the woods a foot to his side. He crawled onto the lawn and approached the house from the shadows behind. Each window was a still photo. He circled the house, climbed onto the porch. Hair stood on his neck and arms. He entered and smelled decay, musty baubles and trinkets, dusty photos and old breath; the faint odor of accumulated years' papers and gifts and memories.

With a start he turned back to the door. No one was there. His pulse pounded at his temples. He breathed carefully. Stepped slowly. The stagnant air was like a physical barrier resisting every step.

The old woman's blood had dripped to the floor. Looking, Jacob found his feet were wet and he'd made tracks. He wetted a rag at the sink and wiped them out, careful to leave the widow's blood undisturbed. Then he wiped his soles.

He found an expended shotgun shell and left it.

Dim lamps lit the dining room and radio room. The stairwell was brighter. He rubbed his palms to his pants.

Lucy Mae had sheltered Jacob from Angus, but her protection had ended last winter. Survival had demanded Jacob learn deception. As he followed Angus's footsteps, what other evidence might he find? Maybe there was advantage in all this.

Jacob neared the top of the stairwell. He stooped with his eyes flush to the floor and looked to the hall. The room on the left was dark. He slipped toward the one spilling light at the far end. Peering around the corner he saw the bed. The air carried a tease of evacuated bowels. The widow was utterly still.

What other clues had his father left behind? From the edge of the hallway Jacob searched the floor, the walls, the blanket. Far away, a gust whistled through the front door. Lightning flashed outside the bedroom window and the thunder boom followed a short moment later. Trembling, Jacob opened the closet. It was unoccupied. He knelt and lifted the blanket from the floor. The space was empty.

He stood beside the body.

Widow McClellan had never been more to him than a crinkled hag with a scratchy voice. He'd only seen her from afar, but her corrugated face, now in repose, seemed capable of suddenly scowling. A faint, shimmering light rose from her like heat. Jacob retreated, raced down the hallway, took the steps two at a time, darted from the front door... forest path... cornfield... to the farm. The truck was parked and unlit; the dogs growled from their pens and the farmhouse was dark. He crossed to the kennel, rested his hand on the corner and caught his breath. His side ached.

Angus killed the widow.

A burst of wind pushed him into the kennel. Lightning flashed and the glow lingered in the clouds above the lake. The wind disappeared, leaving the sizzle of raindrops falling on the lake water and tree leaves.

"Hey Reb," he whispered. "Hey bitch."

Dog tails drummed the chicken wire fence. He wiggled his fingers through the wire and Rebel nuzzled against them. The bitch in the next crate whined. The patter of rain galloped closer.

Wind whipped his shirt and Jacob searched the blank sky. Lightning flashed and an instant report pounded land and lake; the echo rolled. Fat raindrops hit like lead pellets. Cattle bellowed and hogs grunted. Jacob jumped at a bolt of lightning and simultaneous, deafening clap; his ears rang. So close! The strike was at Devil's Elbow! Jacob leaned into the wind and struggled toward the house. His skin tingled with electricity. The gust abated, then whipped him with redoubled fury, shoved him back two steps.

It was like punishment.

Emeline awoke with a dream poised in her mind, the words of the Lord booming from heaven in a deep bass rumble. He said He was about to work and she should watch. She whispered *Yes Lord*, and rolled, snuggling her thin blanket closer to her neck.

A thunderclap jolted her awake.

Emeline twisted from the sofa, braced against the armrest and stood, then followed the wall for support. Another thunderclap ricocheted through the house, rattling windows. The storm was on top of them. Wind rushed under the porch and it sounded like a bawling woman. Rain pattered tentatively on the kitchen window, small droplets that portended giants.

The Lord had said He was about to move.

Where, Lord? What do you want me to do? The basement?

Lightning flashed and outside in the white burst she saw Jacob leaning into the wind and struggling toward the house.

Jacob fought into the gale, squinted against windborne debris and rain. The dogs barked as if challenging an interloper.

Ahead, someone was awake in the house. The kitchen light went on, then the porch light. The door opened. Emeline braced against the jamb. The wind made a black tangle of her hair and she held one arm aloft protecting her face.

"Come inside!"

Lightning flashed. Jacob struggled closer, bracing against a side wind that seemed intent on holding him still.

Halfway to the house, a terrible screech issued from the barn.

Jacob kept his eyes on Emeline and struggled closer. She clutched the screen door but the wind ripped it from her hands and it smacked the house. She fell to the porch and shouted. The wind consumed her words. She pointed to the sky as she rolled flat on the porch. She shouted again and Jacob turned and looked upward.

The heavens were dark. In a sudden claustrophobic instant, Jacob beheld a giant slab of barn roof floating overhead with the lightness of a candy wrapper. The wind stilled and the noise abated; he stood slack-jawed as the roof descended. He ran.

Slipped. The roof crashed to the earth where he stood a moment before, and the consequent wind blast hurled him to the mud again.

"Huuuricane!"

The voice came from the house. Angus ran down the steps in his underwear. Behind, Deet sheltered his eyes with his hand and helped Emeline to her feet.

As suddenly as the storm arrived, it departed. The shrieking calumny faded to footsteps in squishy mud and hands wiping water from arms and naked thighs. The last drop of rain rippled in a puddle. The sky blinked away a fast-moving cloud and the moon peered at them.

"Ripped it right off the barn! I was standing here!" Jacob pointed. "Right here, and it passed like this," he drew an arc over his head.

Angus stalked to the barn.

"Get inside the house," Deet said.

"But I'm already here!"

"Why are you here?"

Jacob hesitated. "I heard the thunder!"

"Where'd it strike?"

"One was at Devil's Elbow. Saw it hit."

Angus marched back to the boys. "Jake, see if anything's on fire. What'd you do to your arm?"

Jacob looked at his bloody bicep. "Musta caught a splinter in the wind."

"Have Em pick it out tomorrow."

Jacob ran to the edge of the lawn toward Devil's Elbow. He looked back. Angus paced to the barn entrance and stared across the field to the Widow McClellan's.

I shove the sliding door open and flip the light switch; the roof over the shop is secure; only the corner above the right side loft is smashed in my yard. Skyward I see stars. The barn frame is intact, but cross members and roof lifted whole, leaving hay bales exposed. Each night, dew will settle. Not worth getting riled about for a night or two, but any more rain and the outside bales will rot. A good soaking will cost me.

"Christ Almighty."

Deet comes alongside.

"You got any tar paper left?" I say.

"Half a roll. Not enough."

"All right. Another roll. Tomorrow I want you to cut and clean five-inch oak crossbeams. Strip the bark. I want eleven-foot poles; looks like, hell, ten of em. Then strip the paper off the roof that blowed off and see what we got to work with. I'm not gonna waste walnut. We'll go to the mill for what we can't salvage."

Deet looks at the ground.

"One other thing. Don't climb that roof without I'm here. I got plans for you."

"Plans, huh?"

I return to the shattered mass of boards and tarpaper lying on the mud. Look from them to the barn to the sky, and wonder at the timing. The illusion of cause is strong, but a snurgle of walnut whiskey'll get my mind right.

Still I study the roof and how it blew Jacob to his face in the mud, and I can't quite fathom any of it.

The first thunder I heard was while the widow choked her last breath.

"Lifted clean off. Just clean off."

Jacob stood at the fifty-foot slope above the lake. His gaze followed the dark shoreline seeking the orange flicker of flames. The air was damp and calm; wet grass tickled his legs. Fireflies had returned to the open air. Stars twinkled, and the scene was one of planetary amnesia: the world had forgotten the storm that smashed into the Hardgrave farm. Jacob ran down the slippery trail.

He whiffed ozone and turned to the forest. The black outline of foliage against the sky had changed. A void had opened in the leaves at the walnut tree. He moved toward the shadows; the scent became burned wood. Feeling along the tree with his hands, he inched forward until pricked by the jagged splinters of an arboreal cataclysm. The massive limb that jutted from the trunk, where he and his father before him had reclined to watch lazy ripples on the lake—had collapsed. He traced his fingertips along the still-hot streak where lightning had blasted away bark.

Eyes open, an image of Lucy Mae's putrefied face flashed into his field of vision.

He retracted his fingers but the image lingered in the dark. His heart thudding, Jacob followed the fallen limb to where branches separated and he could step no farther. The scent became rotten flesh.

Jacob ran back to the farm.

TWENTY SIX Maul

Maul progressed. Although some mavericks fought puppies to condition the dog's minds, dogmen were in general reticent to seed immature dogs in fights. They made a poor spectacle. Ticky Bilger's challenge was to convince an organizer to allow a thirteen-month dog in a sanctioned match. Ticky chose Charlie something or other, from Franklin, a man who'd proven moral flexibility by staging contests between other breeds and pit bulls. If another young dog awaited a match, Charlie might extend an invitation.

Ticky would attend the next fight and plead in person. Charlie, he understood, had a weakness.

Checking Maul one morning Ticky noticed a stray mongrel hound lingering by the yard gate. Though the clearest sign of a bitch in heat was her backside blood, the second best indication was a stray hound's nose. Tobacca was hot.

Ticky did a bit of elementary genetic calculus and decided to breed her with Maul. The worst result would be a couple stillborn pups, but the rest would be killers. The offspring that lived would almost be clones of Maul, Ticky figured. They'd enter training early and once their father proved game, their worth would climb.

The stillborns would've just ended up bait dogs if they lived, so there wasn't any moral consequence to breeding Maul with his mother.

The white powder Vic left made the time pass quickly and improved Ticky's elocution. One night at a bar telling lies with the boys, Ticky's ebullience caused an altercation. Ticky felt his veins bulge and his eyes burn with internal pressure and Marty O'Brien backed down. The next day, after a few hours of sleep and a pot of coffee, Ticky relished the memory. He'd heard of whiskey goggles, which made ugly women pretty. Seemed that white powder made small men big. And smart men smarter.

Ticky fed Maul a plate of liver with a half teaspoon of cocaine mashed into a slice on the side, snorted two lines, and reintroduced Maul to his mother.

He returned three hours later and Tobacca was shredded to her rib bones and half gutted.

"You grinnin' at me you dumb sumbitch? You grinnin'?"

Maul panted, his tongue draped over the side of his glazed mouth.

Ticky stood slack-jawed, beat the pen with his fists and feet. "You fuckin mutt!" Ticky kicked the chain link. "You fuckin cutrate mutt! Bastard! Bitch! Punk! No good murdering fuckin... shit." Ticky clutched the pen and caught his wind.

Maul watched with peppercorn pupils.

Pete joined Ticky at the pen. "He killed Tobacca?"

Ticky clasped the latch. Maul watched, his grin gone. Pete knelt at the front corner.

"Drag Tobacca out, boy."

"You don' think he'll hurt me?"

"He knows better. Go on."

Ticky stood away and leaned forward to the latch mechanism. He eased the cage door open. Pete reached inside. Maul charged and in a mad explosion, knocked Pete on his back, seized his face, shook. The boy screamed as his jaw bone collapsed.

Ticky kicked Maul's exposed neck and groped on top of the crate for a pry stick. He fell to Maul, shoved the oak dowel between the dog's jaws. Expediency demanded force; Pete could die any second. But too much lateral pressure could break a tooth and damage the dog's prospects. Ticky applied gentle, sustained force until leverage overcame brute strength.

Pete wriggled free and kicked backward.

Ticky drove the dowel butt to Maul's skull and shoved him into Tobacca's pen. He slammed the gate with her corpse inside.

Cherry blood smeared Pete's face and neck and trickled steadily from four puncture marks. Ticky wiped it away. "You one lucky bastard."

Pete gurgled, "Illum, illum." He drooled blood and coughed.

Ticky frowned. The way Pete's jaw moved wasn't right.

Ticky attended a fight at Charlie's place in the woods by Franklin. He pulled Charlie aside while the men studied dogs in anticipation of placing bets.

"Found me a match, yet?"

"No one fights pups. You ought to lunge test him."

"He's passed a lunge test, and I put him against the neighbor's two year old blue nose and Maul killed him inside of two minutes. He's ready to go."

"I don't have a match."

"He'll take any dog. I don't care how old or what bloodline. Maul's gonna whup ass, and that's a guarantee."

"You say *any dog?*"

"That's right. Any age, any size."

"You stupid? Fourteen-month dog don't know the tricks. Don't have the track record. Wouldn't be right to the boys or the sport. There's the principle to think of."

"Here's your principle. You got a string of pups for sale. Thunder comes out of retirement for one easy fight, reminds the boys of his glory days. Help them pups fetch a *price*. Maul's only fourteen months. What danger's that?"

"He'd have to be the devil himself to whup Thunder."

"Sounds like we come to accord."

Charlie rubbed his chin.

TWENTY SEVEN

I look at my pocket watch. Twenty minutes late. I pull the F-100 to the side of the dirt road, pour walnut whiskey into my thermos cup and top it with steaming coffee. The new site is around here somewhere—Merle said a mile beyond the last, but with windrows of scrub trees blocking my line of sight and my slippery morning memory, I don't know if I should look left or right. Sipping, I start down the road and watch for tire tracks across either ditch. I hold the cup in my gear-shifting hand and swap to my steering hand with each clutch; my eye torn between the rough road and my splashing coffee.

With the widow's death and my barn roof on the ground, the pendulum swings back and I figure to get the hell out the way 'fore it hits me square. I bounce over a ditch, stop alongside a fleet of trucks on a slick field. The air is wet and the ground muddy. The bastards at Oil City chose a tilled field for the next drill site. My feet stick; suction pops as I swing one leg in front of the other.

The derrick is in pieces; the deck on a single truck, all the machinery spot-welded to the floor. The tower waits on another flatbed, and the diesel motor on a third.

"Get your ass over here, Hardgrave!" Merle leverages a pipe wrench against a cargo strap release that's caked in muck. "Ten minutes more, and you'd a been looking for work. We got to stand this rig."

I gulp the last of my coffee and screw the cup on the thermos.

The drilling rig components was remanufactured after the last job—disassembled, repaired, and moved to the new site. Water beads on the oily cathead spool, but once I wrap the chain four times, a coat of bear grease couldn't keep it from grabbing.

"Thought the company was gonna spring for a new rig."

Merle shakes his head. "You say that every time. Nobody ever said that."

"Still running a four-banger truck motor. Get us a spudder, a Keystone or a Cyclops. We wouldn't be busting our asses half a day bolting the derrick down and traipsing over to the motor to add oil to keep it from burning up. And that's another thing. Karl's putting second sand crude in the crankcase. May as well lube it with chicken shit. How long'll it run like that?"

Merle pries the wrench against the strap lever and it gives, releases a stack of drilling pipe. He backpedals as they tumble, and stoops like he's just outrun a bull. "That little motor's run on second sand five years without a fart of smoke. Shut the hell up and get ready."

Karl's at the head of the thirty-foot tower, and spends a second look at the cable affixed to the frame. He waves his arm upward; the crane operator engages the motor and a steel cable hoists the derrick.

Perhaps now she could write a proper poem; perhaps the mystery of the three missing women would congeal into an appropriate verse—imagine if each wife loved him, pinned her hopes of raising a good family, and his response was to bury them beside a gnarled walnut. There was a poem in that.

The screen door twanged open. Jacob ran to the stairs.

"Jacob!"

He stopped.

"Angus said you have a splinter. Run to the closet and bring me the tweezers."

"It's nothing."

"Jacob."

He continued upstairs, returned a few minutes later, and stood before her.

"Let me see." On his arm, she touched a dimple of a wound with a red center. "A splinter?" she said. "Looks too deep."

"Wind was somethin' else."

"We best dig it out or you'll have an infection. Let me get situated so I can see."

Emeline eased her legs over the couch to the floor, closed her eyes and smiled tightly as pain flared. She took his arm again and squeezed the puncture like a pimple. Blood erupted to the surface. Jacob winced.

"Hold still."

"That hurt."

"Run upstairs and get peroxide, cotton, and Mercurochrome."

"Mercurochrome tastes funny."

She exhaled. Couldn't think of what to say. "Go."

Her leg ached now that she'd moved, but it was the pain of a mending bone, not of burning infection. She closed her eyes and imagined walking barefoot in grass or on pebbles, or even in mud, with tiny brown pillars squishing between her toes. Thank God she didn't have morning sickness or a compulsive appetite. It was good to be warm and fed, trusting the Lord like she promised, and hopeful He would help her unbelief.

Jacob returned. She indicated a space beside her and grasped his arm.

"Stop pulling." She said. "It doesn't hurt yet."

"But it will."

"You let it fester and we have to amputate—then it'll hurt."

She rubbed the tweezers with an alcohol-soaked cotton ball then wiped his wound. "All right." She repositioned him a few inches leftward and squeezed his arm; a rivulet of blood trickled to her hand. He quivered as she brought the tweezers to the mark.

"It hurts!"

"Hurts?" She pointed to her leg. "The bone went clean through and was out in the air. You're practically a full-grown man. You can deal with a splinter."

She pressed the tweezers into the puncture, wormed them farther. Jacob's lower lip rolled over and tears pressed from his eyes.

"I can't feel anything," she said. "You sure there's a splinter in there?"

He shook his head.

She pinched the tweezers and dragged. Nothing. "I've got to do it again. I ought to be able to find a splinter big enough to leave a hole like that."

"That hurts!" He yanked free.

She grabbed his other wrist. "Jacob! Your father has a jug in the hutch. Bottom cabinet. Bring it to me."

He drew back, eyes intent on hers. "What for?"

"Bring the jug and a cup." She released his arm. "I can't chase you, so you better come back."

"Pap don't like nobody touching his whiskey."

"Get the jug."

The humidity-swollen hutch door clucked like a turkey. Jacob returned with the black whiskey cradled in his forearm. He placed it at Emeline's feet and returned to the kitchen. She unscrewed the cap and without bringing the mouth to her nose smelled walnuts and alcohol. Iridescent oil filmed the top and reflected the ceiling light.

Jacob brought a cup. She poured a half-inch.

"Hold your nose and gulp it."

"Does it taste bad?"

"It's a little warm—like pepper. Plug your nose."

Jacob pinched the bridge of his nose and threw the cup back. He gasped. She grabbed his arm, plunged the tweezers deeper. Jacob's eyes watered. He coughed. Pounded his chest with his free hand. Rasped.

"Hold still!" she said, and pressed farther. "I've got something here! Hold still!"

She eased the tweezers out, her forehead hot with concentration.

"Rats!" Purple blood welled out.

"Not again," he said.

"Here, take more." She splashed a second shot into the cup, marking the jug with a bloody fingerprint.

Jacob brought the cup to his lips and swallowed.

"You didn't plug your nose."

"It ain't so bad."

"I found something; got it most of the way out."

He offered his arm and she explored the wound. She closed the prongs. "I got a hold. Be still. What?" She released a BB into her other hand, dabbed it with cotton. "That's a BB. That's from a gun."

"No it's not." Something dark and angry skipped behind his eyes.

"I shoot, and I know. That's from a shotgun."

"So what if it is? The wind blew the barn roof a hundred feet."

"You hold your tongue."

"You ain't my ma!" He wrested free; his heel toppled the jug. Whiskey splashed to the area rug.

"Jake! Pick it up!"

She stretched but couldn't reach; Jacob watched until the whiskey drained even with the opening and no more trickled out. A dreamy, stunned look covered his face, as if his thoughts voyaged far.

"Why'd you do that? You looked like you saw something."

"I was thinking of Ma."

"You miss her."

Jacob righted the jug. Picked up the cup.

"What are you doing? Don't do that."

He drank. Done, he clucked his tongue and smiled with vacant eyes. "She was a bitch." He tossed the empty cup to the sofa; it bounced from the cushion edge and rapped her cast. "Like you."

"You don't mean that."

Jacob backed away, until he spun and ran into Deet at the screen door.

"Hey! Whoa! Where you going?" He seized Jacob by the shoulder but Jacob shook loose and bolted toward the barn.

"What's got into him?"

"I don't know. He just turned mean all of a sudden," Emeline said.

Deet approached, sniffed, telegraphed a question.

"He only drank a little. And spilled the rest."

"That's the whiskey Pap got from the widow. I snuck a gulp; tasted like hog shit—near as I could tell. Jake choked it down?"

"Appeared to like it."

"He'll upchuck in three minutes."

"I dug in his arm for a splinter and gave him a drop of whiskey to settle down. I found a BB from a shotgun. Does that make any sense?"

"I didn't hear any shooting last night—though Jake made it outside before Pap and me."

"Can the wind blow a BB?"

"Did you pick it out his arm?"

She nodded.

"Then the wind can blow a BB." He hovered over the wet mark on the rug. "Pap says anything about this, you tell him I did it. I'll get a rag." Deet paused. "Oh wait."

He stepped to the door and reached outside. "Here. I made this."

He passed a wooden crutch to her. He'd split a piece of ghostly pale maple, secured the bottom with a leather thong, bolted a handle into the middle, and a shaped shoulder rest at the top. She ran her fingers over the curve of the body and couldn't help form the impression he'd given it a special measure of attention.

"Thank you," she said.

"I'll size the handle to you once I get the floor cleaned up," he said.

"There's rags and a bucket in the closet."

Deet gathered the items. Minutes later, he pressed a cloth to the rug and scrubbed. He flipped the rag over and looked at it.

"This whiskey's gonna stain and stink forever. I'll soak it outside." He moved the coffee table, lifted the sofa with Emeline on top, pushed the rug from under with his foot and dragged it to the porch.

Emeline struggled to her feet with the crutch, found it close to the right length, and hobbled to the kitchen. Each forward step pressured her shin and pain flashed, but the kitchen looked dreadful, scattered bowls and plates, bomber-class flies rapping walls and windows. Here was something to do and the crutch gave her the means. But first she'd see to the black whiskey that this very minute stained black the hardwood floor. Emeline drew water in a bucket, and leaning on the crutch, mopped the hickory floorboards.

"That leg ain't knit yet," Deet called through the screen door. "You don't need to be working."

"I've got to do something." She lost her balance and hopped sideways until she bumped into the wall.

Deet entered, stabilized her hip with his palm.

"Why don't you wait until Doc Fleming puts on a permanent cast?" He eased his arm around her waist. "Lean on me." He helped her to the sofa and knelt beside her, arms pinned by her back and legs.

"Deet—"

"Shh." He rested his head at her sternum. "I can hear your heart."

His hair trapped white sawdust chips. His forehead lifted and fell as she breathed. She rested her arm across his, behind his shoulder, and stroked the hair above his ear. "There's nowhere for this to go, Deet."

His arm snuggled tighter below her thighs.

"I can't think for fear of hearing steps on the porch," she said. "This is madness."

"So be it."

"I'm married, Deet. I'm married to your father." She shook his shoulder.

He lifted his head and his eyes were grave. "I'll take you away."

"With a broken leg? We can't even talk like this."

"Then why are you still petting my head?" He pulled from beneath her legs, rested his hand across her belly, sidling a breast.

"Deet—"

He kissed her. She pressed against him, then pulled away. "I'm married—before God."

"You don't love him."

"Deet—I'm pregnant! You and I can't be."

He withdrew his arm. Shuffled backward on his knees and then stood. "Pregnant?" He retreated to the screen door and opened it. Slumped against the jamb, shaking his head. "You ought to kill it."

Jacob's disobedient feet scuffed tufts of grass and he made a giddy game of it. He'd angled toward the segment of barn roof lying in a crushed heap midway to the chicken coops, but a dark curiosity directed him to the lake path. The whiskey opened his mind and he knew what he must investigate with his newfound intrepidness.

The grasses on the bank bore the first tinge of golden dryness at their tips; the blades hung lethargically. A bass floated belly up at the lake edge, its silver underside discernible from the trail. Seeing it, Jacob isolated a piscine odor from the others that pressed upon him: water, forest, and something foreign as death, and recognizable as a rotting roadside groundhog.

The walnut tree commanded him to investigate its broken limb.

He reached the shadow cast by the tree's crown and stopped short. A breeze fluttered leaves and the giant tree wavered. The line of gloom on the ground shifted. Jacob stepped into the shade and his awareness gathered close like testicles in cold water. Something dead and rotten lay near the tree, perhaps crushed by the fallen limb.

Jacob recoiled—but was drawn, and touched the tree again. The vision was gone but a voice arrived as if its journey was long, beamed through some diaphanous membrane and misassembled at his ear.

"Jacob."

It was a woman. He knew her. "What?" He answered even as he placed her timbre. "What?" He looked at trees, the ground. "Where are you?"

His balance wavered and he rested his free palm against the rough bark.

"Jacob!"

He fell; broke contact; regained his feet, ran to the border of shadow and light. As if tethered by a hemp rope around his waist, the walnut tree heaved him. He fell back to it, heart thudding, and pressed the wood. "Ma?"

"Here..."

"Here where? Ma?" He stepped away and spun, searching. Silence. He pressed his hand to the tree. "Where? Where!" She didn't answer.

He shivered; he sensed another ghost, a provider of images. Formless, it made him think of an old man, a giant. It spat words *(fuck!)* at him. Jacob faced the blackness.

"Where is she?"

"Hehehehe."

The presence urged him toward the fallen limb. Jacob clambered over a branch and crawled below the next. The smell of rotted flesh grew until he buried his nose in his shoulder and retched. The earth soaked his knees and elbows; he pressed his belly to the slippy leaves and grass, wriggled under a limb and found another, closer to the ground, and struggled below it. Deeper into the leafy cavern, he pressed tight to the dank earth, closer to the pungent flesh. Bark scraped his bare arm. Twigs gouged his face, brushed his eye sockets; still he squirmed forward.

Wind shifted and the tree groaned; the broken limb, still connected by a hinge of splintered timber, clamped Jacob to the soil. The weight crushed the air from his lungs and he fought to refill them, opened his mouth but his lungs were pressed closed. He kicked; his toes slipped on leaves. He clawed; his fingers drew mud. There was a hole by a limb. If he could reach it he might pull forward and breathe. Yet even as he thought this, his awareness faded. His legs flailed. He saw the *presence,* a man made of sawdust and leather, who grinned as if the wind, the shifting tree, and the subsequent revelation of his form were all his doing.

Blackness encroached upon Jacob's sight. The breeze abated. The walnut groaned and the *presence* disappeared. Free, Jacob gulped air, scampered forward a few inches, panted.

His hand sank deep into the ground in a slippery hole beside a limb, left when the branch shifted after impact. He reached deeper, *(...that's right, Jacob, touch her...)* his bare hand roughed by the bark. *"Jacob..."* Frigid water filled the bottom of the hole. *"I'm here, son..."* His mother's voice...

The mud gave way like over-easy eggs. He shrieked. Smacked his skullcap against the limb. The wind shifted, clamping his shoulder to the ground with his arm in the hole and his fingers probing rotted flesh. His eyeballs bulged and his voice escaped him; he had no air; the tree crushed his lungs. The giant man appeared, gestured him to go deeper. *(grab her, boy! that's a titty!)* Jacob recoiled, shifted and his hand filled with putrid meat and amid the soft stringy mass he found a circular piece of bone.

Or metal.

He grasped it. *"Jacob..."*

"Ma, why?" he choked.

"Angus."

The *presence* howled laughter throaty as a tornado. Jacob connected the words and the breeze abated; the tree shifted, the branch released its delicately wielded weight; he locked the metal in his fist and scrambled back. Mud blackened his arm. Back through leaves and limbs; he ran to the lake, away from the float-ing bass. He splashed and rubbed his forearm in the water, opened his hand and under the surface his mother's wedding ring sparkled.

TWENTY EIGHT

We bolt the derrick erect, fire motors, and sink the bit by mid-afternoon. The surrounding field has dried under the sun but humidity is thick. Mosquitoes hover in a silent cloud beside the pounding diesel motor. I swat but they hone on my breath. I scratch my neck with sodden leather gloves.

Merle waves me away for a quick lunch. A thicket of blackberry grows at the edge of the field in the shade of cherry and oak trees. I press the side of my boot to the thorny stems, kneel at a carpet of ferns. I crush a fistful of leaves in my hands and rub the residue on my neck and arms. Fuckin skeeters.

Back at the Ford I wash a dry sandwich with gulps of walnut whiskey and coffee, and when I finish, top off the thermos cup, and put away the jug in the passenger foot well. I drop a flannel jacket on top and Merle stands at my window.

"What you got?"

"Coffee." The diesel motor chugs forty feet away. "Karl on the rig?"

"He's the two-man, ain't he?" Merle props his elbow on the roof and bites paper-wrapped bread. "We add a section in five minutes, so cut it short."

"We'll hit fifty feet today."

"I want sixty." Merle grins. Walking away he spins. "Charlie's gonna fight Thunder on Tuesday."

"That right?"

"You don't want to miss it. That Thunder—he got a chunk of the devil in him. Eats his own young—killed the last bitch Charlie paired him with. Had to find a bitch meaner than him, and any bitch *that* mean has to add something to the line. Them pups'll be special."

"Sounds like a bunch of bullshit."

"What?"

"He's selling pups."

"You bet against Thunder and see."

"Don't think I'll be for or against."

"Well you oughta pull your wallet out if you want to talk like that."

I drink. "What's the pay?"

"Three to one."

"Who's he matched with?"

"Another red nose. Same pappy as the one that whooped on the dog you took home. Named Maul."

"Maul."

"Head like a fucking rail splitter, they say—and taking on Thunder, come out of retirement—that ain't a sight a man ought to miss."

"Yeah, well my barn roof blowed off last night, damn near landed on the truck."

"Roof blowed off?"

"That's right. Storm come outta nowhere and next thing, I'm standing beside a twenty-foot section of roof, fifty feet from the barn. Tossed the whole damn thing right over my boy's head."

"That's bad luck. Go to the fight and bet on Thunder. Your luck might improve."

"It ain't bad luck when the man upstairs has it in for you. And it ain't good luck when the one below has your back. Luck ain't got jack shit to do with it."

"What the hell's that mean?"

"Anything you want. Now give me some peace if you want to sink sixty feet today."

"I'll get seventy."

I drink. "Wasn't you supposed to shoot a well on the Derry side?"

"They get the nitro, I shoot the well. For today, we're hitting seventy feet. Break's over."

He turns and I swig a long pull from the black jug, cap the thermos. We take positions on the rig, both on the same side. I stand by the cathead, an auxiliary power source from the main drill motor. Done it a million if I done once—break the linkage, insert a new thirty-foot section and reconnect the old to the top of the new. I feed a chain around the pipe and coil it on the cathead, and with a quick pull, friction catches the spool and spins the pipe loose.

I push a lump of chains aside and plant my feet square. Karl, at the top of the A-frame derrick, elevates the shaft until the section break is four feet above deck. Sarge slaps a pair of semi-circle chock blocks around the lower pipe so it don't slip back down the well. Same time, I coil the chain around the upper, just above the break. Lean to the cathead, wrap the links on the spool. The slack chains I kicked aside misaligns and binds.

"Son of a bitch!"

"Come on, for crissakes!" Merle cries over the din.

I tug the chain, kneel, hit the bind with my palm and reach below to the lever that will disengage the cathead from the diesel engine.

"Watch it!" Merle yells.

The bind breaks. The taut chain pops and whistles. In an instant the links pinch my arm to the spinning cathead and flips me to the other side.

A sudden snapping wrench of awareness shoots through me, and my left arm flops on the muddy deck and blood spurts from the ragged meat below my shoulder. I look at the pulpy stump and wriggle past the cathead base to my arm. My hand has a half-open curve, relaxed like it might accept a bottle. Blood soaks my ribs, and all I think is how damn warm it is. The deck is slick and sticky with blood. The sky is blue and mosquitoes zero on my face.

Merle rushes forward. "You dumb son of a bitch!"

He disengages the cathead, secures the chain. "Stupid fuck!" He waves to Sarge. "Get that shoulder tied off somehow, 'fore he bleeds to death!"

I lift my head from the vibrating metal floor. "There goes your fifty feet."

Deet worked at the base of a five-inch oak tree with a one-man crosscut saw. Married! Pregnant!—before he'd even had a chance—a further machination of a Fate that dropped him square in dipshit Pennsylvania to assume the Hardgrave mantle of working like a dog and getting nothing in return.

Saw teeth ripped through pissy smelling timber, spitting white sawdust that fell in a damp, linear snowdrift. He sweated. A squirrel barked at him from a log a few yards away.

"Go fuck yourself," Deet said.

Pregnant! By that prick father of his—that conniving sack of shit bastard drunk. Murderer.

The tree creaked, leaned. Deet stepped three feet back, threw his leg high and pushed. The thirty-some foot tree crashed through adjacent limbs and whooshed to the ground. He denuded the tree of branches with Angus's axe, sawed two eleven-foot lengths with the crosscut, lifted the heavy ends to the crook of his arms, pulled them to the edge of the forest.

He cut ten, and thought of getting the Farmall.

"The Farmall ain't pissed," he said aloud, and with aching shoulders, dragged the logs to the section of barn roof that lay between the house and the chicken coop. He tossed his sweat-soaked shirt aside and with the poles lined side-by-side, adzed long swaths, working each before spinning all a quarter turn and continuing.

When the bark lay in heaps, rough and gray on the outside, moist and yellow on the inside, he remembered he didn't have to be here. He still had a bag packed under his bed. He'd had a plan, and it was time to dust it off.

It was time to head south.

Emeline wiped her eyes. She'd sat on the sofa with the Bible until the words were just words, then hobbled on the crutch to the closet, removed a belt from a pair of hunting pants, wrapped the leather strap around her plaster cast and buckled it. She cleaned the dishes in a performance that recalled her first evening as a married woman, and started supper—roasted chicken and dumplings, gravy, potatoes, corn. She'd finish early—and maybe she'd go for a stumble outside. Maybe visit the neighbors—or neighbor—the only one close enough was the widow McClellan. She should have gone over to properly introduce herself and see to the new widow's needs long ago.

Emeline looked out the window while she held the chicken under running water in the sink, dissolving flakes of ice inside its chest cavity. She saw Deet strip off his shirt. Emeline averted her eyes then allowed them to wander back. The chicken filled with water; the cavity overflowed.

Sarge cinched the blood flow by fashioning a tourniquet with my belt and a crescent wrench secured by a length of twine. I don't know where he found the flesh to cinch. I remember seeing the ball of my arm bone.

Merle hauled me in his truck to Franklin only to find his doctor was away on a house call. Then he took me to Oil City where the company physician stretched a flap of skin over the hole in my shoulder socket and sewed it. I ain't had a sip of walnut in I can't remember. The doctor says penicillin and morphine and he's working two needles and nothing really has too much meaning in my head. But then that company man Dwight Feeley steps in the room and my senses get sharp. He curls his cap brim and looks out the window.

"I feel bad, but it was your own fault. Edgarson's Oil and Gas won't need your labor no longer."

"I come to work fixing to lose my arm, that it?"

"No," Dwight says, "one of the boys brought your truck here. You got a jug in the cab and it stinks of a stillery."

Behind me, a clock clicks with each passing second, as if the man in the white jacket is a man, by God, whose time is important.

"Everybody has a little snorkel here and there," I say. "How the hell's a man to keep his mind on something as miserable dull as drilling holes in the cussed ground?"

Dwight holds up his hand. "I made all the argument on your behalf that's gonna get made. You can't be around a rig missing an arm. Don't make sense to keep jawing about it. Now I'm sorry. I hope things work out."

"That's it?"

"I got your final pay." He digs bills from his shirt pocket and offers them.

"Count em."

Dwight clicks off the tens and ones. "One hundred-fifty-two. That's every hour to the end of today's shift." He offers the bills again.

"Mighty white." I look out the window.

Dwight presses the bills in my hand. He leaves.

I smack my dry lips. The doctor clears his throat.

"You'll need to see your physician tomorrow to follow up on the work I've done. If you were smart, you'd go to the hospital in Dubois tonight. The wound is trimmed clean and I've given you a healthy shot of penicillin to stave infection. When you get around to looking at it, you'll find a drain under the cover that I stitched over the stub, here, to let fluids exit. Make sure your doctor watches for gangrene."

"Right, Doc."

"The men tell me you have a good amount of whiskey alcohol in your truck. Mixed with your coffee, even. You should avoid drinking on your way home, and if that starts bleeding," he points to the gauze-wrapped stub of my left arm, "you'd better get pressure on it quick. You lost enough blood to kill a smaller man."

I close my eyes. Breathe.

"Mister Hardgrave? Are you about ready?"

I flop off the edge of the table; steady myself for the first time missing the weight of my arm and a fifth of my blood. Meet the doctor's eyes. "Go to hell, Doc."

Emeline stood with her crutch.

Outside, the truck door thudded shut. Tonight would be quiet. Angus would be happy—or at least mollified—by the sight of domestic toil. Leaning on the crutch, she forked a chicken leg, added a dumpling and mashed potatoes and waited with the plate in her hands.

She heard his slow footsteps on the porch planks. The doorknob twisted. She stepped toward the table and forced a fragile smile. The door aperture widened and he emerged.

His eye was vacant. His face was ashen; his clothes bloody.

His left arm was gone.

His dinner plate shattered on the floor.

"What happened!"

Angus staggered into the kitchen, leaned against the wall. Looked at the chicken leg, the dumpling squashed like a pale dog pile, the pool of gravy.

"Look what you done." Angus lunged, struck her with his nonexistent left hand, lost his balance and caught himself on the table. His eye had a wild gloss and his breath burned with whiskey. "That's yours on the floor. Now fix me a plate."

He crumpled, grinding his wounded shoulder across the edge of the table. He groaned. His skull clunked against the table, then the floor. He was unconscious.

Angus groaned softly. His knee rested in mashed potatoes and Emeline noticed a long, curved shard of porcelain that drew to a point. His head lolled to the side and she saw the pulse of the artery below the skin. He lay on his side with his good shoulder to the floor and his wounded one on top. The shirt had been folded and pinned and though he'd worn a clean shirt to work it was now crusted with blood and oily grime. From the contour of the cloth she imagined much of his shoulder was gone and while taking it all in, she observed a rapidly swelling circle of darkness, and smelled not just the acrid odor of sweat and alcohol, but the must of blood.

Angus bled.

Emeline looked at the shard of porcelain.

Angus moaned.

Emeline closed her eyes, clenched her jaw, focused.

"Jacob!"

"What?" He leaned against the entryway frame and regarded his prostrate father with a look of careful indifference.

"How long have you been standing there?"

"Just now."

"Run upstairs. I need a needle and thread, bandages, mercurochrome. Just bring everything in the medicine closet."

"I can't carry all that."

"Then make two trips!"

Emeline knelt to Angus and unbuttoned his shirt. She tugged it from his pants and he grinned and mumbled. His shirt free, she pulled until the bandaged stump glowed red and bare. Blood dripped to the floor. Emeline shook her head.

Lord, what do I do? How do I stop something like this?

The Lord was silent.

"Jacob! Where are you!"

She heard him descend the stairs, his feet a rapid patter. He carried an armful of items which he deposited on the table by pushing plates and silver aside with his elbows and opening his arms.

"Get me a clean hand towel from the drawer by the sink and soak it in water."

Emeline unpacked the wound. The doctor had covered the sutures in gauze and held it in place by wrapping a bandage under his opposite arm. Emeline kneeled on one knee, her other held straight by the cast, and grabbed a serrated knife from the table. She ripped through the bandage. The bloodied gauze stuck to Angus's shoulder and Emeline wondered if it was pressed to raw meat.

Jacob stood above her with a dripping cloth.

Emeline took it and swabbed the blood on Angus's chest and side, but more oozed from under the bandage and she realized she was just moving blood from one location to another. She would have to pull off the bandage.

She peeled it from the top of his shoulder. The mesh stuck with blood, not yet dried, but firm like pitch. It sounded like tape. She pulled slowly and Angus's skin pulled with it, a flap that used to be his shoulder but was now a drum skin stretched over an empty socket. It pulled with the bandage. Emeline swallowed and with her other hand applied downward pressure to the skin flap.

"God damn," Angus said.

Emeline stopped. Looked at him.

Lord?

She shook her head in resigned disgust and continued to peel the bandage. It released with a sloppy sound and Emeline unpacked the wet hand towel to find a spot not soaked in blood. She wiped Angus's shoulder and revealed the damage. Falling against the table, Angus had ripped open a row of sutures that held the skin flap in place, and probably broken whatever clotting inside that had stopped the bleeding. The flow quickened, encroaching to her knee on the floor.

Lord, I could let him bleed...

She growled to herself and carried on. "Jacob, did you bring a needle? Thread?"

"On the table."

"Well get it for me."

Jacob passed a needle to her, already threaded. Emeline thought for a moment. The sutures were one-at-a-time, each tied off.

If this was Angus's moment to die, there was nothing she could do to prevent it.

The pressure on her leg issued steady pain and Emeline shifted her hips, lowered her chest closer to Angus's, and relaxed into her work.

"Jacob, get me more thread. This won't do. I need a lot."

TWENTY NINE

Emeline leaned on her crutch at the bedroom door.
Angus sawed an exhalation, rolled, and the blanket
fell from his shoulder. A tiny spot of blood blotched the
bandage she'd applied. Emeline reviewed the contours of his
whiskered face, the shock of hair on his tall forehead. He was
handsome when he shaved, brutish when he didn't. She'd marveled at the stamina that powered him through a full day at the
derrick and then more hours of farm work. On the day they wed,
he looked like a man who could split a tree with an axe or heave
a bag of feed from the barn floor to the loft. How he'd sustained
his pace through a cloud of hangover had been a fearful mystery.

Now as he lay in bed with his arm gone, his eye hollow seemed
dark. She noticed gray hair in his mane. He grumbled in his sleep
as if nowhere could he find peace, and Emeline stood in amazement, realizing that the moment he woke, whatever evil animated
him would seize his tired features, beat back the fatigue and sickness, and deploy him to some form of nastiness or outright harm.
Awake he would be just as fearful as ever.

Would the Lord humble him? All men were in a state of insurrection against the Lord because they wanted to be Him, masters of their fates. Even her father had struggled to trust the Lord would provide. He had worked nonstop, sacrificing all his hours and attention to his business, never seeming to let go and trust the Lord to see to the things he didn't. She loved him in spite of the contradiction between his professed faith and his acted faith.

One time he explained it to her. "It is easy to believe the Lord is good. But how can I know that the Lord wants for me what I think is good? Maybe the Lord thinks something else is better."

It was the conundrum that compelled her father to trust all things to the Lord, and then work like He wasn't there at all.

That, exactly, was her problem. She'd stepped out in faith and though she knew for an absolute fact the Lord was with her, she didn't know what He wanted. She didn't know how to help, and thus, was helpless.

Emeline focused again on Angus. Maybe family time would mellow him; maybe an Adirondack chair, the crisp smell of spruce and the view of the lake he'd bragged about during their courtship—listening to the single car that passed by on the road as if the thrum of its tires was the most interesting thing all day—maybe these would turn his path.

Maybe the Lord took his arm to get his attention.

Though taking his eye hadn't done the trick.

"Angus?" she said.

He choked on a snore and opened his eye to a slit.

"Do you want to come downstairs for breakfast or should I have Deet bring it to you?"

"Hunh?"

"It's ten. Maybe you'd be happier if you took breakfast outside in the air."

"Happier?"

"Do you want to come for sausage and eggs, or have Deet bring them up?"

"Deet, huh?"

"He's at the barn, but I'll call him. I can't carry a tray up the steps on a crutch."

Angus rubbed his eye, wiped his nose. Rolled to the edge of the bed, slid his legs over the side, and drug himself into a seated posture. His organ peeked at her from his boxers. She turned away and when she glanced back, he grinned.

"How 'bout you suck some sausage for breakfast?"

"Don't be vulgar."

"Come over here." He tamped the bed. "Let's see how it's gonna work with one arm."

"Your breakfast is getting overdone." She crutched down the hall and labored down the stairs sideways. Behind her, the bedsprings groaned and Angus's feet struck the floor. She arrived in the kitchen as he clomped down the stairs. She stood at the stove and scooped eggs and sausage patties from the skillet; he wrapped his arm around her and pressed her pubic triangle.

"You notice something?" she said.

"Yeah. I got a pig needs some mud."

"Your pig got some mud."

"Hunh?"

"I'm pregnant."

He released her, sat on the table. Emeline watched his crinkled brow, and his eye, which seemed unseeing. "Can't a doctor get rid of it?"

THIRTY

The special insight came while Jacob leaned against the base of the walnut tree, embraced by clefts of root. Deet worked on the barn roof and Emeline cooked. Jacob couldn't steal whiskey while she peg-legged here and there in the kitchen, but the jug in the cabinet was the only open container. The dozen in the barn were sealed. He rested his head against the bark; draped his bare forearm across the trunk.

His throat was parched. Pap's whiskey tasted like a burning snowball, maybe with flecks of walnut. A sip would be real nice.

In all the times he'd played or loitered at the walnut on Devil's Elbow, Jacob had never seen the *presence*. He'd had a dawning awareness that his thoughts were different when he was there—just like he'd noticed his thoughts seemed more crisp and pleasurable after drinking walnut whiskey. But as he sat now, he was illuminated. The *presence* loitered nearby. Jacob closed his eyes, felt him, almost saw his face, a tan block with hard edges struggling for definition, as if form was of secondary relevance where he came from. With whiskey, things would be clearer.

Jacob shivered. Both the tree and Angus had lost a limb.

"Whiskey."

Jacob remembered his mother, cooing as she cradled him. As if driven by the *presence*, a sharp gust fluttered walnut leaves, issuing a sound like sizzling meat. He wriggled his bare toes, felt the muscles in his neck go taut, and his skin prickle like a needle was about to skewer him. He craned his neck, expecting to see the huge man behind him.

"Walnut Whiskey."

The skin on his face tightened as if he'd stepped into a frosty morning. From nowhere—*(four quarts make a gallon)*—he remembered. In the basement, a cupboard contained canned tomatoes, apples, pears, corn, venison. Empty Ball jars collected dust on the bottom shelf. A nearby bin held heaps of brass lids and threaded rings. There were four, he was sure.

"Plans for you boy. Plans."

Jacob approached the porch and nodded at Angus, who sat on an Adirondack chair with a cup of coffee balanced on his leg, stabilized by his hand. The other arm was gone, the shirtsleeve pinned to the shoulder. Angus had said nothing about his lost limb, nor had Emeline.

But Deet had grumbled while feeding the hogs that he'd be happy once the rest of Angus was torn off by the cathead spool.

Deet and Angus used to be products of the same mold. Deet was cooler, Angus rougher, but they both worked for the same things, griped about the same country problems. Both tore into him if he forgot to shuck corn. They laughed with the same voice the first time he gutted a chicken, accidentally sliced an intestine, and puked at the smell of runny chicken brownies on his hands. But since Emeline came, they were sharp around one another.

Remaining within Angus's good graces, especially now, was important. Deet's failure was Jacob's opportunity.

"You want me to bring more coffee?" Jacob said.

"Nah, fuck off."

"Yes sir."

The front door was open, the kitchen empty. Only fifteen feet and a screen door separated him from Angus. The bottom cabinet held the whiskey. He looked to the basement stairwell. If he waited, he'd have plenty, but he'd think clearer with a nip right now. He turned on the water faucet and grabbed a glass. At the hutch, he rapped the base of the glass to the floor as he popped open the sticky cabinet door.

"What the hell you doing?"

"Drink of water; want me to bring you a glass?"

"Quiet! I got the nerves today."

"Yes sir, Pap." He turned the faucet off and padded back to the hutch, knelt, poured a half-glass, and gingerly situated the jug back in the cabinet, with the thumb ring out and to the left, like he found it. He eased the door to where it stuck.

Since they'd found rattlers in the potato cellar last summer, climbing down the stairwell was a dark and damp terror. Jacob closed the door behind him and stood in absolute darkness. He sipped whiskey, swung his arm ahead, and stepped. The air grew colder, wetter, and he heard only the creaking stairs and the air passing through his nose with each breath. He counted steps and at ten, reached on his tiptoes and groped until he found a thin cord and a knot. He pulled and a yellow light bulb glowed.

A grimy combination of damp dust and mold caked the Ball jars. He'd have to wash them, but the only water source in the basement was a crack in the mortar.

One at a time, careful his feet didn't drum the stairs, he carried the jars to the top and left them on the side where only the most wayward foot might strike them. On the fifth trip, he gathered four rings and seals, pulled the lanyard, and crept back to the kitchen door.

Jacob finished his glass of whiskey, listened, and grew bolder still. He transferred the canning jars to the bottom corner of the closet. He filled the sink with soapy water, washed the breakfast dishes, and one by one, interspersed the Ball jars between.

Emeline struggled to her knees and stretched across the bed. She clasped her hands. *All right, Lord. Where are you? Ask, ask, ask? I've been asking. I've been knocking.*

She lifted herself until the bed corner pressed her abdomen, and imagined the outline of a baby pressing outward, growing. She'd noticed little changes, a slight increase in the heft of her breasts, the small swell of her belly.

I know I deceived him. I know it. You don't have to tell me that, Lord. I know it.

And what was she going to do about Deet? Doctor Fleming— as if he was an angel sent from the Lord—had warned her, but that was like finding a ten-year-old firebug standing in charred rubble and warning him about matches.

I do not encourage him!

She lifted her head, unclasped her hands, looked at the same old things. The broken clock. The wall with no pictures. The open closet, with nothing more than the clothes she'd arrived with on her wedding day. She traced her fingertips across a threadbare quilt, imagined shivering through frosty February nights, and drove the thought away.

I sip piss-warm coffee and watch tree leaves flicker. Giant cloud slugs closer on the horizon, and if it goes any slower I'll get a rifle and shoot it. I've had more bed rest the last two days than any time since the war. I have to do something, anything, but when I stand, my legs feel like the bones are gone and I'm walking on marrow.

My shoulder hollow is tender the way a man's sack might be tender if he slapped it on a stump and pounded it with a chunk of granite. Even the arm that ain't there hurts.

I was careless on the oilrig, a fool to hurry—like when I lost my eye, after Normandy. Woke in a pool of upchuck with Top Bouldin's boot in my ass. After a letter from Adolfina.

To be fair and honest I don't always have the best judgment. I need a shot of walnut shine.

My thoughts turn to the crinkle of bills in my pants pocket— everything'll have to be in my right pocket, now. The money'll need to last 'til something else comes along. I got money saved, but nobody knows it. The farm will sustain us, but funds to carry on with day-to-day living, the electricity, the phone, gasoline, farm supplies, feed—all that needs to come from somewhere else. Let these fuckin parasites put in sixteen-hour workdays.

Lookit that punk on the barn roof, Deet, smirking a hundred yards away. I know what's going on. I was young; I felt my oats. There's a fresh woman in the house—with all the edgy gaiety, the vaginal perfume, somber and urgent as a full moon. Deet smells her, yearns for her.

Deet wants my woman and I want my whiskey.

I rock back and forth as I gather myself from the recess of the Adirondack chair, brace my weight against the wide arm slat and rise on wobbly legs. After a few seconds feeling faint my heart starts pounding and I get a little blood in my head and I feel all right. I cross the lot toward the barn. The dogs see me coming.

"What do you want, hunh?" I lob a small stone, but without my left arm as a counterweight, the rock shoots wide and bounces from the pen. Rebel barks reproof. Bitch in the next kennel is quiet.

"Shut up!" I cup my hand to my ear. The noise jabs; my spine tingles. I press my ear to my shoulder and clamp the other with my hand, move on to the truck. The jug on the floor is empty; I tip it and a black crescent of whiskey lines the bottom corner. I heft it to my mouth and wait as the last drop eases down the jug.

Deet watches from the barn roof.

I toss the jug. Inside the barn, twelve more line the wall at the back left corner. I carry the first to the shop workbench, wipe grime from the cap and neck, buff a yellow square of light on the jug's shoulder. Now we're talking.

How the fuck to open it?

Jacob heard his old man's feet shuffle across the porch floor. He watched from the window as Angus walked to the Ford and then the barn.

Deet worked at the edge of the barn roof with his back to the house. Emeline was upstairs. Jacob slipped his fingers through the mouths of four jars and hurried to the screen door. He glanced upstairs and imagined he heard a Bible page turning, then outside to the shop entrance at the barn. He stepped onto the porch. Deet was climbing down the ladder. The screen door smacked closed. Jacob froze, exposed with a Ball jar on each wrist like a

swollen glass hoof. Deet was half way to the ground. Jacob ran
the length of the porch and leaped over the lakeside end. His heels
dug skid marks as he slid feet first; he scurried back to the porch
and peered over.

Deet stood at the foot of the ladder, facing the house. He
brought his forearm to his brow and entered the barn.

Jacob hid the jars in a huckleberry bush, thirty feet down
slope.

I twist the cap and the jug turns so I drop it in the bench vise.
Two dowels set a foot apart balance the threaded center spindle.
I turn the handle until the jaws expand eight inches, then rest
the jug between. I snug the jaws and twist the cap.

The warm whiskey burns like a gulp of glowing embers; a
nutty, gasoline heat lingers. I gulp, rest the jug on the table, wipe
my mouth with my sleeve. I work one thing at a time, no conser-
vation of motion. No synchronization. No left hand anticipating
and setting the scene for the right. Losing an arm feels like losing
half my brain too.

Deet fills his apron with roofing nails at the bench.

"You ain't done with that roof yet?"

"Why don't you climb up and give me a hand?"

"Best watch your tongue. I only got one arm but I know what
to do with it. And I been watching you."

"Well, I seen you."

A truck pulls in front of the house. Deet twists. "You expecting company?"

I look through the open bay. A man steps out holding a large
book under his arm; he slams the truck door with his boot.

"Who's that?"

"That's the fella said the Farmall was his."

I look at my jug of whiskey. "Tell him I ain't here."

"Tell him yourself."

I swat at Deet but he's already backed away. He circles outside to the ladder and watches from the third rung as I lope across the lot. I get dizzy with being steamed but he won't know. He's climbed the porch steps and looks at the lake.

"What the hell you want?" I plant a fist on my hip at the center of the turning circle, just beyond the stacks of lumber Deet's disassembled from the barn roof.

The man turns. "I'm here to collect a piece of property belongs to me."

"And who the hell are you?"

"Jeb Pitlake. I own the Farmall—"

"You own shit." I step closer.

"I got the proof right here, Mr. Hardgrave, and I'd hoped we could settle this amicably."

"How 'bout I get the shotgun out the house? That *amical* enough?"

"Don't get excited, now. Just take a look at my ledger and you'll see I bought that white tractor you got down by the chicken coops—I bought that when I bought the dealership. It's plain as day."

"Bullshit."

"I matched the serial number when your son had it in town. That's my tractor."

"When you buy the dealership? Forty-seven?"

"That's right."

"And you just now figured out you never laid eyes on your tractor 'til you saw mine?"

"Well, see, that tractor can't be white. Farmall won't allow it—that's a display tractor. I knew I had one on the books, look here," he opens the ledger and points. I stay ten feet away so I don't knock his fuckin head off. "This line right here, and then right here, don't you want to see this—" he tabs to another page, "and every year after. I've been carrying that property the whole time."

"You're some kinda thief." A flicker of motion on the porch, behind Pitlake, draws my eye. Jacob holds a rifle behind the screen door.

"My only recourse is the courthouse."

"I think I'm gonna shoot you."

"You'll lose more than just the tractor if I have to sue you."

I cross him and climb the steps. Jacob opens the screen.

Pitlake hurries to his truck. "You're crazy."

Jacob meets me on the porch and I swipe the rifle from his outstretched hands. I swing the lever like an old west cowboy, flip the rifle and step forward, loaded and aiming from the hip. I ratchet the hammer and squeeze the trigger. The 30-30 barks and jumps. The bullet goes high. Pitlake spins tires in reverse down the lane. I cycle a fresh round, point into the rising dust, and squeeze off another shot.

Deet watched Angus resume his Adirondack seat and rest the rifle across his knees. He still tingled from the excitement. Standing on the ladder, watching his besotted father give Pitlake hell, He'd been ready to join the fight.

On Pitlake's side.

He crawled over the edge and stood on a heavy crossbeam. A slight breeze cooled his skin and he looked at the ground twenty-five feet below. He'd squared the new oak beams a few days before and fixed them to the cross-supports yesterday. This morning he added salvaged boards, starting at the apex. Facing down slope, he'd lost his balance and nearly rolled into the barn—a dozen-foot fall to the loft—before realizing he should start at the bottom and rip the last boards on the table saw.

He looked across his shoulder and saw he rifle leaning on the porch rail. Angus went inside the house.

Deet knelt and resumed where he'd run out of nails, and his eye drifted to the wood shop below. There was a set of tools that could mean a different kind of future for a man like him—a future that beat working a field under an angry sun, or shoveling shit from a pig stall. Or hammering nails into a barn roof.

"I'd take a barn like this," he said aloud. "Sell the animals, the hay, the corn. Spread the shit in the garden, where Em could grow flowers and tomatoes. Fill all that empty space with wood. Hang a big sign out by the road, Hardgrave Hardwood Furniture."

He shook his head. "Emeline could cut those pig-shit flowers every year, and put them on her first husband's grave."

"Don't get into this on your own, you hear?" Looking at Jacob, I nod at a Mickey Mouse glass with a half-inch of walnut whiskey at the bottom. Poising the jug to the tipping point with the strength of my remaining hand, and tickled as shit to find the strength at all, I half-fill a second glass.

A car door clanks outside. I put the jug on the bottom hutch shelf and close the cabinet door.

"Finish that up."

Jake empties the glass in an extended swallow.

Outside, Brad Chambers leans on the hood of his car. He looks up to Deet pounding nails on the roof.

I ruffle Jacob's hair and with my hand on his shoulder guide him to the screen door. I kneel and lock onto the boy's sloshed eyes. "You done good this morning, backing me up with the rifle, you hear? You always got to back me up. That's how a Hardgrave does it."

Jacob nods.

"Get your chores done early and maybe I'll tell you a story about where this shine comes from. All right. Git."

Jacob leaps the steps, stumbles, flops in the dirt. Chambers brays. I step onto the porch. Jacob brushes his knees and limps to the barn, and his head turns as he passes Chambers and I see a scowl to make a father proud.

"What happened to your arm, Mister Hardgrave?"

"You bring rent?"

"That's right."

"Hand it over. Be on your way."

"I got no particular hurry." Chambers fishes crumpled bills from his jeans.

"That's a full month due."

Chambers climbs the steps and passes money to me.

"I seen boys with limbs blown off," Chambers says. "Them gooks was something. Mile after mile of em, mortar rounds like rain, and their officers didn't give a hidy-ho if they was hitting their own, so long as they was hitting ours too. I seen boys—I'll never forget." He drops his chin to his chest.

"Yeah, well them krauts wasn't no slouches neither," I say.

"No they wasn't. You getting by all right? Need anything from town, an extra hand about the place? Looks like you had trouble with the storm this week."

"Blowed that whole corner section to the ground. Deet'll have it fixed today."

"You want to sit for a minute, Mister Hardgrave? Injured man needs rest. You can't let everybody force you back to work so soon."

"Don't I know it?" I sit.

Chambers tests the porch rail for sturdiness and leans. "What happened?"

"Just an accident at the derrick. God forsaken company. Broke equipment, dangerous configurations. If I start bitching now, I'll never finish."

"A man's got to look after himself, these days."

"That's hard when everyone wants a piece of you, and can't think for their damn selves." I thrust my chin toward the barn. "That one wouldn't pull his head out his ass if he was fartin' fire."

"I was you, I'd drive him down to the recruiting station. Make him a man."

"He'd get himself killed or maimed, and hell, I only got one arm; I need his sorry ass here. Turn him into a man myself."

Chambers shifts. "How's your wife? Can't be too easy getting around on a busted leg."

"She's alive."

I sit deeper in the Adirondack, rub the eye patch strap on my left side, which requires a twisting motion that jostles my stump against the chair's arm. Hurts like torture. I smack my hand on the arm slat. Blink a quarter pint of water from my eye. "What happened at the house with Em?"

"I was upstairs and she came charging in. Hell, I didn't know she was your missus; I just heard noise. I come out the bathroom ready to tear into someone, and she let out a yell and fell down the steps. That's the honest-to-God truth. I ran down to help her. Bone was clean through the skin."

"That right?"

"Clean through. I ran and got Doc Fleming. That leg of hers was an awful mess. But who wants a woman for her legs, right? Say, you mind if I get a drink of water 'fore I take off?"

"Kitchen's on the right."

Chambers enters the house.

"I'll do you one better," I call.

I wait a moment, and fail to hear any goings-on in the house due to the steady thudding of hammer and nail at the barn.

"I say I'll do you one better!"

I stand, look inside. Behind the screen, Chambers comes toward me. "You want water while I'm at it?"

"Fetch the jug from the base of the hutch. My glass is on the table."

Chambers returns, sniffs the opening. "Wood stain or whiskey?"

"Bit o' both."

Chambers covers the bottom of his glass with fluid and brings the rim to his lips. He brings the glass down, empty.

"I know you want more."

"Damn! That's a spiteful drink."

"Takes a minute to grow on you. Have another."

Chambers pours an inch in the glass. "You—whew." He pounds his chest and coughs. "You 'still this?"

"Nah. But I could."

Chambers grins.

"Ain't a bad idea," I say. "With bumper crops flooding the market, a fella'd work like a dog and go broke. Lowest prices in twenty years. There's hooch houses in town paying good money for squeezin's like this."

"Tastes like walnuts. What gives it the bite?"

"Them walnuts come from a tree right over the knoll by the lake."

"Well, I don't know. Walnut oil looks like linseed or any other. It ain't black."

"The black comes from the rind."

"Just like stain."

"That's right."

"You know it's making your teeth black?"

"No shit?"

"None. You got the boiler? That's the hardest to find."

I regard him and then watch Deet on the barn roof, his head turned to the side as if keeping the porch in his peripheral sight. Chambers finishes his drink.

Jacob emerges from the bottom floor of the barn with a tin pail dangling from his hand, shoulder bent with the weight, and carries it to the dog pens. "Boiler's nothing but a barrel."

Chambers nods toward the barn. "What you got in the pens?"

"Dog from a fight t' other week—and another."

"Another? A breeder?"

"You gonna tell me you know blood sport too?"

"Maybe. Let me take a look."

I waive. "Have at it. I'm staying here."

Chambers walks to the kennels. I sip. Chambers knows more than he lets on—knows something about dogs. Knows something about stilling shine. You don't know the language without knowing the art. Chambers braces his hands at the top of the kennel and leans close to the wire. The pit bulls are silent. I shift forward. Drink. Chambers moves to the side, hunkers low for a look at the dogs' bellies. He sticks his finger through the chicken wire, looks back at me and shakes his head.

Minute later Chambers sits on the porch. "The bitch—she ain't mean, but that don't matter. You can make any dog mean. But you can't spice a dog's genes, and you can't make a coward game."

I drink. "Just like men."

Chambers nods. "That bitch—she's got some nice lines. Lot of lungs, loose skin at the neck. You want that. I didn't stick my hand in to open her jaw and get a look at her mouth, but I'll wager she's sound."

I grin. "Just about what I thought."

"She's also hot."

"Time to let her get friendly with Rebel."

"Well, that's the rub. That cripple ain't worth a damn, as a fighter. He might whup ass on a collie—or spook a prowler, but he's no fighter. See him lick my finger?"

"That's Jake lovin' on him every day. Flat ruin a dog."

"That's true, but Rebel musta been the runt, or something. Breed him, you'll wish you hadn't."

"Fact is, I saw him fight. He didn't quit for nothing. Passed out, and still clamped on the other pit's neck like he'd die before he'd let up. Ain't nobody knows a game dog till he sees him in a ring."

"Well, that's game, and if you saw it you saw it. Personally, I wouldn't give a turnip's titty for a game dog. You seen men in France, just like I saw in Korea. Some of us got mean enough to do what we had to. Figured we'd sort out our minds later, if we lived that long. And some saw the blood and gore and killing and didn't have the stomach to save themselves. I seen men like that dog—that'd lick a gook's finger, if he offered."

"Maybe." I slouch. "You got some opinions."

"My daddy fought pits, 'fore he died. I know them dogs. I don't give two hoots for a game dog. I want a winner. A mean sumbitch, ain't afraid to shred another. Men talk game like it's more important than teeth. No sir, Mister Hardgrave. You give me a mean, fightin' mad pit—I'll take him over a game no-quitter every day of the week. The game dog won't quit, but he'll sure as hell die."

"Why don't you come by Tuesday? Say, five?"

Finished feeding the dogs, Jacob circled the barn, the field, the house, and found a station at the corner by the spruce tree within earshot of Angus and the fellow in the red and white car. The ground dampened his behind.

Jacob considered running the canning jars behind the house, through the cornfield and behind the barn. While he weighed this alternate route's merits, Angus and Chambers closed their conversation. A car ignition sounded, and Angus tramped inside the house. Jacob crawled to the edge of the porch. Deet hammered on the barn roof.

Jacob stepped back from the siding, looked at Emeline's second story window, and each of the others. They reflected trees and clouds. He'd have to assume no one watched. He ran to the huckleberry thicket, grabbed the Ball jars, and followed a long, circuitous path through the orchard to the barn's lower level. He shushed Rebel at the kennel. The hogs grunted; the corncrib was empty.

Heavy black flies swarmed in the stairway to the second floor; he couldn't swat with his hands covered in Ball jars. They landed on his face, his hair; Jacob rested two quart glasses on the stairwell, beat back the flies, and eased the door open. At the back corner, across the bay filled with shop tools, partly visible from where Deet worked, eleven jugs of walnut whiskey stood at attention like black-uniformed soldiers. Jacob slunk onto the main bay, pressed his back to the wall and looked at the roof. The loft blocked him from Deet's view. Stepping sideways, Jacob circled the shop's perimeter, his eyes fixed on the location of Deet's hammering. When it became apparent Deet wouldn't be able to see him, even if he dangled his head into the opening, Jacob stole to the back corner.

He tested each gallon jug. Too weak to break the rust seal on the first, second....sixth, seventh. Finally one cap spun beneath his fingers. He emptied the jug into the four Ball jars, capping each one tightly before pouring the next. Above, Deet smacked nails through the roof boards. The jug empty, Jacob swapped it for the first and then stood with his hand to his chin. Pap would most likely start at one end or the other—but which end? Jacob wiped sweaty hands on his trouser bottoms, then swapped the first, empty jug, for the fifth.

He peered through a knothole at the house. Pap was inside. Least he wasn't on the porch.

One at a time, Jacob carried the canning jars to the loft and stashed all four vertically between bales of hay. Reconsidering, he carried one back to the shop level, retraced his route along the wall, and cached it on the bottom floor in a dark cubby behind the cast iron bathtub he'd need to fill with corn. That left just one thing.

The walnut tree, the *presence,* had provided the insight. Below the workbench, cans of walnut stain, cherry stain, acetone, turpentine, denatured alcohol, and linseed oil collected dust. Mixed together, they'd look and probly smell like walnut whiskey. Might even taste like it.

THIRTY ONE

Deet nailed weathered boards to new oak rafters on the barn roof. The sun beat his shoulders a shade of bronze and the sweat that collected at his brow dropped like fat rain to the parched planks. He pinched the bridge of his nose and his eyes stung with salt.

Angus's altercation with Pitlake replayed like a movie in his mind. Even with one arm, Angus was a scrappy bastard. Seeing it play out again, the same tide rushed through Deet. If Pitlake would have faced Angus, rifle and all, Deet knew he would have joined the fray. That was the problem. Everything about this place was the problem.

Living here prompted bad decisions.

Angus was bound to lose the Farmall. If Pitlake owned the property, it shouldn't have been part of the Margulies estate. Simple honesty weighed on Pitlake's side.

Deet sat on the roof and absorbed a birds-eye view of the farm. The scope took him aback. To his right, a listless cornfield. Beyond, a wick of forest obscured the widow McClellan's house.

Following leftward, the Hardgrave farmhouse withstood another summer with twenty-year-old paint, and beyond, Lake Oniasant was calm as a mud puddle. His circumstances had a beauty from height that wasn't conceivable from the ground.

Other land, farther out, would be as beautiful. It was time to go.

Deet sat with his arms wrapped around his knees, conflicted.

In an effort to bring more money to the household, he had encouraged Angus to distill liquor. The old family business allured with mystery and profit, but any progress that direction would deepen his subservience to Angus. The wood shop, which he dreamed of owning, was ill gotten.

And Emeline? Another nugget of temptation, and only his most fanciful imagination could concoct a happy ending. He rested his chin on his knee. She made worse decisions than him.

Surely the southern states offered green land and opportunities for a man wanting to build something, and willing to pay in sweat and pain. Maybe one of those states had a beautiful woman waiting for him. An unmarried woman. North Carolina was famous for furniture factories.

The knapsack under his bed still held everything he'd need, minus the two dollars he'd spent on hamburgers. He wouldn't need to slaughter the animals if Emeline would be around to keep them. Resolved, he stood. He'd head out after dark. Every day he waited would make the decision more difficult.

Deet looked toward the sun, checked his pocket watch. Emeline's appointment with Doctor Fleming commenced in a half hour. Glancing over the edge of the barn roof, he saw the Farmall and the wagon with a soft bed of loose hay. He laughed. May as well take the truck. Angus wouldn't be driving. He climbed down the ladder and a minute later, stood at the living room entrance.

Emeline rested on the couch and Angus sat at the kitchen table, hunched over a glass.

"Em, you ready to go?"

She glanced at the kitchen and nodded.

"Where?" Angus said.

"Thought I'd take her to the doctor in the truck."

"You know," Angus said, "it's been—shit—what? Three days since I lost my arm. Feels like I shoved the stump in a nest of hornets. You ain't once volunteered to take me to the doctor."

"You want to come along?"

"That ain't the cussed point."

"You don't have an ornery somebody saying you can't go, like she does. Where's the truck key?"

"Take the tractor."

"Doesn't make sense to take the tractor. That Pitlake fella's looking for trouble. The Ford's sitting out front, and you sure as hell ain't going anywhere."

"I don't know what you two got going on, but it ain't gonna be in my truck."

Emeline perked on the sofa. "What did you say?"

"I don't know." Angus fixed his eye on Deet. "You want to take her, fine. But not in my truck."

"We'll take the tractor," Emeline said. "It'll be fine."

Deet gritted his teeth. Backed away. Outside he hitched the trailer and pulled the Farmall in front of the house. He filled his arms with blankets from the linen closet. Standing in the hay, he whipped them open and dropped them one by one, aware of Emeline watching on the porch, leaning on the crutch he'd made.

"I appreciate you taking me to the doctor," she said.

"It's nothing." Deet carried her down the steps and placed her on the edge bale. "Can you get into the middle on your own?"

"I think I can manage."

She held him as he slipped away and her lips grazed his retreating shoulder. Was he confused? Deet studied her sun-shrunken pupils, the tinge of redness splotched on her cheek. "What's wrong with you?"

He jumped to the tractor seat, throttled up. The tractor lurched and he steered along the edge of the driveway. He pulled onto the road with a wide turn, barely slowing.

"You lost a bale!" Emeline cried.

He looked. She'd braced her arms wide on the bales and splayed her legs. At the rear of the trailer, a bale had fallen to the middle of the road, thirty yards back. He slammed the throttle leftward. The engine settled; he tramped the clutch, disengaged the gear, locked the brake.

The bale prickled his forearms and thighs; he tossed it the last ten feet and avoided meeting her eyes while he secured it behind a walnut slat.

He strode past her.

"Deet! What is the matter?"

He jumped on the tractor and resumed toward Walnut. Pushed the throttle all the way to the right.

"What's the matter?" he slammed his hand to the wheel and the tractor jerked.

She wanted to play games. There'd be jobs in Pittsburg, if he couldn't make it to North Carolina. That's what his buddies always said when they dreamed of getting away—back when he had buddies, before Angus indentured him. The steel mills could always use a body. He imagined the smelters and smoke he'd seen in school textbooks, the noise of clattering pipes, orange sparks from the welders.

Tonight.

Her back to the tractor, Emeline brushed tangles of hair from her face then spread her arms wide on the bales for balance. A familiar stand of trees passed on the right; she turned and the dust blew into her face. Deet never drove so fast. She closed her eyes and tried to retreat to a point of clarity in her mind.

The Lord would protect her from the waxing evil around her. He would. But it would be good stewardship to ask Doctor Fleming to give her a stronger cast—in case the Lord should need her to flee.

The tractor slowed. Town. She watched Deet, erect in the seat, shoulders jutting square. He was angry with her now, but if she believed Doctor Fleming, Deet's anger resulted from not possessing her. He had the same inclinations as other men, and they made him drive like a fool, but at least he didn't grab her hair and alley-oop her to a cave. Or to a car seat. He humored her with respect, which was a step better than having none at all.

How would things have been different if Deet had driven by, instead of Brad?

Chambers and Angus went about their conquests with urgency. Brad pinned her to the seat, smothered her, bit her lip. Angus pressed forward, one moment pointing out Mars, the next, tying her wrists and ankles and ramming through her pubic tangle.

She had avoided Chambers and after a few days discovered he prowled at her home, mirrored her movements in town, laid siege to her window at night. He threw pebbles at the glass and stared at her when she peeked in the darkness. He jiggled the door handles. He climbed the tree by the porch.

Of course the Lord had said to marry Angus.

Chambers claimed her. Angus owned her. And her heart softened for the boy-man on the tractor. What of *her*, though—with a baby in her belly? How could she feed it? What could be more the Lord's doing than providing her a decent man who wanted to work all the time, and only stopped to take her to the doctor, or buy a cheeseburger? How could the Lord desire that she be with Angus? It looked more like the workings of chance and stupidity than the Lord Almighty. She felt like it was almost blasphemy to pray at all.

Deet stopped the tractor in front of Doctor Fleming's, jumped from the seat and offered a flat smile. "Let me help you down." He climbed aboard and stooped; she threw her arm over his shoulder.

"Don't be angry, Deet."

"It ain't a choice."

Doctor Fleming opened the door. "What is this?" Fleming indicated the cast with the belt wrapped for support. "I already had it secure with the ace bandage."

"I have to get around," she said, and wished she had prepared more convincing words.

Deet angled her through the first door, navigated the anteroom and pushed open the second door with his back. He rested her on the table. "I'll be outside."

Fleming closed the door, shuffled beside her.

"You haven't taken my advice."

"You have to give me a stronger cast."

"Too early." Gently, he lifted her leg. He loosened the leather belt, separated the split cast, secured her ankle with his hand. He eased off the cast. She stared at his erratic hair-part, widening to baldness. He looked under the cast, glanced at her face.

"Don't move." He sniffled candidly and peered close at the bandage. She leaned closer. The wound was tingly-numb, purple from knee to ankle, but the flesh was beginning to seal.

"Improvement," he said. "The fracture has set, but this redness tells me the infection will come back if we are not careful. Feel how warm?" He pressed her fingertips to the skin bordering the wound.

Dr. Fleming daubed her leg from ankle to knee with a mildly soapy washcloth, and again with a wet one. As her skin dried, he opened the cast under the light, wiped it out, dried it with a towel, then sprinkled cornstarch inside.

"Another shot of penicillin today, and this cast goes back on for another week. If the infection passes, I'll give you a heavy cast, and you can resume your domestic duties. Somewhat."

"Can't you give me a thicker cast now?"

"The ossification is delicate. I don't want to encourage you to put your weight on it. If you re-break your leg, you'll limp the rest of your life. A week isn't so long, is it?"

"But I need to get about the house—and I'm already—"

He shook his head sideways.

"I have a baby to think about."

Fleming froze, frowned. "Congratulations, I hope. But no."

Jacob said, "Gonna shuck corn for the hogs, Pap."

. "I want you to do something." Angus sat on the Adirondack chair, his head resting against the back. "Corner of the barn, I got a row of jugs. I want you to bring em to me. Every one."

Jacob nodded.

"I want you to take em downstairs, where it's cool all the time."

"On the floor?"

"Nah. Take them suitcases to the burn barrel. Put the jugs on the rack."

"Yessir."

"You ain't much, Jake, but you're the best of the lot. Then bring me that old Remington single-shot twenty two—the one without a shoulder plate—and a box of shells."

"Yessir."

"Get on now. 'Fore your respect and adoration piss me off."

Jacob ran to the barn, surveyed the line of jugs. He reached for the first, paused, stood over the fourth and fifth. The color was off; the dust didn't match. What if Angus wanted to look at them? Or noticed four of the same color and then the fifth was off? Better to take the miscolored one first. Jacob breathed deep, slipped his thumbs through the neck loops and carried the fourth and fifth jugs across the barn, the meadow. Up the steps.

Angus watched. Tipped his cup sideways.

Jacob stretched his step.

"Hold up. I want a porch jug. Tired of walking to the hutch. Gimme that damn jug."

Jacob put the fifth on the floor and handed his father the fourth.

Or was he confused?

Shit.

Angus cracked the seal of the miscolored whiskey. Wiped the jug mouth with his sleeve. Braced the heft of the jug on his thigh.

"Hold my cup, son."

Jacob grasped the cup.

"Hold steady, she won't bite." Angus poured.

Jacob shrank from the smell. "Pap?"

Angus squinted at him.

"Pap, that don't smell like what you gimme me yesterday."

Angus leaned forward and put the jug on the ground, took the cup from his son's hands. Sniffed. Sipped. Spat to the porch.

"What?"

Jacob quivered.

"That goat-fuckin widow!"

"She tricked you, Pap."

Deet stretched Emeline's dress flat before lifting her and seemed to hold his head away as he carried her from Dr. Fleming's office. At the trailer Emeline said, "I want to walk—set me down and give me the crutch. Please."

"Suit yourself."

Deet tipped her on the sidewalk; she reached to a tree while he retrieved the crutch from the tractor.

"Where you going?"

"Prescott's. Can you park by the storefront and let me stretch? I want to buy a few things."

"That's an eighth mile."

"I have a crutch."

He started the tractor and paced her.

"You don't need to putt beside me. Go on, and I'll be there when I get there."

He drove ahead, and stopped. She caught up to him in a dozen yards.

"Maybe I'll walk with you," he said. "So you don't bust your head on the cement." He tramped beside her, thumbs hooked through his belt loops.

"If you like."

"You're not angry?" Deet said.

She stumbled on a mismatched sidewalk panel and he jumped to her; she caught her step and he released her arm. "I wonder how it would be if we'd met in the beginning," she said.

"How you mean?"

"You're decent. That's all."

He tilted his head to maple leaves fluttering upside down. "I'm a game to you."

"That's not true. We share an attraction that we mustn't follow."

"We did."

"We can't just do whatever we want. There are rules."

"Whose rules? Angus's?"

"God's."

"Yeah, well I don't know."

She limped faster to match his stride.

He continued, "All I know is you've got me bollixed, good."

"Slower, Deet. I can't keep up."

He moderated his pace. "You feel it. I see it working you."

"You don't know what you see. I'm going to have a baby. I'm married."

"Well, none of it matters anyway. I've set my mind. There's something I'm going to tell you. Maybe." Deet hesitated as he walked, adding a wobbling swagger to his gait. "What do you think happened to my mother?"

"Oh, Deet... I don't know. Just heard things. You know."

"I know what?"

"She ran away with a man while Angus was at the war."

"She didn't run—with a man, or without. Did Angus say that? Well, no matter."

Emeline sat on a bench. He stood to the side, looking at the sky.

"Do you remember her?"

"Some. She died in December of '46. Angus shot a buck, so I know it was buck season. He didn't poach much back then. I remember the blood stains in the barn and on the snow outside where he drug the deer up from the lake."

"He killed the deer at the lake?"

"Devil's Elbow."

"How old were you?"

"Six, I guess."

"Did your mother say anything before...?"

"No. Don't think she knew what was coming." He kicked a small stone, waited, head angled upward. "A front's coming in. The leaves turn upside down."

"How long was it before Angus married again?" She leveraged to her feet with the crutch.

"We didn't go hungry and Pap don't cook." Deet fell in beside her. "The second Mrs. Hardgrave lasted a couple years, and then he picked up Lucy Mae. Jacob is eight, so Lucy lasted seven years. Reigning champ."

"If you think Angus did something to them, why didn't you tell anybody?"

"How? Ride the tractor to Sheriff Heilbrun and spill my guts? I can't even convince you."

"Do you remember what happened with Lucy Mae?"

"Once Pap finds something that works, he don't have much imagination. It was last December. They'd been arguing long as I could remember, but things changed. Used to be he'd yell and hit her and she'd pipe down, but then it got so he didn't even raise his voice. Lucy Mae started out with a lot of pluck. I used to hide behind her and she'd back Pap into a corner when he was laying into me. By the end, she did what he said. No back sass."

"I see."

"I don't think you do. I know Pap killed Lucy Mae. I've seen him burn through women like a fella smokes cigarettes, putting the flame to one while he stubs out the last. He's done it my whole life, and my mother was the first he ground in the mud. You'll be his fourth, lest you wise up."

Her upper lip was tucked under her lower lip. "How did he kill her—"

"He stuck an ought-six in her mouth."

THIRTY TWO

"You see what I'm doing, boy?" Angus gulped from his mug of walnut whiskey and lifted the .22. He'd long ago stripped the walnut stock and polished a hundred coats of linseed oil to a satin glow. The barrel was silver, the bluing stripped by years of use.

Jacob watched. The rifle barrel rested on the porch rail; Angus leaned with the stock tucked in his shoulder, elbow on knee, finger on trigger.

"I see."

"'Cept you'd have your hand there on the guard by the barrel. When you get old, like me, and wise, you won't need your other arm. So we'll probly get rid of it. But for now you're allowed to use it." Angus blinked. "You see that blue jay on the maple?"

Jacob nodded.

"Keep your eyes on that bird. See, I let out my breath. Squeeze nice and easy. I don't know when it's gonna—"

The .22 cracked and the bird exploded into feathers. It fell.

"Wow! Lucky shot!"

Angus's jaw tightened. "I don't miss with a rifle." He drank from the mug.

"Bet you can't shoot it again."

"That ain't fifty feet. Ain't even a challenge. Run and move him out a ways."

Jacob looked at the rifle.

"Go on, now! Get that bird and move him out."

At the bird Jacob looked over his shoulder. Angus sat in his chair; the rifle rested on the porch rail. Jacob stooped to the blue jay. Its eye was unblinking, its beak open. Tiny talons out-stretched. A great part of it was missing. He lifted it by the tail feathers.

"Run him out another thirty paces—down that sassafras tree."

Jacob stopped at the tree and turned. Angus had disappeared behind the porch rail, only the crown of his head visible, and a shiny silver dot that was the muzzle.

"Hold him out in the air."

Arm trembling, Jacob dangled the bird. Squirming, he bent his hips from the bird. The rifle barrel was a perfect dot.

Jacob felt a tiny amount of urine escape.

"Steady, now."

Tears pressed from his eyes and rolled down his cheeks. His stomach drew tight. The blue jay jolted out of his hand and al-most instantaneously he heard a crack! but he'd already jumped a foot to the side.

"Pick him up again!"

"There ain't nothing to pick up!"

"Guess that means I got lucky again. Hunh?"

"You're the best shot in the whole world, Pap."

"Don't you forget it. Now get back here and I'll teach you."

"I still got to shuck the corn for the hogs."

"It ain't even noon. Get your ass up here."

Jacob ran with his hands cupped at his privates.

"You see any birds around? Chipmunks? Why you holding your mess?" Angus pointed the barrel and pushed Jacob's hands aside. "Get excited, huh. Well the rules are the same now as when you was two. You piss yourself, you sit in it all day. Now go find me another animal."

"They're all scared off."

"Well, they're dumb animals. They'll be back, no time. Grab a chair."

Jacob dragged a second Adirondack, painted green, and sat on the edge.

"That's too low. Run in the house and get a Book of the Year."

Jacob returned a moment later with the 1953 Britannica.

"Slap it on the chair. I guess I don't mind you sitting on the Britannica with pissy shorts. Take this and lay the barrel on the ledge. See how the stock fits in your shoulder? You want it nice and snug." Angus talked him through framing a sight picture. "All right. You got it? Let your breath out and when your belly's empty, pull the trigger real slow."

"I'm not pointing at anything."

"Just pull the trigger."

Jacob released his breath. Pressed the trigger, felt it move beneath his finger, until a spring popped.

"Nothing happened."

"'Course not. Wasn't loaded. But you got the hang of it."

"Can I shuck the corn now?"

Deet watched Emeline recoil. He took her arm. She leaned on the crutch.

"A deer rifle? How? Where?"

"Gonna rain," Deet said. He looked both ways on the sidewalk, tilted his head back and sniffed the air, then glanced ahead. She read the set of his jaw and the way his eyes roamed their path, almost as if he stared into the future and navigated a course through chaos. He seemed cognizant in a way that was beyond Angus's chemistry.

"You saw... Angus kill Lucy Mae?"

"Storm's coming from the east. See them thunderheads?"

"How did it happen?"

"Just like I figure he did my Ma, in the barn." His voice was gritty. "Why reinvent the wheel?"

"You work for him every day."

"What am I gonna do? Tell him I saw it? 'I can't work in the barn, Pap, 'cause you shot your wife and some of her brains is on the rafters."

"That's so terrible. Don't say any more."

"He had ahold of her hair, in the back, and the rifle at his hip. She cried and squealed and begged him not to do it, 'til he shoved the barrel in her mouth."

"Don't tell me."

"She wasn't but four foot tall. Angus was on his knees. By the time I had the guts to help—"

"I can't hear this!"

"I stuck around for you, Emeline! I should have been somewhere else by now. I had it all layed out. But once you showed up, I couldn't stand to leave."

She took his hand.

"I was hunting below McClellan's place. Didn't see hide nor hair all morning. Angus and me hunt separate because he likes to ambush a deer, where I like to stalk one. Give the buck a chance, you know? We'd got a dusting of snow the night before and I was cold. There's a hollow with some thickets where they like to lay about a mile closer to town, as the crow flies. Well I heard a shot at about ten, down by Devil's Elbow."

"I thought that's where Angus shot the deer when your mother disappeared."

"You noticed that? So I decided I'd see his kill and get lunch before heading to the hollow. I got to the house about eleven and I heard him yelling in the barn—thought he'd lost his mind, until him and Lucy Mae come into view, and he let out a punch that dropped her to the ground with a sound I heard seventy yards away. I stood at the spruce. The wind'd already blown the snow off the knoll, so I didn't leave any tracks. I'm twenty feet into a sprint when he grabs his rifle from the wall and gets on his knees so he can shove it in her mouth. He didn't hesitate. It was over. I turned around and hid by the porch with my 30-30 sighted on Pap for ten minutes while he slumped beside her like he was sorry. I wanted to shoot him so bad I couldn't think. I figured I could drag him to the woods and make it look like an accident, except for the mess he'd made in the barn. Ten minutes I laid on the ground, my belly cold and my fingers so numb I couldn't feel the trigger. If I had a do-over, I'd have shot him in the yard, dumped him in the lake tied with a few cinder blocks, and poured water on the boards 'till the blood washed out—but I couldn't think. I kept imagining he'd just killed my Ma—though she's been dead all these years. I saw splotches of blood on the barn floor, and I just watched."

"God have mercy."

"Eventually he carries her down the trail to the walnut tree. Walks right past me, but he's blabbering God would get him someday."

"What about the blood in the barn?"

"He pulled the floor planks and swapped em with wall boards. They're thicker than wall boards, and he had to pair them up to get the width right. They're easy to spot. That's why there's fresh boards on the sides of the barn, and a double-width board beside each."

"He buried her by the tree," she said. "I found the grave."

"It's easy to find. He's been too drunk all year to know. Every time he comes back from that walnut tree, he's got one less card in his deck and some new scheme."

"It's hard to understand."

"You can't understand evil with your mind. You just see it and know it. And kill it if you get a chance. That's what I should've done."

They walked in silence until arriving at the grocery. Deet pulled his hand from hers. "I'll get the tractor and wait here.

Jacob lowered the Ball jar from his mouth. He'd shucked a bin full of cobs and ground the kernels loose. Thinking of the voice he'd heard when he found the ring, and the specter behind it, Jacob slipped his hand to his pocket. The grime between the bands and in the diamond setting—was it dirt, or his mother's flesh? His mind spun. He pulled the ring from his pocket, touched it to his tongue.

He washed away the rotten pungency with whiskey and stowed the Ball jar under the tub. He exited the lower barn floor between the dog kennels. Rebel and the bitch drummed the coop cages with their tails. He neared and their exuberance waned. Rebel backed into the corner and growled. The bitch joined.

The sky had clouded and a fine mist dampened his shoulders. He wrapped his fingers through the wire and pressed his nose. Rebel lurked at the back, his cast smeared black, and his eye a purple scab. His teeth gleamed. Lightning flashed nearby and a clap of thunder exploded; Rebel charged. Jacob jumped. He punched the wire and the dog raged, growled and drove his teeth at Jacob's fist. The bitch snarled in the adjacent cage.

"Hey there boy!" Angus called from the porch. "There you go, son! Grab that prod and jab em in the ribs. Gits em bitter as skunk piss."

A stick leaned in the corner where crate met barn, the green wood whittled to a dull point. Jacob grabbed the shaft and thrust the tip through the fence on the right, Rebel's blind side.

"Hyah!" He stabbed Rebel's ribs.

Rebel seized the prod in his jaws and jerked. The point crossed into the bitch's pen, where she fell upon it, tugging and gnawing like Rebel, until the whole stick was inside. Jacob found a smooth stone under the corner eaves and slung it into the crate. The rock caromed from the wire mesh and rattled inside. He hurled more until a lucky shot struck Rebel and the dog pealed with fury.

"Easy, now, shit for brains!" Angus called.

Jacob turned from the pen with both dogs snarling at his back. He stared at his father on the porch. Since he'd first tasted the walnut whiskey, a certain edgy awareness seemed with him all the time, a sharpness of the mind, a sensitivity, an inability to ignore frustration. He wanted more whiskey right now.

"Well, dumb shit?" Angus boomed. "Fuck with him s'more."

Wind picked up and the raindrops fattened. Angus's laughter swirled around Jacob like the storm. He walked to the lower barn entrance, paused to drink more walnut whiskey, and exited from the opposite side, invisible from the house.

It was a five-minute walk to the Widow's house.

Emeline stood inside the grocery doorway and watched bruised clouds battle white ones. A good soaking might cool her skin, but would spell disaster for bags of flour and sugar. She could stow the groceries under hay and blankets, but a downpour would soak them just the same. She didn't want to think about trying to explain to Angus that the cab of the truck would have better protected the goods.

"Emeline! You're up and about already!"

She twisted to her left. Hannah Kirk.

"I couldn't stand the stillness. Deet made a crutch in his wood shop."

"The Lord's doing."

"No doubt. And Deet had something to do with it too."

Hannah stood so close Emeline smelled the heat from her neckline. "You think about getting out? While you can?" Hannah squeezed Emeline's elbows, her upper arms; her eyes widened and she looked at Emeline's abdomen. Peered into her eyes. "Oh Heavens, Em, you're with child."

"Whatever—"

"No use denying it. I've had eight. Your secret's safe." Hannah stood bolt upright and bounced a look left and right. "Something troubled me since we talked. That question—why did Angus and Lucy Mae marry? I got to gossipin' with Nancy and we both remembered—one thing brought them together and at the time, it was all the talk. It's terrible; I simply can't tell you."

"Maybe you shouldn't."

"But I must. Lucy Mae's father died."

Emeline raised her brows and nodded slowly.

Hannah said, "Well, he sold life insurance. I can't believe Nancy had to remind me—and I shouldn't tittle-tattle, but a story doesn't get told without a kernel of truth. The word went that he wasn't a very good salesman, and had to buy his own product."

"Buy life insurance? On who?"

"Himself, his wife, little Lucy Mae. Well, his wife met her maker in forty-seven, and Lucy Mae's father collected all that money—some said five thousand dollars. He died two years later, and Lucy Mae collected on him. People said she was worth ten thousand dollars, plus the house! I don't know if I ever knew what the house sold for, but Angus got rid of it in a hurry."

"Why would she marry Angus if she had all that money?"

"She wasn't much to look at, for one. And who knows what demons pull what levers in Angus's mind? Everything near your Lake Oniasont is strange, starting clear back with the feud between the McClellans and the Hardgraves over that little strip of land. Spooky, if you ask me. Devil's Elbow. There were even killings."

"Killings?"

"You know Mitch McClellan—just took the bus home? His father Jonah disappeared right after a bar fight here in town, at the Gas Pump Saloon. Of course it wasn't called that back then. Mitch wasn't but a few years old. They called Jonah 'Whale,' to give you an idea. He was tall as a tree and bad to his core, the story goes. They searched high and low and never found him."

"I never heard such a story."

"Your family didn't live here in those times. I was barely a girl. The rest of us would just as soon forget. There was a lot of badness in the air, and it went away with Jonah McClellan."

Emeline glanced to the sidewalk. Deet approached.

"Hannah, you should meet Deet, my step-son."

Hannah seized Emeline, kissed her cheek, whispered in her ear, "You think hard on that. *Hard.*—Dietrich, it's a pleasure. I'll be along now."

Rain pattered corn leaves. Whiskey sloshed in Jacob's belly. Batting the green blades from his eyes, he trotted along a row for a third of a mile and emerged at the margin of forest bordering the Widow McClellan's. Thunderheads blotted the noon sun and it felt like twilight. Entering the woods was like stepping into a closet. He stole over wet leaves, which gave way to brown needles as pines quickly replaced the hardwoods at the field's edge. Amid the trees, he circled the McClellan house and hunkered in the grass at the edge of the dead widow's lawn. He observed the house as if an enemy might have been there in the interim.

A shadow hurled itself against the lamp-lit glass of a second-story window. Wind and rain consumed the sound. Jacob knelt. Instinctive fear waned and drunken curiosity possessed him. It was the Widow's room, and the bogeyman this moment stole her soul.

The beast would pass by the glass again, sure.

A tiny burp pressed from his stomach and he swallowed back the taste. He squeezed his mother's ring in his pocket, rubbed a burr of dried meat with his thumbnail. He released the ring and slipped his finger into the shotgun shell his father had left. Inside the house, clues waited that could make Angus pay. Shooting a bird out his hand.

Shit for brains.

If he was quiet, the bogeyman wouldn't know he trespassed.

Jacob glanced at the road, then back to the upper window. He blinked and the specter crashed against the window like a tornado with a sound like stones on glass. Grass tickled Jacob's inner arm. A mosquito hovered next to his ear. He dashed across the yard and crossed the porch. The door was unlocked.

The upper kitchen cabinets were too high, even on tippy-toes. He opened the first on the bottom row. Candles. Vases. A silver platter. The next door revealed baking pans and cookie cooling racks. The third, opening under the sink, smelled musty. Water dripped from pipe solders in back, and pooled where the rotted cabinet floor bowed under a cast iron skillet.

Heavy curtains sealed the dining room. In the sitting room beyond, a window cast a rectangular bolt of light to the floor. The bogeyman upstairs ignored him.

Jacob shivered.

He parted the curtains above the sink. The forest seemed closer and the dark clouds were like a lid sliding closed over the whole world. He kneeled at the cabinet door by the corner.

Whiskey!

Rust froze the cap; the sharp edge sliced his finger. He sucked the blood and his gaze rambled across the counter. Standing on a chair, he withdrew a cleaver from a knife block beside a Santa Clause cookie jar. The blade spine was as thick as a ball peen hammer.

He ran to the fireplace. Upset a box of kitchen matches. The widow McClellan burned wood year round. He carried a cherry log to the jug, supported the prone neck, hoisted the cleaver and smashed the spine to the glass.

Whiskey splashed his knee and green shards ricocheted from the cherry. He righted the jug, found a drinking glass by the sink. Upstairs, the tinkle of pebbles on glass grew louder. The bogeyman had heard the glass shatter.

Jacob gulped whiskey, lifted the blade, and walked to the stairs.

THIRTY THREE

D eet stared ahead. The Farmall's rear wheels were a blur in his lower peripheral vision. Ahead the sky was black and above him clouds tumbled like boulders downhill. Where would he find shelter, his first night away?

Maybe he'd steal a tarp from the barn and erect a lean-to a few miles away, shoot a deer and spend a couple days jerking the meat. Or something.

A hundred yards out of town, Deet turned to Emeline and called, "Look ahead, Em!" A sheet of rain fell sideways, not a half mile ahead. "Can you cover everything?"

"Pull in here!" she rose on one knee and pointed toward the house she'd inherited from her father. A gust of wind brought rain and drops spattered on her arm. The wind carried leaves and tossed Emeline's hair.

Deet spun the steering wheel and followed the driveway. He turned again and Emeline hunched over the grocery bags, trying to cover them with blankets. Fat raindrops fell, leaving wide wet splotches on her back and making her skin shine.

"Pull into the barn!"

Deet halted the tractor, leaped down, slid the door open, climbed back aboard, and parked in the bay where Margulies' wood shop had been. He killed the engine and wiped his forearms, roughed his hair. He sat on the tractor a moment with his back to Emeline, aware that he inhabited a dangerous place with her. He was at a loss. She would die if he found the nerve to abandon her.

And yet he must.

After a long moment, Deet turned in the tractor seat. Emeline looked up at him and the partly twisted angle of her torso permitted a glimpse of one breast lopsided heavily toward the center of her top. It, too, was wet with rain.

Deet climbed down. "I'm soaked. How'd the groceries fare?"

She shifted a blanket aside. "Dry."

Deet faced away from her at the door. Gusting wind flapped his shirt. "Where's what's his name?" he said.

"Chambers? I don't know his schedule. Angus made the arrangements."

"Angus. Your husband, you mean?"

"I don't know."

"What's that mean?" He climbed on the trailer, sat on a bale. Outside, the uncut lawn had grown shaggy and rippled like a green lake.

Emeline spoke softly. "I mean he's my husband of course. Before God. But I just wonder sometimes if I owe my loyalty to him, or three dead Mrs. Hardgraves."

Deet was silent.

"I'm not running off, if that's what you're wondering," she said.

"Might be best if you did. Go to the courthouse and get the whole thing thrown out."

"Can't. I followed the Lord in my decision and if I change that decision, I'm not changing my mind, I'm changing His. That's not so easy as one might think."

"Well, you ought to run off. If Angus starts something, and I'm gone—"

"Don't say that."

Deet plucked a leaf from Emeline's hair and tossed it overboard. "Look at this tangle." He rested his hand on her shoulder, palm by her neck.

Outside, wind drove rain in slanted bands, separated by rolling shrouds of grey mist. Water splashed from the ground and the barn door beat against the wall. It kept half time against the pounding in his chest. He wanted to plunge his nose into her hair and breathe her in.

He wanted to run. Now.

Emeline twisted away.

"Deet?"

"Wha—" he cleared the huskiness from his throat. "What?"

"Do you ever think about the Lord?"

"I surely wasn't right now." He leaned back, tried to roll with the direction change. "You mean God?"

She nodded.

"Kind of hard, don't you think?"

"What do you mean?"

"Well... look at you. Leg busted. The house you live in. The man you live with. I bet God ain't visited this entire county one time since he made it, whenever the hell that was."

"I think God's not only visited. I think He's right in the middle of everything."

"If you wasn't pretty there'd be no redeeming you. Can't see what's in front of you." Deet swung his legs to the outside of the bale and readied to jump to the floor.

Emeline said, "I asked about your beliefs because I was trying to think of a reason why the Lord might have wanted me in the middle of everything you described, and the only thing I can think of is that He put me here to testify my faith and win your soul—you, and Angus of course—and Jacob. Win your souls to Christ."

Deet slid down from the bale to the barn floor. "You know Em, here's what I think of, when I got time for puzzles. I don't see how you can believe what's in that black book you keep your nose in, and not believe in what's around you every waking minute."

Emeline watched Deet standing in the barn entrance. His profile was rigid, head angled downward, brow tight, as if to firm the thoughts behind it. At least he hadn't been rude. Hadn't the Lord warned that she would be hated, as was He?

Deet would come around. She could see into his heart, a little. Maybe. He was still tethered to the good, and anyone grieved by the difference between right and wrong was only a prayer away from being saved. Deet just needed to learn more and stop rebelling against his Maker.

Dear Lord, I thank you for the blessings you have given me, and the challenges that keep me leaning on You for Your strength. Please Lord soften Deet's heart so that he can hear, and learn. I believe he is capable of being a beautiful disciple Lord, and he's able to see right and wrong, and he wants to make a stand, I can see it. Lord, I just pray that you would give me the words to lead him to You. Amen.

Emeline opened her eyes. Deet was watching her. He turned away.

"I want to check on thing inside the house," she said.

Deet helped her down from the trailer and stood beside her. She leaned to him as they crossed the gravel driveway and climbed the porch stairs, then leaned the crutch to the wall.

"What you looking for in the house?"

"I didn't get to take anything but a suitcase and a bicycle. It'll do me good to see everything sitting where it ought to be." Holding his arm, she bent to a flowerpot and found a key. She gave it to Deet. He opened the door, peeked inside, and they entered. He nodded to a red streak on the wall by the stair landing.

"That's my blood," she said.

"Good of him to clean it," Deet said. "Everything else look right?"

Emeline paused a moment, trying to understand how Brad Chambers could walk past her blood day in and out, and not scrub it off the wall. She imagined him lingering at the stairs, dragging his fingers along red streak.

"Do you want to go upstairs?"

"Now that I'm here, I'm afraid to look. If he's been in my room..."

Deet shifted toward the kitchen. "What's on the table?"

"Drawings?" Emeline took them in; measurements, numbers, quantities. It looked like an engineering project drawn for a price estimate.

"It's a still," Deet said.

"Moonshine?"

"That's a boiler. You build a fire under it. The pipe leads to the doubler—a chamber where steam condenses, and the alcohol passes, then you got the coils over here, probably running through a vat of cold water, and then it spits out whiskey here."

"Not in my house."

"An operation like this doesn't fit in a kitchen."

Emeline remembered her father standing behind his chair at the opposite head of the table, saying grace. Instead of ragged notebook paper, the table was set with china and silver, and the center overflowed with oven-warm bread, gravy, turkey, potatoes, carrots, stuffing. Merry voices bounced from the walls and windows. Women and girls bustled, men and boys marveled at their work, praised and blessed them. She heard chairs sliding and silver clanging, coughing and giggling as family took seats. She was eleven and her father's brothers had converged with their families—one from New York, and the other from Kentucky—for a proper Thanksgiving. It was the first year after her great grandfather and great grandmother died, one three months after the other. The family wanted to be close.

Deet shuffled his feet.

The sunshine and gay voices vanished. Emeline stood at the table and looked to the window, where a film of water rippled the gray reality behind it.

"You want to get moving home before we get another dowse of rain?"

Lord, why did you send me into such a miserable pit of snakes?

Deet touched her shoulder.

"No. I want you to take me up into the field. Take the tractor. It's my field; I don't care what you drive over. No one's using the land anyhow."

"Up in the field?"

"Please just do as I ask."

Deet nodded slowly. "Uh, okay." He spun, leaving her there alone.

Emeline stood.

I don't know what you're doing, Lord. I don't understand.

Hobbling, she crossed the kitchen to the entrance, retrieved her crutch, and locked the door behind her. The rumble of the tractor engine came from the barn. The rain had stopped but the clouds were in turmoil.

Jacob, Angus, and Deet had rejected her attempts to converse about the Lord. They ridiculed her. Is that what He wanted—or was it something else? She would go to where He always seemed to be waiting.

Deet swung the tractor in a wide semicircle and stopped with the trailer positioned in front of the steps. Emeline worked down them sideways, crutch, leg, leg. In a moment Deet lifting her and deposited her in the trailer.

Deet nodded to the field. "You want to go someplace in particular?"

"See that big tree on the horizon? There's a rock I'm looking for in the field, a little before we get to that tree."

"A rock?"

"It's white." She held her hands in an oval.

"All righty."

Deet climbed aboard the tractor as if mounting a horse, throwing his leg high, swinging wide. In a moment the tractor surged forward. She watched him from behind as he stood from his seat to get a better view of the terrain. Seated again he cut the wheel and entered the field beside the tree line.

Lightning flashed. Emeline closed her eyes and counted. *Thousand one, thousand two, thousand three, thousand four.* A long rumbling boom arrived.

Deet turned in his seat and hollered back, "You know Angus been struck three times?"

"No, I didn't know."

"Yeah, he can't carry a pocket watch."

Emeline wanted to pray but didn't. How could the Lord smite him with lightning three times and fail to kill him? Amazing forbearance, giving Angus time upon time upon time to repent of his evil and turn to Him? Or did the Lord have His mind on other matters?

Three times.

Cresting the hill, again Deet stood, now to get a better angle on the ground below. He lowered the engine's tempo and they slowed. "It'll be on the right side," Emeline said. She maneuvered across a bale of hay, looked to the tree for her bearings, then to the ground.

"There it is," Deet said. "Just ahead." He turned the wheel a little to the left.

In a moment she saw the white rock. The tractor stopped and it was immediately below her.

"You want to hold it or something? Or just look at it?"

She looked at him.

""Cause I'll get it for you, is what I mean." Deet jumped to the ground and tromped to the rock.

"Wait!"

Lord, I want so desperately to be obedient but I don't understand anything you're doing. You're infinitely good and I trust you wholly, but I don't trust myself. I don't understand anything and if I don't understand, I can have no peace. I believe—but help me in my unbelief, and forgive me in this act of distrust."

She opened her eyes and nodded to Deet.

Deet bent at his knees. "That's funny. There's paper underneath."

"Paper?"

"Sure. Looks like newspaper, just a little bit."

She hadn't looked closely enough when she'd been here last to notice. How would newspaper be under a rock in the middle of a field? It hadn't been tilled in at least a dozen years. Her father had rented out some of the other land to other farmers, but never this stretch immediately behind the house. There was a tornado two years ago that touched down and bounced to the side hill, and all it did was muss up the grass, rip through a couple of trees, and steal her Bible from the picnic table. It was a puzzle.

"Give me the rock."

Deet palmed the rock and presented it to her.

She inhaled. Exhaled. "Turn it over so I can see the bottom."

She took the stone from his hand and became aware that her mouth hung agape and her eyes strained. A shred of paper, not an inch long and half that wide, clung to the stone as if enameled to it. Her eyes found Deet's.

She mouthed, "The Destroyer."

"What's on there?" He looked to the ground. "Well look, there's more paper." He lifted a sliver and read, " *'and on the two side posts, the Lord will pass over the door and will not suffer.'* That's what it says."

Faint, Emeline laid her head to the bale and blinked. Her eyes filled with tears and her mind with confusion. Joyful confusion and fear. What did it mean? It was like she'd discovered the empty tomb and been confronted by two angels. She felt like she would pee herself and faint. The Lord was real and holy and utterly terrible.

The paper was from the book of Exodus. "On the two side posts, the Lord will pass over the door and will not suffer *the destroyer...* to come unto your houses to smite you."

Rain and wind pounded the McClellan house. Inside, Jacob climbed the steep, narrow stairwell. Boot treads had worn the step edges round. The boards squeaked. He clung to the wobbly banister, then shifted to lightly touching the wall for balance every few steps.

His eyes adjusted to the faint upstairs light. The noise of pebbles on glass waxed. Reaching to the wall, his hand shook. Down the hall at the last room—the Widow's room—a yellow light projected a shadow that could only have come from a demon raging near the dead woman's corpse. Jacob clicked his tongue to the roof of his mouth. He blinked, woozy. He passed the first door on the left, glanced inside, continued. The light at the end of the hall wavered and his ears buzzed with each step. He stood near the doorway and choked on the stench of the rotting widow.

The bogeyman hissed. Jacob inched around the corner.

The corpse crawled with metallic, blackberry-sized flies. A congested armada swarmed back and forth, casting a shadow. They crashed against the window, and as one, turned, and rushed him on glistening wings. He batted them. Flailed. They bounced from his head and arms. Alighted in his hair and dove into his gaping mouth. He spat and screamed and stumbled; caught himself and ran down the steps.

Spitting, *chewing*.

Jacob turned; the flies clouded the landing above and followed him downstairs. He stopped at the whiskey bottle. The broken neck had no loop. Scaly, hairy fly parts coated his tongue. He hoisted the jug, pressed his lips to the sharp glass.

He spat on the floor and gulped again. Ruffled his hair and more of the hairy beasts zoomed around his head.

Fire.

Beyond the dining room, in the sitting room with the floating rectangle of light, a roll top desk abutted the wall. He rushed to it, pulled a lamp chain, rubbed his eyes, tugged a humidity-swollen center drawer, withdrew contents stacked in the center, unfolded a sheet of lined paper. A pencil script titled the page 'Walnut Whiskey.' The tiny writing below resembled one of Lucy Mae's recipe cards, with short bursts of text followed by numbers.

A black book contained names like Spanky Jones and Puss Wilson, followed by two lines of numbers, and a final column with a consistent entry, "pd."

He drank from the jug again. Below the black book lay a photo. A middle-aged ma, made of leather and sawdust posed with a rifle; his narrow eyes leered beneath a fedora brim; the crumpled hat as weathered as the face. His hair draped his shoulders like the painting of Jesus that Pap took down after Lucy Mae... though this man didn't host kindness in his eyes. He had angular cheeks and a wide jaw. Jacob studied his narrow shoulders and hips, muscled and veiny forearms. He could have been Pap's older brother.

It was the presence at the walnut tree.

Jacob drank, slicing his lip from the broken jug.

Fire.

He spat a dollop of blood to the desk. Stuffed the photo, the book, and the recipe inside a tall waxy envelope from a vertical slot, then ransacked each drawer. Coins... a bankbook... a pocketknife... he pocketed them.

Fire.

Jacob glanced over chairs and a radio. Curtains darkened two windows but a third had none. Rain trickled down.

Fire...

Jacob turned a semi-circle. His thoughts wandered and he couldn't keep anything top of mind for more than a moment before something displaced it. *Fire.* But more than anything Jacob wanted to see a fire.

The desire came from somewhere new to him, a thought that floated in on walnut whiskey. *Fire. Fire. Fire.*

At the hearth lay an upended box of kitchen matches. He struck one against the box side. He cupped his hand and held the flame below a burgundy curtain. Yellow licked the cloth. Smoke rose. He sat cross-legged. The match burned his skin and he flicked it away. Flames on the curtain leapfrogged higher. Heat warmed his face. The blaze widened and soon licked the ceiling, fell back, and reached overhead with a wide, orange arm. It roared. It whipped. Smoke thickened above his head. Embers curled below the ceiling and floated across the room. Patches of carpet ignited.

He closed his eyes and the orange light danced.

Jacob opened his eyes. The walls blazed and the chairs looked like devil's thrones, with wavering blue bulbs spitting orange flares. He crawled below the smoke to the roll top, grabbed the waxy envelope and scrambled to the kitchen. The gallon jug sat on the floor. His ears roared and his throat and lungs burned. He pressed the serrated glass to his mouth and drank. An ember stung his neck; he swatted orange flies, circled the table, splashed whiskey into flames. His skin shrieked. He hurled the jug into the inferno and fled, sprinted across the lawn, looking back at the light and heat as he went.

At the forest he collided into a man who clapped a hand on his shoulder.

It was the sawdust and leather man in the photo.

"Aghhh!"

Jacob staggered and the man held his shoulder. Jacob twisted, saw a pinned-up shirtsleeve and quizzical grin.

"Jake!"

The sawdust and leather man became his father. "Guess I don't got to ask what your doing."

"I don't know."

"It's fairly evident. What's in your hand?"

Jacob offered the envelope. "I—thought I should take it."

"Let's stand back a bit. Fuckin thing's hot already."

Angus led Jacob a dozen yards into the woods. Under thick hemlocks the rain dripped in slow, heavy drops. Jacob leaned against Angus and closed his eyes.

A mile ahead, black smoke climbed from the trees and swirled against dark rain clouds. Deet throttled up and ducked into the wind.

"Something's burning!" he called. The wind stole Emeline's reply. He held his hand flat at his brow. "It's our house or the McClellan's!"

Deet opened the throttle. "Come on, come on." He took the curves wide and the straight stretches center-lane. "It's the Widow McClellan's! I can see it." The trailer wobbled and wagged the Farmall. Minutes later he throttled down and halted shy of the widow's lawn.

The back roof had fallen in. Embers swirled skyward like insects from the back corner. The forward roof collapsed as Deet ran a few yards. He turned back from the heat.

"Deet!" Emeline cried, "We're too late!"

"Mrs. McClellan!" Deet cried. "The Widow's inside!" He ran to the side of the house. Flames roared against the windows. On the siding, wisps of smoke grew into sooty orange ghosts of flame. He circled the house. The fire howled like an old woman. She might be just inside, overtaken by smoke.

"No!" Emeline cried, and crutched closer.

Deet darted onto the porch, opened the door by throwing a chair through it. The kitchen seemed clear beyond the wall of flames at the door. If he could follow it quickly, he could find the old woman.

Emeline stood beside a cement birdbath closer to the road. Deet raced toward her tearing away his shirt as he ran. He soaked it in the pool of rainwater.

She seized his arm, screamed "No!"

Flames cried like sirens.

"I got to!" Deet clasped her hand. Removed it from his arm. He wrapped the dripping shirt over his head and pressed a sleeve over his nose and mouth.

He charged into the fire.

I trot through the woods and onto the lawn best I can on a half sober, leaving Jacob in the trees.

"Deet's gone inside!" Emeline shrieks. "I think he fell." She runs on her cast taking strides like Jesse goddam Owens. I've seen women make eyes like that before—cheatin' eyes that don't care who knows.

I reach the porch ahead of her. Orange-black flames billow against the eaves and scale up around. I fall to my knees and crawl, throwing my arm forward, still seeing Emeline's eyes and the kiss she gave Deet this morning on the porch as he carried her to a bed of hay.

"Too hot!" I yell. "It's too hot. I can't get near him!"

Emeline rushed past Angus, dropped, and wriggled to the step. Yellow and orange and blue gasses rippled; smoke layered at the ceiling. Deet lay on the kitchen floor; the flames from the walls mingled with fiery tongues that incinerated his clothes. Emeline inhaled the furnace and choked. Deet's hair was a swirl of singed brilliance; she clutched his ankles and jerked him to the door. Pain shot from her heel to the base of her skull. She wrenched Deet over the step.

Deet lay clear of the flames on the porch and yet the searing pain continued on her skin and Angus tackled her to the grass and rolled on her, jarring loose a burst of breath she'd held since entering the house. She gasped cold rainy air and smelled walnut whiskey and found herself staring into her husband's eye.

She took in his ugliness. His blackened teeth.

"Deet!"

She struggled; Angus wobbled to his knees. She dragged Deet to the lawn and rolled him on the grass. His burned shirt fell away from his shoulders. His scalp was like a charred ham.

"Damn fool," Angus said.

Steam rose from the lawn and the grass closest the house browned and smoldered. Deet lay on his stomach; his back lifted with each tiny inhalation.

Beyond Angus, Jacob crouched at the forest edge behind tall grass. The firelight was queer on his eyes and teeth. He appeared to grin.

"Roll him to his back," she said. "He can't breathe." She heaved Deet's shoulder; his body followed and he flopped over. His stomach was pink and his sides were red and black. His abdomen rose and fell in tight, quick movements.

"Good as gone." Angus squeezed his nostrils together and snapped his hand away, flinging a string of snot.

"He's too close to the fire. Help me!"

Angus stood.

"Now!" She grabbed Deet's left foot and Angus clasped the other; they dragged him closer to the birdbath, where the grass didn't steam.

"He's safe here," she said to no one.

The roof collapsed, sending a spire of sparks into the sky and a blast of heat across the yard.

"He needs a doctor," Emeline said.

"He's gone."

"This is your son!"

Angus slapped her.

Emeline studied his face and Angus stared back into hers. His brow was low and his jaw set, as if he wanted to communicate beyond words. "I'm heading to the house to call for help. You stay with him."

Emeline brought her fingers to Deet's cheek, wavered shy of touching his raw, bleeding flesh. "I'm here," she said. "Deet I know you can hear me and you have to say these words in your heart as you hear them. Lord, I turn from my old ways and repent. Save me Lord. Be my savior. Say it with me Deet. Lord I turn from all my sin and evil. Lord be my savior. Lord I can't go on without you and I need you to save me. Lord please take me from this awful place. Lord? Deet? Say it with me. Lord, I—"

Time slipped from her.

A hand grasped Emeline's shoulder. She lifted her chin from her chest and wiped stringy hair from her eyes. Doctor Fleming knelt beside Deet; another man looked at her with hound dog eyes set on a creased face; he wore a brown and tan uniform. A water-speckled badge gleamed in the waning firelight.

Sheriff Heilbrun removed his hat and said, "Can he make it to the hospital, Doc?"

"He's going to be fine!" Emeline said.

"Mrs. Hardgrave, can you stand? Here you go." Heilbrun stooped and she took his arm. She gauged the depth and goodness of him and pressed her face to his shirt. He stood taller, not uncomfortable, but not relaxing into her either, which consoled her. She closed her eyes. Beside her Doctor Fleming spoke quietly as he studied Deet. Emeline drifted through smoky black images.

Heilbrun rocked slightly. She felt him move his head and imagined his wordless conversation with Doctor Fleming as they stared at each other, at Deet, and back at each other.

Heilbrun led her to his cruiser, helped with her leg and left her in the passenger seat. He returned to Doctor Fleming. They spoke. Raindrops fell like afterthoughts and ash lay soggy on the windshield. Heilbrun returned, stooped before her, hands on his knees.

"Emeline?"

He waved his arm toward the house and his eyes pointed away. He swallowed. "Deet's in real bad shape. Best we can do is make him comfortable. It's his lungs, see? He can't get the air he needs—"

Her mind drifted. She was in her father's woodshop, rubbing wax into the metal to keep it from rusting. She stood before her ninth grade class, reciting Aeschylus. She walked on the sidewalk in the fall with her books pressed to her breast and the light scent of changing autumn leaves in her nose.

"Deet's dying, Emeline, and we can't do anything." Heilbrun's eyes were cold. Angry. "Doc Fleming give him morphine, and it'll make him a little more comfortable. I'm sorry."

Autumn... The clouds were so white, and the blue just beyond—what a delicious blue. Houses displayed carved pumpkins on their porches and a diesel truck rolled by and the exhaust was sweet enough to—

"Emeline?"

She blinked.

"I'm going to put Deet on the trailer here, and drive him to your house so we can try to make him comfortable."

She looked up to him with puckered chin and squinting eyes, but behind them was horror that refused to cry.

Deet had never acknowledged her prayer.

Heilbrun and Doctor Fleming had carried Deet to the sofa. Emeline sat beside him on a kitchen chair that Heilbrun brought out for her. She watched Deet's chest rise and fall; each tiny exhalation caused a quiet whistle. Sheriff Heilbrun and Doc Fleming drank coffee in the kitchen. Their low voices carried talk of the storm, the fire, Deet. She was surprised they lingered. Each had Deet's blood on their arms and chest.

Angus crept behind her but she refused to turn and acknowledge him.

"You don't need to see this," he said.

"Someone has to sit with him."

"Go upstairs and freshen up. You don't look too good."

She touched the inside of Deet's hand. He'd apparently had his fingers curled into fists; the skin was unburned. Deet moaned, but whatever slight awareness she'd stirred settled back below the scorched masque of his face.

Angus breathed hard through his nose. "We ought to roll him on his belly."

"He can hardly breathe, now."

"His belly ain't burned like his back," Angus said. "Needless suffering lying on them burns."

"It's better to hurt and live."

"You need to go upstairs. Seeing things like this don't leave you right, after."

She held her hand to Deet's cheek, close enough to feel heat rising from his flesh, but afraid of the pain she would cause by touching him. She stared at the wall, the window. Propped her head, clutched her hair and pulled until the pain grounded her. She stood and hobbled to the kitchen.

"Do something!"

Somber stares lifted from coffee mugs.

"Emeline..." Doctor Fleming said. Slowly, he shook his head sideways.

She limped back to Deet, touched her fingertips to his palm. His hand shook. He opened his mouth.

She leaned. "Deet?"

Air escaped from his lips; she whispered his name again. His brow clenched and his hand tightened on her fingertips.

She said, "I'm here."

His breath came out raspy and weak like fireplace bellows closing on their own accord. "I ... prayed..."

Doctor Fleming dozed in a heavily upholstered armchair. Sheriff Heilbrun had departed long ago, stating something about the fire didn't feel right. He promised Angus a full investigation. Angus said to keep him abreast, then retired upstairs.

It was two a.m.; Jacob and Angus slept upstairs. The storm stopped an hour ago. The air smelled of Deet—smelled of things that ought not burn.

Fleming coughed, resumed snoring.

Emeline crutched to the front door, then to the porch. The sky was clear and frozen stars blinked. From inside came a gasp and she stumbled back to Deet. His arms stretched stiff. His back tightened and his chin lifted. The veins in his neck pressed against his seeping skin. His eyes were open but unseeing.

She knelt, rested her head on his chest. Her fingertips at his neck. His pulse thumped lighter, weaker; each beat fainter and farther apart. His lungs released. A heartbeat arrived late, and another, but no more.

THIRTY FOUR

The mortician arrived in the morning. He drove Deet away.

Emeline rested in bed all day; Angus didn't seem to mind handling the arrangements. They'd bury him Thursday morning.

Doctor Fleming had treated Emeline's burns; they were mild compared to Deet's, but Fleming slathered balm on her hands and neck and bandaged her, and instructed her to take the Tylenol that he'd given for her leg, which he also took occasion to clean.

Now and again Angus's croaking-timber voice drifted through the house as he talked on the telephone, and she pressed her hands to her ears. The pain from her burns kept her awake, and a new throbbing in her leg—Fleming said she'd stressed the fracture—siphoned clarity from her thoughts.

It was mid-afternoon. Boots clonked on the stairs and a moment later, Angus peered through the open door. A dark circle hung under his eye like a bag of gypsy worms suspended in a silken tree crotch. A splash of color on the flesh at his thumb and forefinger drew her eye—like the brownish green husk of a walnut pod beginning to decay. The skin was turning the color of his teeth.

"Company be here at five. Get off your ass and fix something."

"Company?"

"Kid renting the house in town."

"Why is he coming here?"

"Supper. Get to cooking."

"You cook."

Angus charged. She shrank against the pillow. He towered over her.

"Ain't been a week since I lost my arm, and you ain't doted or said a damn thing. Deet runs into a burning house and the whole world screeches to a fuckin stop. That make sense to you?"

"You haven't shed a tear."

He lifted his arm high, withdrew it. "You best be downstairs in five minutes cooking else you and I'll have the wickedest come-to-Jesus a man and woman ever had."

"I'd love for you and I to have a come to Jesus. I think He's been trying to get your attention over and over, and you're too stubborn to see it. So full of self pity and anger. You walk around moaning the victim all the time and you're a terror to the people around you. So let's you and I come to Jesus right now, you got any courage at all."

Angus slammed the door. His footfalls pounded away.

Four out of four. Women are cunts. All there is to it. Do your best and still end up wishing you'd spent your life fuckin livestock instead. Soon as you even let yourself give a damn, they wave that gizzy up in the air 'til someone tosses a cock in it. That's what Emeline done—waved it up in the air 'til Deet come along.

Son like that's better in the ground.

Woman like that ain't worth keeping around, either. That's all right. Angus Hardgrave don't have to wait 'til buck season. Half the town expected her to run off by now, anyway.

I sit at the kitchen table, watch the wall clock and sip walnut whiskey. The second hand herky-jerks around the dial. Five minutes and not a second more. If she doesn't drag her broke-legged ass down here and cook something, shit's gonna come to a head.

Only so much abuse a man can take.

The minute hand clicks once, twice, a third time. With each circuit I get hotter and hotter 'til steam blows from my ears and eyeball and I slam my fist on the table. Climb the steps two at a time. Throw open the door.

Emeline stands a foot away, on her crutch. Her eyes are red and her face is flushed and splotchy.

"It took a while to get on my feet—I hurt my leg again."

"Get your ass downstairs."

"I'm doing my best to please you."

I back into the hallway. "You oughta started that a month ago."

"I'm just a girl sometimes; I'm trying to do better."

"You getting fresh?"

She stops working the crutch and leans on it. I study her eyes. They're big from having her eyelids all the way back—and a woman only looks like that when she knows you're going to knock her straight or when she thinks she's game to do the same to you. I wave her ahead and she swings the crutch, drags her foot. She lingers at the end of the hall, looking over the stairs. One boot in her ass would guarantee she won't wave that puss in the air.

But I watch her negotiate the steps. Has everything between her and Deet been in my head? I don't feel sharp like I used to. Just a week ago, my life as a country gentleman unfolded in its natural course. The whiskey stillin' idea percolated while the dog business came together. I'd run a wood shop out the barn, with Deet doing the work; and in no time, Jacob'd raise the beef and hogs. Not five minutes since I had a snoogle of whiskey and I can't hardly think optimistic.

Maybe with another shot I'll get a fix on my pretty little wife.

Did she share the gizzy with Deet, or not?

Emeline pulled a slab of sliced bacon from the refrigerator. She'd stowed the iron cookware in the bottom cabinet on the left. Stooped, she recalled her first day in this kitchen. Angus and the boys had cooked fish and left the oil and crusted skin on plates without even soaking them in water. They lived like hogs. She gripped the iron handle with both hands and hoisted the pan to the stove. Forked a dozen strips of meat.

Angus slipped behind her and squeezed her breast.

Her alertness flared and she clamped her mouth.

He pushed her sideways and she clomped her cast and dragged her foot until she stood at the sink. Through the window she could see most of the driveway, the barn, and the top edge of the dog kennels.

"Keep your eye on the window," Angus said. He pushed her forward; bent her at the waist. She crossed her arms at the sink basin. He flipped her dress to her back and dragged down her underwear. He kicked her foot aside with his.

"Where's Jacob?" she said.

Angus's zipper sounded. She felt him against her, searching, probing. She stared at the sink drain hole.

Angus thrust; she grabbed the spigot base. Looked at the knife block, a foot from the sink. Thought of the carbine in the living room. Bacon grease spattered. Facing down, away from Angus, she closed her eyes.

"Yeah, there," she said. She felt him grow.

"All of it, Angus; hard as you can. I've... been bad and... you got to... teach me a.... lesson."

He grunted. The crackling bacon smelled sweet and smoky. A cloud cast a shadow that passed between house and barn like a sliver of night.

"Don't spare me nothing... Angus. You got to teach... a lesson."

"Unh... unh... unh..."

"All you got!" He hit her cervix.

He leaned on her back and bit her shoulder while his arm crossed her belly and squeezed one breast then the other, back and forth, grunting so hard the vibrations rippled through her skin and his saliva wetted her dress.

Lord I know I'm evil but please use that chunk of meat and...

He jabbed and shuddered and squeezed mightily and choking for breath, backed from her, and gave one final slam.

Kill that bastard inside me...

I tell Chambers to drive the truck—the Fairlane won't make it where we're going. Unfamiliar with the clutch and less gutsy motor, he stalls before heading out the drive and turning toward Walnut. We follow 322 toward Franklin. He slouches, one hand on the wheel and the other on the shifter. I drink from a gallon jug braced between my feet and offer him a drink.

"I understand we're headed to a dog fight?" he says.

"That's right."

"Don't mind if I do." Chambers sips, smacks his lips. "Whooey." Passes it back.

I take another pull and cap the jug. Do I imagine—or did some kind of funny business pass between Emeline and Chambers back at the house? She skirted away and never met his face, and he always turned his head and kept her in the corner of his eye. Never addressed her directly—and no man ought to address another man's wife directly—but he wanted to. Slopping down runny eggs and bacon, he wished he was eating Emeline. Is there a man in the county she ain't spread her gizzy for?

"Given any thought to stillin' whiskey of your own?" Chambers says.

"Hunh?"

"Lotta dough."

"Not like in the day."

"Still, better'n feeding corn to cows," Chambers says. "Cleaning stalls for two years, and selling beef. Not that I got anything against a good beefsteak. Just that them darkies in town—they like that cheap liquor. Give their last dime to lick an empty bottle cap. More and more em, every day. I don't know who the hell invites em."

"More n' more? They ain't but a dozen in the county. You just notice when you see em. Naw; I'll sell to white, black, jew, wop, anyone wants a drink. I'd sell to a fuckin nazi. This walnut whiskey opens the mind; ain't a person alive can drink a quart and not feel sharper, and the truth is, after a quart, a man'll have a taste he'll never shake."

"Powerful drink, that."

"I don't know what does it."

Chambers grins. "I've had whiskey all over the damn place and never had any that made me so, well, I don't know. Seems like a pull of *that* whiskey, and I know exactly what I want—and I'm ready to pay the price to get it."

"I got a recipe and a walnut tree. I'm just thinking about how to get the equipment. A fella goes to the hardware and buys fifty feet of copper—if he ain't building a house, it don't take hell of a lot of imagination to see what he's up to."

"Proper still'd only take thirty feet. I made some drawings, best I could remember. Pappy ran a small operation—but I figure that's a good thing. We take a little profit and put the rest into corn next year, build a second operation, a few miles from the first. But here's the thing. We got to find customers can keep their traps shut. Better to drive all over six counties for the right buyers. One snitch'll cook your goose."

"A few miles from the first?" I say. "You can't be hauling that kind of grain around without somebody noticing where you pull into the woods. Don't take but a dog shitting on the side of the road to get tongues wagging."

"I did some looking around," Chambers says. "That back corn-field at your house close to town runs clear for a mile and a half and joins Barnett's place. After that, a field circles 'round the hill and comes out two miles later—and I don't know who lives there, but the path is open. Don't have to drive on roads."

"You mean to set a still on my other property?"

"Two baskets hold twice the eggs. Just an idea, down the road."

"That's a long way down the road," I say. "First off, we need a dozen fifty-five-gallon drums. We got to find two hundred pound of sugar, and fifty of yeast. That's a chunk of dough to come up with."

"We'll find some cash," Chambers says. "But it's equal interest, straight through."

I pull Copenhagen from my pocket and roll it end over end in my fingers.

"You need me to pop that open?"

"I been carrying this for a week and ain't even thought to take a dip." I chuck it out the window, and drink walnut whiskey.

Emeline's mind drifted. She ran hot water on the bacon skillet, wiped grease residue with a paper towel, then propped the pan on the drying rack. A stark memory of Deet tossing his shirt aside at the barn roof sucked the breath from her lungs.

She thought of the white stone and the verse in Revelation, how the Lord would give her a name. The page must have been from her Bible, blown from the picnic table. It must have ripped and been trapped by the rock.

The Destroyer.

Did the Lord send her to destroy the Hardgraves?

She washed Angus Hardgrave's dishes. She coughed loose a wad of phlegm, looked at the dishwater, and hobbled on her crutch to the front door. She spat on the porch. Her nose dripped and her mind hovered above, somehow disconnected from the horror inside.

She smelled charred wood and flesh from McClellan's place.

In a moment she crutched along a footpath. Corn leaves rustled in a slight breeze; the silver tassels smelled like flowers and the clumpy earth recalled a fresh dug grave.

Beyond the path that bordered the field, to her left extended a knoll with scattered sassafras trees and huckleberry bushes. Her eyes followed the shoreline until a giant bough of green eclipsed the water. The black walnut tree. Every halting step carried her closer to the woman buried amid its roots.

A persistent tugging originated from the tree as if it wielded some cerebral gravity. It sought to soften her revulsion. It wanted her to understand. It promised something she couldn't fathom. She steeled herself, focused on the tramped grass and the whispering corn leaves.

Come to me. Let's talk about Deet.

The magnetism increased as she followed the tangent that, at its closest, would bring her within fifty yards of the tree. She dared not look. In her grief the darkness pulled like gravity. She faced the corn as if bracing against a centripetal tether by steering away from it. She passed the closest point and hobbled faster.

I'll show you what to do.

One step after another, she kept forefront in her mind that she knew the Lord, knew good from evil, and recognized the force for what it was: the same animus that inhabited Brad Chambers the night he raped her, that allowed Angus to let his son inhale flames, that turned Jacob into a zombie.

She recognized evil, but the unflagging, gentle offer of understanding confused and overwhelmed. She should go see what it wanted. That couldn't hurt. She swayed toward the walnut.

I'll show you everything...

Emeline froze.

She stepped backward without looking, only sensing the leaves and the fragrance of corn silk as the field enclosed upon her. The walnut's pull diminished with each inch. She crossed row after row, trampling stalks, until the evil lingered more as memory than a presence.

Midway through the field, the parallel rows guided her toward McClellan's. She reached the forest; beyond was the charred hull of the house. Men's voices slipped through the trees. She crept forward. One was dressed in a black suit; two wore denim. They and Sheriff Heilbrun picked through rubble. She watched by a hemlock, her thoughts still ethereal, as if all of this action and pain took place in someone else's life—as if she'd walk back to the house and Deet would call her *Ma*—

The man in the suit stood at the edge of the debris with his head tilted forward; the two in jeans worked their way into the wreckage, removing charred boards and rearranging others. The sheriff walked along the stone foundation. His hands were in his pockets and his dog-jowled face hadn't changed since the after-noon before.

"Sheriff, I think I got something over here," one of the men in denim said. The others angled toward him.

"What?" Heilbrun said.

"Must be the widow."

The others stood at the nearest edge and leaned forward, and Emeline drifted along the path where Angus came from when he rushed to her. The ground dipped and rose; the trail passed be-tween heavy-trunked evergreens.

"Wait a minute, Joe. Is that bedsprings she's laying on?"

"That's right."

"She smoke cigarettes? A pipe?"

"She did not," said the man in the suit.

"She bedridden?"

"Got about fine at church last Sundy. Little bit of limp is all," the suited man said.

"Okay," Heilbrun said, "my mother's eighty-one and wouldn't be caught dead in a bed in the afternoon. Why'd the widow hide from a house fire in her bed?"

"Don't make sense, Sheriff, 'lest she took a nap or maybe felt poorly."

"I know this is a stretch, Joe, but can you see any marks on her? Any holes in her skull?"

"I can't tell. Hell. Just bones and charcoal, and barely that. Musta been a hellacious fire."

"All right. Chief, you see any indications of arson?"

"No way to know. I'd have to pick around the rubble a couple days to rule it out. My money's on lightning."

"Wouldn't that've left marks on the ground?"

"Not if it hit the roof."

The man in the suit touched Heilbrun's arm. "What's eatin' you, Sheriff?"

"I don't like this a damn bit. We got a crew of Pittsburg hoodlums making road trips north to rob old folks, and they always leave their mark. They burn the place to the ground and their victims are always shot in the head with a .22. They haven't hit Walnut County yet, but I got to think this is the first."

"Pittsburg hoodlums?"

"I hadn't heard of em 'til I got a call last week from Roy Stoner, Mercer sheriff. He had an old couple shot and the house burned. Anyhow, he got on the horn with every county sheriff in Pennsylvania, and some in Ohio, and plotted all the victims that fit the pattern. Every one lived three four hours from Pittsburgh."

"I guess if they was coming from Erie, they'd have to be geniuses, something," the man in the suit said. "To get the circle right."

Emeline stood midway along the trail to the house, still hidden. Her wandering gaze settled on the cement slab that used to be a porch, where she'd pulled Deet's ankles. A moment before, at the birdbath, she'd grabbed his arm and he'd reached to her as he sprinted toward his death. Angus had arrived from this direction, as if coming from the farmhouse. He must have finally been up and about, saw smoke, and cut across the path. Came through the yard and saw her cleave to Deet, saw his son's hand linger.

Emeline backed from the house; turned, and spotted an envelope against a hemlock trunk. Though waxy, the bottom was waterlogged and the paper rolled away from the fold in layers.

An oddity—a pair of boot prints next to the tree, the heels dug in and cemented in the mud, as if someone loitered, shifted weight, but didn't move. A man had stood here after the rain started.

Maybe one of those Pittsburg thugs... Emeline twisted toward Heilbrun and stopped. The envelope's flap was open. She withdrew a photo of Angus—Angus, but older. The man might have been his father, or Mitch McClellan's; his hat brim shadowed his hewed cheeks and chiseled nose. His face projected a recognizable brew of pride and arrogance. He was tall, dwarfed the automobile behind him.

It was Jonah McClellan.

She flipped the envelope and read McClellan's address. The post office stamp denoted August—water blurred the day—1946.

Emeline withdrew a black book with names and numbers arranged in a primitive kind of ledger. Last, she unfolded a sheet of paper—a recipe—for whiskey mash.

She looked toward Heilbrun. What's this, he'd say, and she'd say I don't know, but Angus murdered Lucy Mae, and the only witness died in this fire.

And then what? The Sheriff would one day turn those sad eyes at her over Angus Hardgrave's casket, and think, this woman believed Angus killed his other wives—did she do unto him? Did she hasten the *by death do you part?*

Emeline leaned to the hemlock. The recipe. The photo. The book. Walnut Whiskey at the center, and a giant black walnut tree at the center of that. She thought of Lucy Mae's grave, and maybe two others, anonymous under a mat of leaves.

Why there, like some kind of offering?

She recalled picking a BB from Jacob's arm. She'd given him walnut whiskey... *It ain't so bad...* Then, looking out the spare bedroom's window, she'd found Jacob's playground had become the black walnut on Devil's Elbow. Where Mitch had killed himself. Where Angus lounged.

Where he'd had her on their wedding night.

The tree pulled everyone, but only she had the strength to resist. She and Deet. Emeline paused. The hair on her arms stood and a chill coursed her back. Did the tree orchestrate Deet's death? He was the only one unaffected by it. Deet, and her.

"Lord, I'm about to pick a fight."

She quickened her pace along the trail between forest and field. The tendril of attraction from the walnut tree tickled. She firmed her jaw and the presence laughed.

Come, Emeline!

Corn plants resisted her with interlocked leaves.

Closer!

At the field edge, green blades tickled her calf. The tree pulled. She left the corn.

Join me.

She stumbled downslope, caught herself with a painful lunge.

Emeline faced the black walnut. The forest canopy ended with the tree's deep green leaves. Beneath, shade demarked the point of no return.

Touch me.

Her heartbeat thudded under her cast where the break had swollen with recent strain. She wiped sweat from her brow. A cold hand of air crossed over her. Emeline shook. The voice fit the photo of the man who ran whores.

Join us.

She balled her hands into fists. Clenched her jaw until her teeth hurt.

Lord? Guide me.

Emeline placed her palm to the walnut. It was electric, not like last time. An explosion of awareness burst through her, radiated evil in all directions. Everything at the Hardgrave household was within its domain. It wasn't just Jonah McClellan—though he was here too—the evil traced hundreds of years into history— Indians quartered into bloody chunks, hanging from leather straps—and only chose to petrify itself into the form of the man in the photo, Jonah McClellan.

She saw Angus loitering here, filling up his reserves; and Jacob learning to do the same.

She opened her eyes and saw the ground where Angus had taken her on their wedding night, and recalled the grunting of her husband and the groaning of the tree.

Her hand was stuck to the tree bark as some force from within the tree pulled it.

Only a few yards away lay the grave of Lucy Mae—and she wasn't there as Emeline had instinctively surmised, as Angus leaving her there as tribute. She was a prize. The walnut on Devil's Elbow—Jonah—had wanted a trophy to prove his continued virility. The tree kept dead women nearby as rotting symbols of its evil relevance. There were more dead women, here, and the tree wanted more than that.

Her.

Emeline shifted her weight and pulled back from the walnut but it wouldn't release her, as if it held her by dictating the part of her mind that controlled her will to move. It was like waking up from a nightmare and being unable to scream.

She panicked.

"Let go of me!"

Jonah laughed.

Emeline thought of God but couldn't frame a prayer. She felt captive in her own body and battered by waves of evil, sarcasm and rage.

Fighting, Emeline pulled back her broken leg and held it poised, stretching her hip and side. She twisted and released, bringing the plaster cast crashing against the walnut trunk.

Pain like torture flashed through her. In it, her mind was her own and she jerked her hand from the tree and collapsed to the dank ground. She rolled and sobbed. A dozen feet from the tree she stopped and scrambled backward, her lame leg dragging while her other three limbs kicked. Jonah was still in her mind, his laughter and his voice.

I got a spot you'll like.

"Turn here." I say.

A dirt road morphs into a logging trail, kept open by Charlie and his band of dogfighters' continual use. Blackberry bushes border the trail until the gloom chokes them out. Chambers steers along a pair of ruts, taps the gas and the tires spin. The previous day's showers didn't spare Franklin or Oil City; the truck splashes in puddles.

"Easy, now," I say. "Once twenty trucks drive over this, we'll have a rough time getting back out."

"What you got in mind tonight?" he says.

"Couple things."

"You figure to lay money on a dog?"

"Got a sure thing. You want to pick up some dough, you bet when I do."

The truck slips into a rut. Chambers grunts, eases the wheel sideways. The tires fail to grab.

"You don't hafta steer, now."

Chambers releases the wheel and the rutted path channels the tires like inverted train tracks. We follow the corkscrew trail around the hill. Chambers says, "We've gone three quarters around—why didn't we go the other direction?"

"Never thought of that."

"I guess I'll do the thinking in this operation."

This kid's too jolly sometimes. It don't sit. Get the suspicion I'm being had. "How 'bout you shut the fuck up in this operation? How 'bout that?"

The logging road leads away from the hillside at the valley floor, the ruts diverging into choppy dirt and puddles. Evening gloom waxes under the canopy. Chambers pulls the headlight knob. A taillight reflects ahead. "That way," I say, "Pull around with the nose pointed up the hill, close so we can get the trail."

Chambers grins.

I say, "That's right. Just what you think."

A half-dozen pickups circle the fighting pit; Merle's brother Charlie leans on the hood of his truck and men bullshit nearby. A teen boy skitters down a ladder, carries it to another tree, lights a lantern, climbs the rungs and hangs the wire hoop over a spike driven into the tree. Chambers presses the parking brake.

I poke my finger through the jug loop, slam the door with my rear and trudge to Charlie. He smiles until his eyes fall on my folded shirtsleeve.

"What the hell happened to you?"

"Ask your brother."

I offer the jug and Charlie accepts, his eyebrows high. "Merle said you had an accident." Charlie unscrews the cap and sniffs. "Kinda got a funk to it."

"Corn whiskey and a touch of walnut oil."

"Don't know if I should drink it or degrease my engine. This what got your arm tore off?"

"Ah, hell; wasn't nobody's fault; just stupid luck. I don't blame nobody. The company coulda done me better, but that ain't Merle's fault. He be here tonight?"

"Said so." Charlie pauses. Drinks. "You know I'm fighting Thunder?"

"That's why I'm here. Curious about them pups."

"High bid on the male pup is forty-five. Bitch pick is sixty."

"Surprised you're selling the bitches."

"Anything for the breed."

"Don't it hurt business?"

Charlie leads me to the side and gulps from the jug.

I watch a bubble appear in the whiskey. "Looks like you got a good one."

"Shit. Where you get this stuff?"

"I make it. Be in full production in a month."

"I might know a place be interested in taking some off your hands. But about the dogs, see, it's just the bloodline. You got to be able to spot character, and breed to that."

"So what's the secret?"

"I thought you'd ask." Charlie leads me to the tailgate. A wooden crate holds Thunder; I recognize the white patch on the dog's right front leg. A low, disinterested grumble comes from the dog's throat, which ceases when the dog sees Charlie.

"You see that? You think a mean dog has the sense to do that? I'll put a mean dog down. This sport ain't about making a dog full of rage—he's got to be able to use his head in a fight. That's why Thunder's a champ. I'd teach him chess if there was any money in it."

"How you recognize a smart pup?"

"Got to develop an eye. Can't take shortcuts. See here, lookit this." Charlie wriggles his hand between the wooden slats. Thunder licks his fingers. "You try that with Maul, the one Thunder's matched with tonight. That sumbitch'll take your hand off."

"Don't seem like Thunder has much gumption."

"Gumption!" He keels back like I farted green smoke. "That's where you're wrong. He don't waste his strength. He knows it's a fight to the death. Why chew my hand? A champion dog reasons things through. He thinks, I chew ol' Charlie's hand, he's liable to end my sorry life on the spot. So he licks my hand; maybe I'll give him a scrap of jerky. Any champion dog is smarter than the men that bet against him. You remember that."

"Well, you're the professional," I say, "but I'll put my money on the mean dog. You and me, we don't live in a world where you got to be ready to kill right off. We mull things over. Like on a boat chugging to the beaches of France—you got time to build up a good, murdering rage and sometimes it takes years and years. But a dog—he's got to be ready all the time. Thunder might clean up on me in a game a chess, I dunno; but he ain't playing me, and the game ain't chess."

"Whiskey's muddled your brain."

"And I hear Thunder ain't even sharp enough to recognize a bitch in heat. I think you're blowing smoke out your ass with this high-minded bullshit. You lucked onto a decent dog and after that, you put on a circus to sell his pups. My money's on Maul. What's the odds?"

Charlie's lips pucker. "Three to one against Maul."

"You can take my wager right now." I snap a hundred dollar bill from my pocket.

Charlie's face scrunches. "What the hell?"

I tuck the bill in his breast pocket. "You might write my name in your book so you don't forget where you got it."

Charlie retrieves the bill and holds it under a lantern. He holds it toward me. "I can't take your money—look, you come on some rough times. Going broke won't make things better."

"If you ain't got the bank, maybe you oughta let these boys know. Hell, I'd wanna know if I placed a bet with a man couldn't carry a three hundred dollar loss."

"You listen here—"

"I don't think you understand, Charlie. You're the swinging dick, these parts. Take the fuckin wager."

THIRTY FIVE

I sit on a tailgate a few yards from the pit. The business excites but the fight gets tedious. The sound of an occasional breaking bone, the smack of a dog landing on its side in a cesspool of blood and piss—and on the north side of the pit, loose bowels—draws my eye, but mostly I wait. Moths flutter at lanterns that now and again sputter on bad kerosene. Mosquitoes hover near my ears and I pass the hours taking slow pulls from the jug of walnut whiskey and shooting the shit with Chambers. The boy's likable, once a fella gets to know him. Served his country overseas, has the right work ethic, and knows a considerable amount about country enterprises.

"Charlie scheduled Thunder and Maul last just to piss me off," I say.

"Probly have to wake Thunder up and gurney his ass to the pit. Say? You see that other fella, Ticky—what's his name? You see his boy? Kid's face is a mess."

"Didn't see."

"Shit, walk over to the truck. Looks like someone beat him with a porcupine."

I look up from the pit. One of the dogs has turned twice, and the other's ambition stalled. I may as well walk around the pit.

"What happened to your face?"

The boy stares. Man speaks from the shadows beside the truck. "His jaw's wired shut. Dog got aholt him. What happened to your arm?"

"Cathead." I chug a snort from the bottle and offer it. "You the one they call Ticky?"

"That's right."

"Your dog fighting Thunder tonight?"

"Uh-huh. If you're smart, you'll put your money on him."

"Already did. Expect I'm the only one bet against Thunder. Charlie pumps that dog like it's his pecker."

"You seen Thunder fight?"

"Naw."

"He's pure brute, that one," Ticky says. "I seen him. He flat killed every top dog in the state, so Charlie fetched champions from North Carolina, Georgia, New York, even. Thunder licked 'em. These wasn't called fights. Murdered, is the word."

"And Maul's gonna beat him."

"Thunder ain't fought in eighteen months. Ain't trained—he's been dippin' his wick in the bitches, and that can be a fight, I tell ya, but not like bein' in the pit."

I nod. "Two, three differences come to mind, right off."

"Now take Maul," he says. "Prime of his life. Purebred warrior. Muscle lean and strong, and he's got ambition. There ain't a thing alive he don't want to kill."

I glance at Ticky's son.

"You don't worry 'bout my boy," Ticky says. "You just put your money on Maul."

I shake off the few last drops, zip my trousers, lean against a tree. From the periphery the site looks mystical. Lanterns glow orange through low hanging boughs and at any given moment, three or four pickup trucks' headlights point into the center. They switch trucks now and again. Men get drunk on whiskey, beer and exhaust fumes, whoop and curse like fuckin morons or something. They hover close to the pen walls and back away in unison. Charlie's the shaman in the middle.

They watch for blood like they got a need. It ain't curiosity. The way they talk about the sanctity of the sport, the immortality of a champion, a fella could imagine they love their dogs— but he'd be wrong as two boys fuckin. These men are spectators. They've never killed an equal, never made a capital decision. They smell blood and dog shit and watch gnashing teeth and howl at a particularly debilitating wound, but jealousy compels them to the ring, not sport.

They're wrecked men looking for gumption.

Many aspire to breed champions, and several have taken steps—like that idiot Ticky Bilger. They buy into the cult and worship the old breeders like heroes. They believe a champion dog is a perfect alchemy of genes, exercise, and the right mental torments—and maybe it is, but the business hinges on their jealousy of darkness. The business dogman ain't there to enhance the purity of the sport or the breed. His job is to drop evil in a man's grasping hand.

A man tosses a near-dead dog from the pit, climbs the wall, and clubs it. The hypocrisy right there feeds the business. He don't have the stones to club a pit bull 'less the dog is already half dead, yet he falls to his knees to worship the sport.

Dogmen like Charlie corner a narrow market, but I study the theater and the desires it fulfills. Some of these men might pay to be surrogate owners. Hand over cash to take my place beside my dog; feel my pride if the dog wins, club it to death when he loses.

Charlie assumes center ring and barks out Thunder's glorious past, mentions he's got puppies for sale, veritable reincarnations of the greatest warrior dog since the breed baited English bulls. Except for Chambers and me the bets line against Maul. Merle helps Charlie's son unload Thunder from the truck.

Tight cords of muscle glide under Maul's coat. His head floats above his body. His jaw hangs and his teeth gleam a promise.

"Stand back, boys—Maul's got a sense of claustrophobee," Ticky says.

Ticky Bilger holds a pole with a looped rope at the end. Slips it over Maul's head and pulls tight. The device holds Maul six feet away. Maul prances at the end of the truck, stutter-step charging the men who drift close. At the west side of the pit, Charlie holds Thunder and mumbles lullabies into the dog's ear. Thunder licks Charlie's face and turns his head back to Maul.

Ticky maneuvers Maul into place at the east side of the pit, then passes the pole to his son and steps inside the ring. Maul pulls forward, focused on Thunder.

Ticky slides beside Maul, locks an arm around the dog's chest and lifts the rope from his neck.

A tiny breeze carries the ring's death stench. A third man enters, probly another of Charlie's relatives. He holds his right arm above his head, eyes Ticky, Charlie, and drops his arm.

Thunder and Maul catapult at each other, crash together center pit and fall to a writhing, wrestling mass. They slash and clamp until after a few seconds each regains his feet—but unlike boxers in the ring or soldiers on a battlefield, neither studies his enemy or repositions for advantage. The instant one pulls free, he aggresses. Each is a natural force that never abates or surrenders or directs anything but his total self to the destruction of the other.

I lean against the pit.

Thunder has Maul on his back and clamps Maul's face in his jaws. Maul wriggles free. Thunder grapples and reattaches his fangs to the back of Maul's neck. They are on their sides and Maul, for the moment, seems to be resting while Thunder gnaws.

"Thought you called him a fighter," Charlie says.

"What is this, an exhibition?" cries a ringside man.

Finally, Maul snakes loose, flips vertical on his neck, and is free. Men mutter and press to the pen. Maul's haunches fall to the earth. He pushes off with his forepaws, bites and releases Thunder's chest several times in lightning succession, working his way toward Thunder's neck. Within a second of Maul's offensive, Thunder gasps for breath.

"He'd have never gotten away with a stunt like that two years ago," one says.

"Maul wasn't alive two years ago."

"Holy Jesus," someone says, "Thunder's done."

"He ain't done!" Charlie says. "He's gotten out of worse than this."

"Yeah, but look at the jaws on that gray devil."

Thunder drives with his hind legs, spinning Maul a complete circle. Maul holds fast.

Thunder cranes his neck but his teeth fall short and with every effort, Maul's fangs sink deeper. I plumb the dog's eyes to gauge his madness and see if we know one another, see if his past includes his brother's guts flying through the air, spattering the ground like shit dropped from a hemlock; or if the gray dog holds a secret memory of three wives in the same grave, rotting body on body on body. But the dog's eyes speak a different language. The only common vowels are the thrill of murder and the smell of blood up close.

The minutes drag. Maul gnaws Thunder's throat but victory by gnawing can take hours. At times Thunder struggles in spite of what has to be the certain knowledge that doing so allows Maul's fangs to plunge closer to a life-sustaining artery. Men oscillate back and forth seeking a better view; their eyes thirst for the initial spray of arterial blood. Their noise rises with each chomp and grunt.

"You wanna call it, Charlie?" the ref says.

"Call what?"

"Throw in the towel?"

"*Hell* no. Thunder's got this cur right where he wants him."

"You'll eat them words," Ticky says.

"Queer fuck. You'll eat that dog."

I shake my head. Dog fighting is theater. Maul will win—and later tonight another part of the plan will come together. For now, I scan the faces in the crowd.

A man wears a bolo. Thinks high of himself, the way he checks his pocket watch every hour or so and replaces it with a snappy flourish. Maybe a special town lady expects to tear a pheasant with him at a posh Oil City restaurant tonight. He pretends revulsion, and leaves unanswered why he attends at all.

On the other side of the ring stands the bolo man's opposite. He wears rags and another man steadies him from falling into the pit. He whoops with every twist and turn, slaps his comrades on the back and says "blood" in different ways but with the same excitement every time. I might introduce him to walnut whiskey.

The most interesting fella wears work clothes: blue collar, dirty hands and fingernails, rough shave. His open face and eyes say he cleans up real good for church on Sunday, but his soul is tempted here on Tuesdays. He averts his gaze from the gore like a pious man passing a street whore. And then he sneaks a sideways look at her titties. When the others shift to the ring he stands back. And now that Thunder's choking on blood and gasping, mister pious man lips a prayer.

Thunder nears his final moment. Ticky stands with clenched fists, awaiting the fount of blood that'll signal Thunder's demise and Ticky's ascension. Even the boy with the scabbed-over face clutches the oak pallets and leans into the pit. Lanterns sputter like a breeze comes straight from hell.

Maul stands ass high, shoulders low, his body like an archer's bow. We all suck in air and hold our breath, each of us maybe wondering what those teeth would feel like and hoping we don't never find a fate like Thunder's. And after a second, two seconds, three... Maul jerks Thunder's throat open.

Blood spray paints oak pallets. Every man is stone silent. Thunder wheezes blood. History is made. Maul severed the great artery. Thunder quakes and Maul jerks again and again, grunting with each, until Thunder peals with a gurgling whimper and is limp.

Charlie wipes his eyes and says, "He died game. He never flagged. He never turned." Charlie fights to control his face— looks like it wants to crawl someplace and cry. "Thunder died game, you sons a bitches."

The eulogies begin. Thunder's confirmed game death secures his immortality. He passed like a warrior champion; his name will be retired in the state of Pennsylvania; his strength will live forever in his sons.

But I bet if Thunder glances back as he lopes to Valhalla, he'll see a band of cowards standing over his corpse. Nary a one with the courage to take a bite or pull a trigger.

Nary—but one.

"He cheated!" Charlie steps to the center and kicks Maul. The dog growls, jaws still clamped to Thunder. Charlie rears back again, but Ticky scrambles forward and spins his shoulder.

"I'd kick your dog, but he's dead."

"You cheated!"

"How?"

"Poison. Fluffed Maul's coat with arsenic, Slipped Thunder laced bacon. Some damn thing! No way Thunder lost to this gray devil!"

"That devil looks like a champion to me."

"No way, no how. Bets are off." Charlie faces the men. "He cheated."

Men murmur. Most bet on Thunder.

"Thunder was the best there's ever been. Beat by a fourteen-month pup? That never fought before?"

"Was there any way Maul could win fair?" Ticky says.

"No."

"Well ain't you about a piece of roasted shit."

"Bets are off. And you oughtta be lynched, you cheatin' son of a bitch." Charlie rests his hand on the butt of a pistol holstered on his hip.

I gulp walnut whiskey. Clear my throat. "You owe me three hundred, Charlie."

Men stand with clasped hands, looking at Charlie and each other. I scour their faces for a man with stones. You, Mr. Bolo— you pack any rocks? You, Church Sunday—tonight your night?

Chambers shifts to the side. I'd lost track of him during the fight. He approaches Charlie, his arms straight at his side. Metal glints in his hand. There's one other man present, after all. A second later, Chambers stands beside Charlie.

The men hush.

Charlie ain't looked down to see the pistol. His face is a griev-ing snarl. "You best step back, son."

"You made book," Chambers says. "You got to honor it."

"Yeah, well this is my land. These are my boys."

"Your land, your boys—meet my Luger." Chambers points a ten inch barrel at Charlie's face.

"Now hold on." Charlie lifts his hands. "Just hold on."

"I don't expect to leave without my money," Chambers says. "So you may as well pay Angus and Ticky, while you're at it."

"I ain't payin' on a dog that cheated."

"Now it's the dog that cheated?" Chambers squints, cocks his head.

"Does he play chess?" I say.

"I get it," Chambers says. "You didn't balance both sides of the book."

"What do you know about makin' book?"

"I know you're calling foul 'cause you don't have the money or don't want to pay. But you'll honor two bets. I know that."

Chambers backs a step, glances side to side. I step closer and watch Charlie's hand twitch above his sidearm.

Charlie's eyes dart from man to man. "You don't think you're the only man brought a gun?"

"I think I'm the most liable to blow your fuckin head off. Get your book out, Charlie. You owe me sixty, and you owe Angus what—three hundred?"

"Three hundred," I say.

"You want to make that four, Angus, for your trouble?"

"Three hundred." I move to Charlie, pull the revolver from his holster.

"You'll never step in these woods again," Charlie says. "You'll never see another fight."

"Pay up and I'll be on my way."

Charlie withdraws a roll of bills from his breast pocket. He counts three twenties.

"Give it to Angus," Chambers says.

"You might count off fifteen more of those," I say. "Check your book, if you gotta."

Charlie snaps bills through his fingers.

Ticky says, "I bet on Maul. Hey, I bet fifty. You owe me three to one."

Maul breaks his grip on Thunder and sits, then drops to the blood-wet earth.

"You'll never fight that dog again," Charlie says.

Chambers and I back step toward the truck.

Ticky takes the crumpled tens and twenties from Charlie's hand. "Hold on a minute, you two. Gimme a minute."

Pete has looped the rope around Maul's neck and works him to the side of the pit. Chambers holds his Luger on Charlie. I wade into the men, tuck Charlie's revolver into the small of my back and take the pole from Pete. I tell Ticky, "Lift the dog and give him to your boy. I'll make sure Maul don't tear the rest his face off."

With the dog in the truck and Ticky behind the wheel, I lean close to his window. "Stop just before the main road. I want to talk business."

Fifty yards from the road, taillights flash. Chambers stops the Ford a few yards short of Bilger's truck. A shadow climbs from the front seat and Ticky Bilger steps into moonlight.

"He's carrying a pistol in the small of his back," Chambers says.

"You worry like a woman." I heft the .38 used to belong to Charlie, check the cylinder. "Stay in the truck."

I open the door, tuck the gun into the gap between trousers and back, and grab the jug at the foot well. Ticky's truck is a few yards ahead. Maul growls from within his crate. I stumble along the ruts in deep hemlock darkness.

We stand in a sliver of light. Ticky's head moves up and down, back and forth. He's on edge. "'Preciate the hand gettin' outta there. Didn't suspect Charlie'd like Thunder gettin' whupped, but I didn't think he'd go sideways on me, either. What business you got in mind?"

"Have a drink. Tell me if you like it."

Ticky accepts the bottle. His skin is grey and his eyes are pockets of clay. He sniffs and hoists the jug, gulps, brings it down.

"Sheeeit!."

"You like that?"

"Tastes like home." Ticky sways sideways, looks at the truck behind me. "Got some for sale, do you?"

"Only a pint or so left. Take it. I'll come see you after the next batch. If you was to commit to a sizable purchase."

Ticky glances back at his truck. Pete's shadow shifts inside the cab.

"What'll you take for the dog?" I say.

"Aw, shit. He ain't for sale."

"I thought you'd say that."

I pull the revolver from my back and fire a slug into Ticky Bilger's forehead. A black fount erupts like an uncapped oil well, even as he falls. Following through, I fire three shots through the truck window. Bilger's son slumps. Maul erupts.

The jug of walnut whiskey rests in a small depression.

I wave Chambers forward.

"Work quick," I say. I check the boy's body, slip behind the wheel of Bilger's truck and learn to drive with one hand. I get the truck off the trail. Chambers moves my Ford forward, then reverses at an angle to abut the beds. We slide Maul's pen across, then toss Ticky's body in the bed of his truck.

"Lights!" Chambers calls.

"They ain't off but a hundred yards."

"You grab the dough in his pocket?"

"Forgot," I say.

"I'm gonna get it," Chambers says.

"Get the jug, too."

Chambers darts to the body. Behind us, a caravan navigates between the trees; the trucks' headlamps shoot fragmented yellow beams.

"Take the Ford and pull over in the woods, say a half mile toward home," I say. "I'm gonna wait here. See what goes on."

Chambers jumps inside. "You ain't got enough bullets for all of 'em."

I ramble into the woods and hide behind a mossy boulder, huffing with exertion in the cool night air. The headlights near, then by chain reaction starting with the lead vehicle, the lamps go dark as men camouflage their approach to the road. I catch glimpses of the trucks as they cross through a moonlit meadow. To my right, the Ford rumbles as Chambers accelerates on the dirt road.

The trucks weave closer, a snake of shiny grayness slithering between trees. I press close to the rock. In a moment they parade before me. Two pass. The lead stops, a door slams, and Merle calls, "Holy shit they shot him!"

I press lower.

Merle's voice loses clarity amid a dozen truck motors and slamming doors. Charlie steps out of the second truck, splashes through a muddy rut, circles to the front.

"What'd you say?"

Merle points and Charlie halts. "Shit."

"I better check and see if they're alive," Merle says.

"No, don't go over there, less you want to throw your boots away. Don't leave no tracks. I got to think on this."

"Well you know who shot him."

"Who—that fella with Hardgrave?"

"Or Hardgrave hisself, with your gun."

"The dog's gone."

"What do we do?"

Other men materialize and excited voices clamor. Sounds like a bunch of women.

I search the string of trucks behind Charlie's. Nothing moves. No cigarettes burn. I creep around the rock, watch the clusterfuck ahead. White exhaust billows along the ground—the truck burns oil. I peer over the tailgate. Thunder's corpse is in the bed.

The tailgate latch screeches and I pause. The jumble of voices continues. I lower the gate and drag Thunder by his hind leg. The dog falls with a thump. I wait, then ease the tailgate up 'til it barely clicks. I scoop Thunder under my arm and skulk fifteen yards into the trees. A giant beech gives cover. I place the dog on the ground and cup my hand to my ear.

"I'm not gonna have the police on this road, wondering where this truck come from or where it was headed," Charlie says. "We got to move him down the road a ways."

"Why get involved?" the bolo-tie man says. "All we got to do is tell the sheriff what we know, that Ticky and Hardgrave left at the same time, five minutes before the rest of us."

"Son, didn't I just say I don't want them knowing we was back there?"

"You think they don't already? Otherwise, Hardgrave gets off scot-free."

"I got the sport to protect."

"Got to save the sport," another agrees.

"Think of Thunder," someone says.

"All right," Charlie says. "It's settled. Everybody scoots. Tim, you take this truck to the refinery. Drive a ways up Wilson trail, there by the river. And God help me, any you sons a bitches breathes a word of this, you'll find trouble."

Emeline spread an afghan over her bed and rubbed her feet against each other.

The moon suggested early, early morning. She pressed her eyes closed and listened for the rumble of a truck engine or the creak of boots on the stairs.

Since picking a fight with the walnut on Devil's Elbow, she'd realized her struggle wasn't with Angus. He was a minion of the evil gathered unto Jonah McClellan. While touching the tree she'd seen Jonah claim authorship for so many things Angus had done that that she wondered if Angus did anything of his own volition. It seemed as if Jonah was intent on cleaning out Angus and replacing him. It must be hard being caged in a tree, unable to roam. And if Jonah ever succeeded! What horror—pure evil embodied in a man—her husband!

Had Jacob likewise become another underling of evil? Could she trust him in any regard? Couldn't he murder her in his sleep, as easily as Angus?

Her real battle was with the walnut on Devil's Elbow. She lay awake. *But is it my battle, Lord, or yours?* Was she His witness or His instrument? Why make her suffer so much hardship and pain just to watch Him handle the problem? She already knew He was the Lord, so why put on a show? Unless she was to participate.

"He wants me to kill them."

Didn't the Lord have to *command* her to do something like that? But what if He never issued the command? What if Angus jammed a rifle in her mouth?

It's hard to turn the other cheek with a rifle barrel in your mouth.

Her arm slipped to the side of the bed and she rubbed the rounded butt of a knife handle, the blade still sandwiched between mattresses. Would she truly have to wait on Angus to kill her, and only act to save herself once the Lord said it was okay?

Lord, I am in a state of unholy rebellion. I can't lie around and wait for Angus to murder me like he did his other wives. I trust you with all my heart but I don't believe you want me to take no measure to defend myself. If you want me dead then why did you make me? And if I'm going to live, I have to kill Angus before he kills me. I can't wait forever Lord. And you keep saying to have faith but I'm scared. You aren't too clear on your intentions. How can you let so much evil gather in a tree? A tree?

Outside, Rebel's throaty spasms signaled Angus's return. Had she been asleep or awake? Minutes passed. A truck door slammed. The dogs quieted. Emeline sat up in bed and listened. Angus should have entered by now.

She crossed to Deet's room and the hallway light fell across the floor to a canvas sack under the bed. She listened for a moment, then rifled through it.

Slowly she understood the contents. Emeline sat on the edge of Deet's bed and stared out the window. Deet had known his father was a murderer, plotted his escape, and stayed to protect her. She looked out the window through eyes rimmed with tears. The Ford's headlights illuminated the barn and amplified Angus's one-armed shadow. He dragged a sack across the floor.

Emeline returned to bed and lay open-eyed with her hand over the edge of the mattress, fingers tucked between.

Downstairs, the kitchen door creaked.

"Emeline?"

She scarcely breathed.

"I need you down here, Em."

He sounded faint. She lay still.

"Emeline?"

It sounded like a plea.

"Emeline, godammit! Get down here and help me!"

She clunked to the door, cracked it ajar. "I'm asleep."

"Come to the barn. Bring that butcher knife."

The screen door slammed on its springs. His boots thudded across the porch.

Lord, am I your witness or to be your instrument?

Emeline threw a robe over her shoulders. She hammered the butterflies in her stomach with the side of her fist. Downstairs she lifted a cleaver from the wooden block and held it in the window light. Angus honed his knives to a razor's edge on a wet wheel. The way the blade worked on a deer leg bone, it would make short work of a man's skull. She gripped the handle and tested the heft of the blade, waved it side to side, up and down, until the knife felt welded to her arm.

She stood on the porch. The truck's headlamps were dimmer than before. Angus started the engine. Emeline approached. Rebel and the bitch sniffed at the wire fence. Another crate was in the truck bed, and a low growl mingled with the rumbling exhaust. Angus stood at the barn entrance. In the truck's light lay the form she'd seen him dragging. It was a dog.

She stepped closer and observed the animal's bloodied muzzle and blank eyes, his grizzled, torn neck and slashed-open breast.

"He had the other by the throat," Angus said, "and the other had him by the throat."

Her upper lip drew higher.

"Other bastard chewed his neck 'till he couldn't breathe, then split his jug'lar. But he died game. Never let go his hold."

Emeline wiped her eye.

"Uh-huh." Angus knelt at the corpse. "All the boys seen it. I got the other'n in the truck. Acrobat, that dog."

She studied Angus's sweaty neck and the contour of his head, the flat spot on top, where a blade would be unlikely to glance aside. She inhaled. Squeezed the handle. Blood rushed in her ears.

She looked away. Her shoulder ached as if she wielded a cement block.

"What do you want with this?" she said.

Angus looked over his shoulder and she indicated the cleaver.

"We got to skin him an' feed him to the others. Can't waste game like that."

She dropped the blade. It stuck in a plank. She limped to the house.

THIRTY SIX

I look across the toes of my boots, leather permanently damp with accumulated layers of mud and oil, to a steam-like morning mist floating close to the lake. Seems like a long time since I come here for insight.

Touching the tree calms me the way walnut whiskey does, but with a difference of magnitude. A sip of the drink is like kneeling in prayer while a storm rages above. Touching the tree the difference between communication and communion.

The walnut provides images that mark the future with signposts, like an ancestor stands at each fork pointing the direction. I pour an offertory splotch from the jug on the trunk. Can't sit where I used to 'cause the whole limb is snapped and hanging, and it's a minute 'fore I get accustomed to the smell of a dead animal nearby.

I rest against the walnut, arm propped on a comfortable fold of roots, head pressed against a familiar spot of flat bark. First: I ain't yet retrieved the envelope Jacob took from the McClellan house the day it burned. That photo could be a legal claim against the McClellan property—if I want to argue I'm a bastard. Events come and go faster like there's a purpose at hand. Long time ago I thought I did what I wanted for my own reasons.

I close my eyes and see disjointed sequences: three men in a baby-blue convertible, whooping and hollering, spinning out on the dirt beside a macadam road. Rain looming in a grey sky. Wood smoke. I grip the root the way an electrocuted man clutches the current. The image grows strong and clear, and etches itself in my memory.

You got me, Jonah. I got to do what makes sense. I drink more whiskey so I can see it.

Walk away awkward; the leaves are slick with the weekend's rain; once oak and maple leaves mat together, water holds them like glue and they're slick as derrick mud. Only having one arm makes balance something to be mindful of. The going is rough along the lake bank, but a hundred yards ahead I'll find a landing.

Wind comes from the southeast all summer, across the lake and into a wick of forest so narrow, a couple hundred yards at most, that no one'll ever suspect a distillery hides within. Come late autumn the winds reverse. The peculiar thing, said the walnut, is that the wind curls at Devil's Elbow. It crosses the lake, swishes against the hill like against the side of a toilet bowl, and blows right back to the water.

I scan Oniasont, the trail I struck to get here. No footpath will lead here from the road or house. I'll mend the rowboat in the barn and float burlap sacks of corn to the still, and jugs of walnut whiskey back.

A short walk uphill through the wood and I arrive at McClellan's. As a boy I ran through these woods with Larry and though the paths are gone, the contours are familiar. I tromp along looking ahead for a startled turkey or deer. Might be a good idea to shoot a doe down by the orchard where they graze every night. I might mention it to Jacob, now he can shoot.

I arrive at McClellan's from behind. The house has caved in and charred timbers jut from the basement. Mostly it looks like a barbeque pit, with bent black metal mixed with the ashes. I stand at the corner where, in the space twenty feet above my head, the old woman breathed her last under a pillow. I look at the rubble. The bed frame should have survived.

A car door slams. I don't lift my eye 'til Sheriff Heilbrun calls, "That's where we found her."

"A damn shame," I say. "I fixed her cupboard door less'n two weeks ago."

"Is that right?"

"Good old woman, that widow."

"Stopped by the house. Thought you might be here. How you holdin' up?" Sheriff Heilbrun clasps my right shoulder. "Need help making arrangements?"

"Nah. Sendin' him back to the dust tomorrow." I put a hitch in my voice. "It's fuckin hard, Heilbrun."

"Boy had a future."

"Know who did it?"

"Did what?" Heilbrun says.

"Burned this house."

"What makes you say that?" Heilbrun stuffs his hands in his pockets. "That someone did it?"

It's almost like Jonah's in my head giving me the words. "This house weathered a few thousand thunderstorms, no problem. Shit, look at that—it sat on a barn foundation. Them stones is eighteen inches wide. Widow said lightning struck the place all the time, 'fore the turn of the century, before they put up the rods. And I was over at the house the whole time. I'da heard a strike and boom. I'da felt it."

"I came by to ask. What brought you to the house so fast?"

"'Bout all I've done the last week is sit on the porch and try to figger how I'm gonna pull the ends together. Smelled smoke, and when I come down off the porch and looked around the spruce into the wind, there was black smoke over the trees. You stand at my driveway and look, there's only one place on that vector 'til you get to Cal Buzzard's place, six mile off."

"You didn't hear anything suspicious?"

"Suspicious?"

"Car door, shouts. Gunfire?"

"Nah. Well, I shouldn't say that; there mighta been. Hell, the wind picked up, and you know when it whistles sometimes you don't know if you're hearing voices or what."

"Male voices?"

"Hell, I don't know. What are we talkin' 'bout, here?"

"Gunfire?"

"Shit, I don't think so. Though, I had one tied on pretty good."

Heibrun turns away, kicks a dandelion. "There's been a few murders. Two in Jefferson, one in Clearfield, Venango, Butler, Mercer; Christ, all over. Same thing. Old people dead and their houses burned to the ground."

"I knew it."

Heilbrun looks at me.

"Son of a bitch, I knew it. I came up the driveway and a car went tear assin' by. A baby blue convertible, with three boys inside."

"Jigs?"

"Nah. White boys. The one in back was blond. Couldn't see nothing but the shapes of the two in front."

"You saw all that from your driveway?"

"That's right. You sayin' that about the others jarred my memory."

"Gunshots?"

"Not that I heard."

"What kind of convertible?"

"Dunno. Like I said, that car was movin' like a raped ape, and I only saw em a split second."

"You said three of them?"

"That's right. Two in the front, one kind of leaning forward, and that's how I could see the driver. And one in the back seat."

"Well, the other reports say there's only two suspects. You musta seen someone else. You sure there was three?"

"Damn sure. The one in the front leaned forward. You look peaked, sheriff."

Heilbrun studies me and I hold my face flat. He sighs. "I tried to rattle you off a bit. You just confirmed the only thing we know about them—there's three, all right, in a blue convertible."

"That so?"

"You can't guess the make?"

"Big fins, took a bath in chrome."

"Appreciate the help."

I nod. Heilbrun leaves. I cross the lawn to the trail where I'd stood with Jacob, still shaking my head at the profundity of this latest act of walnut providence. The tree showed me the boys responsible for the killings.

I halt, spot footprints in the earth—smaller than mine, larger than Jacob's—and with a wide heel print. I measure it with my boot.

"Five-eighths."

The footprints lead to the envelope resting against a hemlock. Five-eighths the size of mine.

"Where were you this morning?" Emeline said, cognizant of the steak knife beside her plate. She'd passed the semi-delirious hours from last night to this morning sometimes asleep, other times, startled by groaning walls or rustling wind. She'd locked the bedroom and wondered that Angus had never beaten down the door. Never knocked or jiggled the knob.

"Hunh?"

"I didn't see you," she said. "Didn't know when to start breakfast."

"Was out by the dogs."

"Didn't see you by the kennel."

"Maybe I went to the lower corner and took a piss. That all right with you?"

"I checked the pens; I'd have seen you. No matter, though." She moved a piece of ham to her plate. "That new dog's a demon."

"Don't ever get close to that dog."

"I won't love on him, if that's what you're worried about."

Angus chewed with his mouth open. She carried her plate to the sink.

"Love won't touch that dog," Angus said.

She soaped away a spot of egg yolk and grease.

"Dog's name is Maul," Angus said, "and he killed the toughest dog in the state last night. You want to lose your hand, reach for his head."

"Well, I don't know anything about your dogs, and I don't want to. Jacob's the one you'd ought to warn." She placed the plate on the drying rack and touched the skillet to see if it had cooled.

"Goin' out with Chambers today," Angus said.

"We need flour. The rain—"

"Guess I'll get some. Wasn't doing nothin' else."

"Leave me your keys. I'll go myself."

"Don't take a tone. Don't even start."

"What tone? You don't want to take the time out of your day. I'd love to have the chance."

"You're riding my last nerve."

Out the window, Brad Chambers' Fairlane glided up the driveway. "He's here."

Angus walked to the sink and stood beside her. "Put your foot beside mine."

She studied his eye and placed her right foot beside his.

"Five-eighths," he said.

"You can't size a woman for shoes like that."

Angus shook his head and walked to the door. He turned. "You ain't done laundry since Deet kicked off."

"I will."

Angus left. Emeline stood at the window. Chambers watched the house. Angus met him and they ambled toward the truck. Chambers shaded his eyes with his hand and his mouth worked up and down, while Angus looked the other way.

Chambers' baby weighed in her belly like a sack of stones. It would make demands over the ensuing months, and her body would yield. She'd fatten, endure the agony of labor and birth; her breasts would stretch like a cow's teats and her nipples would be gnawed and scarred.

All for the benefit of a baby whose first act in life was theft.

She grabbed a fork at the bottom of the sink, rubbed the tines with her thumb. *Lord, you put* Destroyer *on my white stone. You killed Deet, the best thing about this place. I guess you'll want everyone dead. Is that it?*

A butter knife? No baby could survive a butter knife. Didn't some girls use coat hangers? In her numbness she contemplated impossibly foreign thoughts.

A week ago the baby was both burden and obligation. A child arrived naked and hungry and its mother was responsible. She'd adjusted her preferences to accommodate the reality in her womb. She could see a path forward—the Lord had said to have faith— and that prevented her from the unthinkable. As long as the Lord was with her she would raise Chambers' child so that it had no possibility of growing into its father.

But with Deet gone and the Lord silent her struggle had changed. Evil men surrounded her. Jonah McClellan orchestrated them. A more vital and primitive value system asserted itself. She alone must see to her survival and her only resources were wits and brutality.

Chambers entered the truck on the driver's side and when Angus closed his door, they drove away. Emeline sat on the porch. A cool lake breeze brought bumps to her arms. Jacob stood with a fishing pole by the lake. Maybe, with luck, the imp would slip on a rock and drown. Maybe Brad Chambers would wreck the Ford and both he and Angus would die upside down choking on blood.

Seven weeks since her father had died? Two weeks since she'd escaped Brad Chambers by running to Angus Hardgrave? Only two weeks? She felt a dozen years older.

Was she mad?

Deet said Angus killed Lucy Mae and the others, and she believed him? Deet sought sexual advantage, like all men. What had she actually *seen* Angus do? He was a strong-willed man and rented out her house—but his resolve complemented her capriciousness. He corrected her when he saw the need—but never left a mark. He possessed her body—but hadn't she sworn it to him before God? And didn't the Bible tell her to submit to him?

She was a fool. Deet had sensed her insecurities and fed them. Starving for affection or a hint of understanding, she teased him along though she promised God she'd cleave only to Angus.

But she'd pleaded with the Lord to show her anything to love in Angus. The Lord showed her nothing. Angus wallowed in everything she despised. The foul smell of drink, his temper, his black teeth.

Oh, and he'd murdered three wives.

She'd prayed the Lord would show her she was wrong, but through Deet He warned her about Angus. Emeline prayed for Him to teach her to love Angus, but instead He aimed her love at Deet. And then took him away. Why? Was he a distraction from her terrible purpose?

She paused; illumination shivered through her. Was that the Lord's plan? Why Deet had to die?

The Lord didn't reveal His entire mind, just that small part He wanted her to see. Her duty was to find the context that made sense of it. But all these things weren't accidents. These ruminations on Chambers, Angus, and Jacob were the consonants of a divine command, steeling her for brutal works.

But if the Lord told a person to kill another—or two or three—wouldn't He use a solar eclipse with a booming voice at the moment of darkness, or a discarnate hand scribing Hebrew letters on the horsehair plaster? Why not just kill them Himself? The cathead could have ripped off Angus's head as easily as his arm. The barn roof could have landed on Jacob instead of beside him.

But the Lord had spoken. He named her Destroyer. It was a miracle. Her failure to act was disobedience.

Her faith felt like desperation.

Belief meant trust. She had to know He wouldn't abandon her. If she waited the Lord would deliver her. He tested her faith, her patience, her fealty—as was His divine right. His place was to command and hers was to act. She'd recognize His will by the opportunity He gave her to fulfill it.

Upstairs now, Emeline knelt by her bed. She clasped her hands and brought the bridge of her nose to her crossed thumbs. "Lord, if I am not in your will, tell me."

She opened the closet door and unwound the wire top of a coat hanger. In the bathroom she peered into the mirror, studied her eyes. Placed her hands on the edge of the sink and leaned closer until her breath fogged the glass. She ran water until it steamed, dropped the plug and filled the basin. Soaped, rinsed, and dried the wire. Gathered her dress at her waist. Dropped her panties to her knees, sat on the commode, lifted her unbroken leg through. Elbows folded, the she guided the squiggle-tipped wire inward. She exhaled. It jabbed. She studied the floor. Saw Chambers. Felt him biting her lip. She heard him grunt.

Emeline worked the coat hanger sideways, slowly, blindly, then forward until the point jabbed. Again. With each spike of pain, she withdrew the wire a fraction of an inch, moved sideways, and pressed deeper.

Sweat gathered at her brow.

The stabs came in places she didn't think had senses. She paused, unwilling to retract the hanger and lose the careful progress she'd made, but unwilling to continue stabbing blindly.

Lord what do you want?

She slipped the wire out and threw it, swabbed the bleeding with toilet paper. She made a pad, lined her panties and eased them on. Punched her belly while the dress was high; a new red mark joined the others.

In the hall she whipped open the medicine closet door and rummaged. Rubbing alcohol, aspirin, Tylenol, Mercurochrome, Bag Balm, Epsom salts, and Gold Bond. No paregoric. Emeline recalled the De Ratter, De Mouser in the basement—with the white poison pills. She cold insert one next to the baby.

Lord?

No.

She slammed the door. Pounded and limped down the stairs, crossed the porch and stopped at Chambers' Ford Fairlane.

She'd driven her father's truck along the fields when she was thirteen. The Fairlane wouldn't be much different. She eased behind the wheel and before dragging her broken leg inside, checked the sun visor, where Chambers had left the keys, before. They fell to her lap and she lifted her leg with her arms and jostled into position.

Emeline pulled to the curb at Doctor Fleming's, wrestled the steering wheel and limped quickly to the door. Her eyes were wet but she didn't remember weeping. She crossed the waiting room and opened the door. Doctor Fleming rose from his desk.

He took her hands. "You shouldn't walk without your crutch."

"You have to cut it out."

"Emeline? What?"

"My baby."

His forehead rumpled. "You're misinformed. I don't perform that kind of surgery." Fleming released her hands. Touched her shoulder gently. "Every doctor must seek his conscience for these decisions, Emeline. I've sought mine. I don't play god."

"God made His decision and entrusted it to me."

Fleming rested on the desktop. "If he made the decision the baby would terminate without our intervention. Have you considered giving the child for adoption. Someone else—"

"You don't understand. It's not that I don't want a baby. I don't want this baby to live."

"Good Lord, child. Why?"

"The father."

"Angus..."

"Brad Chambers."

"I see."

"I don't think you do. He—"

"It was against your will?" Fleming said. "That doesn't change anything,"

"If you don't take it out, I'll find someone who will."

"Emeline! Sit... You don't know... I worked at the hospital in Pittsburgh. I saw young women—no! Listen! I saw them arrive, bleeding, dying, because of the work of back alley butchers. Doctors, so called, who used bicycle spokes, coat hangers, Lysol. Knives! I saw a girl, your age, passing feces through her vagina because a butcher put a knife in her. This is what you risk."

"Then you must help me."

"I am not God!" He stood.

She lumbered to the door and slammed it. He thrust it open, called to her as she crossed the sidewalk.

"Emeline, don't!"

She stopped. "Will you help me?"

He raised his wrists as if bound.

She climbed inside the Fairlane, jerked the door. Ten minutes later she swung into a driveway at a small square house with a roofless porch up on cement blocks. A chained dog growled by the steps and a curtain moved. At the door, Jenny Holifield—prom queen—emerged.

Emeline blinked away a film of water on her eyes and opened the car door.

"Emeline? What—you dear! What's happened?"

"You have to help me."

Jenny hugged her. "It's been so long! I heard you got married."
Her face clouded. "What kind of help do you need?"

"I'm pregnant."

"I don't understand."

"I know you can help me."

The hug ended. Jenny recoiled. "I don't know what you
mean."

"You—you and Butch—"

"That's a lie!"

"Just tell me where to go. I'll never breathe a word. You have
to tell me where you went."

"C'mon," I say. "And bring the whiskey."

Chambers stands beside the truck, his arm resting on the roof.
A jug of whiskey sits on the hood. The truck bed is loaded with
empty fifty-five gallon drums.

"We got to get the boat down, and then you can go. I don't
know what kinda work I'm gonna have making it sea worthy."

"Why's that?"

"Got a hole."

"What kinda hole?"

"Maybe a bullet hole."

"Out on the lake fishin' for bass, you run into a U-boat."

"I didn't call it a torpedo-hole, shithead. Musta been a deer
hunter fired off a round in the air and it landed in my barn, is all
I can figure." I twist the cap on the whiskey jug. Chambers
reaches and I pass it.

"Still think we'd have an easier time of it rolling these barrels
through the woods."

"That's why I'm running this operation."

"Who decided to store a boat in a barn loft?"

"Stupid-assed son of mine."

"That's a little harsh. I mean, you bury him tomorrow, right?"

"None too soon."

"What'd he do to get you so riled?"

"Don't worry yourself, y'hear? Just take this rope, tie it off on that beam, and toss the slack over the middle joist. Once you get the boat tied, push out, and I'll belay her down."

"With one hand?"

"All right; I'll hold on 'til you come down and belay."

"What if that support breaks and the boat falls on you?"

"Then it wasn't seaworthy, and we'll roll them barrels through the woods. Gitcher ass up there."

Chambers climbs to the loft, drags the boat to the edge. "You want to toss that rope?"

I pitch the hemp coil. In a minute, Chambers has the boat tied at the mid support, and the rope lobbed across the center joist. I wrap the end around my arm, grip it, and tense up, in anticipation of the falling boat's momentum.

"You ready?"

"Ease her out a bit, and I'll take the slack, see?" I step aside from the boat's likely arc. It teeters on the edge.

Chambers slides the boat into the void and I skip back until it swings across the barn bay, too damn close to the table saw.

"Whoooee!" The jolt lifts me. I kick off and the prow barely grazes my side. Chambers rushes down.

"I got it," he says, lifting the sides. "Cut her some slack..."

"Keep her steady." I let the rope slip around my arm and through my hand, and Chambers lowers the awkward mass to the floor. I flex a cramp out my hand and Chambers studies two holes, one in the bottom and another in the side. Both from the same bullet. Chambers looks at the loft, and then to the boat. He holds up his hand, as if making a few spatial calculations, and rotates his arms while turning his body and craning his neck to watch the loft.

"Your theory's ass backwards. It wasn't a shot from outside coming in and down; it came from down here. See the way those splinters splay in on the side and out on the bottom?"

I face the open barn door. "Well, he musta been standing in the orchard to get the right angle. Hell of a shot."

"If he was aiming at your boat—but shit like this is always accidental. Fella in my unit had a bullet come inside his steel pot, swish around his head, and leave out the front, the same direction it came from. Knocked him out and we thought he was dead. You could see the gouge the bullet left, all the way around the inside of the pot. Luckiest prick I ever saw."

"No shit."

"Mortar took him out a few days later, but bullets couldn't touch him."

I flick splinters from the bullet holes. The wood is solid. Thoroughly fixable.

"How you gonna repair a hole like that?"

"Drill, glue a plug, and reinforce from the inside. Then seal her with a thousand coats of varnish."

"Tonight?"

"Mostly."

"You mind if I run into the house and get a glass of water? I'm about to choke on dust."

Emeline dropped potatoes into a pan of boiling water. A boot slid on the floor. She spun. Brad Chambers stood behind her, close. She stepped sideways and he mirrored her.

"What—?"

He spun her shoulder, seized her wrists so tightly her fingers tingled. She saw his pores and stubble, sweat and dust on his skin; his breath smelled of whiskey and his teeth were gray. He leaned closer until she couldn't bend farther away, and pressed his lips to hers. She clamped tight.

Nose to nose, he said, "Just wanted to tell you we'll be together real soon."

"Let me go."

"I've half a mind to take you right here. You've got to be achin' for me about now, married to that stinking piece of shit for three weeks."

"I'll scream."

"He's in the barn drilling holes. He wouldn't hear, and if he did, I'd step up my plans. Be bouncing you from the bedsprings this very night."

"Why are you doing this? Go away!"

Emeline searched the counter. She stood too far from the knife block. Water boiled on the stove a couple feet away...

"I see your little mind working. Got you thinking. You just don't know how much I love you. I'll be showing you soon. Real soon."

He released her wrists and snugged his forearms around her back; one hand dropped to the round of her behind and he pressed his groin to hers. He sought her mouth. She dropped her chin to her chest and turned her face.

"Go! Leave me alone! Go!"

"Shhh. That's a good girl. Shhh."

"Stop!"

"Shhh. There you go. Easy. I'm gonna loose you, but we'll be together soon. Don't do anything stupid. Shhh. Good girl."

His shirt pressed her face. She smelled sawdust. "The Lord or I one is going to kill you."

He snickered. "Ain't you four aces?

THIRTY SEVEN

A mile back a side road off Route 64 on the other side of Walnut, the town cemetery inters the dead on a hill surrounded by forest. Trees steal in on mossy green headstones that jut from the dirt like hands flagging a friend's attention. Among them are brick-sized markers put up for kids. A dirt lane leads to a wide open field where the newly dead go.

I drive with a bottle of walnut whiskey on the seat between me and Emeline; Jacob rides in the bed of the truck. We ain't spoke since leaving the farm. I swing the steering wheel, hold it with my knees, and ratchet another twist. We bounce around the uphill corner.

Pastor Denny, the cemetery foreman, and the undertaker've been in communication; those three and maybe Sheriff Heilbrun are all I expect to see. No need for a funeral. Deet had no friends and I'd ruther keep the money for a couple things I got in mind. So Pastor Denny'll deliver a few words and then the whole miserable experiment called Dieter will conclude.

Down the hill a casket rests on sawhorses. A pile of dirt sits in front of the grave. Men and women wearing black fill several rows of chairs; more stand at the fringe. I study the vehicles cluttered about the entrance road.

"Wonder who else gettin' buried? Widow?"

I watch the assembly below and swing the truck onto the grass between the first and second rows of headstones. My foot slips from the brake pedal and the truck grinds into a granite marker. Jacob stands in back and falls against the cab's rear glass. Mourners turn their heads.

I circle to the front. A three foot wide stone is on its side. Looks heavy. Rectangle of grime on the pedestal is stark against the polished pink stone. The grass and weeds around the rock base come and go with the season but the rock is close to eternal. Deet, my oldest son, is dead. True dead, never to come back and sass me again. I lean against the front fender and wobble at my shoulders. In the truck, Emeline has her head in her hands.

A minute goes and Pastor Denny touches my shoulder. Sheriff Heilbrun approaches, head down, hands in pockets. He strolls to the front of the vehicle. I watch through the corner of my eye. After looking at the tombstone, Heilbrun opens Emeline's door.

"Who's that group for?" I say.

"They're here for Deet. He was liked."

"Who knew him?"

We walk down the slope. Emeline is at my side using the crutch Deet made. Pastor Denny motions to a row of empty chairs, and we take seats. Denny nods at the group and pulls notes from his pocket.

"Angus, Emeline, Jacob. We are here this morning to express our sympathy. Life always ends too soon. Deet Hardgrave ran into a burning house to save the elderly Widow McClellan, and perished. Words fail us. Our attempts to express sorrow only frustrate us. Though there is a reason Deet Hardgrave died, we are not privy. So let us reflect on his life, console one another, and turn to God's Word for our strength."

Denny lifts his face from his notes, shuffles the top page to the bottom. "Though Deet was not a church-goer, he was a caring and kind young man. He obeyed God and lived a Christian life. He knew one day he would stand before the Lord and accept the gift of unmerited grace. He has already passed through the gates and met his Maker. The scriptures tell us the Lord has found him blameless. In Timothy 4:8 we read: "Henceforth there is laid up for me a crown of righteousness, which the Lord, the righteous judge, shall give me at that day: and not to me only, but unto all them also that love his appearing.

"Death is not sorrow; to the Christian it is triumph. Do not fear death, and do not fear for Deet. He had no fear. He had faith. O death, where is thy sting? O grave, where is thy victory?

"The LORD is my shepherd; I shall not want. He maketh me to lie down in green pastures: he leadeth me beside the still waters. He restoreth my soul."

The assembly mumbles the words with Pastor Denny.

I sit with my back stiff and my head unbowed and recall a couple lines I learned when I was shitting fear on the ship to Normandy. "It matters not how straight the gate, how charged with punishments the scroll; I am the master of my fate; I am the captain of my soul."

Pastor Denny faces me. "Would you like to say anything before we lay your son to rest?"

I'm pretty sure my boy fucked my wife. I look blank at him.

"He was a good son," Denny says. "A good boy."

Four men clad in work clothes stand beside the sawhorses and lift ropes that pass below the casket. With the box over the grave, they lower the rope hand under hand until the coffin settles at the bottom. They withdraw to the shade of an elm.

Pastor Denny grabs a shovel and passes it to me. I drive it into the dirt mound, brace the handle against my side and lever the blade over the grave. Pebbles clatter on the casket.

Emeline pulls my arm. She takes the shovel, rams the point into the pile of crumbly red clay and withdraws a heap. She chucks the load on the casket and fills the shovel again. I touch her shoulder, and Pastor Denny shifts beside her. She bumps his hip aside on the third shovelful. I step back and Doctor Fleming closes in, whispers, "Emeline? You're going to hurt yourself."

"I'm going to hurt *myself*," she says, stopping, leaning on the handle. "You haven't followed very closely, have you doctor?"

"This isn't the time," Pastor Denny says. "Let him go in peace."

I grab Emeline's arm at the elbow and tug her away. She fights. "We're gonna have words on this, woman."

She wrenches free and stumbles. I rear back for a kick and Heilbrun takes my shoulder and I gotto admit I lost my damn cool there a second. I face the men and women who've come to see off my son, and challenge each pair of eyes with my one. They look at me like *I'm* wrong.

Heilbrun leads me up the hill. "Everything all right at home?"

"What you mean by that?"

"You might go easy on her, Angus."

"Might not."

"You good to drive? Maybe I ought to have someone take the truck back for you."

"I got it here just fine."

"Saw a bottle on the seat."

"Didn't want to lug it downhill and back up."

We stand at the truck. "Save that drink for the rocking chair."

"You gonna bring my wife up here, now that you got the whole town thinkin' I don't run my own house?"

THIRTY EIGHT

As Emeline twisted from the sink her eyes sought the rifle that leaned against the trim by the door. Angus drank from a snifter of black whiskey at the table and Chambers sat next to him, between her and the rifle. His gaze rested so heavily on her backside she could feel it.

A car door slammed outside and the chickens raised a ruckus. Emeline looked out the window. "How come the pit bulls don't bark at strangers?" she said.

"They don't think much anything is a threat," Chambers said.

"Who's outside?" Angus said.

"Looks to be that insurance man."

"Ought to see if we can get a policy on Deet. There's an idea."

Emeline scraped the bottom of the iron pan with a wooden spoon and turned the burner lower.

Angus carried his drink outside, shook the short balding man's hand, passed money to him.

The scrape of Chambers' chair focused her. She kept her gaze out the window. The rifle was at the door.

"Won't be long for us, sweetheart," Chambers said. "Every-thing's moving right along. I could've offed him just a little bit ago. I hope you forgive me for waiting. Wasn't the right time. Don't want questions, you know? Has to look right. But soon."

Chambers' eyes were distant. A portal to an inverted mind: she said hate; he heard love. Why tell him anything? God had told her what to do. She mustn't doubt. The Lord would provide the opportunity, and she would act.

Through the window she watched Angus fold her life insurance policy on the roof of the car and tuck it into his pocket. He would now collect insurance money if she died. No matter how she died.

"What's so special about that ugly gray dog on the end?" she said.

"Maul? He's pure killer." Chambers laughed. "That's a story. That's exactly why your old man's gotta go. You think I'm nuts? No, I'm a schemer. I'm patient, and I get what I want. Your old man... he sits down at that tree of his and thinks... and whatever pops in his head, he just goes out and does. Whatever. He thinks an untested dog is going to whup a champ, so he bets a hundred bucks. Then he blows the man's head off to steal the dog. See? Your old man is nuts. Keep your eye on him.

Jacob sat at the table and chewed a chunk of beef tallow. Emeline followed his eyes to Chambers' snifter of whiskey on the table.

"I want that," Jacob said.

Chambers said, "You ain't done nothing to deserve it."

"You wasn't here a couple days ago, Brad." Angus slid his half-full glass toward Jacob.

"Where are you going that you need a rifle tonight?" Emeline said. "Another dog fight?"

"No one's gonna do me the way they done to Mitch McClellan—I'll die before some government thief busts up my works. And that dog ain't gonna fight 'til I find a bitch that can keep from getting killed long enough to breed."

"That why you like him?"

"That dog'll kill anything gets close. If you was smart you wouldn't even walk past the pen. He's a dog killer, a man killer, any damn killer he wants to be. Christ, you burnin' supper?"

"I need you to lift the pot off the burner. I can't."

"You got two arms."

"And both of them hurt from you and everybody else thinking I shouldn't spade dirt on Deet's grave! Look at that mark!" She exposed a flowering bruise on her inner wrist.

"Give her a hand," Angus said to Chambers.

"Look!" she shoved her arm below Angus's eye. "You ever think about how miserable you are, and the Lord only made you to cause harm and hurt?"

Chambers lowered his snifter. "Whoa, Emeline! Glad to help." Moving to the stove, he jostled her hip and stabilized her with a hand on the small of her back. "Easy; don't topple over."

"Just take it off the burner." Emeline limped away and threw an over-shoulder glance at Angus. He watched his drink.

"Angus—"

He looked.

"Slip the chair sideways so I can get in the hutch."

He dragged the chair. She opened the lower cabinet doors, pulled four plates and dropped them on the table.

"Let up on my ears! All right?" Angus said.

"You might make yourself useful and put those plates out. Jacob—silver's in the top drawer. Help yourself, you want to eat."

Chambers stirred the stew.

Emeline sat at her place to Angus's left and folded her arms. Jacob looked to his father. Angus glowered at the stove and Emeline watched them both. Angus clenched his jaw. The basin between his cheek and jaw bones seemed deeper than she recalled. He'd grown gaunt.

"You'll find a ladle in the middle drawer, Brad, and a bread knife beside it. Maybe if you're real sweet Angus'll help you with the plates."

"For Chrissake shut up, woman!"

"For Christ's sake? For His?"

"I'm about to bust your skull."

"Real close?"

"Here you go, Emeline," Chambers said, "I'll serve you first." He rested a plate with a heavy slab of bread slathered in butter, and ladled stew in front of her. He went for the next plate, and she scooped stew on top of the bread and ate. "I already said *my* Grace. You want to know what I prayed, Angus?"

He looked at the stove.

"I didn't expect you did."

A breeze carried the sound of men toiling against metal and wood through the open living room window. She moved to it and looked toward the lake. Angus ground-guided Chambers in the Ford through the tall grass down the bank. Jacob trailed. An upside down boat rocked on top of fifty-five gallon barrels. The bed contained other metal objects too small to discern, pipe, maybe, a toolbox—junk.

Angus resembled the McClellan in the photo, and the items in the truck recalled faintly the shape and intent of the machinery behind him. She thought again of how the two seemed to merge.

Chambers headed toward Devil's Elbow and passed the walnut. At an angle so tight the window glass rippled the picture, Emeline watched Chambers park the truck. Together Angus and Chambers caught the edge of the boat, flipped it bottom side down, and pulled it to the lake.

Chambers rested the first empty barrel inside.

"Easy, now!" Angus called. He scratched his head and Chambers mounted his hands on his hips, and after discussion, they filled the rest of the boat with smaller items. Chambers boarded, took an oar from Angus, and paddled side over side. Angus pulled a rifle from the truck and trudged along the bank until he passed from Emeline's sight. She hurried outside, across the porch, every other step jarring her broken leg. Hidden by the spruce, Emeline watched Chambers oar to shore a hundred yards beyond the Devil's Elbow, at a place where oak and maple leaned over the water and created the shadowy illusion there was no land at all.

Through a gap in the foliage Emeline saw Angus and Jacob unload the boat and then Chambers returned to the truck. Emeline shifted behind the blue spruce.

Chambers had drawn Angus to the project he'd drafted on her kitchen table.

I'm with Chambers and Jacob at the foot of the walnut.

"Jacob—time you run along to bed."

Jacob snickers.

"Get along."

He's drunk and tired and the sound of his pant legs in the grass trails off.

"Brad—I want you to try something," I say. I don't know if it's just the McClellans that it works for. "Come here. Put your hands on the tree."

Chambers is a few feet away, and stubs his toe to tuft of grass. "What you got in mind, Angus?"

"Just try it. Here, like this." I press my palm to the walnut. As if the tree has been waiting, an image shoots through me and I forget Chambers. I don't recognize the house or the room, but Pitlake trembles with pancake eyes, his face broken by the dark silhouette of a pistol's front sight post.

Even as this prophecy fades, another takes shape on top of it, Emeline, pouring whiskey, rubbing my shoulders—

"What the hell you doing?" Chambers says.

I move away. A torn-fingernail moon sneaks through leaf cover, the rest is dark. "I'm gonna handle a problem tonight and I need your help," I say. "I got an opportunity. I need a ride into town."

"What's in town?"

"Business."

Chambers stalks forward, touches the tree with his index finger, then his whole hand. His face is empty. "You're some kind of queer," he says.

"Did you see anything?"

"See what?" He throws his other arm back in a spastic arc. "Wait! I see it now! You're gonna be the president!"

"Fuck you."

We walk to the truck, parked at the water's edge. Chambers says, "I got to know more than you got business in town. You want to buy a cheeseburger, that's one thing. You talk to trees and, well—a fella wonders what you're thinking."

He motors the truck up the hill. We crest the knoll and turn the corner around the spruce. Jake watches partly hidden by the front door. "Stop here," I say.

Chambers waves his hand. "That's a wily boy you got."

"I'll be right back."

Jacob runs and hides somewhere and I pay him no mind. Inside, I swap the rifle for a box of bullets. Climb back into the truck.

"Pitlake." I say.

"You need another tractor?"

"No—just to keep the one I got. Pull over by the Fairlane."

"Keep talkin'."

"Supplies cost money. Yeast. Grain. Pitlake has lotsa dough, probly just laying around. Sheriff said there's been a spate of robberies. Mercer, Jefferson, Clearfield. All over. It'll look like the same fellas did this one."

"What robberies?"

"All over. They musta been a dozen of em and the police in every county north of Allegheny's pullin' their hair out trying to figure who's behind it. We'll give em one more to puzzle. When they catch the other fellas, they charge em with ours."

"Just a robbery?" Chambers brakes beside the Fairlane.

"He's got my tractor's serial number in his books. I take what cash is layin' around and grab the ledger."

"You figure to pop him?"

"Crossed my mind."

"Good times is good times, but the State of Pennsylvania don't have much sense of humor about murder."

"Don't trouble yourself on it." From the glove box, I withdraw the revolver I took from Charlie. Open the cylinder. Four is plenty.

Chambers reaches under the seat and his hand comes up with his Luger.

"Loaded?" I say.

"No use empty. But this is your gig," Chambers says. "I drop you off and come back when you tell me."

"Fair enough."

We ride in silence for fifteen minutes. "Kill the lights. Pull over here."

Chambers drifts to the curb. It's a rich man's street lined with rich man's trees—maple, likely. Roosevelt runs parallel to Main, one block removed. Rightward, at the rear of Pitlake's Farmall dealership, stacks of oak pallets rot and old machinery taken on trade rusts. Leftward, Pitlake's ranch house sits back from the road, fronted by lawn acreage that implies royalty.

I run my thumb against the side of the pistol and slip from the seat, latch the door with a quiet push. I circle the vehicle and lean at Chamber's open window.

"You stay put and I'll be back in no time."

His chin moves up and down. The rest of his face is in shadows. I slink across the street and follow the long driveway close to the hedges. Tires grind gravel and I turn. The Ford creeps down to the bend, out of sight. Brake lights flash a hundred yards away at the corner of the block.

I glance at Pitlake's house, then back to the Ford.

"What the hell you doing, Brad?"

I rub the revolver hammer with my thumb. Chambers is a good kid. Learned tactical thinking in the war. Getting a few yards between him and the house makes sense.

A dog barks with raspy, tick-tock pace, far enough away no one in the Pitlake house will hear. I step on the porch, roll my boot from heel to toe. It creaks dull like it's been soaked in water. I tuck the pistol in my pocket, twist the doorknob. Take the gun in hand and push the front door open with the barrel. Breathe warm, fresh-bread air. I look corner to corner, shadow to shadow, measuring grades of gray for movement.

A man snores in a room down the hallway and in the adjacent living room a clock ticks on the fireplace mantle. I tingle. My stomach growls for some of that damned bread.

Whiskey would steady my nerves. I might dig a flask out of the bureau back home. Strange thoughts with a killing at hand.

My nose guides me to the counter and I stoop at a pair of cooling loaves. Tap the crust with the pistol barrel. Place the revolver on the counter. The bread is warm and greasy with butter on the crust. I rip a mouthful, move to the living room where a hutch-like desk seems the locus of family business. I open a drawer and listen. Pitlake snores. A distant dog bays. Mantle clock ticks.

I find a bankbook with a twenty-spot tucked in the flap, but nothing else save correspondence. Each footstep tempts the groan of a maverick floorboard, but the house is sturdy and I cross to the hallway. Probing the darkness with the .38, I pause at each door and listen for a child's telltale mumbles. Each room is silent. I arrive at the end of the hall. A sliver of grayness marks where the door gaps from the jamb, and Pitlake sleeps within.

Hunting deer as a boy, I sat on stump one winter morning and leaned against a hemlock; behind me, a thicket lined the field's edge. In summer the briars drooped with blackberries. In winter, the thicket and an adjacent seam of ice age rocks funneled deer into a meadow just below where I waited. A savvy old doe knew I was close, but needed proof. So close, her huge eyes reflected snow and trees. She stamped her front legs and swung her head. Turned away and spun back to me, hoping to catch me in motion.

She pitted her intelligence against mine. I relaxed my face. Controlled my breath so the frost trickled over my coat. She was beautiful. She convinced herself I didn't exist, and tiptoed away.

I shot her.

Pitlake stops snoring and a woman voices her sleep delusions.

I exhale like to control the flow of frost over my chest. I touch the barrel to the door. Push.

Nonstop talk. She giggles, says with a mother's tone, *What are you doing?*

My pulse thuds.

Honey, put the frog down. You'll get warts.

Blood rushes in my ears.

Pitlake kicks his blankets. "Warts."

He probly answers her a thousand times a night, conversations like dead letters.

My lands, isn't it though? Up and up. Well bless your heart...

Pitlake groans. The room smells of sweated-out onions. I point. Thumb the hammer. It clicks.

Pitlake sits bolt upright. I see him, a shadow against a deeper hue of black. The woman stops mumbling. She's propped on her elbows.

"Who are you?" Pitlake whispers. "I'll show you the safe. Is that why you're here?" Pitlake shifts.

I hear fear.

"Don't move."

"What do you want?"

"Please, mister," the woman says. "Take whatever you want."

"Matches," I say.

"Cupboard over the stove." Pitlake's voice is clear, alert. "You want to go out and smoke? Talk?"

I fire twice into Pitlake's chest and once into his wife. I have one shot left.

I tuck the .38 in my pocket and hurry to the kitchen. The barrel is hot at my thigh. I tear another bite from the loaf of bread and open the cupboard above the oven. The matches are in a box up front; I dump a few to the counter, strike one, hold the flare to the curtain at the sink window. Carry the box to the living room and ignite stray papers on the desk.

Fire splashes the kitchen in yellow light. I freeze. Chambers stands to my left, his Luger nothing but a shiny dot pointed at my head. He's stark-faced and calm, like I imagine I was a few moments ago.

I see an orange burst.

THIRTY NINE

Emeline reclined against pillows. A shaft of moonlight draped across her legs. Angus had returned from the forest only to depart again with Chambers.

She wiggled lower on the mattress, snugged the blanket at her neck. Timbers ticked and groaned and though she'd had a month to acclimate, the noises struck her as foreign and reminded her she was alien. She lay in an evil bed, in an evil house, about to be consumed.

She climbed from bed and crept down the hall, cringing each time her leg cast touched the floor. Jacob's room was silent. The boy's eyes seemed empty lately. He followed Angus as if making a study of his father's every characteristic. He'd started spitting, without even chewing tobacco. Tssst! It was too easy to imagine Jacob's hollow eyes behind a knife.

Downstairs she clicked a lamp. The rifle Angus had carried into the woods leaned beside the door. She listened. He could be asleep, snoring, anywhere. Or awake, watching her. She looked through the window to the porch, and then from the kitchen toward the barn.

The truck was gone.

Emeline lifted the rifle, broke the lever open and checked the chamber. One in the breech and more in the internal magazine. She carried it upstairs, turned on a lamp, and rested the rifle on the bed beside her. She pulled her new diary from between the mattress and box spring. Pen in hand, she wondered what to write.

She moved the rifle between her legs. The hours passed and nary a word issued from pen to page. Leaves rustled in wind. Branches groaned. She imagined a complementary flurry of noises: a car door, footsteps, fist pounding on door, and the inevitable confrontation. It would surely happen tonight.

He had life insurance on her.

Emeline stood at the window. The moon had passed and the lamplight painted her reflection on the pane. She lifted the window and cool outside air carried the sounds of crickets and frogs.

She needed a hiding place for her diary. Angus had probably already found it. Could he read? How could she not know if her husband was literate? He had volumes of books but never opened one.

She pulled the string dangling below the closet light bulb. The horsehair plaster flaked at the corners and a crack descended from the ceiling, but the surface was inviolate. She pushed clothes aside. At foot level she saw a gap between plaster and timber, barely wide enough for her diary. She could slip the book along the floor, far enough to be invisible, and fish it out with a toothbrush handle.

Emeline knelt and shifted her shadow from the gap. Something dim and gray reflected within. She pressed a pinky into the slot and withdrew a leather-bound volume.

Emeline lifted the cover to the first page.

Lucy Mae Hardgrave. My Diary.

She turned a leaf. No dates. Terrible penmanship.

"I'm so lucky to have a man as clear-headed and far-sighted as dear Angus Hardgrave. And sophisticated, for a country man. Already bought me a life insurance policy—and me just a woman!"

A bullet cracks past my ear. Behind me there's a thud like a baseball bat hitting meat. Smoke hangs at the ceiling. The walls ripple in flame. Chambers fires again, just missing me a second time. I twist. A boy collapses against the wall and a deer rifle drops from his hands. His eyes waver in firelight.

"He had a bead on you—and you was chewing bread," Chambers says.

"What are you doing here?"

He tilts his head like I'm a dumb shit.

We run out the front door. Flames lick the windows and cast light to the lawn. A half-dozen dogs bark across the neighborhood, but fifty yards stand between this house and the next in either direction and darkness covers the farthest territory of the lawn. Neighboring houses flash porch lights and slam doors.

"Quick," Chambers says, "around the back."

"Why?"

"That' where I parked. C'mon, damn you!"

We navigate to the west side and follow a windrow of trees. My lungs are hot. The exhilaration recalls Normandy. Some neighbor gets nosy, I'll plunk him.

A man shouts.

We reach the truck and Chambers tools along without head-lamps. He turns right, goes a short block, and then right again. He turns on the lights.

"Shit!" I say. "You're driving right past it!"

"No one knows this truck."

"Course they do."

"We got to get back. Or would you rather I take 322 and waste an hour?"

"Just go faster."

"Normal person'd slow down and lend a hand. Maybe we ought to pull over."

"That's about fuckin stupid," I say.

"Think on it. Or you want to ask your tree?"

"What reason we got being out this time of night?"

"Something in Oil City. Play it cool. Thought you had a back-bone, for crissakes."

Chambers swerves to Pitlake's lawn, stamps the brake and the truck slides. He jumps out. I slam the pistol in the glove box and join him at a gathering of men and women in nightclothes.

"Anyone gone inside?" Chambers says to a man in boxer shorts and boots.

"You'll burn alive!" a woman says.

"Don't!" another woman shouts. Others join from the flanks. "There's nothing anybody can do. Didn't younz hear the gun-shots?"

"Gunshots?" Chambers says. "From here?"

"Afore the blaze," a man says. "Say, ain't you the fella at London Cleaners?"

"That's right." Chambers looks closer. "Joe Bandman—didn't recognize you in your skivvies. You say there was shootin' in there?"

"Uh-huh. Two men come out and followed them trees back to the byway there. Long gone by now."

"Is anyone inside? You sure no one's inside?"

"I heard four shots. There's four Pitlakes." Bandman shrugs.

"Four Pitlakes?" I say.

"That's right."

"Well, we got to try." Chambers turns on his heel.

"You'll die!" a woman hollers, "like that young fella not a week ago."

Bandman places a hand on Chambers' shoulder. "There's nothing we can do, son."

A fire truck arrives. We watch with the others. More neighbors gather.

"Hardgrave—what are you doing here?"

Sheriff Heilbrun stands a few feet away, hands on hips, head level, badge glowing orange.

"Came from Oil City and saw the fire. Chambers here was driving, and pulled in to see if we could lend a hand."

"Oil City?"

"That's right."

"Just come from down east a ways myself." He rests his hand on my shoulder and leads me from the group. "You see all them deer in the field by Shuggart's place—musta been a thousand glowing eyes. You see that?"

"Wasn't lookin'. Dozed off. Long night."

"What's going on in Oil City?"

"Oh, a little speculation."

"Why you coy? I'm trying to figure out why I'm seeing you at a house fire again, and you ain't telling me a damn thing I need to hear."

I lower my voice. "There's a crew in Oil City fights dogs. Spent half the night looking for a turnoff that don't exist. I got bum directions, and that's a separate score. But me and Brad here pulled in to help. If that ain't the truth, God can strike me down."

Heilbrun removes his hat and brushes hair from his forehead. "These damn Pittsburgh boys, again. I'll lay odds the Pitlakes are inside with .22 caliber holes in their heads."

"No one we talked with saw a getaway car, but that fella Brad knows—"

"Joe Bandman."

"—Bandman said he saw two fellas take off around the back."

He gets drinking and he's different... Down the page: *It's like the tree is his mistress. Or Master. I can't tell. When I first came here he said he didn't like to tarry at the Devil's Elbow. Now it's where he finds his rest.*

Emeline rustled back to a page two-thirds of the way through the diary. She pressed her thumbs to her eyes, blinked several times.

He said, 'you're getting on my last nerve.' He beat me, again. Again. Who can I tell? Willard Prescott? I'm trapped. Cooped up in this god-awful house, don't know anyone, anymore, and Jacob's going to have the same life.

The final entry, the only one with a date:

December 6, 1956: I told Angus I'd take Jacob someplace, instead of having him grow up with an evil fool for a father. I'm leaving when he goes hunting. If I can make the truck start. He bought it with my money, anyways.

Deet had said Angus shot Lucy Mae during buck season.

Emeline climbed out of bed and tucked the volume into the closet corner. She placed her diary on top, and slid both back until shadows hid them.

A slight gust lifted the curtain and she collected her thoughts. The truck door slammed.

Emeline hobbled to bed and drew the covers. Footsteps echoed from the porch and the front door groaned. She should have locked Angus outside the house, but that would've only made him mad. Maybe he was drunk and would sleep on the couch.

Footfalls pounded the stairs.

She looked at the door—the lock was upright! His boots grew louder in the hall. The doorknob twisted. The door swung open.

Angus stood with his head low and studied her. He looked at the rifle in her lap, pointed vaguely his way. "I was lookin for that."

"Why?"

"What you need with a rifle?"

"I heard noises outside—I'm not used to living so far away from everything."

"Well, gimme that, 'fore you shoot yourself."

"You ain't angry?"

"Why the sam hell'd I be angry?"

"You stand back a bit." She waved the rifle at his belly.

"You lost your damn mind?"

"I haven't lost my mind. It's you that's been acting crazy and I'm through with you. Sit in that chair and we're going to discuss some things."

She rested the rifle on her legs again, with her finger inside the trigger guard. Angus studied the hammer, then his gaze found her face.

"It ain't cocked," she said. "But that don't take but a second."

"I done right by you. You're about to piss me off."

"What happened to Lucy Mae?"

"Cunt run off."

"I heard you shot her."

"Who said?"

"Deet."

"And you believed him!" Angus rapped the dresser side with the base of his fist. "I knew he was after you. And I knew you give him what he wanted."

"That's not what we're talking about."

"I'm talkin' about it." He stood. She lifted the rifle. He stepped closer. "I say we're talking about it. I treat you good. You're the damn fool busted your leg and trot that pussy in front of Deet's nose."

She ratcheted the hammer. "You remember when the marriage is over, right? Death do us part? You ready for your freedom?"

Angus combed his hair with his hand. "I know things've been rough with your leg, but damn, Emeline; you was coming around. And look at my arm. This ain't been a picnic."

"I'll be on my way tomorrow or the next day. I'll move myself, thank you, and send some boys with the pastor to come get the tools from the shop, and it'll be like you and I never saw each other. Until then, you can sleep on the sofa downstairs, and cook for yourself."

He stood. "Why don't you put the gun down, Em?"

"And you'll need to tell Chambers to move out of my house. Tomorrow."

"Maybe we'd best sleep on it. Look, I'm a-backin' away. Put that down?"

Angus stepped through the open door into the hall. He smiled, closed the door, and his boots clomped down the hall.

Emeline listened, leaned forward, and when the house was silent, lowered the hammer to half-cocked. Heart racing, she limped across the room as quietly as she could. As she reached to the lock, the bedroom door burst open. Angus lunged through, punched her jaw. She sprawled to the floor. The rifle spilled from her hands and slid. She felt a loose tooth in her mouth, tasted blood. She spat both to the floor.

Angus clomped into her path to the rifle. She kicked away on all fours.

"You gonna pull a gun on me in *my* house?"

His foot lashed to her hip and she pitched. He lifted the rifle. Pointed at her.

"I oughta end this! I swear I oughta right this very damn second."

"Do it." She looked past the barrel sight to a black pupil circled with a bloodshot white. The lamp cut steep shadows in his cheek hollows. She glimpsed Jacob at the door.

"Why don't you?" she said. "Show your last son how a real bastard handles his wife."

Angus glanced at the door, and Jacob. "Outta here, boy." He leaned the rifle into the molding at the closet, tossed a blanket from the top shelf over his shoulder. Looking at the floor, Angus grinned.

He stood over her and reached down. She shrank. He picked up her bloody tooth and held it up so she could see. "This is the toughest thing in your body," he said.

Angus placed the tooth back on the hardwood floor. He grabbed the rifle from the wall and vertically smashed the stock butt to the tooth. He lifted the butt and with his index finger wiped away the gritty residue. "That's a lesson in frailty, Em. There's nothing stronger in you."

Rifle in hand, he left.

Shaking, scarcely breathing, Emeline listened to his footsteps fade. She climbed to her feet and locked the door.

Emeline woke with a start to silence and a warm breeze through the window. Her jaw ached. Her hip was tender and her eyes were swollen. Her first thought was of Lucy Mae's diary, her second, the likelihood Angus would shoot her the minute she stepped outside. Would he at least try to get her on the grass? She crept to the bathroom and splashed water to her eyes. The house was empty and the Fairlane was parked out front. The truck was gone. They must have gone out for more supplies, more barrels.

She thought of the envelope with the old photo and the machinery—the still. That's what Angus was doing. That's why he took the rifle to the woods.

Why hadn't he already killed her? Was it him, or Jonah deciding her fate?

Emeline lifted the telephone. She dialed the operator and asked for Hannah Kirk.

"This is Emeline. I need a favor."

"How are you, Dear? Are you okay?"

"Who are those people that go looking for moonshiners?"

Emeline parked Chambers' Fairlane in front of the bank and entered. The echoes of her feet on the floor brought to mind the last time she was there. She half expected Angus to grab her wrist. The same teller stood behind the same brass grill.

"I'm here to withdraw a hundred dollars."

"Do you have your bankbook?"

"I don't have one. But that didn't stop you last time."

"But, what account? I don't know that you have an account."

"Angus Hardgrave."

"Hmm." He turned, opened a card catalogue drawer, flipped through tabs. "No, Mrs. Hardgrave, I'm afraid Angus never added you. Just takes a short form, but it'll have to be him that takes out the hundred dollars."

"Look, you fool. He just lost his arm and buried his son. You think he's up for running errands? No. I'll tell you why—"

"Hold on, now..."

"He's holed up in the house and won't come out, and if I don't get my hands on that money, Deet's funeral doesn't get paid, Angus doesn't get his medicine, and his eight-year-old boy doesn't eat."

"Now, Mrs.—"

"Do you know how embarrassing it is for a man that can't read nor write, other than to scratch his name? Can't you be decent, for once?"

"One hundred. Just a minute. Please."

Emeline drove the Fairlane to a small lot by the Walnut macaroni factory and parked where forty cars camouflaged it. Maple trees lined the sidewalk; their roots lifted and cracked the cement slabs. Keeping her focus on the uneven surface, she limped a block and a half to the one-screen Orpheum Theater. The marquee read, *An Affair to Remember.*

She studied it a long moment.

The adjacent alley turned to cobble and emptied onto a parallel backstreet. Opposite, a block of brick houses with four-sided roofs, each a perfect replica of the next. She limped to Main and looked north and south, then at the end of the alley, leaned against ragged clumps of mortar.

She turned to a rumbling engine and the sound of tires on gravel. A car with dual headlamps and a bumper like a dark smile swerved from the brick street into the alley. She pressed to the wall.

The car stopped; she leaned to the open passenger window. The man looked straight ahead. His hair was grey and oily and too long, and his chest seemed propped on his belly.

"You Emmy?"

"That's right, Doctor—?"

"You got the hundred?"

She nodded. He didn't see. "I do."

"Get in."

A boy walked by on Main Street, turning his head as he passed. She touched the door. Hesitated.

"You want help or not?" he said.

She thumbed the release and opened the door.

"Sit in the back. Lever's on the side."

She flipped the seat forward, and struggled into the back.

"Cover your eyes." A black wool scarf lay on the seat. "Either that or get out."

She wound it around her face, smelled salt and sweat, wondered how many other girls' tears the weave had absorbed. The car moved forward.

"Lay flat on the seat."

She leaned. Wool fuzz prevented her from focusing through a gap at the bottom of the scarf. The car turned right and accelerated. North. After a short while, the driver swung left and she recognized the curve. The speed didn't change for a long while. He was taking her to Dubois.

The car turned right, drove straight, then left. Every few seconds it rocked a different direction. Finally, the car slowed, climbed a small grade, and the motor noise reverberated as if they had entered an enclosed space.

"Sit up. Take off the scarf."

She slipped it over her brow. The car door opened and a woman peered in, maybe the man's mother from her corpulent face and triple chin. Her eyes judged; her lips were blue.

Emeline worked her leg out of the car; the old woman yanked her arm. Glared. "Don't dilly-dally all day. We got to get you inside."

The man had stepped around the car and entered the house, leaving the front door open. Emeline stood under the carport and looked across the hood. The slope of the terrain and the boxed-in houses confirmed she was in Dubois. Oaks besieged the hillside community as if the settlement had been built before the land had been cleared, and afterward, removing the trees was too burdensome to bother. Not a single house had a lawn or garden.

"What happened to you?" the old woman said.

"I broke my leg."

The woman shook her head as if suffering a fool. The man stood inside the house. He wore a suit jacket with a baby blue tie that had brown food stains. He left the kitchen before she could study his face.

"Inside, tramp." the old woman said.

Emeline climbed the cement blocks and crossed the threshold. The pungent combination of odors was hard to place. Maybe feet, maybe garbage. A long, thin, silver instrument gleamed on the sink drying rack, the only clean item in the kitchen. It caught light from the single bulb overhead. The woman followed and closed the door. Emeline felt a growing awareness that darkness surrounded her, as if upon entering the house, she had stepped into the shade of the Walnut tree.

"Where's the money?" the woman said.

Emeline pulled the bills from her purse. "What's your name?"

"Doctor'd go to jail if people found out he helped girls like you. Girls like you never think of that, do you? A barn owl breaks wind and a tramp like you spreads—"

"Mother!" The man called from the side room.

"Give me the money," she said.

Emeline passed the bills

"Take off your underwear and lay on the table. Put your legs up. You're used to that, right?"

The table had a marble pattern with a rim of shiny aluminum. Emeline pushed and it wobbled; the pole legs slid on linoleum. She searched for grime or blood. The top, at least, was clean.

"Press it up against the wall," the woman said.

"Right, okay." She pulled her panties to her knees, slipped her good leg out, and slid over the edge of the table. Heat spread across her face. She looked at the door, at the drawn curtain. The lock.

She reclined to her elbows, then all the way back. The weight of her hanging legs pinched her lower back. At least her dress covered her. The old woman lifted Emeline's ankles to the platform and shoved her back. Her leg throbbed. She bit her lip, tucked her quivering hands below the arch of her back.

The man shuffled into the kitchen—his soles scraped the floor as if rolling on sand. He stood at the end of the table, between her feet. "This will only take a minute."

Lord, if it's your will, take this baby into your arms. I know I'm terrible but you made me. And if you don't want the baby then I suppose it'll wait for me in hell.

"In a moment I'm going to install a small dose of a medicine. You won't feel anything, not for the first twelve hours. After that, you'll curse your existence. It will hurt like nothing has ever hurt you." He nodded at her leg cast. "Worse than that."

"Will you take... it... out?"

"You'll deliver a stillborn. You're a couple months along—it will look like very heavy clotting."

The doctor applied a cold and slippery lotion to her, then stepped away. She heard him off to her left—maybe at the sink. Something clattered.

"Maybe next time you'll think," the old woman said.

Emeline closed her eyes and tears pressed out. She imagined holding her baby close to her breast, peering into its bright eyes and smelling its innocence.

THE MEN WILL DIE.

She heard the voice but from where she couldn't tell. It was like in the field talking to the Lord but more real, more present. *What? Is that you?*

FAITH, EMELINE.

Lord?

She recoiled. Something cold and smooth slid inside her. The instrument from the sink. The poison.

Lord, where have you been? You used to talk to me all the time. You said to trust...

BEHOLD...

Emeline could almost see the Lord—she groaned. Her mind seized. She suffered a blinding flash of awareness, like staring into dazzling white heat and peering for the source.

YOU LOVE ME BUT YOU DON'T TRUST MY LOVE FOR YOU. DESPITE ALL I ACCOMPLISHED TO CLAIM YOU, YOU REBEL.

Emeline saw the white stone with Destroyer underneath, and in sudden series of images observed herself preventing the judgment of the Lord. As a tornado hurled the barn roof toward Jacob, Emeline turned on the porch light and screamed. The light allowed Jacob to escape. She saw Angus collapse on the floor after the Lord smote him at the oilrig, and she prevented him from bleeding to death by sewing him back together. She saw herself with her palm to the walnut on Devil's Elbow and shame crashed through her. In that moment at the walnut tree she had decided she couldn't trust the Lord to prevail. That was her greatest sin: professing her trust and immediately relying on her own ingenuity instead of the Lord's promise. She frustrated the Lord at every turn, saving lives the Lord wanted rid of—and only His forbearance gave her another opportunity to be obedient. She had taken different footsteps than those the Lord had prepared, yet his grace reunited the divergent paths at the abortionist's table.

TRUST THAT I ALREADY SAVED YOU.

The fight had never been hers. She had aggravated the Lord greatly. The decision she made now would determine her fate.

Emeline would trust the Lord in all things, in suffering, in death if it was His perfect will.

GIVE ME YOUR LIFE AND I GIVE YOU EVERYTHING.

She opened her eyes and saw the stains on the doctor's blue tie. He stood between her legs with his arms moving toward her.

"Just another minute and we'll be done."

"Stop!" Emeline kicked away. "Don't put the poison in me! Stop!" She clasped her knees and pain exploded in her broken leg. "No! I can't! I can't!"

Emeline wriggled back, then sideways, and locked her good leg around her other. She rejoiced in the pain of it.

The doctor stopped. "There's no refunding the hundred dollars."

"Just take me back to my car."

"That's a good girl," the old woman said.

FORTY

Chambers parks the Ford by the barn. The bed contains two fifty-five gallon drums, a mess of copper, three hundred pound feed corn, several five-gallon buckets of sand, bricks, a bag of cement.

"I'll be back with the torch," I say. "Jake—run down the basement and get the hoe."

"Where'd she take my car?" Chambers says.

"Hell if I know. Didn't think she could drive."

Chambers slaps the hood of the F-100. "I'm liable to straighten her out."

I fix my eye on Chambers. "Piece of advice. Don't ever tell a man you'll correct his woman." I sip from the jug. "She won't take your car again."

I enter the barn and return a minute later with a butane torch, clicker, and a roll of solder. Jam them into gaps in the cargo. Jacob sticks a hoe handle in a bucket of sand and climbs to the sacks of feed.

Chambers drives down the slope, does a three-point turn and backs to the boat, which rests upside down at the bank. We right it and load cement bags until water approaches four inches from the side.

"That's enough," Chambers says.

I pass him an oar. "You still got that pistol?"

Chambers reaches to the small of his back.

"Gotta get real careful," I say. "You never know who sees something you did, or who wants to curry favor by turning you in."

Chambers shoves off. I hoist a bucket of sand from the bed and angle for the woods. "Jacob, grab the shovel and the rifle from back of the seat."

Jacob runs to the truck. "You want I should bring this?"

I turn. Jacob holds the .38. "Careful, now. Stick it in your pocket."

A breeze kicks up with a smell that's electric, almost. I look across the lake. A thunderhead gathers at the horizon a thousand yards off. The walnut's leaves are upside down. As Jacob closes in, I plant my hand on the bark. "C'mon, talk to me, old man."

I close my eye and trees surround me, the picture is clear in the middle and opaque at the edges. A man stands with a grimace and a rifle. The image rushes away and another follows. A second man, sprawled on a rock, bleeds.

"Whatcha doin', Pap?"

"Git on, boy. Leave me be."

I hear Jacob's feet in the grass. The image is gone. I press the tree until my hand holds the bark pattern. "What is it? C'mon! C'mon!"

Nothing. Jacob's gone ahead following yesterday's ruffled leaves. I trail him and we meet Chambers at the shore. The boat unloaded, Chambers returns to the truck for more while Jacob and I carry the load farther into the woods.

Pausing near an oak, I wipe my brow. Have a taste for the bottle—damn near a certifiable *need*—but I left it at the truck.

A twig pops. I hold my hand up and Jacob halts. "Y'hear that?"

"No, Pap."

"Yeah." I cock my head, search the trees, the undergrowth. A squirrel chatters. A crow caws. "Run and fetch Rebel on a twine lead."

We work, enclosed in semi-darkness. The coming storm brings muggy air. By late afternoon Chambers ferries the last haul to the bank. I've carried most everything a hundred yards from shore to a draw with a stream at the fold. At the last load Chambers hefts a sack of grain and follows me to the site.

Carrying a bucket of sand, I lean hard to the right. My eye searches the trees, rocks, each fallen log or bump of land. I feel eyes on the back of my head. I twist and catch Chambers with my peripheral sight. He grins.

Hair stands on my neck.

The crick bed's eroded two feet into naked roots and rocks. At the low end of a long pool, a mossy ring suggests a dam constructed by boys who rolled the heaviest stones they could find within a hundred yards either direction, and pasted the gaps with mud.

"That your doing?" Chambers says.

"Nah. Mine washed away thirty-five years ago. Deet did that."

"Hell of an engineer."

"Fuck." I drop the bucket of sand and slap a deerfly on my neck. "I hate these fuckin things."

My senses tingle. After the first haul I took the .38 from Jacob and shoved it in my pants. The front sight post rubbed my ass raw so I stuffed the pistol in my crotch, considered the freak chance of a misfire leaving my family jewels in the mud, and laid the gun on a stump. I'd trust Rebel's ears and nose. This early into an operation, the top reason for security is to establish the habit. That last vision at the tree is probly a few days, or weeks off. Still, I can't shake the sense an adversary is nearby.

"Where we building?" Chambers says.

"We'll put the boiler here." I scratch my neck. "Back far enough the side won't erode from under. We dig a pit for the fire, twelve inches deep, lined with brick and cement, with an open channel to the crick. When we're done, a bucket of water'll carry the coals to the stream. We put a doubler two feet off and coil the copper through the second barrel. We got a release valve for the water at the bottom, and we keep it full of cool crick water when we're in a run. That'll be a full-time job for Jake."

I stoop to a jug of whiskey and see Rebel. His muzzle is on the dirt; his good eye probes the woods. Leaves rustle and a sparrow darts from limb to limb. Rebel's ears perk. He jumps to his feet and strains against the rope, his tail straight and still, chest twitching.

I gulp whiskey. "Somethin' spooked Rebel."

"Rebel?" Chambers says. "What, a chipmunk?"

"I don't like it."

Sunlight speckles glide back and forth on the ground with the sway of trees and as I look overhead the sun disappears behind storm clouds.

"You got the jitters, is all." Chambers says. He steps back, his legs spread shoulder-wide. "Something I wanted to mention to you. Been eating at me, you know?"

I hear his tone.

"You want to get a hole dug, right about here?" I indicate where I want the boiler. My gaze falls on Jacob. The deer rifle leans on an oak beside him, and a few feet to his left is the .38.

"Well, that's just the thing," Chambers says. "I don't think I do."

I face Chambers. His smile don't match his eyes. "Plenty of daylight. Don't slack now."

"I like the way you thought all this out. I kinda had a plan like this. Fact, this is just about the way I'd a done it." Chambers reaches to his back. "But we got to talk about something else, altogether."

He holds his Luger at his side. "You see, here's how it is. Emeline—"

"YOU THERE! Don't move! Federal officers!"

A dozen yards away, a man steps from behind a car-sized boulder and aims a shotgun from his hip.

Rebel finally growls.

FORTY ONE

Chambers jumps behind a line of mash barrels. Jacob hunkers at a stump.

"What of it?" I call, and glide behind the tree with the rifle. I glance at Chambers—he signals one finger, then two, and shrugs.

"Aw, come on out," the man says. "Hands in the air."

"Got us surrounded, do you?" I crack the .30-30 lever open, view brass in the chamber. Close it and pull the hammer. Chambers crawls along the row of barrels. Rebel whines. Lightning flashes and after a four-count, thunder sounds.

"That's right."

"Then you shouldn't have no problem coming and getting us," I say.

"No reason to get hostile. Just want to talk."

"Talk *ransom*, is what you wanna talk." I watch the man through wavering leaves and sneak a look left and right. Chambers, still behind barrels, scans the terrain behind our position. Jacob watches me with bug-eyed expectation.

"That's how it is with you people," I say. "A man puts his back and his money into an enterprise and you fucks come along."

"We want to talk about your intentions with all this equipment."

"We, hunh? You federal?"

"Department of Revenue."

"I knew it. I never seen a bunch of folks that do so little and take so much."

"I'm an agent of the law, Hardgrave, and I'm losing what patience I brought. I'm not a fool. You don't have six mash drums for personal use."

"I drink more'n you think."

"Now come out from behind that tree so I can see you. Same for your buddy by the barrels."

A thistle bush—the kind my mother used for making gumdrop trees at Christmas—obstructs my line of fire. But the .30-30 is a brush gun—shoots fat slow bullets that locomote through all kinds of shit. Like thistle. I poke the barrel through a notch in the tree where a branch splits from the trunk. The man looks back and forth and his shotgun drifts toward the ground.

"You're bluffing," I say. "You're alone."

"You think what you want. But touch that trigger, and you'll bleed from more holes than you can count."

That's me. Dumb hick can't count bullet holes.

I line the sights on the revenuer's chest and fire. The man pops backward and claws the ground. I crouch and watch for motion between the tree trunks. The clap of a heavy-bore rifle rings from the left; I scamper around the tree.

"Shit!" Chambers calls. "My leg!"

I crawl backward and slide over the eroded creek bank. Keeping to the dry side of the bed, I low-crawl toward the lake.

Another shot sounds and Chambers cries, "You can shoot the dog all day," Chambers laughs. He squeezes off several rounds from his Luger.

"Where they at, Brad?"

"Eleven o'clock," Chambers calls. "But that last shot was someone different."

I bang my knees wriggling thirty yards on rocks. Where the streambed curves, I turn up a small wash that carries runoff from the upper cornfield. I peek over the bank then slither forward. Leaves rustle against a backdrop of moans and the pounding heartbeat in my ears. I stop, and raise my eye over a knoll.

At my left, Chambers rests on the ground with his shoulders leaning against a barrel. His hands hold his leg. Tree limbs sway. Above, the sky grows blacker. I recall the images from the walnut tree, hours earlier. Chambers said he counted three men, but my vision was of two.

I don't know what to expect.

Finally, motion. The lawman lays prone across an up-sloping boulder with a rifle trained at Chambers. I press the .30-30 stock to my shoulder, rest the muzzle against a cherry tree, and fire.

The man screams and flips over, clutching his ass.

"That's for the dog!" I shoot again. This one goes high and destroys the man's neck.

"Chambers!"

"Hey."

"Any more 'em?"

"One. Last shot was above me, but he could be anywhere by now."

"Stay down 'til I scout a bit." I've used up my visions; I'm on my own.

I step forward, careful of twigs and leaves. Each crunch triggers a shiver down my back. I stalk along a wide circle, holding the rifle stock in the crook of my elbow with my finger looped across the trigger. My breath comes in long pulls; I wish to hell I had two eyes, but all I'd see is the impending storm. A gust crackles through the limbs above; I glide from tree to tree, pausing at each to survey the terrain.

I recognize the pop of Jacob's .38.

Three rapid shots follow, heavier caliber than before. I search, see the flash of a man's face, and sight my rifle. The man swings his head around like a wary doe and I fire. His head snaps sideways and he falls. He jiggles a bit and is still.

I crouch. If a fourth man lurks, he ain't betrayed himself with speech or gunfire—but I've given away my location. The thought of being in another man's rifle sights makes my nuts scrunch. I crawl to a boulder and look behind, seek the sheen of metal or the outline of a head, shoulders, and elbow.

"Angus, you better come," Chambers' voice trails.

I am still.

"They shot your boy and they shot me."

The storm drops its first volley of raindrops and they patter the leaves.

"Shot me real bad."

I wait. A breeze flows downhill. A fat drop lands square in the middle of my back; the sudden coldness is electric like a bullet and I grin. Alive.

"Angus, I'm bleedin' hard," Chambers moans.

I study trees, brush, rocks.

"I think Jake's dead," he says.

I am still. Rain drips from the leaves. Twigs fall around me. Each noise draws my eye. A rock below my groin presses against a vein and my leg tingles. Still I wait. A half hour passes; I'm getting cold. The storm is digging in for a long slog. Chambers has been silent and nary a squirrel has moved for an interminable time. I wiggle sideways and blood rushing through my leg makes it burn. I crane my neck left and watch until the muscles ache, then turn right for an equal time. Finally I climb to my knees, then stand. I advance, careful of twigs, and study the topography. I wonder about Emeline, where she drove off to. About the Sharps above the mantle. Could've rigged it to blow up in her face, but plum didn't think of it. I'd hear her, walking with a cast and a woman's piss poor instincts in the woods. I walk and even after getting Em in context I still expect a bullet to knock me on my ass.

I stand over the last man I shot, who fell with the exit in his skull exposed. His brain looks like a big mess of fish guts with no heads or tails.

Thunder booms. My knees are rubber. I make a circuit around the still site, stopping at each dead agent, kicking a foot, stepping on his back. I get lost in the third's gemstone eyes. I shot him in the head and the back half is gone and both his eyes are half shit out their sockets. Wish I knew how to keep one and maybe get some use of it. Have to ask Jonah about that.

I orient on the fifty-five gallon barrels and hurry my step.

Chambers' face is like ashes in a fire pit. The fire's out, but embers glow. He's fashioned a tourniquet with his belt but to little effect. Blood soaks his thigh and the leaves beneath. There's more blood than a man might believe he carries. He smiles. I touch the rifle trigger, and point at his belly.

"Thought you'd leave me here to die," he whispers.

"Might, yet. Where's Jake?"

His eyes point straight ahead. I swipe the Luger from his hand, stuff it under my waistband and cross to the stream bank. Jacob is face down in Deet's brook; his hair stretches on a surface clouded pink with blood.

I watch Jacob float. The storm picks up and rain strikes the pool like June bugs. I wade in; drag Jacob by his collar to the bank. I put my fingers to his throat. Nothing. Press his eyelids closed. They won't stay, and Jacob stares.

I return to Chambers.

"You was gonna say something about Emeline."

"That wasn't nothing."

"You fuck her too?"

Jonah ain't showed me anything about Chambers. If he was set to be a problem today I expect I'd have known about it.

"I got to pick up your leg." I brace Chambers' foot at my groin, lift, and cut the trouser above the gunshot with his boot knife. I drink walnut whiskey then flush blood from the entry side.

Chambers grunts, "That shit tastes better 'n it feels."

"Passed clean through—but left a hell of a hole." I rub whiskey into the exit wound. "I'm gonna patch you up then I got work to do. One more piece of business needs done and ain't never going to be a time like now. Here, take a drink."

I pin Chambers' pant leg with my knee, cut two lengthwise strips and bind a wad of cloth to the exit side. In a couple of minutes, he's ready to travel.

"I gotto get you out of here, but you got to help. Brad?" I tap his cheek. "Stay awake. You ain't hit bad, but you lost a bucket of blood. C'mon now; wake up."

I snake my arm behind Chambers' back, wrestle him to his feet. We stagger through dells and over hillocks to the water. I lean him over the boat edge, and flop his feet in. Lightning flashes at the far side of the lake. The boom echoes across the water.

"Don't sink me," he says.

I board and sit with the oar in my hand. Paddling with my right arm will propel me to the center of the lake. I'd have to turn around, and alternate strokes. I look skyward. Plunge the oar into the lake until water reaches my elbow. Finding bottom, I jump over the side. The water reaches my chin. Slipping on mud, I tug the boat along the edge, and tow it ashore at the Ford.

"You got to help me," I say. "C'mon." Chambers' head lolls to the side. He lays in red water. "Shit, boy. C'mon."

Chambers straightens his neck. "My ass is wet."

"That's nothing. C'mon." I hug him and lift. My back muscles twang like guitar strings. The boat rocks. Chambers gains his feet and falls. On my knees I maneuver him over my shoulder and stagger to the truck.

"You got to drop the tailgate," I say. "I can't let go."

Chambers pulls the latch. The gate drops and the chains plunk taut. I buck him onto the bed.

"Lay back. Let your feet hang."

"Hurts."

"Pain is proof you're alive. You keep awake and we'll get you patched up. What the hell's wrong with you?" I hold Chambers' head aright and peer into his glassy eyes. His lips pull back in a quiet snarl.

I slip into the driver's seat, start the truck. Grind the clutch. The engine races. I look back. Chambers' head slumps sideways and his chest deflates like he barters for life but the deal goes south. "'Cause of your bad living," I say.

I motor up the grade and Emeline stands on the porch.

"Gimme a hand here." I hurry to the tailgate, pull Chambers off and support him hip to hip, but Chambers slips to the ground. I hoist him over my shoulder, again. Lug him up the steps. Emeline opens the front door and I dump him on the kitchen table.

"The wound is clean. You got to stop that bleeding."

Emeline hovers at the living room door.

"Damn you Emeline, we don't have time for games. Get your ass over here and plug these holes, 'fore he bleeds to death."

She cants her head. A gust brings a smattering of rain to the roof. "You better get Jacob inside," Emeline says. "Merely a suggestion."

"S'pose so. You patch him up."

I stride to the door, and as I pull it, Emeline says, "I'll take care of you, Brad."

Got a spark in her eye since she pulled that stunt with the rifle last night. I'll settle with her after bit. I can't look after Chambers, and Doc Fleming won't overlook a gunshot wound. But first, three dead men litter my woods. I steer the truck to the edge of the forest, gather Jacob and carry him to the walnut tree. I lean him in the folds of the trunk then return to the still site.

How did the revenuers know to find me in the woods, right there?

I grab the first lawman's boot, curl my wrist and pull. The man is too heavy. I slip my arm below his shoulders. Thick bastard. I fight him to the water's edge. His feet float; his back is on rocks. Gusts blow rain across the choppy water.

I find the jug of walnut whiskey we had at the site before carrying the second man to the lake's edge. He's lighter or the whiskey makes me strong. The water reaches the shore in six-inch waves. How the hell is this going to work? If I take him out deep and the boat upsets, can I swim with one arm, in boots?

If I hold a gun on Emeline, she can row and throw the men overboard with cement blocks tied to their ankles. Fish'll strip them clean in a month, maybe. But Emeline's proven the moxie to bead a rifle on me. She might dump the boat and take her chances. What good is a pistol if I'm paddling with one arm?

Only thing that will work, and only for a short while, is to drag the bodies far as I can from shore, or maybe tuck them under some low-hanging branches. Come back in late fall, dredge up whatever's left and burn it.

I shift a corpse into the water. Lightning flashes on the opposite hill and the boom arrives after a two-count. I don't like being in the water with so much lightning but I got to figure I'm damn near indestructible. And if heaven or hell wants me dead they either lack the power or they got a special death in mind.

I slip in the mud to deeper water and the body floats just below the surface. Soon as the man's open mouth fills his lungs with water he'll sink. I tow him to a fallen tree that's created a shelter of oak leaves. A mild current eddies here, trapping leaves and green detergent foam.

I wedge the body under the timber and return for the next.

Jacob stares. I climb from the water and stumble to the walnut, touch the bark, shy like my wet finger will conduct a shock. The bark crumbles. I press my palm, curl my fingers. Close my eye.

"I got to know what I'm gonna do."

Lightning flashes and thunder claps. I press my eyelid tight and half imagine, half dream I see Deet, shaking his head, and Jacob, pleading. My old man, Mitch McClellan, weighs me with a judge's stare. The widow looks away.

But none of this is from the walnut.

It all fades like a dream and now that I've had a play vision the walnut says it's time and a man with a terrible grin and a face hewed from ironwood studies me. He turns sideways like to view a spectacle, but my eye is stuck on his frame. It is another version of me, or some distillation of everything strong in the McClellan line.

It is my grandfather, Jonah.

Gramps shakes his head sideways and the feeling I've had all along—someday becoming the country gentleman, money and power, and special insights—that feeling is gone. Gramps shakes his head and I'm out. One eye, one arm, everyone around me destroyed.

Jonah stares and I follow his gaze.

I see my kitchen. Blood on the table. Chambers is gone—and Emeline? She pours me a drink.

Emeline cleaned Chambers' leg with a towel and hot water.

Chambers held her arm. "I always saw us like this, you takin' care of me."

She slipped free of his feeble grasp. "Brad, the bullet that cut through your leg nicked an artery. Your leg is dead. Won't be long until the rest of you is too."

Emeline stepped to the front door. She passed Chambers on the table. His eyes were closed; his skin was pale. Whatever amount of blood he'd lost, it wasn't enough. Bracing herself on the countertop, the refrigerator, the wall, the banister, she made her way to the basement, pulled the lanyard, and in the back room lifted a blue circular device with *"de-ratter—de-mouser"* stamped in the base. A glass globe on top, screwed upside down, contained a half-gallon of Warfarin pellets. She flipped it sideways, toggled the pedal and a dozen white pills fell to the floor. She cradled them by her womb.

But hadn't the Lord commanded her to wait, and watch what was about to unfold? He'd spoken clearly. He could have told her she would have to stuff Chambers' leg with rat poison—but He didn't. Emeline returned the poison to the blue *de ratter* and climbed the stairs.

"Let's keep our eyes on the Lord, Brad. Things are going to turn out perfectly," she said. "I'm checking your wound. We have to try to stop the bleeding." She held her finger below his nose. He was unconscious.

Angus had fashioned a tourniquet. She touched the knot. It was tied poorly and Blood flowed from Chambers' thigh to the table and dripped to the floor. Emeline grabbed a mixing bowl from the cupboard and placed in on the floor.

Emeline sat at the table. Chambers shuddered from his loins and his hands clasped the side of the table. He gulped short breaths.

She waited. His chest rose and fell, but the pace was slight and the sound almost non-existent. Finally his back arched and he wheezed. His back fell to the table and the air rushed out. His whole body clenched.

Emeline leaned forward, close to his face. His eyes opened, though no breath came through his mouth, and his countenance was utterly blank. His pupils were empty.

Emeline dumped the bucket of blood into the toilet.

Thank you Lord for helping me in my unbelief.

The telephone rang. Emeline answered.

Emeline sat on the same chair from which she'd watched Deet in the barn. Angus stepped to the porch, swung the screen door open and entered. His clothes dripped as if he'd been swimming.

He was alone.

"Chambers bled out," she said.

Angus leaned against the wall. "Damn near filled the boat with blood." He stared at the floor. His face was tired.

She said, "Where's Jacob?"

"Down by the tree."

"Why'd you leave him?"

"I got to bury him."

"I should take the Bible down and say a few words."

"I thought you might." He rubbed his temple under the eye patch strap. Ruffled his soaked hair. "I feel just about dead. We got anything to eat? You want to fix some pancakes and gravy?"

"We'll have to move Chambers off the table."

The table was wet from her scrub brush. Angus sat in fresh, dry clothes and chewed buttermilk flapjacks.

"Someone called a few minutes ago," Emeline said. "He said his name real fast and I didn't hear. Said you had his dog and he was coming to get him."

"Who?"

"I asked, but he yelled he knew what you did."

"Charlie? Did he say his name was Charlie?"

"I think that's right. Charlie." She gulped water from a glass.

"When's Charlie coming?"

"He said tonight."

"Not in the storm."

"Well, he knew it was raining—said he had to get off the phone before the lightning zapped him."

"We got to move Maul."

"You move him. He's too mean. I tried to feed him this morning and he about took my hand off. Isn't that what you said the other night?"

"Two of us can do it. We'll tie him out in the woods, and when Charlie comes he'll be none the wiser. I'll show him the pens and run him off."

"What's the secret? How come you got Maul so much meaner than the other fellas get theirs?"

Angus studied her face. "The others stop when a dog aggresses them. They don't take em far enough."

"But you do."

"Damn right."

"You think that bitch outside is worth breeding with him?"

"Not her." Angus drank again and Emeline poured more. "We got to go," he said, and finished the glass. A blue-white flicker lit the room, and the thunder crash lingered.

"Angus, about last night—" She withdrew a new jug of whiskey from the cupboard. His eye followed the bottle. She filled his tumbler and placed it before him.

"Yeah?"

"I married you for good or worse, and if you're willing to accept it, I owe you an apology. I haven't been a good wife to you." She reached slowly, touched the strap of his eye band, dragged her fingernails lightly over his ear.

He sat straight in his chair.

"You lost your arm, and what did I do? Loafed around and complained. I'm a terrible complainer—and a broken leg's no excuse. Deet died and I didn't think about how you must have felt losing your oldest son. I never realized how cold I've been until tonight." She touched his shoulder, shifted her hand down to his chest.

"You need to take a drink of this." He held the glass to her.

"I didn't like it much, last time."

"Last time it was straight whiskey. This has walnut. It'll change your perspective."

"Well, I just changed my perspective. Don't know I want any."

"You're a hard woman to trust."

"I don't have the stomach, but if you want me to, I'll drink it. The Lord says I'm supposed to obey my husband and I will, though it'll make me sick and hurt the baby. I'll obey my husband."

"That's what the Lord says." Angus propped his chin with his hand.

Emeline gulped whiskey and her stomach turned. She spewed the whiskey into the sink. With half of the glass remaining, she said, "I'll try again if you need me to."

"That's enough if you're just going to spit it out." He stretched to her, pinched her breast. His pupil was a void and his head swayed as if something weighty rolled loose inside. "Just one thing."

"What's that?"

"You got to call me 'Mister'."

"When?"

"Now. Forever."

"Okay... Mister Hardgrave." She helped him to his feet. "Whoa, there, Mister... Let me get my coat and the lantern." She stepped to the closet, braced her arm on the molding. She grabbed the lantern. She'd leave her coat; the rain would keep her alert.

Angus watched from the living room door, braced against the jamb. Emeline primed the lantern at the kitchen table, lifted the globe, struck a match.

"Watch your step," she said.

"I ought to be suspicious, you bein' so nice."

"Lots of women don't have it near as good."

She opened the door. The lantern sputtered. Across the lawn, two pairs of eyes reflected green. Lightning flashed. The barn was a huge, black shadow. Lighting flashed again and the forest appeared white, green, silver, and was suddenly black again. Fat raindrops stung.

She took Angus's arm and they crossed the lawn. "I only see two dogs in the pen," she said.

"Reb's dead. There's a neck pole against the kennel, topside. We use that to keep our distance."

"How's that?"

"Slip the loop at the end of the pole on his neck and he can't get at you."

"I don't know how you mean. Steady, there." She heaved against him as he slipped.

"I'll do it. I just need help getting the chains on him afterward. That's what's gonna be tough."

They entered the barn and Angus angled to a box of towing chains at the back of the white Farmall.

"This'll hold him."

They stood at the kennel a minute later. Maul glowered at the rear of the cage.

"He's a brute," she said.

"A piece of work, for damn sure. I'm gonna put that loop on him and once I got him, I'll pass it to you."

"All right, if you're sure." She placed the lantern above the pen.

"That sumbitch Charlie ain't left me no choice." He stopped. Looked as if a thought struggled to take shape, and said, "Nah."

Angus opened the pen door. Maul remained in the back, his head low and a perceptible stiffness lifting the hair on his back. "Easy boy. Easy."

Angus pushed the staff into the pen. "Move the light to the side a little. I can't see him." The rope loop was parallel to Maul's head.

"Shit."

"What?"

"He won't put his cussed head through the loop."

"Can you jiggle it?"

"You think he's susceptible to jigglin'?"

"What if I go to the side? Will he look at me?"

"Take that stick by the barn and prod him a wee bit."

Emeline lifted the staff from the grass, rammed the sharp end through the wire into Maul's neck. Maul latched with his teeth and broke it with a violent twist. Angus jabbed with the loop, but missed. Maul clamped the pole in his teeth and jerked. Emeline prodded him with the splintered staff.

"Hold on, Em; we don't want him *too* riled."

"You missed him. Choke up on it."

His arm already in the pen, Angus followed inside with his head, shifted his hand closer to Maul.

Emeline glanced at Angus's feet. He was bent at the hip with his shoulders inside the kennel.

"I'll get him looking this way," she said, and stabbed Maul with the stick.

"No!"

Maul whipped his anvil head, shouldered Angus's arm aside and charged.

Maul's teeth glow—never seen anything so beautiful. His muscles ripple in a flash of lightning and as I behold the fury of his attack, a secret, *walnut* part of me cheers. This killer makes no bones. Maul's shoulder collides with mine and my head bounces from the chicken wire. Before I can move, Maul sinks his teeth into my neck and a million tons of pressure collapse my windpipe.

I am flat-out fucked.

The pain paralyzes and I understand with each subsonic grunt that Maul is ripping out my throat. Maul loosens and snaps tighter, closer, with a gentle rumble passing from his throat to mine. A love song. Maul heaves; his tremendous neck tosses me side to side, cuts my brow against the chicken mesh. He growls with the intimacy of killer to prey, as if to say, soon enough you'll join my flesh. Then you can kill.

But I've killed. I've killed so much!

My mind floats and I see Jonah McClellan. He pays me no mind. He swats like there's deerflies around him, keep stinging him. He looks to the sky with wrath. Jonah the whale tormented by something bigger. *Why'd you lead me wrong, Jonah? Why'd you set me up for failure? Why you let my boys die?*

Jonah stops swinging at his tormenters and stares stupid at me.

Maul squeezes with force I cannot comprehend. Blood drains warm into my throat, my lungs, and I gag without air.

Emeline says something. I try to hear as blackness presses in from the sides. She says it again.

"You're dying, Angus."

Of course I'm gonna die. We all gonna die.

A red light forms at the center of my sight. It overwhelms Maul's stinking coat, the blood, the lightning. But not the darkness.

The light grows redder.

FORTY TWO

As Maul growled and thrashed about the pen with Angus, Emeline retreated to the house. Angus's body blocked the exit. She wanted to do this while all the blood and electricity in the air gave her clarity. She dragged an end table to the fireplace, struggled on top, and withdrew the Sharps rifle Angus had told her never to fire.

As she arrived at the crate she found Maul wriggling to escape, his head barely squeezed through the narrow gap between Angus's torso and the gate. She pressed the rifle barrel to Maul's head and pushed him backward. The dog scrambled.

The carbine locked in her folded arm, she took Angus's hand and checked his pulse. Emeline released his hand and lifted it again, starting over. Again she pressed for his pulse and felt the faintest pressure, a tiny beat, as if the heart of an infant struggled to keep alive the decrepit and addled body of Angus Hardgrave. Emeline held her fingers to his wrist and after a few moments, felt another beat arrive, fainter than before. She waited and felt no more.

"If life handed anyone a raw deal it was you, Maul. But I'm not having you around a baby."

Emeline cocked the carbine, drew it to her shoulder and pointed toward Maul's head. She squeezed the trigger and the rifle erupted. The barrel pulled and she heard the bullet impact bone and mush. Through ringing ears she listened for Maul's breathing but heard nothing. She shifted around the kennel and on the side, pressed the barrel through the wire and prodded him.

While she peered lightning flashed so brightly the sky was illuminated like day. She beheld Maul's shattered head and turned while the lightning still flashed, a single jagged bolt that seemed ten feet wide, a fiery white electrical spear that crashed into the land beyond the house and dazzled her feet with electricity.

Emeline left the rifle propped in chicken wire and limped alongside the edge of the porch. She looked over the hill to Devil's Elbow. A tower of flame consumed the walnut, as if the purpose of the lightning bolt was not to strike the tree, but to ignite all of it at once. The smoke was acrid, like a rotten offering, and the flames grew higher as she watched. She listened to the crackling as if hoping to hear confirmation that Jonah McClellan suffered within, but like the rifle ended Maul instantly, she suspected Jonah McClellan was no more.

Emeline circled to the steps and climbed. From inside she took the blanket she slept with and returned to the porch. She turned the Adirondack chair to face the burning tree and sat in it.

The sun climbed over the horizon and mist floated above the lake. Emeline turned the Adirondack chair to face the orchard instead of the ash of the walnut tree, but after an hour with Angus's hind end protruding into her peripheral view, she realized there was yet another dog to deal with.

Emeline retrieved the rifle from the chicken wire and shifted several cages lower and stood in front of Widow McClellan's bitch. Emeline cycled another round and cocked the hammer.

She released the crate door and stood back.

The dog growled but remained in the back of the crate.

"You can stay here if you want. You start to look or sound like the other, then you'll get what he got. If you stay here, you'll sleep in the house and your name will be Ruth."

Emeline backed away. Half way to the house she again drew the rifle. Ruth had come to the front of the crate and peered at her.

"You can come and go as you please."

Ruth leaped to the ground and trotted toward the burned McClellan house.

Back on the porch, with the sun fully above the horizon, Emeline telephoned Sheriff Heilbrun.

Ruth returned ten minutes later, and after a few growls, allowed Emeline to scratch her shoulders. She lay at Emeline's feet.

Would Emeline move to the town house or stay on the farm? This place had potential. Crisp beams of gold warmed her bare arms. The farm was silent save Ruth's thumping tail, and the chickens. The cattle... birds... frogs.

Perfectly silent.

Emeline shifted her broken leg out and nestled into the chair. Her coffee cooled, barely sipped, in a mug cradled on her lap.

Ruth perked her ears and lifted her neck, then climbed to her haunches. She watched a black and white car park by the Fairlane.

Standing beside his car door, Sheriff Heilbrun spent a long moment studying the ass and legs hanging out of the dog kennel, then approached the porch. He looked at her hands. He walked slowly.

"You said you had a rough night. That Angus in the kennel?"

She nodded. "That's Mister Hardgrave."

"You want to say what happened?"

"He was trying to take the dog out and got mauled."

"Where's the dog?"

"Still in the pen. Angus's body blocked him in. I got a rifle and shot him."

Heilbrun nodded, sat on the porch steps. "What else?"

"Angus said Jacob was down by the lake. Shot in the chest, but I didn't see it, so I don't know who did it. Brad Chambers—that's his Fairlane—he's in the barn. He was shot through an artery in the leg and bled out. By the time Angus brought him in from the woods, there was nothing I could do. We had him on the kitchen table until he died, then moved him to the barn. Angus wanted pancakes. I don't know where the other dog is, and I don't know who else might be dead in the woods. I didn't look. I figured if Angus came back, he'd killed anybody that came for him."

Heilbrun studied the cast on her leg. "You seeing Doc Fleming on that?"

"Not for a week."

He nodded while he exhaled. "Both McClellans. Deet, Angus, Jake, Chambers, and four Pitlakes—all dead inside of two, three weeks. And you, or this farm, at the center."

"The Pitlakes?"

"House burned to the ground night before last. All four died in the fire. Three had bullet holes in them. I talked to Angus and Brad that night. They happened to be passing by at one in the morning. I did some poking around and found Pitlake filed at the county seat to get a white Farmall he said he bought with the dealership in 1947. The dealership he bought from your daddy."

"I was seven then, and not part of this farm 'til a month ago."

"That's about when everything went to hell. No, I'm not saying anything. I talked to Doc Fleming and you being on your feet is a small miracle. I don't imagine you could coax Angus to poke his head inside the pen of a fighting dog unless that's what Angus wanted to do. As to the others, we'll match the bullets up and sort it all out. You mind if I pour a cup of coffee and use your phone? I got a feeling this is going to take a while."

"Help yourself. I'll be right here."

FROM THE Author

NOTHING SAVE THE BONES INSIDE HER is an Indie published novel, which is another way of saying I published it. The novel has no significant marketing budget, no publicist, no team of Big Six publishers trying to figure out how to earn back the two million dollar advance they paid. In short, this book will pass away more quickly than most unless its readers keep it alive.

How? By spreading the word.

Before I mention a few things that are helpful to authors in general, let me point out that *Nothing Save the Bones Inside Her* is a moral story, as was my debut novel *Cold Quiet Country*, and my upcoming release, tentatively titled *Dead Honest*.

I believe in absolute right, meaning, I believe a divine being created right and wrong, and that in the end, right will prevail. God will prevail. Each of my novels rests on the foundation that evil is real, wrong is wrong, and the struggle to defeat it is a heroic struggle, whether the outcome is secure or not.

I don't subscribe to hopeless writing. I love rural noir because the darker the dark, the lighter the light. I hope that's what you take away from this and all of my work... that the impossible fight is always worth fighting.

If you found value standing beside Emeline as she overcame her internal and external foes, please consider doing any or all of the following:

Tell a friend. Tell ten, or two hundred, that you enjoyed *Nothing Save the Bones Inside Her*.

Go on Twitter, Facebook, or some other social media forum and spread the word.

If you belong to a book club, suggest this title.

Follow me on Twitter (@claylindemuth) and consider retweeting some of my tweets. Or friend me on Facebook—I accept all requests.

Write a review on Amazon, Barnes and Noble, or Goodreads. Or all of the above. Even a couple of lines about what you enjoyed about the story can help others make a decision. One of the most difficult obstacles for a self-published work to overcome is the reader's worry that the work will be inferior, poorly formatted or edited, or just boring as hell. An effective review might address some of those concerns.

Write a blog review, or contact a blogger you know who is on the lookout for Indie creativity.

Or, if you know someone in media who likes to interview authors...

Whatever you do, please know that I am very grateful to you for purchasing *Nothing Save the Bones Inside Her*. I truly hope you found value in it, and I will feel deeply indebted if you help spread the word. Thanks—ten million thanks—

—Clayton

ACKNOWLEDGEMENTS

This story would not exist but for the early encouragement of my wife Julie Lindemuth, and my great friends Loren Fairman and Dan Youatt.

My wife Julie has been a constant champion of my efforts, a dedicated beta reader, an insightful sounding board, and an all-around advocate of my career as an author. Of all the many blessings I've received in life, I am most grateful to God for her.

While I wrote the first version of this novel, Dan Youatt read it page by page and always came back telling me it sounded like a real story. As every author knows, hearty support like that is priceless. Thank you, Dan.

No one could ask for a better beta reader or friend than Loren Fairman. His insights increased clarity and cleverness, but most all I am indebted for his unflagging support. For the last six years he has been a true friend in good times and bad, and I am grateful.

Another great champion of my work has been Jedidiah Ayres. Aside from delighting me with his devastatingly evocative prose, he has gone out of his way as an ambassador of noir to introduce me to local and national authors, invite my participation in Noir at the Bar events, and drink beer and coffee while bullshitting about the art. Although I wrote six novels before meeting him, I didn't feel like an author until he brought me into the community. That's pretty cool. Thanks Jed.

Although I have always been a great believer in Emeline, Angus, and Maul's story, I have also been too close for objectivity. I am deeply indebted to the authors, reviewers, and readers who answered my call for help in deciding whether to publish this novel. Although their voices were not unanimous they gave me tremendous insights into the story and its audience. To them I am indebted for their honesty, advice, and generosity:

Rob Pickering

Aaron Reed

Judy Erslon

David Odeen

Ashley Tschakert

Jen at ChicksDigBooks.com

Lee French, (author of *Dragons in Pieces*)

Gonzalo Baeza, (author of *La ciudad de los hoteles vacíos*)

Philip Thompson, (author of *Deep Blood*)

Les Edgerton, (author of *The Bitch, The Rapist*, and more)

Gabino Iglesias, (author of *Gutmouth*)

ABOUT THE AUTHOR

Clayton Lindemuth writes noir because that's where he lives. He runs marathons. Reads economics. Is a Christian apologist, a dog lover, and eternally misses Arizona. Clayton is the author of *Cold Quiet Country*, *Nothing Save the Bones Inside Her*, *My Brother's Destroyer*, and other volumes not yet released. He lives in Missouri with his wife Julie and his puppydog Faith, also known as "Princess Wigglebums."